THE YEAR'S
BEST
MYSTERY AND SUSPENSE
STORIES
1987

Other Books by Edward D. Hoch

The Shattered Raven
The Judges of Hades
The Transvection Machine
The Spy and the Thief
City of Brass
Dear Dead Days (editor)
The Fellowship of the Hand
The Frankenstein Factory
Best Detective Stories of the Year 1976 (editor)
Best Detective Stories of the Year 1977 (editor)
Best Detective Stories of the Year 1978 (editor)
The Thefts of Nick Velvet
The Monkey's Clue & The Stolen Sapphire (juvenile)
Best Detective Stories of the Year 1979 (editor)
Best Detective Stories of the Year 1980 (editor)
Best Detective Stories of the Year 1981 (editor)
All But Impossible! (editor)
The Year's Best Mystery & Suspense Stories 1982 (editor)
The Year's Best Mystery & Suspense Stories 1983 (editor)
The Year's Best Mystery & Suspense Stories 1984 (editor)
The Quests of Simon Ark
Leopold's Way
The Year's Best Mystery & Suspense Stories 1985 (editor)
The Year's Best Mystery & Suspense Stories 1986 (editor)

THE YEAR'S BEST

MYSTERY AND SUSPENSE STORIES

1987

Edited by Edward D. Hoch

WALKER AND COMPANY
NEW YORK

First published in the United States of America in 1987 by the Walker Publishing Company, Inc.

Published simultaneously in Canada by Thomas Allen & Son Canada, Limited, Markham, Ontario

The Library of Congress has cataloged this serial publication as follows:

The Year's best mystery & suspense stories.—1982-   —
    New York: Walker, 1982-
        v.; 22 cm.
    Annual.
    Editor: 1982-   E.D. Hoch.
    Continues: Best detective stories of the year.

    1. Detective and mystery stories, American—Periodicals 2. Detective and mystery stories, English—Periodicals. I. Hoch, Edward D., 1930-   . II. Title: Year's best mystery and suspense stories.
—PZ1.B446588—   83-646567   813'.0872'08—dc19
Library of Congress [8406] AACR 2 MARC-S

ISBN:0-8027-0945-1

Printed in the United States of America

10 9 8 7 6 5 4 3 2 1

For Nancy and Hugh Schick,
After 25 Years

CONTENTS

Acknowledgments

INTRODUCTION

The year 1986 saw renewed vitality in some aspects of the short mystery story. Women's magazines like *Redbook, Ladies' Home Journal,* and *Woman's Day* published mystery and suspense stories for the first time in years, and there were more mystery anthologies published here and in England than at any time in the past quarter century.

Still, there were no additions to the ranks of the regular mystery magazines, and at the beginning of 1987 it appeared likely that *Ellery Queen's Mystery Magazine* and *Alfred Hitchcock's Mystery Magazine*—now almost equal in circulation— would soon be the only two digest-size publications in the field. The two-year-old *Espionage* announced that it would convert to a larger format, approximately 8½ by 11 inches, effective with its issue of May 1987. While maintaining its commitment to fiction, the magazine also planned to use more nonfiction than in the past. *The New Black Mask,* encountering legal problems over the use of the Black Mask name, announced that issue number eight would be its last under that title. It planned a rebirth in May 1987 as *A Matter of Crime,* with its format changed from trade paperback to the smaller mass-market paperback size. We hope neither of these changes will result in fewer short stories being published during 1987, and we can hope that both publications will gain in display space and circulation.

Death claimed a number of major mystery writers during 1986, including two past presidents of the Mystery Writers of America, Stanley Ellin and John D. MacDonald, and the world-famous Argentine author Jorge Luis Borges. These are recorded, along with a couple of deaths that went unreported in previous years, in the Yearbook section at the back of the book.

The stories chosen for this year's volume, representing the best of 1986, mark the arrival of a new wave of modern mystery writers. Eight of these authors have never appeared in an annual *Best* volume before. Three of them—Robert Barnard, B. M. Gill, and Sue Grafton—are well known for their novels, but the other five—Thomas Adcock, Doug Allyn, David Braly, Nell Lamburn, and Robert Sampson—will be new names to most mystery readers. In their different ways they all demonstrate the vitality of the mystery short story.

Again, my thanks to the many people who helped with this year's volume, especially Ed Wellen, Eleanor Sullivan, Ruth Cavin, and my wife Patricia.

Edward D. Hoch

THE YEAR'S BEST

MYSTERY AND SUSPENSE STORIES

1987

THOMAS ADCOCK
THROWN-AWAY CHILD

Thomas Adcock is the first of the relatively new mystery writers in this volume. He's the author of Precinct 19 *(Doubleday, 1985) and an increasingly frequent contributor to* Ellery Queen's Mystery Magazine. *One of his stories, "Christmas Cop" (EQMM, 3/86), was nominated this year for an Edgar award, but I prefer this tale of the strange ways of death and religion in a section of New Orleans. It finished second in voting for the EQMM Readers' Award.*

The little room in back where Perry stayed was "nothin' but a damn slum the way that no-'count keeps it," according to his Aunt Vivian. She had a long list of complaints about her nephew, most of which were shared by most people who knew him. But she and Perry were still family and so she loved him, too, in a quiet and abiding way.

Vivian lived in the rest of the place, a wooden cottage of four narrow connected rooms built up on hurricane stilts, with a high pitched roof, batten shutters over the windows, and French louvered doors on either end. The front steps were scrubbed every morning with a ritual mixture of steaming hot water and brick dust to keep evil spirits at bay. The back steps led from Perry's squalor to a tiny fenced garden of thick grass, a chinaberry tree, and a lilac bush. In appearance and infirmity, the cottage was nearly the same as the forty or so others crowded into a rut-filled dirt lane between lower Tchoupitoulas Street and a levee almost crumbled away from years of flood and neglect.

The neighborhood was one of many that tourists in the city were not encouraged to visit, a neighborhood where pain and fears from the hard past overlapped a generally despairing present—a haunted part of New Orleans, some claimed. Which

1

was why, among other customs, the front steps were washed down with brick dust every day.

On most afternoons, the people in the lane would go to the levee for the coolness of the river breezes or to catch themselves a dinner of Mississippi catfish. There, ancient Creole men and widow ladies—with *tignons* covering their hair, the Madras handkerchiefs favored by voodoo women with seven points carefully twisted heavenward—would talk until dusk of the old days and the old ways.

Long ago, Vivian and her husband had been terribly proud of the cottage. It was truly theirs, no thanks to any of the banks or mortgage companies—bought and paid for with the saved-up wages of a yard man and a cleaning woman whose ancestors had once been shackled to posts in the public squares above Canal Street and sold as slaves. But on a sunny day in March of 1948, Vivian and Willis Duclat took title to a little wood cottage and became the first of their families to own their own home.

It was a long way up in a perilous, hostile world, and Willis and Vivian were pleased to be gracious about their ascent. Almost everyone else in the lane shared generously in their reflected joy. One who did not was a tall, sour-faced woman next door to the Duclats, a spinster known as Miss Toni. "Ain't goin' to be no comfort to you or the rest of us down here to be buyin' your own place when it's the last one that ain't owned yet by Theo Flower. Theo wants the whole lane bad and he means to get it, one way'r other. He knows the mysteries, so that's how he'll get you yet—one way'r other."

Vivian said to pay no mind to Miss Toni. "She only says those poisonous things 'cause she's lonesome and miserable."

The pride of the Duclats was brief.

Toward the end of '48, the parish tax assessor came calling. He smiled quite a bit and seemed genuine. He shook hands with Willis, same as he'd shake a white man's hand. And he addressed Vivian properly as Mrs. Duclat. The assessor was there to explain how he had some important papers for signing, papers that would bring paving and curbing and a sewer hook-up. The Duclats didn't understand quite all of the small print on the man's papers, but since he'd been so respectful Willis and Vivian trusted him and signed where it said "Freeholder." Then by

Christmas of '49, when they'd fallen impossibly far behind on the special surcharges for modern conveniences levied against them by those important papers, the Duclat's home was seized by the sheriff and put up for sale in tax-forfeiture court.

At the auction there was only one bidder—the Church of the Awakened Spirit, in the person of its pastor, The Most Reverend Doctor Theophilus Flower. At last, Theo Flower and his church owned every last cottage in the lane. Pastor Flower wasted no time. He called on the Duclats the very day he put down the cash money to retire the delinquent surcharges, plus the customary plain brown envelope full of money for his friend, the smiling tax assessor.

Pastor Flower drove straightaway from the courthouse to the Duclats' place in his big white Packard motorcar, one of the first post-war models off the Detroit assembly lines. When the neighbors saw the Packard roll in from Tchoupitoulas Street, they went to their homes and shut the doors until they knew Pastor Flower had gone away.

In the parlor of the newly dispossessed Duclats, Theo Flower was courtly and sympathetic. The pastor had no need for meanness when he bought somebody's home out from under them—the law made it all so easy and polite.

"Now, I know you can understand that our church has many missions," he said in his deep, creamy preacher's cadence, "and that among them is providing what we can in the way of housing for our poor and unfortunate brothers and sisters."

Willis sat in a caneback chair in a sort of shock, still as a stone while Pastor Flower talked. He didn't appear to hear anything. He'd hidden from his wife for days before the court sale so that he could cry, and now his eyes looked like they might rust away with grief. Vivian sat next to him and held his big calloused hands. She looked at the floor, ashamed and resigned, and listened carefully to Theo Flower.

"I surely don't want to see fine people like you having no place to live. You see, though, how we must serve our members first? Now, I've been giving this predicament of yours a lot of my thought and some of my most powerful prayer and I do believe I have come upon a solution—"

When at last Pastor Flower was finished, he collected twenty dollars on account toward the first year's tithe to the Church of the Awakened Spirit. And the church's two newest members, Vivian and Willis Duclat, signed some important papers their new pastor happened to have with him, pressed inside the red-leather Bible he always carried. They signed where it said "Tenant."

After scratching his name to Theo Flower's lease, Willis rose from his chair and crossed the room angrily, tearing himself away from Vivian's grip on his shirt. He stood towering over the preacher and his black eyes came alive again. Duclat's huge hands, made hard and heavy from his work with shovels and stone and earth, clenched into dark fists. His voice sounded as if it were a thousand years old.

"I ain't no educated man," he said to Flower, "and I ain't well spoken like you. But I ain't simple, neither, and I can sure as hell figure you just done somethin' crooked here. I'm goin' to think on this, then I'm goin' to figure some way to bring you down for what you done to me and my wife, and prob'ly other poor folks besides."

The Most Reverend Doctor Theophilus Flower only smiled. When he did, Vivian saw a flash of gold at the back of his dark-brown lips. Then Flower stood up, no match in physique to Willis. He folded the lease into his Bible and answered the big angry man with the clenched fists: "It won't do to talk like that, brother. I know you're a troubled man today and I'm sorry for you, truly. But you'd best not take an adversary's tone against a man who knows the mysteries like I do. You understand what I mean, don't you, brother Willis?"

Willis understood only too well. Since he was a boy, he'd heard of Theo Flower's abilities, how he could call forth the dead from beyond, how he could "fix" an enemy, how his power came from the evil fangs of river snakes. Willis felt something cold on his neck, something like a wet wind.

Then the pastor drove off in his Packard. And later, in the silent night, Willis awoke from a nightmare with a violent fever and pains that shot through his chest and neck.

Willis never worked another day, nor did he sleep well. Then three months into the new year of 1950, on the very day that Perry was born to his younger sister, Willis Duclat dropped dead.

It happened despite his precautions. Convinced that mortal danger lay waiting in the alleyway in the form of water moccasins or copperheads that would sometimes slither up from the levee, Willis had begun a new daily protective routine. He would mix a batch of quicklime and cayenne pepper into the boiling water left over from scrubbing the front steps and pour the potion in two parallel lines along the inside of the fence that enclosed his garden. One of the old *voodooiennes* assured him he would be safe now, back as well as front.

Just before he died, Willis was sitting on a step out back, smoking a morning pipe of tobacco. Vivian was on her way to a mansion on St. Charles Avenue, where she had a job minding three children, cleaning some, and cooking for a doctor who ate far too much. Across the river, meanwhile, in the parish of Algiers, a midwife pulled an infant boy into the world from between the legs of his very young and frightened mother.

Willis's left leg dangled off the side of the pine steps and his bare foot swung back and forth, toes brushing through the dewy grass that he'd coaxed into growing from muddy soil. Then suddenly, his body convulsed with a spasm so overwhelming it threw him to the ground, where he twisted around for a few seconds in mute torture before his heart stopped. Vivian found him when she returned home in the afternoon. He was sprawled on his back in the grass, his face covered with bits of blossoms, the white and purple petals that fell from the chinaberry tree.

She ran to a confectionery shop where there was a public telephone and rang up the doctor's house. Her employer drove over right away, breaking the speed limit even though Vivian told him that Willis was dead and already cold. The doctor examined the body there in the garden and after a minute or two pointed to a blue-black welt on Willis's left ankle. "He's full of venom more than likely," he said.

"No, sir," said Vivian. "Somebody's gone and hexed my man."

The lane was never paved, nor was it ever so much as named. And through the decades, Theo Flower bought up hundreds more ragged neighborhoods in New Orleans, building up his church membership and the sort of respectability money from any source whatever buys in the entrenched power structure of a southern town.

Along about the middle 1970s, the federal government mandated sewer hook-ups for even the lowliest neighborhoods in any city that expected revenue-sharing funds. So New Orleans obliged people like Vivian Duclat, finally. For his part, Theo Flower hiked her rent since the property would become more valuable with the addition of a modern convenience.

In July of 1983, Perry Duclat was paroled out of the Louisiana State Prison at Angola after serving half of a seven-year sentence for grand theft—auto. He'd been convicted of "borrowing" a Rolls-Royce that belonged to the doctor where his Aunt Vivian worked. In his defense, Perry told the judge, "I was helpin' out my aunt one day at the big house and the man was out of town for the weekend and there was that nice big car of his just sittin' in the garage goin' nowhere. So naturally I borrowed it. How else is a man like me ever goin' to have any style in his life? I put it back right where I found it and I never hurt it one little bit, no sir." Perry had borrowed many things in the past, many of them yet to be returned, so the judge threw the book at him and lectured him on how he'd probably never amount to anything with that sort of thieving attitude. The defendant only smiled.

And even so, even though the doctor told her she could never work at his house again, Vivian took Perry in when he was released from Angola with nowhere to go. She took him in because they were family, no matter what; because he was born on that terrible day her husband died; because in the years he'd been at Angola he'd taken on such a strong resemblance to Willis.

Every day but Sunday, Vivian would get up early in the morning and go off to work someplace. Perry would get up right after that and attend to the chores, which included keeping his aunt's part of the cottage meticulously clean and scrubbing down the front steps because she believed most of the old myths even if he didn't. By ten o'clock or so, he would be back in his own room watching television.

In the three months he'd been there, Perry's room had become wall-to-wall beer cans, hundreds of them, under a film of cigarette ash. He would light cigarettes and leave them burning on the windowsill or at the edge of the dresser. Holes were burnt into the sheets of his bed, where he sat day after day watching television game shows, talk shows, soap operas, meaningless news and witless comedies and endless commercials on a portable black-and-white set with a wire coathanger for an antenna. He liked to crush the cans after draining them, then he'd toss them aside, anywhere. Mostly, he drank Dixie beer, in the white cans with red-and-yellow lettering, or Coors in the gold cans when he had a few dollars extra.

Some days he'd stroll down to the levee. But Miss Toni had whispered around that Perry was an escaped convict, so very few neighbors would have anything to do with him. The old-timers talked to him, though, especially the widows in their *tignons*, garrulous old magpies always happy to pass along the legends that meant everything to them and practically nothing to the disrespectful younger generation.

Sometimes he would tend his late uncle's garden, where Miss Toni would spy on him from a window, ducking out of sight when he turned his face in the direction of her cottage. Or he'd sit on the back steps and read a book, which Miss Toni considered most highly suspicious. Perry had two big stacks of books in his room, one on the dresser and another that filled a corner, floor to ceiling. Sometimes, too, he would write or draw in a tablet. About once a week, he would set off by foot all the way up to the library on Rampart Street.

But mostly Perry watched television, drank and smoked and drowned himself in thought. By noon, his eyes were boozy slits and his fingers stank of nicotine. He would watch the flickering idiot box until it went dark in the wee hours of the next day. He ate very little, though he did enjoy whatever his Aunt Vivian cared to cook or bake.

The two of them seldom talked. The chat was pleasant when Vivian spoke of Perry's late uncle, when she'd show him photographs of Willis or bring out a box of Willis's personal effects or tell Perry again about the day he died, what the doctor said, and how she thought that was "nothin' but medical yap." But then it would lead inevitably to the subject of Theo Flower and their chat would quickly become an argument loud enough for Miss

Toni next door to hear every word of it, even without her big
ears at the window.

"That nigger Flower's nothin' but an old-timey conjure man,
nothin' but a slick and cussed old fraud who's gots lots of little
old ladies like you and Miss Toni and all scared out of your
bloomers 'cause he's supposed to 'know the mysteries,' " Perry
would say, eyes rolling and his voice heavy with sarcasm. "Haw!
Y'all must be crazy."

To which Vivian would reply, her jowls quivering and a finger
wagging up against her nephew's nose, "You best shut that sassy
trap, boy! In the first damn place, we're beholden to Pastor
Flower for this house we're in. And in the second damn place,
well, let's just say you ain't lived near long enough to understand that precious little in this ol' world is actually what it
seems to be."

She never quite told him so, but Vivian thrilled to her
nephew's boisterous arrogance on the subject of Theo Flower.
She supposed this might be a womanly fault of hers, enjoying
the antagonisms of men at dispute where she was concerned, so
she kept quiet. But when Perry would inveigh against Pastor
Flower and his church, Vivian's eyes would mist over some, and
through that prism of tears and remembrance she sometimes
thought she was looking at her husband again. God bless poor
black men for what little arrogance they dared show the world,
she thought.

And Vivian didn't care a hoot whether Miss Toni heard them
carrying on—which she did, and which she dutifully passed
along nearly word-for-word to Pastor Flower himself, who
maintained a pervasive interest in the personal lives of his
home-indentured flock.

Perry's irreverence greatly disturbed Theo Flower. His un-
ease was compounded by the unnerving physical resemblance
he saw in Perry to the late Willis Duclat, who was about Perry's
age when he died. Perry had taken to attending Sunday services
of the Church of the Awakened Spirit and he sat right down
center and never took his eyes off Pastor Flower, never registered any expression, just stood and sat down when requested.
Never had a nickel for the collection plate. But there he sat
anyway, unembarrassed, looking for all the world like Willis

Duclat with his hot black eyes, taut olive-brown skin, high forehead, and straight hawklike nose. And those wide shoulders and thickly muscled arms, with big hammer hands folded in his lap.

"You better come do somethin' on that boy here," Miss Toni warned Pastor Flower on the telephone. "I tell you, I believe Perry's got some kind of trouble-makin' designs. I see him some days on those back steps, lookin' over to my place and starin' at me and wonderin' lord only knows what! Now, you know how we don't want no trouble here. We mean to keep in our houses, Pastor Flower. Please do somethin' on him!"

"Yes, yes. You're quite right," he told Miss Toni. "We will have to stop any trouble before it has a chance to begin."

Pastor Flower said yes to a drop of brandy in his coffee and asked permission to light a cheroot in Vivian Duclat's parlor besides. "Oh my, yes, go right ahead," she said. "My Willis was a smokin' man, you know. La, yes, he had to have that pipe of his from mornin' to midnight."

"Yes, I do recall that." Flower fired a sterling Tiffany lighter and touched the yellow-blue hiss of flame to the blunt end of his cigar. In the flash of light, Vivian saw again the gold crowns sparkle in the back of his mouth.

It was a Sunday twilight and a heavy blackness moved across the sky, overtaking what was left of the day and the week. Perry's television set droned from the back of the cottage.

"Sister Vivian, I come here to talk with you tonight on a delicate matter, one that causes me grave concern as to your welfare."

"What in the world can that be?" Vivian had enjoyed several drops of brandy in several cups of coffee before the pastor's call and her voice was thick.

"Well, Sister Vivian, you know how people will talk. Many of your neighbors and friends are worried sick about your being all alone in this house with a man fresh out of prison, a man who I am told lives like some sort of wild animal in the back room of this cottage and who does nothing besides drink all day long. Now, I must worry about this for your sake—and for the sake of the church's property, after all."

Vivian touched her lips to hide a smile, which she thought Pastor Flower might well interpret as contemptuous. "I think I know maybe just one neighbor who'd gab like that and maybe she's over there listenin' now. Besides, if I had to worry 'bout ev'ry man 'round this neighborhood who'd ever been locked up, well, shoot, I'd be a mighty nervous old hag by now. So don't worry none 'bout my nephew Perry, 'cause *I'm* sure not worryin' and you can tell Miss Toni the same if you want."

"Well, I only mean that your husband Willis was a hardworking, sober man and this Perry is a layabout. That is what I'm told." Flower coughed, then opened his red-leather Bible and spread it out on the parlor table. "You know very well from the scriptures how the devil works through wicked drinking men and other idle folks."

"Maybe I know that," Vivian said. "I do know for sure that the devil works through schemin' folks."

She poured herself another brandy and spotted it with coffee out of respect for the ministry. The ministry accepted one for himself.

"Let me set your mind at ease some, Pastor Flower. You should know a little of Perry's story, then maybe you'd understand him like I do. He's not a dangerous young man, no more than any other young man. He is sloppy, though. I'd be shamed to have you see where he stays.

"But look here, Perry's been bruised all through his life and them bruises come one right after the other. Ain't none of them healed up completelike, which is maybe why he lays 'round all the day long. Sometimes he shows some spunk, but if he's dogtired from life most of the time, then I figure he's got the right.

"His mother—that would be Willis's sister—was nothin' but an ignorant teenage girl livin' over in Algiers in a shack all alone near a coalyard. How d'you s'pose a girl like that made out in the world? Well, you can imagine right enough. Anyway, she gets herself in the family way and then come runnin' over here with the baby, not even knowin' her brother Willis had passed on. Not that she'd care 'bout that, mind you, not any more'n she cared for that baby she just plopped down on me.

"But I minded the child for a while and loved him. I named him, too, you know. Maybe I might have gone crazy without the baby 'round me to take my mind offa how Willis died like he did—" Her shoulders shook and she cried softly. Pastor Flower moved to comfort her with his hands, but she backed away from his touch.

"And you know all 'bout that," she said to Flower. "Anyway, Perry's mama went up to Chicago, so I heard. She wrote how fine she was doin' up North and how she wanted to send for Perry and all. But then the man who did her come by one day with a new wife and says he wants to take his baby and raise him up over to Algiers. That's what he did, took Perry away from me and wasn't nothin' I could do 'bout it.

"But Perry started comin' back here regular when he got older, just as soon as he could get by on the ferry on his own. An' I started noticin' how beat-up lookin' he was. I got it out of him what was goin' on over to his daddy's house. His daddy's lady would be all the time hittin' him, or burnin' him with cigarettes or shamin' him in front of the other little boys by comin' after him with a belt and whuppin' his head till he'd fall over bloody, then whuppin' some more until he messed his pants.

"I tol' his daddy all this when he would come for him to take him back, and that man said his boy was possessed 'cause he wouldn't never do nothin' right or what was told him. Then he finally put little Perry in a home someplace out in the country.

"Next I heard, Perry'd busted out of that home, which was more like some prison than a home, which it never had any right to be called, and he headed north lookin' for his mama. He found her, too. He come back and tol' me how she was nothin' but a whore and a dope addict, how she looked like death itself and didn't even know Perry was her kin.

"Well, he was right. Later on, we heard from some city health official up North how she was dead from heroin and askin' us did we know her birthday. They was so shocked to learn she was only thirty-six.

"Perry figured he'd better stay over with his father, else his daddy'd make trouble for me. But the man tossed him out soon's he showed up over there to Algiers.

"And so, you see, Perry's had trouble all the time in his life. What do you expect? He was nothin' but a thrown-away child.

Least that's what he think of himself anytime he's away from
here."

Pastor Flower folded his hands over his Bible. Vivian ran her
fingers through her hair nervously. From the back of the house
where Perry watched television came the added sound of a
beer can popping open, an empty being crushed, then the
clatter of it when it fell to the littered floor.

"I'm sorry for you, Sister Vivian, but I cannot stand by idly in
this matter."

Her voice rising high, Vivian said, "What do you mean? Don't
you be takin' my Perry away! Don't you be takin' another man
from this place!"

"Quiet woman!" Flower's voice thundered. There was stillness in the house. "What I shall do here is convene the spirits
and consult the wisdom of the other side. I shall call out your
own husband, Willis Duclat!"

Vivian shrieked, and her cup and saucer crashed to the floor.

"Yes," Flower said, "I shall call out the spirit of Willis Duclat.
He—and only he—shall guide us on the matter of your
nephew!"

Pastor Flower closed his Bible and the sound of it echoed in
the parlor. He stood up and moved to the door, put on his hat. "I
shall request that everybody in this lane come to service next
Sunday. You come, too, Sister Vivian. I know you wouldn't want
to miss hearing your husband's voice."

The tall dark woman at the side of the altar began chanting in a
low, melodious voice. She started in a *français africain* dia-
lect—

>*"Danse Calinda, boudoum, boudoum!*
>*Danse Calinda, boudoum, boudoum!"*

Pastor Flower, in a scarlet robe covered with *gris-gris*—dolls
made of feathers and hair, skins of snakes, bits of bone—rose
from a pit beneath the altar in a great plume of white-and-gray
smoke. Beaming at the congregants in front of him, he turned
and knelt at the altar as the woman's chanting grew in volume
and tempo. He rapped the floor and then lit the black crucifix-
shaped candles. He turned again to face his flock and he picked

up the chant himself, raising his arms, commanding all to join in the calling out of spirits from beyond life.

Bodies swayed in the pews of the Church of the Awakened Spirit and the chanting rolled in waves, the single line of African French pulsating stronger and stronger through the sanctuary and out the open door into the liquid air of a savagely hot, humid Sabbath morning in New Orleans. Hands kept time and feet moved from muffled accentuation to a steady, rhythmic pounding.

Vivian Duclat, tears streaming down her face, for she had slept little during her week of anticipation, slapped her hands together determinedly and pounded her feet. She would hear her man, maybe she would even see her Willis—it didn't matter if the image were no more real than the times she thought she saw him in Perry's face. But what would Willis say of Perry? Would he send him away from her? Would Willis, too, throw the child away?

The tall dark woman stepped forward from the altar, moved her arms in an arc, and then switched to the Creole patois and to the uninhibited, throaty *canga*—

"*Eh! Eh! Bomba, hen! hen!*
Canga bafio, te,
Canga moune de le,
Canga do ki la,
Canga li!"

All joined the chant, their massed voices now storming and frenzied, so full of pathos and longing that it became impossible for anyone to remain free of the swing and the narcotic influence of the ancient words. Everywhere, people were prepared to believe it all, for the first time in many cases. The eyes of the young were no longer disrespectful, they were full of proper fright—the old-timers clung righteously to *gris-gris* charms of their own they'd brought along to the ceremony, their little "conjure balls" of black wax and bits of their own skin or bleached lizards in glass jelly jars or dried-up rooster hearts—the curious things they kept under lock and key at home, out of embarrassment and fear. Pastor Flower then began the dance of the Voudou, the leader.

He raised a bottle of brandy from the alter, dashed some of the liquid on each side of a brown bowl full of brick dust, then tossed back his head and took a long pull of the liquor. Then he started the slow hip shuffling, moved his feet backward and then forward, accelerating his movement up to the speed of the hypnotic *canga*. Without ceasing a single step of his dance, Flower poured the rest of the brandy into the bowl, then ignited it with his silver Tiffany lighter. The bowl flared up high over the altar and still he danced the maddening *canga*, his powerful voice starting to rise up over the waning strength of all the others:

"I call out Willis Duclat! *Eh! Eh! Bomba, hen! hen!* I call out Willis Duclat! *Eh! Eh! Bomba, hen! hen!* Willis Duclat, speak through me—"

And suddenly, a tall young man covered in a brilliant red-and-black robe and hood ran crazily from somewhere in the back of the church, whirling and leaping and howling like a dervish until he reached the altar and a stunned Pastor Flower, who tripped and fell to his knees. The mysterious figure then vaulted over a railing and turned to the panicked congregation.

He tore the hood from his head, then the robe from his body, and stood before the assembly, his olive-brown body naked and oiled, his handsome face with the straight hawklike nose held high. Women screamed, but they did not avert their eyes, for the figure before them was a perfect masculine beauty. He raised his big-fisted hands and cried out over the nearly hushed church.

"I am Willis Duclat! I *am* Willis Duclat!"

And from the pew next to Vivian Duclat, a trembling Miss Toni stood up and screamed, "Jesus, Mary, and Joseph, it's him! Oh la, it's him!"

The old ladies in *tignons* began fainting away and children squealed. Men stared, gape-mouthed, unable to help the women and the young. The tall muscular naked man grasped the shoulders of a terrified Theo Flower and lifted him several inches off the floor, then dropped him, crumpling, to a twitching heap. He turned again to the congregation and roared, "I, Willis Duclat, have come out!" He then knelt to Pastor Flower and whispered to him, "Time for you to blow town, chump, 'cause your number's up here."

He stripped Flower's robe of his *gris-gris,* which he dropped into the bowl of flaming brandy with elaborate gesticulation, so that all in the church could see he meant to destroy Theo Flower's control over them. "Be gone, the impostor's fakery!" he shouted.

He asked for silence. Then he raised an arm and slowly directed it toward Miss Toni. "You," he said, "were in league with the impostor cowering at my feet. *You* placed the snake below the steps where you knew it would strike at me. You murdered me! It could have been no other way!"

Vivian sobbed.

"La, gawd-a-mercy!" Miss Toni screamed.

"Yes, yes, it was you! You and the impostor, this man called Theophilus Flower, who has oppressed you and cheated you all so cruelly for so many years since my death. It was you, Miss Toni, who killed me—to keep me from telling the truth that I do today!"

"La, mercy! Mercy! Oh la, please!" Miss Toni fell to the floor, gasping and writhing and consumed with her guilt, which took the form of what the hospital would later diagnose as massive cerebral hemorrhage.

The man then tore a lock of hair from his head and held it high over him so all could see. "Today I have destroyed the power of the impostor Theophilus Flower, who was foolish enough to call me out. I tell you all now, you must shun him! This hair I hold is the most powerful *gris-gris* of all, the hair of one from beyond. I shall give it to someone who lives amongst you. I shall plant it in his head this very night as he sleeps, and there it will grow. I shall give the power to a thrown-away child, now a grown man in my image, so that you shall always know him!"

Then he disappeared into the pit below the altar.

"Thank you for receiving me here, sir. I would have understood your refusing me."

"Well, son, I look at it this way: you done the crime and you done the time. Now that's just so much water under the bridge, don't you know. B'sides, you intrigue the hell out of me."

"Yes, sir. Thank you again." He brushed lint from the top of his sharply creased charcoal-gray slacks, part of a Parisian suit he'd had made for him by a tailor at Gauchaux's on Canal Street.

The fat man offered him one of his cigars, which he declined in favor of a pipe that used to belong to his uncle. He lit the pipe and the fat man's cigar, too, with a sterling lighter that used to belong to Theo Flower.

"Tell me," the fat man said, "how's Vivian doin' for herself these days? We all loved her so much. Damn me for casting her out like I did just 'cause of what you did."

"Nice of you to inquire, Doctor. My aunt's doin' just fine now. She had a little excitement at church a while back, but she rested lots afterward and I was able to take care of her, now that I'm runnin' the church myself and all."

"She's welcome to come back to me any time, you know."

"Thanks again, Doctor. I'll send her callin', but, you know, she likes her retirement now and she's earned it, I'd say."

"Of course, of course." The doctor shook his fleshy head. "Damn me again! Perry, I'm sorta sorry now for havin' that judge crack down on you like he did."

"That don't matter much now. You might say you straightened me out by catchin' me. I had lots of time to think things through in prison. It was sorta strange, actually. All kinds of thought just sorta took over me, and I couldn't do much more'n think, day in and day out. Finally, I figured that I had to watch close for somethin' to come along that I could grab onto to make life good for me and my aunt for a change."

"Well, sounds to me like you did a fine piece of thinkin'. Just how'd you manage to take over the church, though? I mean, Theo Flower didn't strike me as a man ready to retire, like your old aunt. All of us fellows downtown were sorta surprised when he lit out for Baton Rouge like he did, without even a bye-you-well."

Perry smiled. "He had a change of spirit, you might say. Decided on greener pastures maybe. Anyway, I was around and interested in the church, you know. Spent lots of time readin' up on it and all and figurin' how I might make my contribution.

So, the moment come along when I figured I might grab on, so I done that."

He smiled again. "Of course, I had to first prove to Pastor Flower that I understood all the mysteries of his divine work. He musta been satisfied, because he signed everything over to me."

Perry emptied the contents of a satchel onto a table between him and the doctor.

"It's all legal, I didn't have to steal anything—or 'borrow,' I should say." The doctor laughed and Perry went on. "See here, it's all the deeds and titles and bank accounts—everything. That's why I come to you, sir, for some guidance in handling this all."

"You can count on me, Perry."

"I'm so glad."

"Where do you want to start?"

"Well, first thing," Perry said, "I want all the cottages down there in that lane off Tchoupitoulas deeded over to the tenants, maybe for a dollar apiece, some token like that that'd be sure to make it legal and then—"

DOUG ALLYN

THE PUDDLE DIVER

Doug Allyn was the 1985 winner of the Robert L. Fish Memorial Award, presented each year by the Mystery Writers of America to the author of the most promising "first story" in the field. During 1986 Allyn more than fulfilled his promise with four stories in Alfred Hitchcock's Mystery Magazine, *three of which I've listed on this year's Honor Roll. The best of them is this suspenseful novelette of murder in a sunken ship on the bottom of Lake Huron, which earned the author an Edgar nomination from MWA.*

It's possible Charlie Bauer's siren saved me from serious bodily injury. One of my regular customers had started a shoving match with a line-backer-sized tourist at the pool table. I'd charged out from behind the bar to try to break it up when the whoop of the approaching siren and the shriek of rubber in the parking lot mellowed everybody out. We couldn't be sure what the siren meant, of course, since the only windows in the Crow's Nest face Lake Huron and the harbor; still, ask not for whom the horn toots.

Charlie Bauer stalked through the back door a moment later, looking extremely unhappy, which made me unhappy, too. At six six and 270, Charlie's moods would be contagious even if he weren't the county sheriff. He may not be solid muscle anymore, he's pushing fifty, going a little gray on top and bulgy in the middle, but he's still big enough to make people uneasy, and a giant surly cop is not what I needed to perk up my afternoon trade.

He motioned me back to my office, followed me in, and closed the door behind us.

"Mitch, I've got a problem, and I need help. Looks like we've got a body down."

"Who?" I asked.

"Addison, I think his name is. Harvey Addison? Andrea Deveraux's fiancée."

"Sweet Jesus," I said softly. I didn't say anything for a moment. I couldn't. "What happened?" I managed at last.

"Nobody's sure. Addison and Terry Fortier were diving on the *Queen of Lorraine.* Terry came up, Addison didn't. Baggers Gant was down with them videotaping the dive, but he didn't go inside the wreck. I want you to go down after the body."

"I thought the department had a contract with Bill Atkins for this sort of thing."

"He's down on Saginaw Bay diving on a light plane and we're supposed to get a three-day blow tonight. I need somebody to go out there right now."

I glanced out my office window. Across the harbor the sky was darkening and Lake Huron already looked rough, with three- to four-foot seas. Typical weather for August. Tour Michigan, the water wonderland, the brochures say. What they don't say is that only half of the water is in the lakes. The other half will fall on your head at frequent intervals.

"Sorry," I said, "you'll have to get somebody else, Charlie."

"What the hell? You helped us out once before."

"Right," I said. "Once. A lot of guys will dive on a body—once. It's not something you ever want to do again. Besides, I've got a business to run here."

"The *Queen*'s at two hundred feet. Do you know anybody else who can work that deep?"

"Yeah," I said. "Terry can, or even Baggers. And they're already out there."

"I don't want either of them going back down. In fact, I've ordered them to stay out of the water."

"What the hell is that supposed to mean?"

"Maybe nothing," he said stubbornly, "but Terry and Addison went down together and Addison didn't come back. Terry and Andrea were pretty tight at one time, as I recall. Real tight."

"Nuts, Charlie, if you suspect every guy who's had the hots for Andrea Deveraux sometime or other, you'll have to arrest half the clowns that grew up in this town, including me. Terry's always been a little wild, maybe, but not that way, and you know it."

"I know he's a friend of yours, Mitch, so I'll put it to you straight. We're not talking about just anybody here, we're talking about Andrea Deveraux's fiancée. I can't take any chances with this. If you won't go down, I'm going to hold Terry on suspicion until Atkins gets back. I've got to cover myself. You know what old man Deveraux's like."

Charlie had a point. In that long ago summer when I'd been Andrea's latest, and temporarily welcome at the Deveraux estate, I'd gotten to know Jason Deveraux in passing. He was my fantasy father-figure, tall, distinguished, head of DevCon Paper Mills, the Deveraux Mills Fleet, the Deveraux Institute. A charming, glib, vindictive son of a bitch. I liked him a lot. And Bauer was right. He was not someone to cross.

"Come on, Mitch," Bauer pleaded quietly, "I haven't been keeping score, but you must owe me at least one. And if not me, then Terry. I don't want to lock him up, but I will. How about it?"

"I guess I can get Sharon to come in early to tend bar, and keep an eye on things," I sighed. "You've scared off half of my customers anyway. I'll get my gear and meet you at my boat in twenty minutes."

"Good," Bauer said. "I won't forget this, Mitch. This ah, Addison," he added, pausing in the doorway, "did you know him?"

"I met him once," I said.

"And?"

"He seemed nice enough," I shrugged. "Andrea's always had good taste. I'll see you at the harbor. Twenty minutes."

I'd met Harvey Addison a month earlier, Fourth of July weekend. The Crow's Nest was packed with wall to wall tourists, but I noticed him right away because he came in with Andrea. Even after all these years I still get a visceral twinge whenever she walks into a room. First loves are like that for everyone, I suppose, but I think she has a similar effect on most people. She's a striking woman, broad-shouldered with dark, tousled hair. Her features are too angular to be considered conventionally pretty, but there's a feline magnetism about her, a restlessness, that more than compensates. For me, at least.

Naturally, I checked out the latest of my successors. He was depressingly handsome, tall, trim, and tan, with sandy hair, wearing a linen blazer that cost as much as air fare to Australia. He looked early thirtyish, maybe a year or two younger than Andrea, although she never seems to change. They conferred for a moment by the door, then she wandered off to talk to friends and he came straight back to my office, rapping lightly on the door before he stepped in.

"Mr. Mitchell?" he said, offering his hand. "I'm Harvey Addison. I understand that among other things, you're the dean of the local scuba divers."

"I don't think I'm old enough to be a dean yet," I said, "but I know most of the people in the area who dive, and I've been known to get wet myself. What can I do for you?" His handshake was firm, but not a contest. Score one for him. He eased into one of the captain's chairs in front of my desk.

"I'm interested in chartering a boat for a month or so. I'm told there are some interesting wrecks in the area."

"A few," I nodded. "There are nearly a hundred wrecks within fifteen miles of where you're sitting, and over six thousand major wrecks in the Great Lakes that we have record of. God only knows how many smaller ships there are. The big lakes are hard on boats. And people, too, sometimes."

"Actually, there's a specific wreck I'm interest in, the *Queen of Lorraine.*"

"The *Queen?*" I said, raising an eyebrow.

"That's right. Do you know anything about her?"

"Some. She was built in 1926, flagship of the Deveraux Mills Fleet," I recited. "She was bound for Chicago out of Erie with a cargo of rolled steel in November 1968 when she was rammed by a Swedish freighter, the ah . . . the *Halmstad.* Her captain apparently didn't realize how badly she was damaged and tried to run her for the beach on North Point. He didn't make it. She rolled and sank. Most of her crew got off, but at least a half-dozen didn't, including the captain."

"I'm impressed," Addison said. "You've dived on her, then?"

"He hasn't," Terry Fortier said from the doorway, "but I have." He'd wandered in during the last few moments of our conversation. I'd been expecting him. He'd been shooting pool in the lounge and I knew he wouldn't miss a chance to check out Andrea's latest. They were quite a contrast, Addison, the fair-haired WASP, and Terry, compactly built, hawk-faced, dark as a pirate.

I introduced them and Terry parked a hip on the corner of my desk, resting the hilt of his pool cue on the floor.

"The *Queen's* at two hundred feet," he continued, "upside down, with her masts and stacks buried in the mud, right in the middle of the Huron Bottomlands Preserve."

"Preserve?" Addison frowned.

"The legislature passed a law back in '80 outlawing any plundering of the wrecks," I explained. "You need a permit to dive on any ship in the Preserve. The law's difficult to enforce, though, and there's still a black market for ships' 'jewelry,'— running lights, wheels, portholes, things like that. In fact, I heard a rumor that some of the jewelry from the *Queen* was on the market recently."

"Yeah," Terry said blandly, "I heard that, too. Why the particular interest in the *Queen,* Harvey? There are plenty of wrecks out there."

"She belonged to my fiancée's family, the Deveraux. Perhaps you've met Andrea?"

His innocence was unfeigned, so apparently she hadn't told him about Terry. Or me. Or any of the others either, probably. I wondered how well he really knew her.

"Sure," Terry said, "we went to high school together. You remember Andy, don't you, Mitch?"

"Vaguely," I said. "Nice kid."

"I think so," Addison said smugly. "In any case, it seems there was a large bronze plaque bolted to the wall of the passengers' salon when the ship was launched, and my future father-in-law is pretty keen on recovering it for the Deveraux Institute museum. I have a picture here," he said, retrieving an old photo of the *Queen of Lorraine* from an inside pocket of his sportcoat. "The lounge is all the way forward here, in the bow. From the blueprints, it looks like the only way to get into it is down a long corridor from the main entrance amidships." He passed the photograph to Terry. "What do you think? Could we get in there?"

"I don't know," Terry said, frowning at the photo. "I haven't been inside at that end of the ship, but her bow area's clear of the bottom. Maybe."

"You said 'we,' Mr. Addison," I said. "Are you planning to dive on the *Queen* yourself?"

"Of course," he said, "that's the whole point. I want the plaque as a sort of wedding present for Mr. Deveraux. I've never been down two hundred feet, but I'm a quick learner and I've done some diving."

"In the Great Lakes?" I asked.

"No, mostly in the Caribbean and off the Florida coast, but I don't imagine there's much difference."

"Actually there's quite a bit," I said. "The lakes are dark and dirty and cold as a witch's kiss. The visibility's lousy because of the silt, and the currents can be tricky as hell. The wrecks are usually in good shape, though. They don't deteriorate in fresh water, which makes them seem deceptively safe sometimes. They're not."

"And, of course, there may be a body or two," Terry said, "which is why Mitch here hasn't been down to the *Queen* himself. How do you feel about bodies, Harvey?"

"There was a skeleton on one of the wrecks off Florida," he said. "I managed."

"I'm not talking about skeletons," Terry smiled, "I'm talking about bodies."

"But the *Queen*'s been down nearly twenty years, surely—"

"At two hundred feet the lake temperature only varies from thirty-four to thirty-eight degrees," Terry said, "so the bodies don't deteriorate, and lake fish don't scavenge that deep. The *Griffin* went down in 1689, but if she's deep enough, whoever went down with her is probably still aboard, and in one piece. More or less."

"You've got to be kidding," Addison said.

"I'm afraid he's not," I said. "There may be six men still aboard the *Queen*. It's something to consider."

Addison eyed us with obvious suspicion. "Look," he said stiffly, "I know it's probably a local custom to have a little fun with the new kid on the block, but I'm dead serious about diving on the *Queen*. I'm no puddle diver. I've worked at a hundred feet and I can handle two hundred with a little training. I want to hire a boat and an experienced diver. Now, is either of you interested or not?"

"Don't let these louts get your goat, Harvey," Andrea said, leaning over the back of his chair, her lips brushing the air beside his cheek, "they're experts. The class clowns of Huron Harbor High. And don't get up on my account, gentlemen, if the thought had even occurred to you." She eased gracefully into the captain's chair next to Harvey's, drew a cigarette from her handbag, and waited for him to light it for her. Which he did with not quite unseemly haste.

"Mitch, Terry," she nodded, blowing a plume of smoke in my direction, "how are you? It's been a long time."

"You wouldn't know it to look at you," I said honestly, "you look terrific." And she did. Almost. She was wearing an unbleached muslin sunsuit that showed her figure to good advantage, but the tequila sunrise in her hand looked suspiciously like a triple to my practiced eye, and she'd kept her sunglasses on, even though the Crow's Nest is dim as a dungeon. I'd heard her mother was summering in a posh sanitarium for substance abusers, and I wondered if Andrea was going to make it a family tradition.

"I'm surprised to find you back in town and running the Nest, Mitch," she said.

"Why surprised?" I said. "Some of my best friends are saloons."

"I don't know, I remember you as being irritatingly ambitious. I thought you had your eye on bigger things."

"I still have, in a way," I said, indicating the window.

"You mean the harbor?" she frowned, following my glance.

"No," I said, "the lakes."

She puzzled over that for a moment, then dismissed the idea with a shrug. The talk turned to the difficulties in obtaining a salvor's permit from the DNR, but I didn't pay much attention. A moot point. Her father could probably finagle a permit to cede Alaska to the Bulgarians if the mood struck him. Instead, I played a little game.

I switched on an imaginary slide projector in my head, and tried to align my undimmed images of Andrea from the summer after graduation with the woman seated next to Harvey. They didn't match. The changes were slight, but significant. The cigarette, the tequila triple, the lines of petulance etched permanently around her mouth. But then my little projector went out of control and the memories came rushing over me in a flood, Andrea in my arms at the senior prom, Andrea on the foredeck of my first little sloop, wearing an electric blue bikini that caused me physical pain, Andrea by moonlight, the lake spray glistening on her shoulders as we made love for hours on a tattered beach blanket with the surf a symphony of thunder in the background. And, of course, Andrea enraged, coldly furious at my demand that she miss the July Fourth beach party because I had to work. She'd gone to the party, and out of my life, and as it happened, into Terry's that same night. But only briefly. In September she'd gone off to Bryn Mawr and—

They were staring at me expectantly.

"I'm sorry," I said, "I was . . . woolgathering. What—?"

"Harvey asked if he could charter you and the *Bonita* exclusive for a month or so," Terry said. "If you're too busy, I'd be happy to take him on. I can use the charter."

"Maybe that would be best," I nodded. "I'm, ah, pretty well booked up, and since you've already been down to the *Queen* . . ." I was having trouble breathing. My chest was constricted by a long forgotten ache, one that had nothing to do with the woman in front of me, only with the one I'd lost.

"Good," Harvey said, rising. "It's settled, then. I look forward to it. It's been a pleasure meeting both of you." Andrea walked out without a word as we made our goodbyes.

Terry watched them make their way through the afternoon crowd, Andy moving a bit unsteadily, I thought, then he crossed to my liquor cabinet and poured two snifters of Courvoisier.

"Here," he said, passing one to me, "you look like you need one."

"Was I that obvious?"

"Probably only to me. She hasn't changed a bit, has she?"

"It's been a long time," I said. "Everybody changes."

"Not Andy," he said, sipping the brandy thoughtfully, "she's like one of the deep water ladies. I don't think she'll ever change."

It occurred to me that Terry probably had a few memories of his own, so I sipped the brandy, letting the warmth of it soothe my pain, and said nothing. And maybe that was a mistake.

Charlie Bauer was waiting on the dock, staring doubtfully at the *Bonita* when I pulled up.

"Christ," he said, "are we goin' out there in this thing? I've seen wrecks on the beach lookin' better'n it does."

"She was a wreck," I said, "a Chris Craft Sea Skiff, built in '58, sunk in a storm in '76. I salvaged her out of the deep channel in the Charlevoix inlet and fixed her up."

"It don't look like you fixed her up much," he said, frowning.

"No reason to," I said. "Divers' boats always look crappy anyway, what with tanks and weight belts and salvage bangin' around. She's seaworthy enough."

"I'll bet the first guy who owned her thought so too," Bauer grumbled. He chucked his hat into his prowl car and helped me transfer the three sets of double eighty air tanks from the back of my Jeep to the racks of the *'Nita*'s gunwales, handling the 125-pound packs with ease. You can never have too many spare tanks on a dive boat, but I probably wouldn't need them today. The sky was darkening rapidly and the wind was rising. I'd only have time for one dive before the storm hit.

I fired up the *Bonita* and her Chevy inboard grumbled to life, coughing and hawking like an old man in the morning. "Grab my duffel bag out of the Jeep and cast off while I warm her up," I shouted at Bauer over the mutter of the engine.

"You got a radio aboard?" he yelled back.

"Ship to shore, marine band. Your office can monitor us on channel sixteen."

"Good enough."

I checked the gauges and the radio while Charlie called his office from his prowl car. The *'Nita*'s fuel tanks were topped off, and everything else read normal, which was good. The *Queen of Lorraine* was three miles offshore and I didn't like the look of the bay at all. My duffel bag thumped on the deck behind me. Bauer cast off the mooring lines and scrambled aboard with all the grace of a waltzing bear.

I eased the *Bonita* forward out of her berth, keeping our

speed to a crawl to avoid rocking the other vessels at their moorings. As soon as we cleared the harbor mouth, I opened the throttle and she sprinted out into the bay, bucking her way through choppy five-foot seas, waves that could be thirty feet high in a few hours but not much farther apart than they were now, ship killers that hammered major vessels to pieces and swallowed them down, from the *Griffin* to the *Edmund Fitzgerald.*

"Take the wheel," I shouted at Bauer, "I've got to get my gear on."

"Maybe you better keep it," he said, shaking his head, "I don't know squat about boats."

"Just keep her pointed the way she is now. You'll see Terry's boat when we clear North Point. Head right for it."

He nodded reluctantly and took over. I moved cautiously to the stern, unzipped my duffel bag, and stripped down to my swim trunks. I hauled my "woolly bears" out of the bag and slipped them on. The fluffy long underwear suit probably looked ludicrous for an August afternoon, but where I was going it's always deep in dark December.

The full-body Viking dry suit was next, a bulky, bulgy, neoprene outfit that makes you look like a pregnant walrus. I felt Bauer cut the throttle as I finished giving my equipment a quick once-over. Terry's twenty-seven-foot white Bayliner, the *William Kidd*, was fifty yards or so off our port bow, bobbing like a tethered kite in the choppy seas.

I took the wheel from Charlie and eased the *Bonita* alongside. The *Kidd* is her exact opposite, sparkling new, fiberglass, top of the line, with twin Volvo engines and a fair-sized cabin. Baggers Gant, a towheaded kid from Ohio who works oil rigs with Terry in the winter and as his gofer and safety diver in the summer months, tossed Charlie a line. We moored the boats together, ten yards apart.

"What happened?" I shouted.

"I don't know," Terry called back. "We got into the main salon okay, found the damn plaque and got about half the bolts out of it. I figured we'd need another dive to finish anyway, so I signaled Harvey time's up and made my way out. I thought he was right behind me. Baggers swam over to one of the salon portholes and signaled with a light, but we couldn't see anything inside and we didn't have enough air to go back in."

"Why didn't he follow you when you signaled?"

"How the hell do I know?" Terry shouted angrily. "Maybe he figured he could do the rest of the bolts himself and cut it too fine. I just don't know. He wasn't much on following orders, though, I can tell you that."

"What's it like down there?"

"Bad," Terry yelled, "the weight of her cargo's gradually crushing her superstructure. The passageway and the main salon were tarted up with a lot of gingerbread, and all that crap's coming loose because the bulkheads are buckling. There's about two inches of silt all over everything and it clouds up if you look at it crossways. It's as bad as I've seen."

"How do I get into the passageway?"

"Follow the line down. We're moored to the railing beside the main deck entrance. We ran a lifeline in from there."

"All right," I nodded, pulling on my neoprene helmet. "I'm going down. I'll need a backup."

"I'm coming," Terry said, "my gear's—"

"No," Bauer said, "Baggers can go down."

"Now look, Charlie—" Terry began.

"Knock it off, dammit!" I interrupted. "I don't give a rip who follows me down, just so somebody's there with a line when I come out. And move it. If we get caught out here in that blow we'll all wind up swimming home. Charlie, gimme a hand with my damn tanks!"

The dark water of Huron Bay closed over me in a soft green explosion. The weight of the tank harness disappeared into neutral buoyance, and I felt only the mild drag of the weight belt as I safety-checked my regulator, then found the half-inch nylon mooring line that trailed from the *Kidd* to infinity below.

I began to swim slowly down along the line, gliding gently through a murky green fog, pausing every fifteen feet or so to swallow hard and pinch the bridge of my nose below the mask to adjust my ears to the pressure change. Visibility was especially poor because of the rough weather above, and after the first fifty feet I couldn't see the boats above any more, or anything else below, only the nylon line, faint as a thread, leading down into the haze. There were a few fish, of course, small and indistinct, darting through the green mist, most of them moving downward with me, a sure sign of a serious storm coming on the surface.

At a hundred feet I paused at the deflated inner tube Terry'd snubbed into the line as a shock absorber. I cleared my ears, then did a quick doublecheck of my equipment, for safety and to remind myself that I was in an alien, hostile environment now, no matter how enchanting it was. It's a game all divers play. Deep water, like the sirens of old, can lure you on in a thousand ways, but there's only one way you can ever truly belong down here. The *Queen*'s way. And now Harvey's.

I left the inner tube and continued down. At this depth, the temperature had already dropped to ten degrees Centigrade and was still falling. My Viking suit, so bulky on the surface, was sleek as a second skin now, form-fitted by the pressure. A wet suit would compress to the thickness of a plastic garbage bag at this depth, and be just about as useful. Suddenly I instinctively grabbed the line, startled by a dark shape looming out of the murk below, huge and formless, stretching away beneath me as far as I could see. A great fish glimpsed from above. The keel of the *Queen of Lorraine.*

She was upside down, her stern buried in the ooze. Her forward hull, supported by her crushed stacks, towered above the lake bed like a mountain. Patches of moss adhered to her metal skin, giving her a scrofulous, unhealthy look, but other than that, I could see no rust, no deterioration. She was frozen in time, unchanged since that terrible November night when she'd been mortally wounded by the bow of the *Halmstad* and plunged to the bottom, only minutes from the sanctuary of the north bay shore.

I switched on my helmet lamp and the huge vessel instantly disappeared as the light haloed in the turbid water around me, limiting visibility to eight or ten feet. The *Queen* reappeared moments later as I followed the line down past the gash in her side. It hardly seemed big enough to have killed such a giant ship, no more than fifteen inches across at its widest point, but the angle of collision was such that when the captain swung her into that last desperate dash for the beach, her own speed had forced the water through the gap in a torrent. And she'd rolled. And died. And yet she seemed so untouched by time that she might have lurched to the the lake bottom only hours ago, not twenty years.

I found Harvey's swim fins tied neatly to the main deck rail a few feet from the grappling hook at the end of the *Kidd's* mooring line. A second even more slender line led from the railing across the deck, and disappeared through an open bulkhead door.

It was an odd feeling to look *down* from the main deck at the bridge and wheelhouse below. The *Queen's* masts were buried in the muck and her stacks had collapsed, but her superstructure was otherwise undamaged, supported fifteen or twenty feet above the lake bed.

A flicker of movement below caught my eye. The wheelhouse door was moving, swinging gently in the current. The area around the doorlatch was dented, and the scratches on the metal were still bright. That hadn't happened twenty years before. The marks were fresh.

I slipped my flippers off and tied them beside Harvey's, a cave-diving technique that would tell whoever followed me down that I was inside the wreck. The fins would be useless in there anyway. You have to move very slowly in a wreck; a snagged hose or a bang on the head can finish you, and flippers only roil up the silt, making visibility worse.

I tied the end of my own lifeline next to Terry's. It would unwind automatically from the safety reel on my belt. I would follow Terry's line in, but I didn't know what was on the other end. And apparently it hadn't helped Harvey much.

Keeping one hand on Terry's line, I swam cautiously toward the open doorway. The weight of the great ship with her cargo of steel looming over me made me even more aware of the pressure at this depth. Every seam of my clothing, every wrinkle, would leave a welt on my skin that wouldn't fade for hours. Even sound is compressed in deep water. The rumble of a passing freighter would whine like a buzz saw down here, and the normally comforting burble of your breathing regulator is strangled to a squeak. Or a scream.

The doorway was alive with motion. Dogfish, dozens of them, three to four feet long, their ugly tentacled heads too large for their slimy, leather-skinned bodies. With a storm coming, the wreck would be infested with them. They're harmless, their rows of tiny teeth dangerous only to crayfish, but they trail you through the murk like clumsy submarine zombies, inhaling the silt in your wake.

I hate the damn things.

A rush of anger surged through me like an electric current, anger at myself for letting Charlie Bauer talk me into this, at Harvey for getting himself killed, at the captain of the Swede freighter for ramming the *Queen* in the first place.

I pushed through the doorway, ignoring the bumps and brushes of the dogfish as they lumbered awkwardly out of my way. I'd entered some sort of anteroom. Metal stairways led up—or rather down, now—to the bridge, and to the engine room and cargo holds above. I followed the lifeline through a second bulkhead doorway and stopped.

Christ. What a mess.

I was in the ship's central passageway, a long narrow hall that ran its full length. The *Queen* was the flagship of the Deveraux line, a freighter but with lavish accommodations for company officers and their guests, though fortunately she'd carried no passengers the night she sank. Her steel bulkheads had been paneled in lacquered hardwood with ornate light fixtures every ten feet or so, but the weight of her cargo bearing down from above had buckled the walls enough to tear it all loose. The fixtures dangled from the walls like grappling hooks, panels and furring strips stuck out at odd angles like jackstraws, each with its own row of protruding nails. Most of the cabin doors had either popped from their hinges or splintered in half. Overhead, long strips of hardwood flooring had given way, hanging down like spiked tentacles. And through it all swam the dogfish, their greedy mouths sucking in the muck Terry and Harvey had churned up earlier.

Terry was right. This was as bad as I'd seen, too. And if Harvey hadn't been somewhere forward near the end of that lifeline, I wouldn't have gone another inch. But he was. And Terry'd made it in and out in one piece.

I checked the time. Ten minutes left on one tank, a full fifteen on the other. Plenty of time. No excuse there. Cursing silently, I began to swim down the hall following Terry's line, promising myself that if I lived through this I was going to beat the living bejesus out of Charlie Bauer with his own nightstick, providing I could figure a way to tie him up first, of course.

The hallway wasn't quite as bad as it looked. The obstacles, vicious though they were, were farther apart than they'd appeared from the doorway, and as long as I moved slowly, I was able to work my way past them. I covered the first thirty feet or so with no problems. But then everything began to disappear.

There was a dark cloud of roiled silt at what I assumed must be the end of the passageway. Dogfish were moving through it, feeding, and Terry's lifeline led into it, so there had to be something beyond, probably the salon. But I couldn't see a thing in there. Terrific.

I slowed my progress to a crawl, inching my way along the line into the cloud. Visibility diminished rapidly until I could see no farther than the length of my arm, maybe less. I could only see the lifeline, occasional pieces of debris, and the dogfish as they blundered into me out of the murk. And then I reached the end of the lifeline.

It was tied around a doorknob at the end of the hall, holding the door open. I felt a surprising rush of relief, both at finding the door and finding it open. Maybe Bauer's suspicion was contagious, but I think I'd been half-afraid it might be closed.

The interior of the salon was even more turbid than the passageway. It was beginning to look as if Harvey'd made a basic, puddle diver's mistake. He'd lost the door. My problem was, the main salon was a large room and several suites opened into it. He could be anywhere in there.

First things first. They'd been working on the dedication plaque, and it was directly opposite the door. I snubbed a loop of my own lifeline over Terry's on the doorknob to take up the slack, and started in.

The room was a shambles, furniture, flooring, bookshelves all tangled and smashed on the ceiling below me, the whole jumble covered with a fine layer of sediment that roiled and swirled around me as I swam slowly above it. A shattered crystal chandelier glittered crazily below for a moment, scattering and reflecting the light from my helmet lamp like a pool of diamonds.

I had to admit the plaque was impressive, a three-foot square of hammered brass listing the company's officers, ships' captains of the Deveraux fleet, and with a bas-relief of the *Queen* herself. It must have cost a bundle even in 1926. It had been secured to the wall with a dozen brass bolts. Eight of them had been removed and placed neatly in a bag on the ceiling below, and a ninth was halfway out.

But no Harvey. Not a sign of him. I checked my time again. It had taken four minutes to get to the *Queen*, four more in the passageway, sixteen minutes total transit time then, minimum, on thirty minutes of air. Soon. I'd have to find him soon.

I tried to concentrate, to put myself in his place. I've lost the door, I'm running out of air, I'm—his light. His air would be long gone, but his helmet lamp should still be working. I reeled in a few feet of lifeline, pulling myself back to the chandelier in the center of the room. Then I turned off my helmet lamp. And waited.

After a minute or so the walls began to glow faintly, and I could make out the pallid green gleam of the portholes, four on each side of the room. And off to my right, a brighter yellowish glow. I took a bearing on it as best I could, switched my own lamp back on, and swam cautiously toward the light.

He was kneeling against the outer wall, his mask pressed against the porthole glass. Maybe he'd been trying to get it open, although it was too small to get through, even without his tanks. Or maybe he'd watched Terry's and Bagger's lights gliding away up the mooring line, leaving him behind or . . .

It didn't matter now. I tugged him gently around. He stared at me through his mask, but there was no life in his eyes, no expression. He was dead. His equipment was all right, no signs of violence. I didn't expect any, but I knew Bauer would ask, so I checked.

Time to go.

I tweaked the valve on his flotation vest, allowing just enough inflation to make him buoyant, then unwound a piece of lifeline from his reel, the line he hadn't bothered to use, and tethered his body to my weight-belt. I tried to get a fix on the door, but the water was just too cloudy, I couldn't see three feet. So I unhooked my lifeline and began to reel it in, following it toward the door.

It was slow going. Harvey dragged behind me like a sea anchor. Dead weight. Since I couldn't see well and Harvey couldn't see at all, he kept bumping into things. Twice he got hung up on dangling flooring strips, but I managed to pull him free by tugging gently on the line. Then, as we neared the door, his regulator hose snagged in a tangle of wiring and I had to stop and work it loose, wasting precious time and slicing my right palm open in the process. Cursing my luck, and Harvey, and this damn deathtrap of a ship, I started moving toward the door again—and suddenly I was staring into a face straight out of hell.

His skin was bloated and gray, his blind eyes milk white, teeth bared in a grimace of agony. His uniform jacket had been gouged through, revealing a terrible wound, clotted with gore and bits of protruding bone.

And I panicked. And ran.

Or tried to. I scrambled backward, a scream strangling in my mask, shoving Harvey aside, clawing my way mindlessly through the wreckage on the ceiling, so shattered by terror I even forgot to swim. But Harvey's corpse hooked on the wiring again and jerked me sidelong into a jumble of furniture. A searing blaze of pain exploded above my heart as something ripped through my suit and deep into my chest. Bone deep. Instantly, instinctively, I knew I was badly hurt. Maybe finished. Icy water surged through the puncture, hammering what little breath I had out of me like a second blow. My consciousness was out of control, skittering about like a cockroach on a hot griddle. *Trapped*, it was screaming, *it's dead, it's dead, get away, you're trapped.* I grasped the lance in my chest with both hands and pulled it out.

A table leg. A splintered table leg. I stared at it with no comprehension at all as blood began seeping through the rip in my suit, clouding the filthy water. I'd crashed into a broken table and speared myself. On a table leg. And I was going to die. I'd seen a body. And panicked. A body. Nothing more. He was dead. And dead is dead.

And now he'd killed me, too.

No. I'd killed me. I panicked. And wounded myself. And tore my suit. But worse than that, I'd dropped my lifeline. I was going to die down here. Like Harvey. Like . . . the other one. Because I'd panicked. Because I'd lost the door. Like an amateur. Like a goddamn puddle diver. I came down after Harvey, and now somebody would have to come down for me. That should have made me angry, but somehow it didn't seem important. What little I could see of the room was flickering and fading as the blood oozed from my chest and my awareness dimmed and I began to fall, down and down into December.

Someone tapped me on the shoulder.

The jolt of pure horror that shot through me brought me instantly awake as I tried to pull away. But it wasn't *him*. It was only a dogfish. A dogfish. And I wasn't dead, yet. Almost, though. Almost.

The wound in my chest was going numb, chilled by the icy water. It didn't hurt as much now, and I was glad of that. Maybe dying wouldn't be so bad, only . . .

I didn't want to die in here. In this terrible place that killed Harvey with the silt and the dogfish and that *thing*. Out in the hall would be better. They'd know I tried if I could just make it out into the hall. I came down to take Harvey out of here. I should at least do that much. Maybe I'd be able to swim better without him, but if I was afraid to die in this place, then he must be, too. It would be wrong to leave him behind. And Harvey was trying to help. He'd floated free of the wiring all by himself.

I checked my pressure gauge, but I couldn't make sense of the numbers. It didn't matter. We were lost anyway. Somehow we had to find the door. Maybe I could find a wall and follow it around, but I wasn't sure how big the room was, and there were other doors. If we went into another room . . .

Or maybe I should just find a porthole for one last look at the world like Harvey did. The portholes. That seemed to make sense. If I could find the portholes . . .

Switching off my helmet lamp was very hard. Maybe the hardest thing I've ever done. But I did it. And we waited in the dark. And in a while I could see the pale glow of the portholes again. Four of them to my right, four more, much fainter, ahead and to the left. And a dark area in between.

I fixed the dark area in my mind, switched my helmet lamp back on, and swam slowly toward it, with Harvey following faithfully behind. And we found the plaque. And the plaque was directly opposite the door.

I explained the situation carefully to Harvey. We had to swim straight. My chest hurt terribly and my right arm wasn't working right. He had to help me. And if we ran into that thing again, we mustn't be afraid this time. He couldn't hurt us now. Dead is dead. But we had to swim straight.

We placed our feet against the plaque and pushed off, swimming for the door. And we saw the thing again. A couple of times. Only he wasn't as scary now. He wanted us to wait. He didn't like it in here, either. He didn't belong in here. He wanted to go with us. But we couldn't take him along. I'll come back for you, I said. I promise. But we can't stop now. We have to swim straight.

And we did. Or Harvey did, anyway. I banged into a wall, but Harvey drifted past me, pulling me through the doorway into the passageway.

It was much worse than before. Harvey kept stopping, banging into things, getting hung up on nails. I told him to stop it, but he wouldn't listen. So I jerked him free and dragged him along.

But we were too slow. My regulator was already choking off when we made it to the anteroom. I tried to slow my breathing to stretch it but it was too late. Too late. And I yelled at Harvey that we were out of air. We had to get up now. And as soon as we cleared the outer door, I hugged him close and twisted the valve of his flotation vest wide open, and he surged toward the surface, carrying me toward the light, faster and faster.

And then Terry was there. He had his back to me, staring out the window into the dark. I started to ask him if Harvey was okay, but my chest hurt too much.

And then it was afternoon. And a nurse was there. And she asked me how I felt. I said I felt like I'd been eaten by a bear and shat by the side of the road. And she smiled and left, shaking her head. And in a little while Charlie Bauer came in.

"Hey, Mitch," he said, tossing his uniform cap on the foot of the bed, "how ya doin'? Gonna live?"

"I don't know," I said honestly. "What happened?"

"What happened? You scared me out of ten years' growth is what. You came bustin' up outa the water with Addison's body like some kinda guided missile, bleedin' like . . ." He ran a freckled paw through his thinning hair. "Mitch, what the hell went on down there? Christ, they needed twenty stitches to sew you up. You had the bends from comin' up too fast. . . . You damn near died. What happened to you?"

"It was a mess down there," I said simply. "I found Harvey, but I lost the door myself. And I rammed into something. A table leg, I think. Stupid. Really stupid."

"Is that what happened to Addison, you think? He just lost track of the door and couldn't get out?"

"I've had a lot more experience than he had, and I lost it."

"But you got out," Charlie said.

"We got lucky," I said. "Harvey helped me find it."

"Yeah, um," he said uncomfortably, "I guess."

"It's okay," I smiled. "I'm not gonna wig out on you. Things got a little crazy down there at the end is all."

"Yeah, I imagine they did. Look, I almost hate to ask you this but—you kept saying there was somebody else down there. That we had to get him out."

"There was another body," I nodded slowly. "One of the crew from the *Queen.*"

"I thought that must be it," he said. "You seemed pretty positive about it. 'Course, you also said he talked to you."

"Did I? Well, maybe he did. Maybe after the storm passes we can . . ." I trailed off, confused, staring at the window. It was late afternoon. And the sun was shining. Charlie was watching me intently. "How, ah, how long have I been out?" I asked.

"Three days. You lost a lot of blood. The storm blew out yesterday. I sent Bill Atkins and a team from the Coast Guard Auxiliary down to the *Queen* this morning. Didn't Terry tell you?"

"I didn't talk to him. I mean, he was here, but . . ."

"He stayed with you almost the whole time. He was about half crazy himself. Said if you died he'd kill me for sendin' you down there. I think he meant it, too."

"Did Atkins find the body?"

"No, he didn't," he sighed. "They didn't find anything hardly. The *Queen*'s cargo apparently busted loose in the storm and smashed down through her decks. There's nothing left down there but the hull and twenty thousand tons of rolled steel buried in the bottom."

"No," I said softly, "that's not right. I said I'd get him out."

"You, ah, you better get some sleep," Charlie said, picking up his hat. "Look, I just want you to know I'm sorry as hell about this, Mitch. If I'd had any idea . . . Anyway, I owe you one. A big one. I won't forget it."

"I know," I said. "I won't forget, either. I promised."

Terry came in a little while after Bauer left. He said he was leaving, something to do with Harvey, but I was groggy and it didn't make much sense.

Two more days passed before I felt human again. I still felt a little wobbly, but I'd had enough of hospital rooms. And besides, I had unfinished business.

I called Sharon Hess, one of the barmaids at the Nest, and asked her to drive me to the Deveraux Institute. She gave me a hard time but she agreed after I promised to go home to bed afterward. I said I'd call a cab when I finished, but she said she'd wait and I didn't have the energy to argue.

I like the Deveraux Institute. It's a combination research library and nautical museum that occupies most of a city block in downtown Huron Harbor, land that Jason's father had donated as a park fifty years ago. It's a pleasant building, modern, open, with a lot of glass but with plenty of wood showing in its counters and shelves, too. And even in the library section, the walls have huge displays of historical artifacts of Great Lakes shipping, everything from canoe paddles to a cross-section of the *Edmund Fitzgerald*'s turbine.

I spent ten minutes with the library's data terminal, making up a list, then took it to the counter. The girl on duty, young, with a complexion problem and a mouthful of braces, frowned at the list.

"Are you a historian?" she asked. "Accredited with the Institute, I mean?"

"My name's Mitchell," I said. "I'm doing some recovery work for Mr. Deveraux."

"Oh," she said, brightening, "I'm sure it'll be all right then. Some of these books are restricted access, but . . ." She disappeared into the stacks, still muttering to herself.

I glanced around the room while I waited. I'd been here often, of course, but I'd never really realized how *many* artifacts they had on display.

"Here you are," she said, placing a small stack of books on the counter. "I'm afraid most of these are restricted. You'll have to study them here."

"No problem," I said. "I wonder if you could help me with something else, though. If the Institute acquired a new artifact, say a large bronze plaque, maybe three feet square, where would it be displayed?"

She looked at me blankly. "I'm sure I wouldn't know," she said. "There are several large storerooms in the basement filled with stuff we haven't room to display now."

"I see," I said, picking up my books.

"They still acquire things all the time, though," she added helpfully. "The family's quite wealthy, you know."

"Yes," I said, "I've heard that."

His name was Stanley Joseph Maychek. I found a picture of him posing stiffly with a group of company officers at the Soo Locks in 1964. He looked much younger and healthier than when I'd seen him last. He was the second mate on the *Queen of Lorraine,* signed aboard in '63. He had a wife and two kids in Saginaw, and parents still living, or at least they were in '68 when the *Queen* went down. His picture on the page blurred and swam before my eyes for a moment.

"I'm sorry," I said softly, "I'm very sorry."

The librarian was staring at me, then quickly looked away. It didn't matter. His name was Stanley Joseph Maychek. And he'd told me the truth.

I didn't return to work at the Crow's Nest for a few days. I lazed around on the beach behind my cottage, soaking up the pale August sun, listening to the seagulls and the surf, feeling my strength gradually seeping back. But somehow it wasn't as tranquil as it should have been. There seemed to be a sense of urgency in the relentless pounding of the waves, especially at night, when sleep was hard to come by, troubled by dreams of chaos I couldn't quite recall in the morning.

I went back to work on Thursday, but I felt uncomfortable tending bar and mixing with the customers, so I spent most of my time in the office, catching up on paperwork. Charlie Bauer came by to see me the first day, but we didn't have much to say to each other, and he didn't stay long. And on Saturday afternoon, Terry rapped lightly on the door and stuck his head in.

"Hey, Mitch, glad to see you're still alive. How ya doin'?"

"I'm all right. Actually, I think I look better than you do."

"You might be right," he said, slumping into one of the captain's chairs. "I've been runnin' my ass off. Sorry I haven't been around sooner, but Jason asked me to accompany Addison's body back down to Miami and talk to his folks. I wasn't crazy about the idea, but Jason can be a pretty persuasive guy."

"Jason?" I said, raising my eyebrows. "Are you two on a first-name basis now?"

"Ah, yeah, we are, as a matter of fact," he said, trying not to look smug, and failing. "I've been spending some time out at the estate. Andrea's been pretty bummed out by this whole thing. In fact, that's one reason I stopped by. She wants to fly down to Acapulco this weekend and I guess I'm gonna tag along." He tossed a key ring on the desk. "The marina's closed till Monday. Can you see the *Kidd* gets beached and stored for me? I'd appreciate it."

"It's a little early in the season to be packing it in, isn't it? What about your charters?"

"I cancelled 'em all and cut Baggers loose. I, ah, I expect I'll be pretty busy for a while."

"With Andrea," I said. It wasn't a question.

"Looks like that's the way it's going. No hard feelings, I hope?"

"About you and Andrea?" I said, "No. Not at all. In fact, I think we should have a drink on it. You want to do the honors?"

"Absolutely," he grinned, crossing to the liquor cabinet and pouring two snifters of Courvoisier. "Hey, I'm really glad you're taking it well. Tell you the truth, I was a little worried. I mean, we been friends a long time, but I knew how you felt about her, and, anyway—" he handed me the glass. "You're all right, Mitch. You always were."

I stood up, facing him, and raised my glass. "A toast," I said formally. "To Stanley Joseph Maychek. God rest his troubled soul."

"To . . ." Terry paused with his glass halfway to his lips. "To who? Who the hell's Stanley—whatever?"

"You don't recognize the name?" I asked. "You should. He's a friend of yours. He's the man who helped you kill Harvey."

He went suddenly pale, as though he'd been struck. "What the hell are you talking about?"

"I'm talking about Stanley J. Maychek, the second officer of the *Queen*. The guy I met in the salon. You should have warned me, Terry. I might've been okay if you'd warned me."

"You were raving about a body when we pulled you out," he nodded, "but I didn't see one. Christ, the way the room was silted up, there could've been an army in there and I wouldn't have seen 'em."

"But you knew Maychek was there," I said. "You put him there to guard the door to keep Harvey from getting out. Only he didn't belong in there, Terry. He said so."

"He said . . . ?" Terry echoed, staring at me.

"It doesn't matter," I shrugged. "I would have figured it out anyway. He was the second mate, and there'd been a collision. I don't know where he was when she rolled, maybe down in the hold checking the damage, or maybe aft warning the crew, but the one place he wouldn't have been was all the way forward in the passenger salon. The room's a dead end and there weren't any passengers. My guess is he was on duty in the pilot house. I noticed the door'd been pried open. Is that where you found him?"

"It, ah, doesn't really matter now, you know," he said carefully. "There's almost nothing left of the *Queen*. No way to . . . prove anything. Have you talked to anybody about this?"

"I'm talking to somebody about it now," I said. "Truth is, I'm worried about you, Terry. You don't look good. Murder's a little out of your line. I don't think you're going to handle it well at all."

"It wasn't murder," he said, tossing off his brandy with a single swallow. "It was a joke. Or it was supposed to be."

"Strange place for a joke."

"I didn't say it was a good joke. It—went wrong, that's all." He fumbled a pack of cigarettes out of his jacket, extracted one, and lit up, pulling the smoke deep into his lungs. Odd, I'd never seen him smoke before, him or any other diver. We rebreathe too much of our own air.

"Anyway, you're right," he nodded, "we did find the body earlier this year, in the wheelhouse. Me and Baggers."

"And you didn't bring it up?"

"How were we supposed to explain it? We had no permit to dive on the *Queen*. We could've wound up in jail. We were scavenging 'jewelry' out of the pilot house so we moved the body into the last cabin off the hall, next to the salon."

"And later you decided to use it to play a not-so-practical joke? Like in high school? Only two hundred feet down?"

"Dammit, you didn't really know Addison," Terry flared. "He was a fourteen-carat phony. Mr. Bigbucks, only with Andrea's money. Just because he chartered me for a month I was supposed to jump every time he said 'frog.' Especially when Andrea was around. He'd snuffle after her like a goddamn lapdog and then expect me to call him boss. Christ, he wasn't man enough to shine my gear. He was nothin' but a puddle diver, and a lousy one at that."

"You killed him because he was a puddle diver?"

"I didn't kill him at all! He killed himself. Because he panicked. How the hell did I know he'd lose the door? He could have made it out. You did."

"But not without some help from Harvey," I said. "And I don't believe you were joking around down there, either. There were too many bolts out of the plaque, Terry. Nine of 'em. And you only had twelve minutes of working time in there. Even Jacques Cousteau couldn't jerk nine bolts in twelve minutes. I think you deliberately worked into your safety margin. Harvey was green, he wouldn't notice. Then you slipped away, easy enough to do in that murk. And you shoved Stanley in to guard the door on your way out. And when Harvey realized you were gone and tried to follow, *if* he found the door at all, he ran into Stanley. And he probably panicked. I sure did. And he hyperventilated, and used up most of his air in just a few seconds. . . . And right then he was a dead man. Even if he'd found the door he had no chance at all. None. And that was no joke, Terry. That was murder."

"Look, I'm sorry as hell about what happened to you down there," Terry said coldly, grinding out his cigarette in the ashtray on my desk, "but I didn't ask you to go down there, Bauer did. So what happened wasn't my fault. And you're wrong about the bolts. We only got three or four out. No more."

"I'm sorry you're going to play it this way," I sighed. "I'd hoped . . . well, I guess it doesn't matter." I picked up his key ring and tossed it back to him. "I think you'd better have somebody else look after the *Kidd* for you. Ask a friend."

"Fair enough," he said evenly, "I'll do that. But if I were you I wouldn't talk to anyone else about—"

"I'm afraid it's a little too late for that," I said. "Too many people know about it already."

"Like who?"

"You. And me. And Harvey. And Stanley Maychek."

"You really *are* crazy, you know that?"

"Maybe a little," I conceded, "but I know you, Terry. I've known you all your life. You won't be able to handle this. Eventually, it'll destroy you. And I don't think you'll make much of a lapdog either."

"And that's really the bottom line here, isn't it?" he said, his eyes hard, and a bit feverish. "It's Andrea. That's what's really eating you. You're jealous. You never got over her, either. Only you didn't have the guts to go after her and I did. And I'm going to have it all, too. Andrea. Everything. You think I murdered Harvey? Fine. You'd better keep that in mind. And from now on, stay the hell out of my way!"

He stormed out, slamming the door behind him. I watched him through the glass as he shouldered his way angrily through the afternoon crowd. For a man who had everything, he didn't look very happy.

Or maybe he's right. Maybe I'm just jealous.

But I don't think so. In fact, I hope he gets exactly what he wants. All of it. He's earned it. And he deserves it.

Only I don't think it'll be enough. The girl he really wants doesn't exist any more. She's a mirage, a dream from a long lost golden summer. We all need our dreams, I suppose. The trouble is, that if you hold on to them long enough, and your luck is bad enough . . . sometimes they come true.

ROBERT BARNARD

HAPPY CHRISTMAS

Robert Barnard is a British author whose novels and short stories have been appearing with increasing frequency and critical acclaim since 1974. He's earned four Edgar nominations since then, and this dark tale of obsession and murder shows him at his best. It's not a story for everyone, but it's a memorable tale even by Barnard's own high standards.

"The people I'm sorry for at Christmas are the ones with children," said Crespin Fawkes, in a voice that rang round the Waggon of Hay. "It must be dreadful for them."

He looked around his little group from the corners of his bright little eyes, registering their appreciative chuckles. Then he took another sip of vodka and tonic. "Think of it—the noise, the toy trumpets, the crackers, and the computer games! Much more appropriate, one would have thought, as a celebration of the crucifixion."

This time the appreciation was more muted. The joke would have been better if he had left it alone. Crespin never had been able to leave a good thing alone.

But they had all enjoyed the joke, and like all good jokes it went home to them. They all, in their way, faced a future when their Christmases would be alone. The Waggon of Hay was one of those pubs where what are today called the sexual minorities tended to congregate. Several of Crespin's group were old boyfriends of his, or occasional partners, and most of the ones who weren't were so because Crespin had very definite ideas about what he fancied and what he didn't. Then there were Joan and Evelyn, who definitely had a relationship but who enjoyed male company, and there was Patty, who nobody could quite pin down.

Still, the fact was that they were all, except Crespin, young. Almost all of them would in fact be going home to families for

47

Christmas, however much they might profess boredom, reluctance, or irritation. Joan, or Evelyn, would ring home and say, "Can I bring my flatmate?" and Mummy would say, "Of *course,* dear!" The others would go on their own, probably, bearing sophisticated presents from the metropolis. For three or four days they would be back in the bosoms of their families, cherished and chaste. When you got to Crespin's age you didn't have a family with a bosom to go back to, but that was something in the future for the rest of them. Crespin had always preferred to keep company with young people.

"You're not going down to your sister, then?" asked Gregory.

"My dears, no!" said Crespin with a theatrical shudder. "Not after last time. And to be perfectly frank, she didn't ask me. She has Teenage Boys, and the fact is she doesn't trust me with them—though last time I saw them they promised to be both pudgy and spotty, which is something I can't *abide.* And her house and grounds are positively country gentry, which is not *me* at all. You expect to see mummers on Christmas Eve, all madly tugging at their forelocks and talking Thomas Hardy. 'Thank 'ee koindly, squoire'—all that stuff. Oh dear, no. Not even for a twenty-pound turkey with all the trimmings would I betake myself to Priscilla's. I *much* prefer my own company, and *la cuisine de chez* Marks and Sparks!"

Once more there was a gratifying laugh. Crespin sat back, his performance over for a few minutes as he let the younger ones take over. As their talk about who was going with whom washed over him (Crespin had had a lifetime of who was going with whom—had figured in it as often as not), he let his eye rove around the bar. There were the Chelsea locals—for there was a straight clientele as well—there were the blacks, the lesbians, the kinks, and the rough trade—these last all friends of Crespin's.

And there, over by the bar, was a boy by himself. Boy? Young man? Somewhere on the border, Crespin judged him. He was eyeing the company speculatively—listening, absorbing. His shirt, dazzling white, looked as if it had been bought that day, but his cardigan, which he had taken off and draped over his arm, was pure home-knit, his jeans were chain store, and his shoes might have been bought for him by his mother for his last year at school. There was about him an indefinable air of newly-up-from-the-country. As Crespin looked at that face, intently absorbing the ambience of the Waggon of Hay, it suddenly struck him that he'd seen it before and knew it, if only slightly—that somewhere or other he had come across this young man as a child.

The young man's eyes, roving around the bar, suddenly met his, and there seemed to Crespin to come into them a flash of recognition. Then he turned to the landlord and ordered a fresh half of lager. Crespin turned back to his friends. This was the last Saturday before Christmas. He wouldn't see them again for quite a while and the stimulus of their laughter and admiration would be missed. Crespin did need, more so as he got older, laughter and admiration. As for the young man—well, no doubt an opportunity would present itself. It so often did, Crespin found.

In the event, it wasn't so much opportunity that presented itself as the young man himself—"on a plate, as it were," as Crespin said wonderingly to him. There was a ring on his doorbell on Christmas Eve, and there on the doormat he stood, dark-haired, thick-eyebrowed, strong-shouldered, altogether capable. Crespin warmed to him at once, to the mere sight of him, and smiled his very friendliest smile.

"I hope you'll excuse my bothering you," said the young man. "I saw you in the Waggon the other night, you see—"

"And *I* saw *you*," said Crespin.

"And I saw you in the street the other day, too—you didn't see me—and I followed you here."

"Flattering," said Crespin. "Almost invariably, nowadays, it's the other way around."

"You see, I think I know you—met you once or twice, years ago. And your picture's on your sister's piano. The boys are always saying, 'That's our uncle who's in television.' "

"So much more distinguished than 'who's *on* television.' Are you sure that's *all* they say?"

The boy smiled, twisting his mouth. " 'That's our uncle who's queer and in television.' "

"Exactly. Don't bother with the censored version. But this leaves open the question of who *you* are."

"My father's the gardener. I always used to help him in the school holidays. That's how I met you."

By now they were both in the hallway of Crespin's awfully amusing flat, and quite naturally Crespin had removed the boy's duffel coat and taken his inadequate scarf. They understood each other so well that no invitation, no pantomime of reluctance, was necessary. Quite soon the boy was sitting on the sofa with Crespin in the armchair close beside him, they were both clutching drinks and talking about anything but what Crespin really wanted to talk about, and the boy's eyes were going everywhere. For all that there were slight traces of the bumpkin about him, Crespin decided at once that he was an awfully noticing boy. There was almost nothing in Crespin's living room that escaped his wandering eye.

"You like it? My little nest, I mean?"

"Yes, awfully. It's not like what I'm used to. Even at your sister's—"

"My *dear,* I should think not. Don't even *mention* my sister's in the same breath if you want to stay in favor. Of course, she has the odd good piece—could hardly fail to have in a house as old as that—but everything she's bought herself has been the purest Home Counties. Now *I* rediscovered the thirties ten or fifteen years before anyone else. I bought, bought, bought, quite ri*dic*ulously cheaply, dear boy. I wouldn't like to tell you what some of the things are worth today."

As he said it, Crespin noticed on those sturdy country features a gleam come into the eye.

"This Beaton, for example. *Only* a photograph, my dear, but in its original frame, and signed to the subject, who was a *quite* minor poet—well, someone offered me four hundred and fifty only the other day. And I paid ten bob for it back in the days of Harold Macmillan, in a little shop in East Finchley."

All the time the boy's eyes were watching, waiting for him to go on to another item. Crespin, characteristically, decided to play with him. He sat down beside him on the sofa.

"But don't let's talk about my little knickknacks. Let's talk about you. I don't even know your name."

His name, it turned out, was Stephen Hodge.

At home, he said, things hadn't been "all that bad," but on the other hand he hadn't got on "all that well" with his parents. His father had been old-fashioned and heavy-handed and had insisted on his leaving school at sixteen. "Don't want you loafing around there for the rest of your life, learning things that won't be no use to you," he had said. Stephen had wanted to stay on. He was middling at most things, but he had definite talent in certain directions.

"Art and that," he said. He had wanted to get an education to get away from home, find new horizons, "meet exciting people." And he added: "Get new experiences."

By now they were in the kitchen and Crespin was preparing one of his risottos. "Something light," he said. "We want to keep our appetites for tomorrow."

Over the risotto, Crespin returned to the absorbing topic—absorbing, in fact, to both of them—of his flat and his possessions.

"When we've eaten, dear boy, you shall have a tour of the flat. A personal conducted tour, led by the chatelaine. Then you can feel truly at home here for the festive season. Where are you living, as a rule?"

"I've got this camp bed at a mate's," said Stephen, eating hungrily, as if he had little desire to save his appetite for the morrow. "He's away for Christmas."

"Then we are saving each other from some perfectly ghastly festive days. I shall conduct you around my nest and my things, so that you will know them as you will know me." He smiled at the boy, who slowed down the pace of his eating. "I can see that you have an eye for fine things."

This last was said with a touch of malice, but it went unperceived. The boy said, "I think I do. But I don't have the training and that. I need someone to show me."

After Crespin had found some ice cream in the fridge, which Stephen had wolfed down in a way that suggested the schoolboy that showed through some of his clothes, Crespin put on some coffee and they began the tour of the flat. The eye that Crespin had noticed almost from the beginning went everywhere, and the brain stored every item of information. The living room was thirties, but the rest of the flat was pleasantly crowded with more conventional objects. Often Crespin noticed that Stephen wanted to ask the value of something, but managed to refrain. Sometimes Crespin would give it to him, sometimes not. He began to drop prices and sale values, but ambiguously. ("Would you believe me if I said fifteen hundred?") He was already playing with his guest—beginning the games that would be conducted more roughly in the bedroom.

Soon a refinement of the game suggested itself to him. Instead of being ambiguous, his assertions of value became downright mendacious. His valuable things—oh, yes, ducky, he did *have* valuable things—were commended as amusing trifles, no more. The highest commendation and implied value were lavished on pieces whose worth was at best sentimental.

If *that,* said Crespin to himself, as he held—gently, as if it were Ming and he a museum curator—a piece of nondescript china inherited from his Aunt Molly, which looked as if it had been purchased from Woolworth's in the twenties.

"Exquisite," said Crespin. "And beautifully kept, you notice. Trust my Aunt Molly for that, dragon that she was. I wouldn't like to tell you what my friend Henry at Chez Moi Antiques round the corner would offer me for that if I ever told him I'd sell."

He saw the boy, in some space behind his eyes, file the information away. For a moment, Crespin felt himself washed by a wave of nausea and ennui. So many young men—tough, capable, greedy. So many nights of delicious brutality, followed by less delicious humiliation, depredation, loss. He shrugged the feeling aside and went on with the tour. Crespin was a magpie. Only a fraction of his things could be shown that evening. There would be plenty left to talk about the next day.

After coffee, and after all the china and glass had been safely tucked away inside the dishwasher, the games started again— but this time they were more physical, and this time it was Crespin who was victim. And in these games Stephen understood what was going on. It was amazing how quickly he got the idea. But then, he had been in London some weeks. Crespin had no reason to think he was the first of his kind that the boy had been with. If he frequented the Waggon of Hay, after all—

But it was a pleasure to encounter a lad with that sturdiness of physique, yet that delicate inventiveness of mind. They started with the schoolboy stuff, with the arm twisted behind the back, but then they proceeded, sometimes Crespin suggesting, sometimes Stephen improvising, to more serious brutalities. Halfway through the games, both of them sweaty, Crespin a little bloody, they stopped for a neat Scotch. By this time they had very little in the way of clothes on, and some of Crespin's, lying on the floor, were torn and dirty. As he drained his glass, Crespin plunged his other hand down Stephen's schoolboyish Y-fronts and the games began again—until they climaxed, gloriously, on the bed, Stephen's big hands around Crespin's throat as he lay on top of him.

"It's been one of the most wonderful nights of my life," Crespin said, after Stephen had roughly taken him for the second time.

The next morning Crespin was up early, showering away the dried blood and gazing with satisfaction at the discoloration of his skin as bruises began to show. Before going into the kitchen, he went through the lounge and drawing room, looking for something sufficiently masculine to present to Stephen on Our Lord's birthday. He found nothing that satisfied him, and in the end wrapped up a really beautiful Georgian silver cream jug. In his gifts, at least, he would be generous, he thought. He made tea and toast, set out the tray for two, then put the present on the tray and went into the bedroom. Stephen was awake and sitting up. Crespin thought he had never seen anything more beautiful. He set the tray on the boy's lap, presented him with the little parcel, then sat himself cross-legged on the end of the bed.

"It's beautiful, really beautiful," Stephen said, gazing at the silver object.

"Nothing—a mere nothing," said Crespin with his characteristic wave of the hand.

"And I have nothing to give you."

"Do you imagine you could give me anything more wonderful than you have given me already?" asked Crespin. Stephen looked pleased, and Crespin added: "Dear boy."

They had a quiet morning preparing lunch. The cookery of Mrs. Marks or Mrs. Spencer did not need long in the oven and Crespin was pleased to find that he had *two* packets of stuffed turkey breast in the deep-freeze. He would feed Stephen up. He knew the boy was hungrier than, so far, he had been able to satisfy. He peeled a mountain of potatoes and carrots, set out the cranberry sauce on a pretty Meissen dish, opened the tin of National Trust Christmas pudding. Stephen's eyes sparkled at this: he still had a child's love of sweet things.

While this was going on, Stephen did his bit around the place, clearing up from the night before and setting the table, at which he proved surprisingly adept. In between, they watched bits of the Christmas-morning service on television.

"Are you religious?" asked Stephen.

"I converted to Rome when I was eighteen," said Crespin, with some signs of pride. "Inevitably, with my name, I suppose. Such a relief after the middle-of-the-road Anglicanism of my childhood—the middle-of-the-road down which my dear sister and her family still happily plod. But somehow the conversion didn't last. I regret it. And you?"

"I don't know. I don't go to church and that. But sometimes I watch it on television and it seems to—have something. But I'm not religious. It doesn't sort of—go, does it?"

"Go?"

"With us. With the sort of lives we lead."

"No," agreed Crespin sadly. Soon he went back to the kitchen.

They ate about two o'clock. The meal was a great success. Stephen ate about two-thirds of the turkey and was clearly pleased with a Christmas dinner that was all breast and no leg or wing. He made significant inroads into the vegetables and seemed to enjoy Crespin's cream on the Christmas pudding in place of the custard he always had at home.

Before the meal, they had a glass of sherry—Reina Victoria. Stephen said it was like no sherry he had ever had before, inspected the bottle, and asked how much it cost. As they ate,

Crespin gave him his little lecture on Moselles. How often had he given it before, over dinner, to a bored, contemptuous, or frankly dimwitted companion? Stephen followed him, asked questions, stored up the answers.

He will take everything I have to give him, thought Crespin.

"Do you want to ring your family?" he asked.

"No," said Stephen awkwardly. "No. They don't know where I am, you see."

"I'm not pressing you. That's your business."

"Will you be ringing your sister? Don't say anything to her if you do."

"I shan't ring her. She won't be expecting it. Nobody will. Outside my job I have nobody." Crespin paused, then said deliberately, "I could lie here dead for days—weeks—and nobody would know."

He registered, unmistakably, a tiny glint in the boy's eye.

They went back to the living room for coffee, and as he poured it and handed his to Stephen, Crespin said, "This has been a Christmas to remember."

"For me, too," said Stephen.

"Two days wonderfully marked off from the humdrum round."

"Maybe we could do it again."

"Dear boy, repetition, even if it were possible, is not advisable. Exquisite pleasure is a once-off thing. With your inventive mind, you should understand that."

Stephen smiled slowly. "You think I have an inventive mind?"

"I know you have. I'm in a position to pronounce on the subject."

Stephen stirred his coffee. "I could stay."

"Dear boy!" cried Crespin, fluttering his hand. "Do you imagine I could stand excitements like last night's every day?"

"We wouldn't need to go at it like that every day."

"If you were here with me, how could we not? Come, you've never seen my study. Let me continue with your aesthetic education."

So Crespin resumed yesterday's game, with renewed zest. He had the boy at an ideal stage. He was quick but ignorant. In a year's time—if he remained at large—this particular fun would no longer be possible. He would *know.* Now he was anxious to learn, but did not know. Thus Crespin could wave aside a rare, intimate conversation piece by John Singer Sargent that hung over the mantelpiece as "a mere daub, dear boy—hardly worth the canvas and oil. I keep it for sentimental reasons."

He paused, as an idea seemed to strike him. He looked up at the stalwart man, the worried wife, and the three girls of the picture.

"My great-grandfather, the Admiral. And his three jolly-tar daughters. Imagine—that his blood should have diluted itself into mine. Funnily enough, I remember one of the daughters, in old age, chivvying me into manly sports. The Admiral, I always suspect, would have gone in for more drastic remedies— probably have had me drowned at birth. He was never one for half measures."

Crespin, watched by the boy, tore his eyes from the exquisite "daub" over the fireplace and took, very casually, from on top of a bureau a large, silver-encrusted nineteenth century firearm. "This was his. Isn't it handsome? And characteristically assert- ive. Feel the weight of it."

The boy took it, and in his surprise nearly dropped it. It was as heavy as death.

"It's not a gun at all, in fact. Really more of a cudgel. He had it made to his own specifications. He always said that if you shot an intruder, some damn fool was going to ask questions. With this, you could either terrify him or bash the daylights out of him if that didn't work." Crespin looked at Stephen and took the weapon from his hands. "It's one of the best pieces I own. I always think it might come in useful someday, to somebody."

Their glance at each other held a brief flash of understanding. Then they went on to other things. As before, Crespin praised cut-glass vases and commercial prints as if they were priceless objects the Victoria and Albert was itching to get its hands on. The pleasure was redoubled because, in addition to observing the pricing-and-cataloguing going on behind the boy's eyes, Crespin had a sense of something more—of the boy screwing himself up to something. When he put his hand on his arm, or

delicately round his waist, he could feel it was already manifest-
ing itself physically in a bodily tenseness.

Those brief touches, those affectionate squeezes, inevitably
began to lead to something more, but Crespin wasn't anxious to
start on the serious business yet. He wanted a cup of tea. He had
always enjoyed tea, and served it in a ceremonious way that
reminded him of his mother. He would enjoy one more cup.

The boy's tensions had relaxed by the time they both drank tea.
For a moment Crespin wondered whether he had changed his
mind, but he was reassured to notice a tiny smile of anticipation
playing around his lips: he was relaxed because he had decided
to do it.

Conversation between them was strained and spasmodic, as it
had never been since Stephen had arrived. Now they had
between them an unspoken contract. Any mention of it could
only render it ludicrous and void. So they must talk about other
things, though other things scarcely came. In the end, Crespin
put an end to it after one cup. Second cups were always less
than perfect. He turned toward the boy beside him on the sofa
and began gently to unbutton his shirt. Stephen, at least, must
look kempt when he left the flat.

His own clothes were another matter. God knew he hadn't
exactly been cautious in the past. Now there was nothing he
wore that could mean anything to him again. But as the game
hotted up, no item was given up without a struggle. The shirt
went as he was held back forcefully over the sofa, his head being
pummeled by one fist as the boy's other hand tore at the
flaunting pink silk.

Other items went as they fought across the table, chased each
other round the kitchen, sank into violent clinches onto the
floor. There were intervals of something like tenderness, almost
peace, as their naked bodies came together in something other
than struggle. There was a moment, on the rug in front of the
gas fire, when it almost seemed as if the contract between them
might be forgotten.

It was Crespin who ended it. He slapped Stephen ineffectually
across the cheeks.

"Pig!" he shouted. "Yokel! Rustic yob!"

Stephen's fists began brutally hitting him about the head, first left, then right, leaving Crespin breathless. Then Stephen unclenched his hands and felt for the throat. It was this that had always excited Crespin, but he knew that this time he couldn't give way to his excitement. That was not the way he had to go. It had to be by the Admiral's gun.

He writhed on the rug, twisted, and turned within those strong hands. The bodies came together, then slid off one another until suddenly Crespin managed to knee the boy in the groin. With a wrench, he struggled away as Stephen let go his hands, then he ran for the bedroom. "Come for me!" he shouted. "Come for me!"

He slammed the door, but it swung open again. He stood there in the darkness, panting, aching, watching the light from the living room as it filtered through the opening in the doorway. The boy was not coming.

Wait. He heard a floorboard creak—the one just inside the study door. He was going for the weapon. Perhaps he was looking round at the things he would take, the things he had marked off in his little inventory, the things that would fetch the odd pound when he hawked them round the antique shops as soon as he dared.

Crespin's breath was coming more easily now. Let him come! Let him not break the rhythm! He heard the floorboard creak again. He heard soft footsteps across the carpeted floor of the living room. He was coming after all. The game would be played through.

And as he saw, in the lighted doorway of the bedroom, a large, dark shadow, there flooded over him an overwhelming feeling of excitement and fulfillment. It had been the happiest Christmas of his adult life.

LAWRENCE BLOCK

AS GOOD AS A REST

There is a certain type of mystery that has always appealed to me when it's skillfully done. I'm thinking of one in which things are never quite what they seem, in which the reader is not sure where the author is headed until the very last page. This story by the popular mystery novelist and Edgar-winning short story writer Lawrence Block is a fine example of what I mean.

Andrew says the whole point of a vacation is to change your perspective of the world. A change is as good as a rest, he says, and vacations are about change, not rest. If we just wanted a rest, he says, we could stop the mail and disconnect the phone and stay home: that would add up to more of a traditional rest than traipsing all over Europe. Sitting in front of the television set with your feet up, he says, is generally considered to be more restful than climbing the forty-two thousand steps to the top of Notre Dame.

Of course, there aren't forty-two thousand steps, but it did seem like it at the time. We were with the Dattners—by the time we got to Paris the four of us had already buddied up—and Harry kept wondering aloud why the genius who'd built the cathedral hadn't thought to put in an elevator. And Sue, who'd struck me earlier as unlikely to be afraid of anything, turned out to be petrified of heights. There are two staircases at Notre Dame, one going up and one coming down, and to get from one to the other you have to walk along this high ledge. It's really quite wide, even at its narrowest, and the view of the rooftops of Paris is magnificent, but all of this was wasted on Sue, who clung to the rear wall with her eyes clenched shut.

Andrew took her arm and walked her through it, while Harry and I looked out at the City of Light. "It's high open spaces that does it to her," he told me. "Yesterday, the Eiffel Tower, no problem, because the space was enclosed. But when it's open

59

she starts getting afraid that she'll get sucked over the side or
that she'll get this sudden impulse to jump, and, well, you see
what it does to her."

While neither Andrew nor I is troubled by heights, whether
open or enclosed, the climb to the top of the cathedral wasn't
the sort of thing we'd have done at home, especially since we'd
already had a spectacular view of the city the day before from
the Eiffel Tower. I'm not mad about walking stairs, but it didn't
occur to me to pass up the climb. For that matter, I'm not that
mad about walking generally—Andrew says I won't go anywhere without a guaranteed parking space—but it seems to me
that I walked from one end of Europe to the other, and didn't
mind a bit.

When we weren't walking through streets or up staircases,
we were parading through museums. That's hardly a departure
for me, but for Andrew it is uncharacteristic behavior in the
extreme. Boston's Museum of Fine Arts is one of the best in the
country, and it's not twenty minutes from our house. We have a
membership, and I go all the time, but it's almost impossible to
get Andrew to go.

But in Paris he went to the Louvre, and the Rodin Museum,
and that little museum in the 16th arrondissement with the
most wonderful collection of Monets. And in London he led the
way to the National Gallery and the National Portrait Gallery
and the Victoria and Albert—and in Amsterdam he spent three
hours in the Rijksmuseum and hurried us to the Van Gogh
Museum first thing the next morning. By the time we got to
Madrid, I was museumed out. I knew it was a sin to miss the
Prado but I just couldn't face it, and I wound up walking around
the city with Harry while my husband dragged Sue through
galleries of El Grecos and Goyas and Velasquezes.

"Now that you've discovered museums," I told Andrew, "you
may take a different view of the Museum of Fine Arts. There's a
show of American landscape painters that'll still be running
when we get back—I think you'll like it."

He assured me he was looking forward to it. But you know he
never went. Museums are strictly a vacation pleasure for him.
He doesn't even want to hear about them when he's at home.

For my part, you'd think I'd have learned by now not to buy

clothes when we travel. Of course, it's impossible not to—there are some genuine bargains and some things you couldn't find at home—but I almost always wind up buying something that remains unworn in my closet forever after. It seems so right in some foreign capital, but once I get it home I realize it's not me at all, and so it lives out its days on a hanger, a source in turn of fond memories and faint guilt. It's not that I lose judgment when I travel, or become wildly impulsive. It's more that I become a slightly different person in the course of the trip and the clothes I buy for that person aren't always right for the person I am in Boston.

Oh, why am I nattering on like this? You don't have to look in my closet to see how travel changes a person. For heaven's sake, just look at the Dattners.

If we hadn't all been on vacation together, we would never have come to know Harry and Sue, let alone spend so much time with them. We would never have encountered them in the first place—day-to-day living would not have brought them to Boston, or us to Enid, Oklahoma. But even if they'd lived down the street from us, we would never have become close friends at home. To put it as simply as possible, they were not our kind of people.

The package tour we'd booked wasn't one of those escorted ventures in which your every minute is accounted for. It included our charter flights over and back, all our hotel accommodations, and our transportation from one city to the next. We "did" six countries in twenty-two days, but what we did in each, and where and with whom, was strictly up to us. We could have kept to ourselves altogether, and have often done so when traveling, but by the time we checked into our hotel in London the first day we'd made arrangements to join the Dattners that night for dinner, and before we knocked off our after-dinner brandies that night it had been tacitly agreed that we would be a foursome throughout the trip—unless, of course, it turned out that we tired of each other.

"They're a pair," Andrew said that first night, unknotting his tie and giving it a shake before hanging it over the doorknob. "That y'all-come-back accent of hers sounds like syrup flowing over corn cakes."

"She's a little flashy, too," I said. "But that sport jacket of his—"

"I know," Andrew said. "Somewhere, even as we speak, a horse is shivering, his blanket having been transformed into a jacket for Harry."

"And yet there's something about them, isn't there?"

"They're nice people," Andrew said. "Not our kind at all, but what does that matter? We're on a trip. We're ripe for a change . . ."

In Paris, after a night watching a floorshow at what I'm sure was a rather disreputable little nightclub in Les Halles, I lay in bed while Andrew sat up smoking a last cigarette. "I'm glad we met the Dattners," he said. "This trip would be fun anyway, but they add to it. That joint tonight was a treat, and I'm sure we wouldn't have gone if it hadn't been for them. And do you know something? I don't think *they'd* have gone if it hadn't been for *us.*"

"Where would we be without them?" I rolled onto my side. "I know where Sue would be without your helping hand. Up on top of Notre Dame, frozen with fear. Do you suppose that's how the gargoyles got there? Are they nothing but tourists turned to stone?"

"Then you'll never be a gargoyle. You were a long way from petrification whirling around the dance floor tonight."

"Harry's a good dancer. I didn't think he would be, but he's very light on his feet."

"The gun doesn't weigh him down, eh?"

I sat up. "I *thought* he was wearing a gun," I said. "How on earth does he get it past the airport scanners?"

"Undoubtedly by packing it in his luggage and checking it through. He wouldn't need it on the plane—not unless he was planning to divert the flight to Havana."

"I don't think they go to Havana any more. Why would he need it *off* the plane? I suppose tonight he'd feel safer armed. That place was a bit on the rough side."

"He was carrying it at the Tower of London, and in and out of a slew of museums. In fact, I think he carries it all the time except on planes. Most likely he feels naked without it."

"I wonder if he sleeps with it."

"I think he sleeps with her."

"Well, I know *that.*"

"To their mutual pleasure, I shouldn't wonder. Even as you and I."

"Ah," I said.

And, a bit later, he said, "You like them, don't you?"

"Well, of course I do. I don't want to pack them up and take them home to Boston with us, but—"

"You like *him.*"

"Harry? Oh, *I* see what you're getting at."

"Quite."

"And she's attractive, isn't she? You're attracted to her."

"At home I wouldn't look at her twice, but here—"

"Say no more. That's how I feel about him. That's exactly how I feel about him."

"Do you suppose we'll do anything about it?"

"I don't know. Do you suppose they're having this very conversation two floors below?"

"I wouldn't be surprised. If they *are* having this conversation, and if they had the same silent prelude to this conversation, they're probably feeling very good indeed."

"Mmmmm," I said dreamily. "Even as you and I."

I don't know if the Dattners had that conversation that particular evening, but they certainly had it somewhere along the way. The little tensions and energy currents between the four of us began to build until it seemed almost as though the air were crackling with electricity. More often than not we'd find ourselves pairing off on our walks. Andrew with Sue, Harry with me. I remember one moment when he took my hand crossing the street—I remember the instant but not the street or even the city—and a little shiver went right through me.

By the time we were in Madrid, with Andrew and Sue trekking through the Prado while Harry and I ate garlicky shrimp and sipped a sweetish white wine in a little cafe on the Plaza Mayor, it was clear what was going to happen. We were almost ready to talk about it.

"I hope they're having a good time," I told Harry. "I just couldn't manage another museum."

"I'm glad we're out here instead," he said, with a wave at the plaza. "But I would have gone to the Prado if you went." And he reached out and covered my hand with his.

"Sue and Andy seem to be getting along pretty good," he said. Andy! Had anyone else ever called my husband Andy?

"And you and me, we get along all right, don't we?"

"Yes," I said, giving his hand a little squeeze. "Yes, we do."

Andrew and I were up late that night, talking and talking. The next day we flew to Rome. We were all tired our first night there and ate at the restaurant in our hotel rather than venture forth. The food was good, but I wonder if any of us really tasted it?

Andrew insisted that we all drink grappa with our coffee. It turned out to be a rather nasty brandy, clear in color and quite powerful. The men had a second round of it. Sue and I had enough work finishing our first.

Harry held his glass aloft and proposed a toast. "To good friends," he said. "To close friendship with good people." And after everyone had taken a sip he said, "You know, in a couple of days we all go back to the lives we used to lead. Sue and I go back to Oklahoma, you two go back to Boston, Mass. Andy, you go back to your investments business and I'll be doin' what I do. And we got each other's addresses and phone, and we say we'll keep in touch, and maybe we will. But if we do or we don't, either way one thing's sure. The minute we get off that plane at JFK, that's when the carriage turns into a pumpkin and the horses go back to bein' mice. You know what I mean?"

Everyone did.

"Anyway," he said, "what me an' Sue were thinkin', we thought there's a whole lot of Rome, a mess of good restaurants, and things to see and places to go. We thought it's silly to have four people all do the same things and go the same places and miss out on all the rest. We thought, you know, after breakfast tomorrow, we'd split up and spend the day separate." He took a breath. "Like Sue and Andy'd team up for the day and, Elaine, you an' me'd be together."

"The way we did in Madrid," somebody said.

"Except I mean for the whole day," Harry said. A light film of perspiration gleamed on his forehead. I looked at his jacket and tried to decide if he was wearing his gun. I'd seen it on our afternoon in Madrid. His jacket had come open and I'd seen the gun, snug in his shoulder holster. "The whole day and then the evening, too. Dinner—and after."

There was a silence that I don't suppose could have lasted nearly as long as it seemed to. Then Andrew said he thought it was a good idea, and Sue agreed, and so did I.

Later, in our hotel room, Andrew assured me that we could back out. "I don't think they have any more experience with this than we do. You saw how nervous Harry was during his little speech. He'd probably be relieved to a certain degree if we did back out."

"Is that what you want to do?"

He thought for a moment. "For my part," he said, "I'd as soon go through with it."

"So would I. My only concern is if it made some difference between us afterward."

"I don't think it will. This is fantasy, you know. It's not the real world. We're not in Boston *or* Oklahoma. We're in Rome, and you know what they say. When in Rome, do as the Romans do."

"And is this what the Romans do?"

"It's probably what they do when they go to Stockholm," Andrew said.

In the morning, we joined the Dattners for breakfast. Afterward, without anything being said, we paired off as Harry had suggested the night before. He and I walked through a sun-drenched morning to the Spanish Steps, where I bought a bag of crumbs and fed the pigeons. After that—

Oh, what does it matter what came next, what particular tourist things we found to do that day? Suffice it to say that we went interesting places and saw rapturous sights, and everything we did and saw was heightened by anticipation of the evening ahead.

We ate lightly that night, and drank freely but not to excess. The trattoria where we dined wasn't far from our hotel and the night was clear and mild, so we walked back. Harry slipped an arm around my waist. I leaned a little against his shoulder. After we'd walked a way in silence, he said very softly, "Elaine, only if you want to."

"But I do," I heard myself say.

Then he took me in his arms and kissed me.

I ought to recall the night better than I do. We felt love and lust for each other, and sated both appetites. He was gentler than I might have guessed he'd be, and I more abandoned. I could probably remember precisely what happened if I put my mind to it, but I don't think I could make the memory seem real. Because it's as if it happened to someone else. It was vivid at the time, because at the time I truly was the person sharing her bed with Harry. But that person had no existence before or after that European vacation.

There was a moment when I looked up and saw one of Andrew's neckties hanging on the knob of the closet door. It struck me that I should have put the tie away, that it was out of place there. Then I told myself that the tie was where it ought to be, that it was Harry who didn't belong here. And finally I decided that both belonged, my husband's tie and my inappropriate Oklahoma lover. Now both belonged, but in the morning the necktie would remain and Harry would be gone.

As indeed he was. I awakened a little before dawn and was alone in the room. I went back to sleep, and when I next opened my eyes Andrew was in bed beside me. Had they met in the hallway, I wondered? Had they worked out the logistics of this passage in advance? I never asked. I still don't know.

Our last day in Rome, the Dattners went their way and we went ours. Andrew and I got to the Vatican, saw the Colosseum, and wandered here and there, stopping at sidewalk cafes for espresso. We hardly talked about the previous evening, beyond assuring each other that we had enjoyed it, that we were glad it had happened, and that our feelings for one another remained unchanged—deepened, if anything, by virtue of having shared this experience, if it could be said to have been shared.

We joined Harry and Sue for dinner. And in the morning we all rode out to the airport and boarded our flight to New York. I remember looking at the other passengers on the plane, few of whom I'd exchanged more than a couple of sentences with in the course of the past three weeks. There were almost certainly couples among them with whom we had more in common than we had with the Dattners. Had any of them had comparable flings in the course of the trip?

At JFK we all collected our luggage and went through customs and passport control. Then we were off to catch our connecting flight to Boston while Harry and Sue had a four-hour wait for their TWA flight to Tulsa. We said goodbye. The men shook hands while Sue and I embraced. Then Harry and I kissed, and Sue and Andrew kissed. That woman slept with my husband, I thought. And that man—I slept with him. I had the thought that, were I to continue thinking about it, I would start laughing.

Two hours later we were on the ground at Logan, and less than an hour after that we were in our own house.

That weekend Paul and Marilyn Welles came over for dinner and heard a play-by-play account of our three-week vacation— with the exception, of course, of that second-to-last night in Rome. Paul is a business associate of Andrew's and Marilyn is a woman not unlike me, and I wondered to myself what would happen if we four traded partners for an evening.

But it wouldn't happen and I certainly didn't want it to happen. I found Paul attractive and I know Andrew had always found Marilyn attractive. But such an incident among us wouldn't be appropriate, as it had somehow been appropriate with the Dattners.

I know Andrew was having much the same thoughts. We didn't discuss it afterward, but one knows . . .

I thought of all of this just last week. Andrew was in a bank in Skokie, Illinois, along with Paul Welles and two other men. One of the tellers managed to hit the silent alarm and the police arrived as they were on their way out. There was some shooting. Paul Welles was wounded superficially, as was one of the policemen. Another of the policemen was killed.

Andrew is quite certain he didn't hit anybody. He fired his gun a couple of times, but he's sure he didn't kill the police officer.

But when he got home we both kept thinking the same thing. It could have been Harry Dattner.

Not literally, because what would an Oklahoma state trooper

be doing in Skokie, Illinois? But it might as easily have been the Skokie cop in Europe with us. And it might have been Andrew who shot him—or been shot *by* him, for that matter.

I don't know that I'm explaining this properly. It's all so incredible. That I should have slept with a policeman while my husband was with a policeman's wife. That we had ever become friendly with them in the first place. I have to remind myself, and keep reminding myself, that it all happened overseas. It happened in Europe, and it happened to four other people. We were not ourselves, and Sue and Harry were not themselves. It happened, you see, in another universe altogether, and so, really, it's as if it never happened at all.

DAVID BRALY

THE GALLOWGLASS

*If you've been missing those fine old locked-room mys-
teries complete with stormy nights, old Irish houses, and
talk of ghosts, here's just the thing for you. David Braly
happens to reside in Oregon rather than Ireland, but that
really doesn't matter.*

Sergeant Brian Sullivan set the brake and cut the engine. When
he turned off the headlights, everything around the small police
car was enveloped in black except for small squares of yellow
light from the windows of the house. Some of these yellow
squares appeared to go on and off like ship blinkers because of
the violent swaying of the tree limbs between them and the car.

"This is the place," Sullivan told his passenger, John McNamara.

"How do you know in this storm?" asked the locksmith. "It's
too dark to tell a cottage from a castle."

"It's the only house on this part of the shore."

Sullivan forced open his door against the strong wind. The
wind and heavy rain struck him like the blast from a fire hose
when he stepped out. The wind's howl was so loud that Sullivan
couldn't hear the car door when he slammed it shut.

Sullivan looked out toward the sea. He could not see it nor
the beach. All that he could distinguish when he squinted his
eyes toward the sea-bred storm were the black forms of nearby
trees swaying against a black sky. Everything was black, windy,
wet, and caught in the mournful howl of the storm.

Lightning flashed, followed immediately by a tremendous
explosion of thunder.

Sullivan pulled up his raincoat collar, then pulled down his
visor to secure his cap. He stumbled to the front of the car, then
to the opposite side, pushed by the wind.

"Worst storm I've seen in my life!" shouted McNamara when
Sullivan reached him.

"Aye!" shouted Sullivan.

Sullivan grabbed McNamara's arm and they hurried toward the house. Its front porch was seventy feet away at the end of an ancient stone walkway that ran past an equally ancient stone wall. From a previous visit—it was too dark to see it now— Sullivan knew that the wall was only a crumbling, moss-laden ruin.

Wind-driven into a trot, Sullivan and McNamara quickly reached the porch. Sullivan carried his lead-encased, five-battery flashlight and McNamara a small metal toolbox filled with the gadgetry of his trade. The porch wasn't shielded from the wind, and horizontal rain continued to pound them.

"I'm surprised they still have lights," said McNamara. "Winds half this strong usually bring down the wires."

Sullivan nodded, then grabbed the brass knocker and pounded.

They waited.

No one answered the door.

Sullivan knocked again. After a half minute, he did it again, as hard as he could. Still no answer.

Sullivan put his hand on the doorknob, tried it. The knob turned.

The sergeant pushed the door open, then glanced at McNamara. McNamara shrugged. Sullivan stepped inside. McNamara followed and shut the door behind him.

"I hope we don't get nabbed for housebreaking," quipped McNamara.

Sullivan ignored the remark. He looked down the narrow, dimly lit hallway that led to the stairs. No one was in sight. Nor could he hear the sounds of human presence over the now muted roar of the storm.

"Hello!" yelled Sullivan. "Is anyone home?"

Seconds later a white-haired woman appeared at the end of the corridor in front of the stairs. "Who's there?" she called.

"Sergeant Sullivan from Bandon, ma'am. Are you the woman who phoned about some trouble?"

"Yes, yes. Please come here."

Sullivan hurried down the hallway, followed closely by McNamara. The ancient oak floorboards creaked at their every

step. Old candleholders were screwed into the walls, but the
light came from dim overhead electric bulbs, three of which
dully illuminated the sixty-foot corridor. At the corridor's end,
Sullivan found a stairway straight ahead, and another corridor
that led away from the main one at a forty-five-degree angle.
The woman had come from this second corridor.

She was small, plump, and wore glasses. She looked like the
sort of pleasant person who was normally happy and optimistic.
She had that kind of face. Even now, when she appeared
confused and frightened, Sullivan could see that normally she
looked happy.

"This way, sergeant." She led them down the second corridor.

"Sorry to have walked in," said Sullivan. "We knocked hard
but got no answer."

"I'm glad you came in. I don't know what I'd do if . . . I didn't
hear you. . . . This wind."

She stopped abruptly in front of a door. Like the other doors
in the huge house, it was tall and wide. The elaborate carving of
the oaken woodwork revealed its antiquity.

"Here," she said. "George went in right after dinner. He's been
in there ever since. When I tried to enter, I found the door
bolted. George never bolts the door. Never. He has no reason
to. We're the only ones here."

Sullivan tried the door. It wouldn't open.

"You said he went in after dinner," said Sullivan. "What time
was that?"

"We finished about eight."

Sullivan glanced at his wristwatch: it was twelve past ten.

Thunder cracked overhead.

"Are you sure he didn't come out and go into some other part
of the house without your being aware of it?" Sullivan asked her.

"Quite."

Sullivan tried the door again, and of course it still remained
immobile. He nodded to McNamara and stepped back. McNamara walked to the door and knelt before the knob. He placed
his toolbox on the floor and opened it.

"This is John McNamara," Sullivan explained. "He's one of the
best locksmiths in County Cork—and in any case the only one
we could rouse tonight."

McNamara—sifting through his tools—looked up and nodded.

"Pleased to meet both of you," she said. "Forgive my lack of manners. I'm Mrs. Harrogate."

"Quite understandable," said Sullivan. "And everybody knows that the famous Dr. George Harrogate lives here, so naturally I knew who you were."

The lights blinked twice.

"Oh, no," said McNamara. "Not now."

The wind outside continued to howl, but the lights remained on.

"Is this Dr. Harrogate's study?" asked Sullivan.

"Yes," she said. "A library and office. He usually retires here after dinner to work on his current book or his sea camera plans."

Thunder banged overhead; the huge house shook.

"We've lived here for three years," continued Elizabeth Harrogate, "and this is the worst storm we've had."

"I've lived here all of my forty-seven years," said Sullivan, "and it's the worst I've seen."

"I can top you both in years." McNamara was busy worrying a file between the door and jamb. "And I can't remember a storm this bad—ever."

The lights blinked again.

"They're going to go out for sure," said McNamara. "Keep your flashlight handy."

McNamara continued to pry at the bolt. Finally he dropped the file back into his box. He scrounged around in it for a minute and lifted out a thin chisel. He inserted it between the door and jamb near the knob.

"It isn't budging," he said.

The lights flickered four times, then went out, leaving everything as black as the inside of a coal mine.

Sullivan clicked on his flashlight and turned its beam onto McNamara's chisel.

"Trouble in threes," said Elizabeth Harrogate. "First the storm, then George not answering, and now the lights. All I need now is for the ghost to appear."

"Ghost?" said McNamara. "Is this old place haunted?"

"It's supposed to be. But we've never seen the naughty fellow in the three years we've been here. That was part of our attraction to it, too."

Sullivan knew the story of this particular ghost. Supposedly a MacSweeney gallowglass had remained in the area after being wounded at the Battle of Kinsale. He had built the original house that formed the center of this building, and had lived to be almost a hundred years old. MacSweeney had taken up arms again in the 1640s despite his advanced years, and all four of his sons had been slain then, fighting under Black Hugh. The story was that MacSweeney had sworn he would kill every Englishman he saw from the day of the oath "till the crack of doom." After he died, and ever since, the house's occupants had claimed that MacSweeney's ghost walked the hallways and stairways at night.

"It isn't coming, not even by a millimeter," said McNamara. "That's one good bolt you have there, Mrs. Harrogate."

"Can you cut it?" asked Sullivan.

"I have a tool that can."

"Well?"

"It's electric."

Sullivan turned to Mrs. Harrogate. "You said that the windows are nailed down?"

"Yes."

"On the inside or the outside?"

"Oh, the outside. Whoever nailed them down didn't want to ruin those beautiful oak frames. I imagine that's why when times became bad enough to secure them they decided to nail them down on the outside instead of installing latches."

"Do you have a claw hammer in the house, Mrs. Harrogate?"

"I've got one," said McNamara. "Shine that light on my box."

Sullivan did, and McNamara rummaged around until he found a small, wooden-handled claw hammer. He handed it to Sullivan.

"Are you going through one of the windows?" asked McNamara.

"Oh, sergeant, it's wet out there."

"The only alternative is to break open the door," said Sullivan. "A door like that wouldn't give easily, and the woodwork near the bolt would be damaged."

Three minutes later, after following Elizabeth Harrogate's directions about how to reach them, a cold and wet Brian Sullivan was standing at the library's multipaned windows. There were two, and as Mrs. Harrogate had said, both were nailed down on the outside. Sullivan tried to lift each in turn, but couldn't. Five nails held down each window.

Sullivan shone his flashlight into the room. The drapes were open and he had as clear a view as the tobacco-stained glass permitted. He could not see anyone inside.

Lightning suddenly lit up everything around him, then thunder boomed.

Sullivan focused the flashlight beam on the nailheads of one window, then on those of the other. The nailheads holding the first window looked slightly larger, which would give the claw a better grip. Sullivan decided it would be those nails he would pull out.

It took several minutes. The nailheads were flush with the wood, making it difficult to get a hold. He had to dig into the wood with the claw points to get the grip, then press hard against the body of the nail to avoid tearing off the rusty nailhead. The hammer slipped many times, scarring the wood and chewing up the nailheads.

Eventually he managed to remove all five nails.

He lifted the window, which went up surprisingly easily.

Sullivan climbed through rapidly, then lowered the window again. He did it to keep out the rain before he realized that the rain could not enter because the wind was blowing it elsewhere.

The room was warm. Not as warm as Sullivan remembered the corridor's being, but a wonderful improvement on what he'd just left.

He shone the flashlight beam around the room. He aimed it at one object, then another: the rows of books in the bookshelves, the large old wooden desk, the globe, the oil paintings, the wooden filing cabinet, the fireplace, the old wooden radio, and the door.

Sullivan did not see Dr. George Harrogate.

Lightning flashed; thunder shook the house.

In the second that the lightning illuminated the room, Sullivan had seen something odd on the floor.

He aimed his flashlight at it.

A man.

Sullivan swallowed hard.

The man was lying upon the floor, his eyes half-shut in death. He was of medium height and build, had thinning gray hair, wore brown slacks and a blue sweater, and was covered with blood. The blood had also soaked the carpet around him. The cause of the blood was evident: a battle-axe was buried in his chest.

"Sergeant?" called Mrs. Harrogate. "Are you inside yet?"

"Uh, yes. Yes, I am."

"Have you found anything?"

Sullivan turned toward the door. He examined the area near the knob to see how the bolt above it had been slid into place. The bolt itself was large, black, iron. Really solid.

Sullivan turned around, his back to the closed door, and swept the room with his flashlight beam. No one was in the room except the corpse and himself. To be sure, he slowly swept it again and again, overlooking nothing.

Sullivan stepped away from the door. He looked under the desk, up into the fireplace chimney, and around the bookcases. He examined the windows for signs of entry other than his own. There were no hidden spaces, no exits other than the door and windows, and the other window was as firmly nailed down as the one he had entered.

And yet the man who Sullivan recognized from newspaper photographs as Dr. Harrogate lay on the floor with an axe in his chest.

An impossible way to commit suicide. It had to be murder.

But the room had been locked up, sealed from the inside! Not by Dr. Harrogate because his wife had said that he never locked the door.

Lightning flashed, briefly illuminating the eerie room again, sending a chill down Sullivan's spine.

"Sergeant?" called Elizabeth Harrogate again.

"I'll be right out, ma'am."

Sullivan walked over to the corpse. He stood at its feet, quietly examining it in his flashlight beam for almost a minute. There had to be an answer to how Dr. Harrogate died. Had to be.

The battle-axe was embedded deeply. Harrogate could not have wielded the axe with such force upon himself, even if the handle had not been pointing downward. Nor would the axe have come down with enough force to penetrate deeply if Harrogate had tossed it up and let it fall on him. The low ceiling wouldn't allow that much momentum.

Sullivan bent down and rubbed his thumb over the point opposite the embedded blade.

Dull.

It would require another person swinging the axe to bury it that deeply, for surely bones had been broken. Probably it would take another man to do it.

Someone knocked on the door. "Sergeant!" called Elizabeth Harrogate.

"Coming," said Sullivan, still looking down at the body.

He turned and walked to the door. Sullivan threw back the heavy bolt, then opened the door. When he stepped out, he kept Mrs. Harrogate and McNamara back and closed the door behind him.

"What's wrong, sergeant?" asked Elizabeth Harrogate. "It's George, isn't it? Something bad has happened to him."

"Is there any other exit from that room?" asked Sullivan.

"No."

"Any way to bolt that door from out here?" Sullivan asked McNamara.

"None."

"Mrs. Harrogate, I must ask you to show me to your telephone. John, will you watch that door?"

"I'll stand here and lean against it, but I can't 'watch' it."

"That'll be adequate . . . Mrs. Harrogate?"

"Why do you want to use the phone? What's happened?"

"I need to call the station." Yes, thought Sullivan, call 41145 and let them call Dublin. Dublin because part of being a good police officer is knowing when to step aside and when your own colleagues should step aside because they too lack adequate skill to handle an investigation.

"We need a thoroughly trained, thoroughly experienced detective down here."

"Then George is—is dead?"

"I'm sorry, Mrs. Harrogate, but he is. He's been murdered."

Gardai Detective Chief Inspector Phelim Kane arrived in Bandon by motorcar late the following morning, having first flown to Cork from Dublin. Kane was pleased to find that the storm had passed out into the Atlantic and that only broken tree branches and mud puddles remained to recall it to memory.

Kane had never been to Bandon before and found its quaint architecture, its many bridges, and its rolling, very green hills a visual pleasure. He had been told before he flew down that two churches here were the oldest and second oldest Protestant churches in Ireland, and Kane was interested because he himself was a Presbyterian. He felt less of an outsider in Bandon than he normally did in Dublin.

"The house is on the coast," Sullivan was saying as he started the police car. "That's a short drive from here."

Kane settled back to enjoy the passing scenery. Soon Sullivan began talking about the strange murder and Kane was unable to concentrate upon the view.

Sullivan was a talker.

Kane respected silent people more than habitual talkers, but Sullivan did sound knowledgeable. And he was probably rich in experience. Kane judged his age to be forty-seven. Every inch of him looked the copper: he was tall, although shorter than Kane; muscular, although not as muscular as Kane; weathered, where Kane's broad face was smooth and pale; lean, where Kane was stocky; and his steel gray hair reinforced the impression of strength, where Kane's brown hair conveyed neither strength nor weakness.

"Haunted?" Kane said suddenly.

Sullivan's narrative stopped. "Uh . . . what?"

"Did I hear you say that the house is haunted?"

"Aye, that's the local legend, although McNamara, who's older than I, professes never to have heard it. The story is that there was an Irish gallowglass—you know, a mercenary soldier who fought for land grants as his pay—who bore the name of that most illustrious of all gallowglass clans, MacSweeney. He fought at Kinsale—which is just south of here—and remained in the area after the Irish and Spanish forces were defeated. Later he fought for the Stuarts and lost all his sons in the cause. The legend says that this old captain swore he would kill every Englishman he ever met until the crack of doom."

"Yet this was the English stronghold of seventeenth-century Ireland," observed Kane. "I would've thought that a gentleman who felt as Mr. MacSweeney did about the English would've moved to a more Irish section of Ireland—if the legend be true."

"Aye. But they say that no Englishman ever called upon him. In any case, the Harrogates tempted fate. Mind you, sir, I don't believe in ghosts myself."

"Why was Dr. Harrogate living in Ireland?" asked Kane.

"Taxes. Not just the usual Englishman seeking a lower rate. Although Dr. Harrogate was a famous scientist and inventor, he earned most of his income by authoring textbooks and science fiction novels."

"And Ireland doesn't tax authors," said Kane.

"Exactly. . . . He should've paid. He would've been able to live in a nice English manor instead of that old hodgepodge, and he wouldn't have fallen prey to a petty thief like Stritch."

"Ah, yes, Mr. Stritch. You told me at Cork that you'd arrested someone."

Kane saw a tiny smile of satisfaction form at the corner of Sullivan's lips.

"Aye," said Sullivan. "We questioned the neighbors and one told us that he saw Stritch last night. Pinned him in the beams of his headlights when returning home from Bandon. Stritch was on a bike, he was. Pedaling along the Bandon road while the rain came in a horizontal torrent. He's an old hand at thievery, is Stritch. Mostly petty stuff. Never any violence until now."

"What was taken from the Harrogate house?"

"According to Mrs. Harrogate, the doctor's plans for that new invention are missing from the library. She can't really be sure that they're stolen until she has time to search the entire house, but she says they should have been in that room. We searched it carefully sir, and found no sign of them."

"Did you find them on Mr. Stritch?" Kane looked out the side window at the ruin of an old cottage. "Or in Stritch's domicile?"

"No. But then we wouldn't, would we? I mean, Harry's a petty thief but he's nae stupid. He would hide them someplace or give them to someone to hide for him."

"I shall look forward to meeting Mr. Stritch."

"Uh, good. . . . Of course, we've got him already. What we really need is your help in discovering how he did it. That sealed room, I mean."

In a firm but pleasant voice, Kane replied: "I'm here to investigate *all* aspects of the case, sergeant."

"Well, yes, of course. All I meant was—ah! The house will come into view now, sir."

The motorcar came to the end of a long, elevated hedge. When it passed the end of the hedge, an enormous old two-story house surrounded by the ruin of a crumbled stone wall came into view. Beyond it was what appeared to be a steep drop bordered by ancient trees, then the ocean.

"It's beautiful, that old white house near the ocean, isn't it?" Sullivan looked at Kane.

But Kane was gazing over his shoulder at the hedge.

Less than a minute later they pulled up in front of the house. Both men got out of the car.

"Looks peaceful now," said Sullivan. "But not last night during that gale."

Kane nodded. He stood beside the car a minute, studying the house. It was surrounded by the crumbling stone wall. The old central portion of the house had been built of stone and mortar, while the two wings were brick. Ivy covered most of the older wall, and the sagging middle of the second floor roof was laden with lichens.

"Where is the library?"

"You can't see it from here. It's on the east side. The house is shaped like a topless square. We are at the bottom of the square, on the south side."

"Which side of the house was hit by the gale winds?"

"The south."

Kane followed Sullivan up the stone path that led to the porch. Sullivan pounded with the brass knocker; a woman answered the door and let them in. The sergeant introduced her as Elizabeth Harrogate.

"Nobody could sneak through this house," observed Kane as the three of them walked to the library.

Every step upon the old warped oak floor caused a creak. Sometimes even the walls along the narrow corridor creaked, their own peace upset by the movement of the floorboards upon which they rested.

"George always said that the crackling floors and creaking doors were this house's best burglar alarms," said Elizabeth Harrogate. "But you couldn't have heard a gun go off last night."

"Aye," said Sullivan. "The roar of the wind was so loud that the locksmith and I had to housebreak when we got no answer to our knock."

"Really? And you used that big brass knocker on the front door?"

"We did, sir."

Inside the library, Kane meticulously examined every piece of furniture and the bookcases. He used his fist to make soundings of the walls, the floor, and the ceiling. He could not find evidence of any secret passages into the room, and Sullivan assured him that his own measurements precluded that possibility as far as the walls were concerned. Sullivan occasionally pointed out something to Kane, but generally he observed. Mrs. Harrogate watched Kane's inspection in silence.

"What was here?" Kane pointed to hooks projecting from the wall.

"The battle-axe," said Sullivan.

"Was it genuine?"

"Aye. Mrs. Harrogate told us that it was here when her husband and she moved in, so I contacted the widow of the previous owner, Hugh O'Kennedy, and asked about it. Mrs. O'Kennedy said that her husband's father bought the weapon at an antiques auction in Dublin. She wasn't sure of the year, but it was during the Great War."

Kane walked to one of the windows. He tried to lift it. It

wouldn't budge. When he tried the other window it lifted easily, noiselessly. Then he knelt down and examined the floor beneath each window.

"No trace of moisture damage, even from your entrance," Kane said at last. "Of course, if the wind blew from the south and this window faces east, there probably wouldn't be. No rain would blow in. The killer, although perhaps as wet as you were, probably wouldn't leave any trace."

"He couldn't have used the windows," said Sullivan. "The one you opened just now was nailed down as solidly as the one you were unable to lift. I know because I tried them both."

"Yes, well . . . You say the door was bolted from the inside?" asked Kane. Sullivan nodded. "Can it be bolted from the outside?"

"No," said Sullivan. "The locksmith couldn't move the bolt at all. I had to throw it back after I was in the room."

Kane looked at the chimney.

"We examined the chimney thoroughly," volunteered Sullivan. "It's too small for even a child to come down."

"And the fireplace interior? Did you examine it for catches or panels which open or . . . You didn't?"

Kane spent the next half-hour examining every potential entry or exit point, starting with the fireplace. Carefully he inspected every brick, the damper, and a blackened metal plate at the rear. He paid special attention to the damper, trying to move its handle in every direction and even pushing and pulling upon it.

Next he examined the heavy wooden door. Kane closed and opened it a score of times, attempted without success to pull its old hinges up, and tried unsuccessfully to open it after the bolt had been slammed home. It was possible only to pull back the bolt on the inside; there was no way to gain entry from the outside. Just as important, there was no way to slide the bolt home while standing outside the door.

Kane went outdoors to inspect the tall, tobacco-stained windows. He looked for footprints below them, but the ground was too stony. Kane picked up and examined the five nails that Sullivan had pulled out of the window stools and dropped onto the ground. Then he examined the nailheads in the other window. The five heads were rusty; the wood was weathered, the paint having long ago peeled off. There were no holes in the frame where other nails had been, and only the five holes in the first window. Kane tested the strength of the panes and the wooden parts. All were firm. Each window was a solid whole.

Kane climbed up an unsteady old wooden ladder to the roof. He examined the portion above the library and found that there was a boundary visible there that was not visible from inside the house. One section of the house ended and another began at the north wall of the library. It took the form of two separate roofs, one a meter higher than the other. Elevated above the newer portion was part of the original wall of stone and mortar. Decades of poor drainage had weakened it, and Kane opened up a hole in the wall simply by pulling out a large stone.

"Sullivan!" he called. "I've found the entrance. Bring up your flashlight."

Sullivan fetched the flashlight from his car and climbed up. His eyes widened when he saw the hole.

"You *have* found it," he said.

Kane clicked on the flashlight and climbed through the hole. He had anticipated encountering spiders and webs, but there were none. The space (one meter high and fifty meters across) was empty. There was no indication that any living thing had ever penetrated the area. The roof above this space, like the ceiling below it and the meter-high walls around it, was strong and solid.

Usually Phelim Kane was verbally restrained, but he left the strange crawl space sputtering strong words.

The area beneath the library proved inaccessible. Elizabeth Harrogate's statement that the house had neither basement nor cellar was confirmed when Kane's probing proved that the old building had been erected atop a stony ledge as solid as the foundation of a castle.

"That settles it," said Sullivan after he accompanied Kane back to the library. "I don't care if Stritch was near, MacSweeney did it."

Kane smiled. He glanced around the library, hunting for anything strange, anything he had not seen before.

But now it was all familiar.

"I think it best," said Kane, "that I turn my investigation onto a different track, before *I* start thinking that old MacSweeney is guilty."

Kane looked at a nearby chair, but then he glanced down at his filthy tweed suit and remained standing.

"You said that some plans were stolen, sergeant. What plans?"

"The plans for Dr. Harrogate's latest invention. Or at least it would've become his latest invention if he'd ever got it invented. He'd been working on it for a longer period of time than he'd lived in Ireland. I think about five years. He'd given press interviews about it and mentioned it several times when speaking as a guest lecturer at universities."

"So these are not secret plans?"

"It's well known that he's been working on these plans, and from what I understand it is the subject of some amusement in less creative scientific circles on the Continent. But the details of the camera itself are secret."

"He was working on a camera?" asked Kane.

"That's what he called it: the sea camera. Actually, sir, it's a computer. The idea—as I understand it—was to mount this contraption on an airplane or satellite and point it at large bodies of water. By some combination of photography and computer radar which Dr. Harrogate hadn't perfected, the machine would take a picture of the water and this picture would be free of particles, sand, salt, shadows, and all other obstructions. In other words, the developed photograph would show a lake or sea as being transparent. This will mostly be done by computer, much the same way NASA uses computers to sharpen images in blurred photographs."

"Remarkable. I've never heard anything about it myself, but then I don't follow scientific news very closely. We could finally learn if there is a monster in Loch Ness or if ruins of Atlantis exist in the waters near the Bahamas."

"Actually, Dr. Harrogate wanted to use it to mine ocean mineral deposits."

"Ah . . . so the sequence of events can be summarized as follows: Last night, during a fierce gale, someone murdered Dr. Harrogate and stole the incomplete plans for an invention that potentially could be worth millions, perhaps billions, of pounds. The killer committed the crime in this room. He—or she—then bolted the door (assuming that it was not already bolted) and left. Except that the only way to leave is the door, and if the killer had used it he or she could not have bolted it. And of course there is the murder weapon. A battle-axe."

"And Harry Stritch."

"Yes, your prisoner Mr. Stritch. A thief, you say."

"Aye. A petty thief with a long record. He's never before committed violence, but obviously Dr. Harrogate walked in on him and took him by surprise."

"Being surprised would explain why he grabbed the battle-axe," said Kane.

"It would. Stritch would never carry a weapon on him. He knows it would go hard with him if we ever caught him carrying one under those or any other circumstances."

"What sort of things has Harry Stritch stolen in the past?"

"Money, jewelry, appliances, that sort."

"Never any scientific plans or other papers?"

Sullivan shook his head.

"Has Stritch ever been here before, to your knowledge?"

"I thought of that myself, especially since the handyman also has a record, as it happens, but Mrs. Harrogate said that she'd never heard of Stritch or seen a man answering his description. I also asked Mrs. O'Kennedy about him during our phone conversation. She said that she did not recall the name, and that she didn't remember ever seeing a man answering his physical description."

"I'll want to interview Harry Stritch," said Kane. "Now about this handyman?"

"Ron Pihilly. He's been the handyman and gardener here for about fifteen years. It's one of many small jobs he has. Comes out one to four times a month, depending upon the season. His criminal record is for some burglaries and a confidence scheme he ran years ago. Now he's an informer."

"Steady?"

"Aye. We hear from him about three to four times a year. His information is always good."

"Hmmm. I'll want to interview Pihilly, too. First I wish to talk to Mrs. Harrogate—but not in here."

The two policemen left the library. They found Mrs. Harrogate sitting in the living room, off the corridor near the front door.

The living room was square, large, and had a higher ceiling than other rooms in the house. Its walls were painted blue, although the other walls in the house were papered. The furniture was modern here, and included a large television set.

Kane asked Elizabeth Harrogate to describe what had happened the previous night. While she talked he watched her closely, seeking any irregular eye movements, and listened for every tonal alteration.

"We finished dinner about eight," she said. "George left the dining room immediately, saying that he had work to do in the library."

"Was it normal for him to work there after dinner?" asked Kane.

"Usually he spent an hour there, then come into the living room to watch the telly. . . . But last night he didn't come, so I went to the library to tell him that one of his favorite programs was on. I found the library door locked. I knew instantly that something was wrong. I knocked and called his name, but he didn't answer. Thinking—hoping—that the noise of the storm had simply drowned out my efforts, I called and knocked much louder. I stood there for perhaps ten minutes pounding and shouting before deciding that it was useless. I already suspected that he was . . . but I was thinking of a coronary or stroke, not murder. That's when I phoned the Bandon police. That was about 9:30, I think."

"Did you notice anyone around the house yesterday?" asked Kane.

"No one. George and I were alone here all day. There were no visitors, and nothing out of the ordinary happened other than that dreadful storm."

"Are you usually at the house?"

"Always."

"Always?"

"Yes," said Mrs. Harrogate. "One or the other of us is always here. I don't believe that the two of us together have been absent from the house more than twice during the last year."

"That clears up one mystery," said Kane. "It explains why the thief didn't wait until you were absent to break in, especially since he would have to keep the house under constant surveillance if he wanted to enter while you were gone."

Kane rose from the sofa and thanked Mrs. Harrogate for her cooperation.

"How long were they married?" Kane asked Sullivan when they were back in the police car.

"About thirty-five years."

"She holds up well. Not a tear."

The statement hung in the air for a long time. Then Sullivan turned the ignition over. "Where to?" he asked.

"First our informer friend Pihilly, then a trip to the jail for a chat with Harry Stritch."

Ron Pihilly lived in a cottage halfway between the Harrogate estate and Bandon. It was a trim little place, painted white, with an old blue Ford motorcar parked in front of the picket fence that surrounded the house. Flowers grew along the cottage walls; the yard was kept up nicely.

Mrs. Pihilly—a short, dumpy woman with suspicious eyes— answered Sullivan's knock. She showed the officers to two armchairs in the living room, then went to fetch her husband. He'd been working out back on someone's cabinet.

Ron Pihilly flashed a broad smile when he entered the room. "Why, sergeant," he said, "what gets you out of bed before noon?"

Sullivan introduced Kane to Pihilly and informed him of Dr. Harrogate's murder.

"He was a fine man, even though English," said the handyman. "He asked only what I could do and paid me my wage promptly, and that's more than I can say for some."

Kane watched Pihilly as he spoke. Pihilly's words sounded sincere and the man looked sincere. But there was something too smooth, too glib about this weathered little man.

"Where were you last night between eight and ten o'clock?" asked Kane.

Pihilly looked surprised by the question but smiled easily. "Now where would I be but in my own home?"

"You were here the whole time?"

"I was."

"Will anyone vouch for that?"

"The wife—at least for the time after eight thirty."

"Why not before eight thirty?"

"She was at her sister's, in Bandon."

"So until 8:30 you cannot prove that you were home?" said Kane.

"That's correct."

"If you were, say, to drive off somewhere in your motorcar and not return until, say, 8:20, no one would know. There are no neighbors close enough to see your departure or return, nor to hear it."

"That's right. . . . Are you accusing me of killing Dr. Harrogate?"

Kane smiled. "At this time, I'm accusing no one."

"Good. Because I've not killed old Harrogate or anyone else. I've done some dark deeds in my past, stupid things, but that was years ago and I've learned the error of my ways. The sergeant here can tell you that I work closely with the police now. I'm a special consultant to them, and my advice and independent investigations have led to over fifty people going to prison. Right, sergeant?"

"Aye."

"Aye! The way I figure it, inspector, is that I can use the knowledge I acquired when I was operating outside the law to help the law now. I'm a professional crime-fighter just like you. The difference is that you're paid more and your professional status is recognized, whereas I don't receive recognition."

Sullivan grinned. "Do you want recognition, Ronnie?"

Pihilly smiled, "Nae, sergeant, I do not. At least not as long as I'm a consultant instead of an officer."

"Do you hope to become an officer?" asked Kane.

"I have a record. I doubt that I could ever be accepted into the force. Still, I read a great deal of fiction about police detectives and secret agents who were once on the other side. I see no reason why reality should not copy fiction when the idea is good. It's not fair for a man with my knowledge and talent to spend his life as a handyman. I deserve better. And, considering my understanding of crime and espionage—not all of which was gathered in detective and spy novels—I think I would be worth the salary."

"I know where your first-hand knowledge of crime comes from," said Kane. "But what's this about espionage?"

"In my younger days I had my hand in. It concerned subversives here in Ireland. I can't reveal more. Perhaps Dublin can fill you in, if they're willing to declassify the files."

Kane was certain that Pihilly's talk of having been a secret agent for Dublin was nonsense, and he decided not to pursue this part of the conversation.

"When were you last at the Harrogate house?" asked Kane.

"Last week."

"Did you know about the invention Dr. Harrogate was working on? The so-called sea camera?"

"Everybody did. It was a combination camera and computer that was supposed to make water in photographs transparent. The Cork newspaper had a big article on it some months ago because of him living in the country and all. . . . What does the invention have to do with his murder?"

Kane told Pihilly that he had no further questions.

"We'll speak to Stritch after lunch," Kane told Sullivan as they drove back to Bandon. "First, I want to call Dublin."

"To find out if Pihilly ever did intelligence work?"

"Exactly."

"It would be significant if he did," observed Sullivan.

"It would be more significant if he didn't."

Kane did call Dublin and a high-placed friend at the Castle promised to call him back with information within an hour.

Kane had called from Sullivan's small office, and had only just rung off when Sullivan returned. The sergeant looked like a man who had received a shock.

"It's the autopsy," explained Sullivan. "The report isn't ready yet, but they say—unofficially—that Dr. Harrogate wasn't killed by that battle-axe."

"What!"

"They say he died from a blow with a blunt instrument on the back of his head. The axe was probably buried in his chest less than a minute later."

"What sort of blunt instrument?"

"From the impression made upon Harrogate's skull, they're positive that it was a hammer."

"A hammer. No hammer was found in the room, was there?"

"No hammer found, sir."

Kane rose from the desk chair and began pacing the floor of the small office. "A hammer," he said. "A hammer, a hammer, a hammer . . ."

"A handyman would have—"

"So would every adult male in Ireland, sergeant. No, we cannot approach this from that angle. Rather, we must ask for what purpose a thief would carry a hammer? And how would it fit in with the other elements of this case?"

Both men were silent for several minutes, deep in thought.

"We'll go to lunch now—it's already late," said Kane. "At least now we can be certain that Harrogate did not commit suicide."

"Aye, it would be a bit difficult."

"Have one of your men phone the previous owner—what was her name?"

"Mrs. Hugh O'Kennedy is the previous owner's widow."

"Have her phoned and asked if any windows in the house, especially those of the library, were ever regularly opened during the time she lived there. Perhaps to air the old place out now and again."

There was no message from Dublin Castle or from Mrs. O'Kennedy when Kane and Sullivan returned from lunch, so they had Harry Stritch brought into Sullivan's office.

Stritch was a lean dark man with stringy black hair. He walked into the office with his back slightly bent forward, head up, and long arms dangling at his sides. His smile revealed tobacco-stained teeth. Stritch nodded at Sullivan, but examined Kane with suspicion. "Have a seat, Harry," said Sullivan.

Stritch sat down in a chair facing Sullivan's desk. Sullivan was seated behind the desk, Kane beside Stritch in a narrow office chair like Stritch's.

"This is Detective Chief Inspector Kane from Dublin, Harry. He would like to ask you a few questions about last night—if you're willing to answer them without having your attorney present."

"You know I'll answer," said Stritch. "I want to get this mistaken charge dropped so I can get out of this rat-infested icehouse."

Kane looked at Sullivan.

"Cold perhaps, but no rats here," said the sergeant.

Kane turned to Stritch and asked: "Last night why were you riding a bicycle during a storm?"

"I was riding for pleasure earlier in the day. I got caught in the storm, that's all. It struck sudden, it did."

"Did it?" Kane asked Sullivan.

"Aye, but the day was no pleasant one. Cloudy, chilly, and generally uncomfortable. All in all, sir, not a day that anyone would go biking in the country, especially the likes of Harry here."

"But that's what I did," insisted Stritch.

"Do you often bike in the country?" asked Kane.

"Yes."

"No," said Sullivan. "We know Harry's habits, and biking isn't among them. Harry hates exercise. Even if he overcame that aversion for one day, I don't picture him riding down all the way to the coast through a damp chill."

"But I did."

"I don't believe you," said Kane.

"But—"

"Forget it. I don't believe a word you say. If you want to get out of here, Mr. Stritch, I recommend that you tell us the truth."

Stritch said nothing.

"Have you ever been to Harrogate estate?" asked Kane.

"No."

"Ever met Dr. Harrogate?"

"No."

"Ever hear of the invention he was working on, this strange camera-computer?"

"Of course. Everybody around here has."

"You realize that even the incomplete plans for such a device would be worth millions of pounds?"

"I hadn't really thought about it."

"Hadn't you?"

"Why would I? It's none of my business. I mean, well, sure I've got a record. We all know that. But tell me what I would do with a bunch of papers. I mean, well, I know where to fence most property and I sure do know what to do with any cash that might find its way into my hands, but papers . . . I wouldn't know what man or company would be interested in them. And I don't kill people. And if I tried to swing one of them old battle-axes, I would probably end up chopping my own foot off."

There was a sharp knock on the door.

"Come in," said Sullivan.

A constable entered and handed two sheets of paper to the sergeant. "You said that you want to know when these messages arrived and they were both just now phoned in, one right after the other," said the constable.

After the constable left, Sullivan read the messages and handed them across his desk to Kane.

The first read: "DUBLIN SAYS NO RECORD RONALD PIHILLY EVER EMPLOYED IN ESPIONAGE OR COUNTERESPIONAGE WORK BY GARDAI OR ANY OTHER IRISH DEPT."

The second read: "MRS. O'KENNEDY - SAYS SEVERAL WINDOWS OPENED IN SUMMER TO AIR HOUSE, INCLUDING ONE IN ROOM CURRENTLY USED AS LIBRARY."

Kane stood and handed the messages back to Sullivan.

"Mr. Stritch," said Kane, "I must leave now, so you have only one last chance: why were you riding a bicycle near the Harrogate estate late in the evening during a storm that ranks with the worst in County Cork's history?"

"I told you," snapped Stritch.

"I was just caught in the storm during a pleasure ride."

"And would you be willing to take a polygraph test on that question?"

Stritch paled. "I want my attorney," he said.

A constable was called to accompany Stritch back to his cell.

"See what I meant?" Sullivan said to Kane.

"Yes, but I still doubt that Harry Stritch is our man."

"Why?"

"For one thing, I can't believe that he would go all that way on a bicycle to commit a burglary. Especially for papers. He's probably telling the truth when he claims he wouldn't know where to sell them. True, someone could have hired him to pull the job but . . . Another thing: the entry—or perhaps the exit—showed ingenuity on the killer's part. Harry Stritch doesn't impress me as ingenious."

"Then why won't he tell us why he was out riding a bike during a gale?"

"Probably because he was doing something else illegal or immoral, sergeant. I suggest you release him."

"Release him?" Sullivan stared at Kane incredulously. "Not unless you show me better reason than you've given, sir!"

Kane smiled. "I think I can, sergeant."

"Until you do, sir, Mr. Harry Stritch remains in our jail."

"It will necessitate another trip to the Harrogate house, but I was about to suggest that anyway. We will need to take along a claw hammer and a very sharp knife."

Sullivan got the tools, then drove Kane back to the Harrogate estate.

"We have three suspects," Kane said after they parked the car and began walking toward the house. "All three are suspicious."

"Granted," said Sullivan. "Say, aren't we going to the front porch?"

"No. To the library windows."

"Shouldn't we inform Mrs. Harro—never mind. I see her watching us from the living room window."

Sullivan and Kane waved at Mrs. Harrogate, and she nodded back at them.

Kane resumed his explanation: "Harry Stritch is suspicious to us because he is a known thief who was seen nearby riding a bike during a torrential storm. But that fact itself casts doubt on his guilt. Would he ride out here on a bike in order to commit a burglary? He wouldn't know that Dr. Harrogate would interrupt him. The burglary could have gone easily, but been discovered rapidly. That would lead to the early arrival of the police down the Bandon road—the very road Stritch had to pedal down in order to return home. Also, he allowed himself to be seen. Notice that I say 'allowed.' In a storm like last night's he would have seen those approaching motorcar headlights long before the vehicle's occupants saw him. He had ample time to ride off the road and lie in the grass or even on the flat earth. He would never have been spotted at night in such a storm had he done so."

"Then why didn't he?"

"Obviously, because he had nothing to fear—or thought he had nothing to fear. That means not only that he had no hammer or stolen papers on him, but that he had no knowledge of any crime's having been committed. I think it's a safe bet that with Stritch's record he would have hidden from everyone if he'd known of any crime hereabouts, whether he had a hand in it or not."

They rounded the corner of the house. The library windows came into view.

"And Mrs. Harrogate?" said Sullivan.

"My only reason for suspecting her at all was her lack of emotion when discussing her husband's brutal murder. There may be many psychological reasons for that. The most important fact about Mrs. Harrogate is that she is obviously not strong enough to plant that heavy battle-axe so deeply into her husband's chest—even when the man was flat on his back dead at the time."

They reached the nearer window. "And Pihilly?" asked Sullivan.

"He has a motorcar and lives nearby. He could have easily murdered Dr. Harrogate sometime past eight and driven home before 8:30 with nobody the wiser. That hedge along the road that prevented me from seeing this house until we approached it could have concealed his motorcar from the Harrogates. Pihilly could have parked the vehicle on the other side of the hedge as a precaution, come here on foot, and then hurried back to the motorcar after he murdered Dr. Harrogate. Mrs. Harrogate couldn't have heard the motorcar's engine because of the storm. She apparently didn't hear your motorcar's engine that same night when you drove it up to the front of her house."

"But if Pihilly did do it, *how* did he do it?"

Kane used the knife to dig around the head of one of the nails holding down the window. When he had exposed enough of the head, he used the claw hammer to extract it. The nail was three inches long, bent, and old.

Kane walked to the next window, followed by Sullivan.

"The central problem in this case has been how the murderer left the room," said Kane. "He couldn't have gone out the door, nor up the chimney, and both windows were nailed down."

"Right."

"But then we learned that the battle-axe was used only to make sure Dr. Harrogate was dead, not to strike him down. A hammer had been used for that purpose. And I kept asking myself, why would a burglar bring a hammer to a house he intended to rob?"

Kane pulled a plastic bag from his pocket containing the five nails Sullivan had extracted from the window.

"Then," continued Kane, "I remembered that although each of these windows was held down with five nails, the size of the nailheads had been different. Did you notice that?"

"Why, yes. The larger size of the nailheads was why I extracted nails from this window instead of the other. Firmer hold, you know."

Kane withdrew a nail from the small bag. It was four inches long, bent, and old.

He held the nail he'd just extracted from the other window beside it.

"It's longer," observed Sullivan. "But just as old."

"You can draw old nails out of any fence or building and reuse them. Remember what Mrs. O'Kennedy said? One library window used to be opened occasionally to air out the room. That means that one of these windows should have slid up easily— and without the nails' being extracted. An old nailhole is always larger than the old nail that fits into it if the nail has been lifted out several times when the board it was driven through was raised."

"But I tried both windows that night. Neither one would budge."

"One should have. Obviously when the window was raised to air the room in former times, the nails were left inside the frame and raised from the ledge at the same time as the window. Then, when the window was lowered again, the nails fitted back into the nailholes of the ledge. It would've ruined the window frame to renail it every time."

"You're saying that someone extracted the five nails in this window the night of the murder and replaced them with five longer nails?" said Sullivan. "Why would he bother?"

"The burglar knew that if the police realized that the window of entry could be opened easily they would suspect someone familiar with the house—someone aware that it would open easily. He therefore wanted the window shut again, and he wanted it shut firmly in such a way that the police would never realize it could have been easily opened before. He decided to renail it. And he decided to use longer nails because the old nails would not hold it down if someone tried to lift it. The longer nails would enter fresh wood, stick solid, and the police would never suspect that they were not the nails that had been there all along."

"An interesting theory."

"More than a theory, I think." Kane turned to the window ledge. He began cutting away at the portion that covered the hole of one of the nails Sullivan had extracted. For several minutes he cut and sliced, until at last he reached the hole itself. He cut away one side of the hole, leaving what looked like a cross-section. "There," he said when he finished. "Examine it carefully."

Sullivan did.

"What do you see?" asked Kane.

"A half-section of a nailhole."

"And you see where the metal of the old nail has discolored the wood?"

"Yes . . . yes! For about two inches but not for the last inch."

"Precisely. After deducting the one inch of nail that was in the window, there should have been three inches of discoloration in the three-inch hole, but instead we have only two inches. The three-inch nails that were originally there were pulled out the night of the murder and replaced by four-inch nails, but the killer overlooked the fact that metals leave residue on wood when contact exists for many years. The longer nails had no time to leave a trace. Or, if Pihilly did think of it, he was unable to do anything about it and just trusted that we wouldn't catch on."

Sullivan shook his head and chuckled.

"He may have even put cloth over the heads while he was driving them in," continued Kane. "That would muffle the noise and prevent chipping through the rust into a fresh part of the nail, which would've then shone through."

"But that you can't be sure of because I damaged the heads so badly when I extracted the nails," said Sullivan.

"Right."

Kane dropped the two nails into his plastic bag.

"So, it's all clear now," said Kane. "Pihilly parked beyond the hedge, walked up to this window, and lifted it. I don't know whether he pulled out the old nails before he entered the house or after he left, but I think it was after he left. That's probably why he bolted the door: so that if Mrs. Harrogate *did* hear the hammering, she wouldn't be able to enter the library and discover what had happened. He may have planned this long ago and waited for a loud storm to arrive before implementing his scheme. In any case, he got in and stole the papers. But Dr. Harrogate came in, perhaps catching him in the act or perhaps not realizing that Pihilly was there. Pihilly hit him with the hammer, then took the battle-axe and used it to make sure that Harrogate was really dead. That indicates to me that Harrogate had seen him. Pihilly went out the window, nailed it down with the longer nails that were also wider and that held the window fast. Of course, Pihilly knew that this particular window could be raised easily because he had often seen it open when he worked here for the O'Kennedys."

"You keep saying Pihilly. But how do you know it was Pihilly?"

"The facts I've mentioned. That and the hammer. The hammer shows planning. I read Pihilly as a much better planner than Stritch."

"Surely there are other reasons?"

"Don't worry about insufficient evidence, sergeant. We'll nab him with the plans when he goes to Dublin. We could get a warrant and search his house, but considering Pihilly's experience and his love of intrigue, I think it's safe to assume that he's found an enormously clever place to hide those papers."

"Why would Pihilly go to Dublin?"

Kane smiled. "That's where the foreign embassies are. I

spotted that part of the scheme the moment I heard about the camera and before I knew of Pihilly's involvement. Pihilly's character fitted that part of my conception of events perfectly."

Pihilly paid the taxi driver and walked toward the Soviet embassy.

"May I have a word with you, Mr. Pihilly?"

Pihilly turned and found himself facing Kane.

"Well, well. I haven't seen you in three weeks, detective chief inspector." There was sarcasm in the words.

Two sergeants walked up. "Take Mr. Pihilly down to the station," said Kane. "Search him well."

"What!"

"We have a warrant." To the sergeants: "If the papers aren't on him, search every inch of his hotel room."

The papers weren't on Pihilly.

Nor were they in his hotel room.

Kane was surprised—and embarrassed.

Then he remembered the old Ford that Pihilly had driven up in and had it torn apart.

The papers were there.

Phelim Kane was in his office later that afternoon reviewing a gun-smuggling case in Donegal when the call came in from Sergeant Brian Sullivan.

"The espionage angle was really the simplest factor of all," explained Kane. "Consider Pihilly's personality, his character."

"You mean his love of spy fiction?"

"More than that. He was financially ambitious, yet strapped for cash. He wanted to be a professional, claimed to be a 'police consultant' instead of an informer with a criminal record. Pihilly even claimed that he had once been involved in intelligence work when in fact he had not."

"In other words," said Sullivan, "he wanted to be a cop or a spy."

"And obviously he could never become a cop. Not with a criminal record. But anyone with access to information that a foreign government considers valuable can become a spy."

"And the valuable material was the incomplete plans for a combination camera-computer to make water appear transpar-

ent in photographs? Why would the Russians care about the
Loch Ness monster or Atlantis? I admit, mineral deposits
would—"

"None of the above, sergeant. Such a device would be valuable for another purpose. An obvious use that Dr. Harrogate
may never have thought of but that our espionage-loving friend
recognized immediately."

There followed a long silence while Sullivan thought. Finally
he gave up. "What was it?" he asked.

"Tracking American nuclear submarines."

B. M. GILL

A CERTAIN KIND OF SKILL

B. M. Gill is a Welsh writer who has attracted a great deal of attention with her first four novels, published in this country by Scribners. Winner of the Gold Dagger from the Crime Writers Association for The Twelfth Juror *(1984), which also brought her an Edgar nomination from the Mystery Writers of America, Gill shows her talent for suspense writing with this tale of a man who learns he has less than a year to live and decides to commit a long-overdue murder. Earlier authors have dealt with similar situations, but none has achieved an ending quite so unexpected and satisfying as this one.*

Alex listened to the death sentence with cold calm. He had been expecting it. Ten years of controlled behavior were about to end. The murder could now take place.

"Thank you," he said.

The consultant surgeon had heard that response before. Patients were innately polite. When the news was good they put a brake on their soaring spirits, exhaled softly, and smiled. They didn't throw up their arms and whoop with joy. When the news was bad they didn't accuse you of incompetence or rail at fate. They thanked you for telling them.

He waited for the inevitable question.

Alex sat forward in his chair. "When? How long have I got?"

The surgeon gave the usual palliative replies. The tumor was malignant and inoperable, but great strides were being made in cancer research. Life, at the best of times, was a gamble. People got killed in traffic accidents. In natural disasters. Et cetera. Et cetera.

"I have a family," Alex explained patiently. "I need to make plans. My daughter is in her first year at university. The boy is due to start prep school in September."

"The boy." Not "my son." The surgeon, only dimly aware of

99

the change of inflection when "the boy" was mentioned, told
the patient that his affairs should be put in order within the next
six to eight months. "It's always wise to see to the necessities
while you feel strong enough to cope."

Alex began to see the future in more detail. Sedation would
be stepped up as time went on. He would become weaker.
Fuddle-headed. His law practice, inherited from his father,
would have to be disposed of while he was still sufficiently
astute to get a good figure for it.

And the other act of disposal—the one he'd thought about for
years—that would have to be soon.

In the meantime his wife mustn't be told that his illness was
terminal.

Anna was glancing at the glossy pages of *Country Life* in the
waiting room when he joined her. A mean wind had been
whipping through Harley Street when they had arrived half an
hour ago and her dark curly hair was windblown. The room was
warm and she had taken her coat off and loosened the blue and
white silk scarf at her throat. She enhanced her surroundings
with a casual understated beauty—even these surroundings.
Somehow she removed the menace.

She looked up, saw him, concealed her anxiety, and smiled.
There were other patients waiting, emotions mustn't be shown.
He helped her on with her coat and they went outside.

"Well?" she said and slipped her hand in his.

The wind felt cold on his skin. It was still gusting and there
was a scatter of dusty rain in it. He didn't feel strong enough to
cope with the underground to Paddington. Too many people.
Everything too fast. Too loud. It would be good to be home
again in the comparative quietness and clear salty air of the little
Devon town.

"It's raining," he pointed out, prevaricating, uneasy about
having to lie. "We'd better get a cab."

Her voice was sharper, "For goodness sake, Alex—come on—
tell me!"

It took an effort to smile convincingly, but he managed it. "All
the hospital tests were okay. No operation. No drastic treatment. Rest. A few pills that Brian can dole out. The consultant's
writing to him. They were in medical school together. Well, you
know. Brian told us. The bloody thing isn't malignant."

She couldn't speak for a moment or two. She wasn't a crying woman, it was just that her voice couldn't come easily at moments of stress.

He sensed her relief—incapable of expression—and squeezed her hand gently.

Before catching the train home to the West Country, Alex put a call through to Jenny at Liverpool University. He had always been very close to his daughter and the lie in this case was a kindness, not a stratagem. She would know the truth soon enough. Smiling, Anna listened as he spoke to her. "And now a few words to Jeremy," she said, "just to say we're on our way home."

"Oh, the boy," he shrugged, "he'll be out playing with the lads. He's too young to be concerned."

She took the receiver from him and began dialing. He wasn't that young. He was ten. He *was* concerned.

"We'll need to get some newspapers and magazines," Alex reminded her. "They're pretty busy at the kiosk, and the train is due to leave soon. I'll see to it."

"I'll give him your love." Her voice was determined.

"Oh yes," he said coolly, "of course."

Being cuckolded in a small town is more painful than being cuckolded in a city. Everyone knows you. Jeremy—an abominably prissy name, but he had been too angry to care what she called him—had been conceived when Alex was absent on a golfing weekend. On the return journey the car had crashed. No way can you make love to your wife when your leg is broken and hoisted up on a pulley. No way can you call a lusty full-term infant premature when he quite obviously is not. You can, of course, divorce your wife. But you don't if you love her. You don't even confront her with your pain and your rage. She might leave. Had the boy looked like Anna, accepting the situation would have been less difficult. Had he been dark, or even blond, he would have merged into the family background. But his hair was red. A bright, coppery red. Like his father's.

If you had a twisted sense of humor, and most of the townspeople had, you were amused at the joke fate had played on Anna. You concealed your amusement, of course. Alex, aware of it, pretended not to be. Anna was indifferent. What the hell did it matter what people thought? Jeremy was important to her. She loved her son. And her daughter. And, believe it or not, her husband. The family, somehow, must blend together as one unit. It wasn't easy. It wasn't, in fact, possible. But she kept on trying.

As the train sped homeward she watched him covertly from the opposite window seat. He was very thin. His normally plump cheeks had fined down so that the cheekbones were prominent. On his good days he had the air of an aesthete, gently bemused by ordinary beautiful things. On bad days he looked conquistadorial, darkly forcing back pain, saying sharply that he felt nothing. Not to fuss.

She had warned Jeremy not to fuss. Especially not to mind. "If he snaps at you, he doesn't mean it." The child hadn't pointed out that Alex's behavior—sick or well—had always been the same. Toward him.

Alex became aware that she was looking at him. What could she see? The gray hairs amongst the black ones at his temples? Premature grayness, had it occurred a few years ago, would have been a kindly concealing touch from nature. But nature's hand wasn't kind. Or was she looking deeper that that—trying to fathom his mood—wondering why he wasn't happier?

He forced a smile. "It's our silver wedding on the twenty-first of June—just a month away."

She nodded. Congratulations to us both, she thought ironically, but was wise enough not to voice it. They were still together. A feat of love and enormous tact. Most of the time.

An idea was forming in his mind. "Let's celebrate," he suggested. "Let's make a really wonderful day of it."

He tended to withdraw from social occasions and she looked at him in astonishment. And then she smiled. He was celebrating his reprieve, of course. And why not? What better reason? He was going to be okay.

"Great," she enthused. "I'll start planning it."

He didn't say that he would start planning it too. The logistics of murder were difficult. First set the scene and then catch your victim. A month should give him reasonable time.

Alex preferred discussing his medical condition with his friend Brian on the golf links rather than in Brian's surgery. To disappear from the clubhouse for a mythical round of nine holes also gave the impression that he was getting better. The time was spent in a summer-house set near the fourth hole. It was out of sight of the clubhouse and in the lee of a gorse-covered hill. Very private, unless the players came close. Here Brian read him the surgeon's letter. He read it reluctantly, but there was a time for truth and this was it. Brian thought Anna should be told. She needed to prepare herself. Why build up hope for no reason? It was a mistaken kindness.

Alex said he would tell her after the silver wedding party. It would be a day to remember. A high point.

The doctor was worried. It was like offering her a glass of champagne and then throwing it in her face. "If I were in your shoes I'd tell Anna now. If I were terminally ill, I'd tell Belle."

"Your wife happens to be a nurse. She'd notice anyway."

Brian had married Belle, a local girl, soon after he had taken over his father's practice. She had been his nurse-receptionist for a while and still helped out occasionally. They had three children, twin boys of twelve who were friends of Jeremy, and a son of nineteen.

"Does Belle know I'm going to die?"

The question was blunt and Brian was startled. "I certainly haven't told her."

"She stands in for your receptionist sometimes. She might look at my medical records."

"She might, but she wouldn't. If she did, she wouldn't speak of it." It was an embarrassed jumble of contradictions.

"Promise me that she won't tell Anna. They natter a lot together. When the time comes, I'll tell her."

"I promise she won't tell Anna." He had already warned Belle not to. The warning had annoyed her. Damn it, she was discreet, wasn't she? When, during the twenty years of their marriage, had he had occasion to doubt it? Never, he had soothed, and changed the subject.

A golf ball plopped into a nearby bunker and a few minutes later the golfer appeared over the hill. Both men watched in silence as he chipped it out on the fairway. His three companions joined him and they all moved on.

Brian said, "Remember how you and I and Duggie used to hide in the high grass over there and steal the balls?"

Alex stiffened. Didn't answer.

Brian was grinning at the recollection. "You were the look-out. Duggie stole them for himself. I stole them for Duggie. He used to flog them back to that caddy chap—can't remember his name."

Alex said coldly, "It was a long time ago. We were kids."

"Appalling snotty brats. Well—he was snotty. Why did his nose run, do you suppose, and ours didn't? Because ours were middle-class?" Brian, unsure if he were wise to talk about Duggie, nevertheless blundered on. "It was a bloody awful class-conscious town in those days. Even worse than now. Not easy for him."

Duggie had been their pal. They had first met in primary school and the friendship, though beset with difficulties, had grown. Duggie lived at the wrong end of town. His mother, a woman of vast proportions, cohabited with a small, skinny man who swept the roads. Duggie, small and skinny and with dirty, tangled red hair, was their son. At eleven he had passed the entrance exam to the grammar school, but couldn't afford the uniform. Brian's parents and Alex's parents had chipped in to buy it. More fools they, they had complained bitterly, when Duggie's mother had spent the money on booze. He went to the secondary modern school and the family disappeared, no one knew where, when he was thirteen.

At Duggie's departure the two boys had felt a sense of loss.

His return, years later when they were in their thirties, had been dramatic. The one-time ugly, deprived duckling had swanned back to the town of his youth driving a high-powered Bristol. He had bought one of the more expensive houses on the headland as an occasional residence and had, in the vernacular of his rivals, pulled the local birds.

Including the married ones.

Including Anna.

"Would you happen to know his address?" Alex asked Brian on the way back to the clubhouse.

Even though the conversation had been steered away from Duggie, Brian didn't have to be reminded who Alex was talking about. The question was heavy with hate.

"Well—Seawinds, locally," he said, "but he's hardly ever here.

He came to see me a few years ago, just before his divorce. He was living in London then. He moved to Liverpool, I believe, after being abroad for a while. Why do you want to know?"

"I'm thinking of asking him to the silver wedding party—a surprise for Anna."

"By God!" Brian stopped in his tracks. Had Alex's medication started affecting his brain? "Do you think that's wise?"

Alex looked at him coldly. Wisdom was for those who might incur a life sentence if things went wrong. In his case it didn't apply.

"Under the circumstances," he said, deliberately vague, "it seems the right sort of gesture."

Local inquiries, made with some caution, failed to come up with Duggie's address. An advertisement in the *Liverpool Daily Post*, however, might draw the victim. Alex worded it simply, confident that no one here was likely to read a Northern paper: *Duggie contact Alex. Urgent.* He gave his office telephone number; the code pinpointed the town. There would be many readers called Douglas who might know an Alex. There was only one Duggie. *Urgent* might force a response.

It was a long shot that worked.

Duggie phoned on the following Friday afternoon. And caught Alex in a spasm of pain. Duggie's Devonian accent had been ironed out over the years, but there was still a trace of it when he was anxious. Alex didn't sound normal. Had something happened to Anna—or Jeremy? Had there been an accident? He asked Alex sharply if anything was wrong. "Why are you talking like that?"

Because my goddamned gut is being eroded. Because in a few months I'll be six feet under. Because you'll walk in on Anna—and the boy—when I'm not around. Or you would. If I let you.

He took a sip of water before answering. "I'm sorry—a fit of coughing. Okay now. Is that better? Can you hear me?"

"Loud and clear." A pause, then very puzzled: "Family all right?"

"Oh, fine, marvellous. Jenny is doing well at university. And the lad—Jeremy—he's growing at the speed of knots. The fact is, Anna and I—it's our silver wedding anniversary on the twenty-first of this month. We're throwing a party for old friends. We'd like you to come."

Duggie, seated at his antique desk in his very plush office, made doodles on his notepad. He had been in awkward situations in the past and had been quick-witted enough to talk his way out of them. This situation smelt wrong. Though accusations had never been bawled out all those years ago the friendship had been karate-chopped. Understandably. So why this sudden *urgent* need for camaraderie now?

"I don't know if I can shelve my commitments at such short notice," he said smoothly, "much as I'd like to."

Alex, expecting this response, tried persuasion. It didn't work. "All right," he said tiredly, "let's start again." He told him about the cancer.

Duggie, a canny poker player, was aware that he was being dealt a different hand. This one looked genuine. Alex was tidying up the past. Healing old wounds. Forgiving trespasses. Getting a touch of religion, perhaps. No harm in that. Poor Alex. Poor sod.

He said he would come and added—quite genuinely—that he was sorry.

Alex replaced the receiver and smiled with profound satisfaction. Duggie, quite soon, would be a hell of a lot sorrier. The next stage could now be planned.

Anna, an excellent cook, made the anniversary cake herself. It was a smaller version of their wedding cake and triggered memories. On the whole, she told herself, as she piped rosettes of icing in the familiar pattern, she hadn't been too bad a wife. Alex had a lovely home. She had cared for his comfort. Above all, she had loved him. Oh yes, there had been sexual lapses— the last one rather obvious. The libido was heightened when middle-age began to loom. Now, forty-five and sexually more quiescent, temptation was resistible.

She placed a silver bell in the center of the cake, looked at it critically, and removed it. Bells rang out joyful carillons. They also tolled. The little silver container for a tiny bunch of flowers made a better centerpiece. Not ambiguous. Alex was supposed to be getting better. He didn't look better. She cooked him tempting dishes and he ate what he could of them, but not enough. His so-called rounds of golf only covered a few holes—so Belle told her. Belle, she sensed, could tell her a lot—the sort of things she didn't want to hear. Their friendship was a frail affair, socially convenient. Her two younger boys played with Jeremy and they got on well enough in a quiet, well-behaved sort of way. A very different trio from the Alex, Brian, and Duggie trio in the days of their youth—according to what she had heard of it. She had stopped hearing about it when Jeremy was born. Some silences positively screamed. That one had. It still did, now and then.

"Brilliant!" Alex said, coming into the kitchen quietly and surprising her. "You've made a fantastic job of it." He beamed at the cake and went on praising it lavishly. His overreactions could be disconcerting. The illness was doing something to his nerves. He had begun talking in his sleep, but unintelligibly.

She told him she needed the very large crystal cake stand that was wrapped in tissue paper in the loft—the one that wouldn't fit into any of the kitchen cupboards. She had no head for heights, she reminded him, and couldn't stand on the loft ladder and push open the trap door. It meant taking her hands off the ladder. If she did that, she would fall.

The long unnecessary explanation was a reflection of her own state of nerves. Alex's slow drift from normality was something she sensed but refused to acknowledge. So block it out with babble. He was strung up and tense. Sick, but improving. He had to be. *Believe it.*

While Alex was up in the loft fetching the cake stand he had another look at the gun. It had been issued to his father during the war and probably should have been returned to the army years ago. When his parents had retired to their bungalow in Exeter, and left him the family home, they hadn't bothered clearing the loft. A gun—minus bullets—wasn't a valuable asset. They had probably forgotten it was there.

Alex, crouching on the dusty floor, held it in his right hand. It was a heavy, alien object. Even unloaded it looked menacing. What sort of bullets did the goddamned thing fire, he wondered? Where could they be bought? How were they loaded? What happened if you just winged your victim? How could you learn to shoot straight? For a mind only trained to deal with conveyancing, divorce, and the usual peccadilloes of a small town, planning a murder wasn't easy. It required a certain kind of skill. The hazards of being caught and convicted didn't worry him. A life sentence, in his case, would be a joke. But the shame and horror would be no joke for his family. And that he had to think about.

Death by gunshot was messy, unpredictable, and left no room for doubt. Definitely murder. Death by drowning in the clean, salty sea was more acceptable. It could look like an accident. There would be no stigma. Anna's widowhood wouldn't be blighted by his guilt. Nor Jenny's youth by shame. As for the boy—well, the boy—none of it was his fault.

But how do you entice your victim into the sea? He might be persuaded to come for a sail in the dinghy around the cliffs and out of sight of the shore. But having got him that far—what then? Even if he were boozed up—or drugged (drugged with what, for God's sake?)—a polite request to step fully clothed into the ocean wasn't on. It wasn't like stepping off a bus. Jumping off a cliff presented similar problems. Not a voluntary action.

A gun, however, could be persuasive.

Alex ran the palm of his left hand over the muzzle. It was brutish. A cold snarl of a weapon. Had his father, a mild-mannered solicitor metamorphosed into a major, ever used it? Or had he just carried it around for effect? Presumably pushed into a holster. A gun in the context of war wasn't remarked upon. It was part of the uniform. But how, forty years on, in these days of civilized suits and innocuous leisure wear, could one conceal a murder weapon? It was too big for a pocket. A holster under a jacket would be bulky. And he hadn't a holster. They probably weren't made to fit this model any more. He couldn't parcel up the gun and unwrap it carefully when he was ready to use it. So what could he do?

The answer came to him suddenly and he grinned at the sheer simplicity of it. He had bought Anna a silver bracelet as an anniversary gift. She was still wondering what to buy him.

He put the gun back under the eaves and carried the cake

stand carefully down the ladder. While Anna was washing it he told her what he wanted.

"You know I like to take the boat and watch the puffins nesting on the cliffs," his voice was staccato sharp and full of controlled glee, "well, the best anniversary present you could give me would be a pair of binoculars—large ones—with a big waterproof carrying case. My others are too small—not much good."

She put the dish to drain. "Jeremy gave you the small ones at Christmas. If I got you others now, so soon afterward, wouldn't it be rather hurtful?"

He felt himself going hot with frustration and anger. The boy. Always the boy.

"All right," she soothed, noticing his expression. "I'll say the new ones are a stand-by—that you need two pairs."

At dawn on the day of the anniversary it rained heavily and then just after eight the clouds cleared. By nine o'clock the lawn steamed gently under the warm sun. Anna brought Alex a cup of tea to bed and drew back the heavy brocade curtains at the window. The view was a constant delight. The bay across the road was a neat slice of sand creamed with foam. The dinghy, moored a little way off shore and in the shelter of the cliffs, cast upside down reflections, white on blue. This was a nice place, as near to perfection as one could get. When Alex was better they would go sailing again. Not out into the rough water beyond the cliffs—not until he was stronger—just a gentle messing around where the waves weren't big.

"Happy anniversary." She sat on the bed and leaned over and kissed him. His hair was wet. She smoothed it back from his forehead. Sweat? No, rainwater. The pillow was soaked. What, in God's name, had he been doing?

"You've been up, haven't you? Where have you been?"

He told her he hadn't been able to sleep. "I took a walk around the garden. Checked that the marquee was all right."

"That's ridiculous. There was no wind. Why shouldn't it be all right?" She noticed that there was wet sand on his shoes. He had been down on the beach. To take a walk along the shore in the dark, in the wet, was crazy. A bizarre cure for insomnia. What was he doing with the sleeping pills that Brian gave him? Hoarding them? Either that, or they weren't working. It wasn't the first time he had been up in the night. She looked at him anxiously. Brian had better be told.

"You should have woken me," she reproached him gently, and left it at that. It was wise not to seem worried—not to nag. Today was their special day, it must be cloudless in every sense.

The caterers came at midday and set up the buffet lunch on the trestle tables. Family and friends began arriving. Jenny, home from university the previous evening, helped her mother and fussed over her father. His looks shocked her. Not only did he look ill, but he seemed to be having some sort of personality change. He was edgy. Falsely cheerful. Talking too much. Only his attitude to Jeremy remained the same. He continued to ignore him.

Lunch was due to start at one o'clock. Duggie, always an excellent time-keeper, drove up to the house at ten minutes to. He could have left his car at Seawinds and walked, but it was a brand-new Ferrari Mondial and had cost him over thirty thousand quid. So why hide it?

The guests, he noticed, were the usual bevy of bank managers, accountants, solicitors, teachers. The professional breed. An unmistakable genus. They had their own clean smell, their own sharp sound. He knew most of them and remembered their parents. Above all, he remembered their parents' patronizing gifts—their kids' cast-offs. When he was ten he had stuffed a tattered pair of his ma's bloomers into Brian's ma's golfbag, and stolen her anorak. An act of retaliation against unwanted charity. Brian had approved. Alex hadn't. A cautious law-keeper, old Alex, even then.

Alex, who had been hovering near the parking area, walked over to the car and greeted Duggie stiffly. "It's good of you to come."

"Good of you to ask me." It was an amused parody. He hadn't expected a "Hi there, old mate." Ten years of aggro—even silent aggro—couldn't be forgotten. So trot out the polite clichés. Play the chit-chat game. He was less amused when he observed Alex more closely and realized how thin and drawn he was.

Alex, returning his gaze, became uncomfortably aware of flesh. The idea of Duggie had become the reality of Duggie. It gave his hatred a new dimension. He could hear him breathe. See the hair on his wrists. If he shook him by the hand—which God forbid—skin would be warm on skin—bone hard on bone. This man would bleed real blood. This man who had bedded Anna.

He tried to distance himself in his mind. Turn off the emotion. Behave normally. He told Duggie that Anna didn't know his illness was terminal. "Only you and I and Brian know. She mustn't be told—yet." The three of them had shared secrets in the past. It seemed odd to be sharing this one. "And she doesn't know I've asked you to come."

Duggie frowned. Alex being devious? Obviously. Why? No doubt reasons would be revealed. The next hour or two could be interesting. He had brought an anniversary present and fetched it from the car. It would sweeten Anna. If she needed sweetening.

Anna, confronted by her unexpected guest, was shocked, angry, hurt. In that sequence. When she saw the two men walking across the lawn toward her, she instinctively took a step or two back, and then held her ground, her heart beating, her throat dry. Alex, her tame tabby, had unsheathed tiger's claws. Today of all days. Had he battered her all those years ago, she could have borne it. But this sly slashing of her emotions now was unforgivable.

Alex, flinching from the pain in her eyes, her censure, mumbled a few meaningless phrases before walking away and leaving them together. The guests, standing in groups near the marquee, were watching them covertly. Anna, aware of the audience, regained her composure and then nearly lost it again when she unwrapped the parcel. The gift was dreadfully pretentious. A silver salver. Huge. Ugly. Unsuitable.

"Thank you, Douglas. I'll take it indoors and put it in the dining room."

"Duggie," he said. "And it's solid silver. Flog it if you don't like it."

She hadn't aged very much, he thought. He had seen her at a distance a few times when he had been weekending at

Seawinds. But never this close. No gray hairs. A few lines around the eyes. The yellow sun-dress with matching yellow and white jacket became her. A good figure still. She hadn't let herself go.

He asked how Jeremy was.

"All right. He's playing in the garden somewhere." She cut the conversation short. Left him.

Jenny waylaid her as she was about to go into the house. "Who's Croesus?"

"Crusoe? What are you talking about? Isn't this awful!" She was almost crying.

"Croesus—the rich, small, fat bloke who gave you that."

"A friend of your father." Small and fat? Yes. And the famous red hair was thinning. If he was small now, then he must have been small when they'd gone to bed together. Small and lean in those days. Muscled. Not flabby. Sexually desirable. Though not all that desirable, even then. They had made love once.

When Anna returned to the marquee the meal was about to start. Duggie, she saw, had seated himself between Brian and Belle. The two men were in strong contrast to one another. Brian had become distinguished in his middle years—lean body—high cheekbones—beaky nose—floppy brown hair streaked with silver. He seemed to be listening with more than a hint of boredom as Belle chatted animatedly to Duggie. She had always been voluble. Duggie's expression was polite rather than enthusiastic. Had he gone to bed with her, too, in the days when she'd been pretty? Probably.

Alex took the chair next to Anna's at the head of the table. "Brian will propose the toast." He spoke at her rather than to her, his head averted.

"Will he? To our happiness?" It was a bitter little whisper.

He winced. He hadn't meant to hurt her. Or had he? Perhaps a little. Not this much. It had been essential to get Duggie to come—at any cost.

Jeremy, along with Brian's boys, arrived late at the marquee. They had been running and were hot and untidy. Blinking the sunlight out of their eyes they made for the buffet table.

Jeremy helped himself to sausage rolls and then glanced around for somewhere to sit.

Duggie stopped listening to Belle and looked at the boy. Alex watched Duggie looking at him. And now Jeremy was looking at Duggie. The two were regarding one another with great intentness. Jeremy raised his voice so that the man with red hair could hear him. "I think that car of yours is fab—super—fan*tas*tic!"

Duggie nodded, smiled. Afterward, when the meal was over, he'd take the kid for a ride in it.

Two red heads in a red Ferrari can't make an unobtrusive exit. Duggie didn't ask permission to take the boy. He just mentioned casually to Belle that they wouldn't be long. "A spin along the coast road. Tell his parents."

By this time most of the guests were ready to leave too. They stood around in the drive making polite comments about nothing in particular and surreptitiously eyeing Anna and her husband as they watched the car depart. Of all the silver weddings they had attended this one was proving the most interesting. Bastardy had rarely been so blatantly displayed. Nor parenthood so obvious. What would be the next chapter of the drama, they wondered? It was a pity that politeness prevented their staying to find out.

Alex, frustrated and angry, felt helpless and inadequate in a situation he couldn't control. Anna's accusing eyes, her terrible anxiety, her absolute certainty that something awful was going to happen to the boy, filled him with guilt. Had he been accomplished in the craft of murder he would have done something to the brakes of the Ferrari while the others were in the marquee—and made sure the boy didn't go anywhere near the car. But he hadn't that sort of knowledge or technical ability. It was easy to set the scene in your mind—to feed on hate over the years—but when the victim appeared everything began sliding out of focus.

And Alex was worried about the boy too. The drive was lasting too long. Oh Christ, he chided himself, why do I keep calling him "the boy"? I'm worried about *Jeremy.* There was no reason why he shouldn't be all right—why he shouldn't come back in one piece. Duggie wasn't likely to abduct him. Or was he? And if he did . . .

If he does, I'll kill *him!*

Same brash words. Easy to say. Hellishly hard to do.

It was difficult to look at Anna. Impossible to speak to her.

The house, too, was inimical—full of anniversary cards, flowers, gifts that pointed up contrasts, made a mockery of everything. He had to get out of it. Go down on the beach for a while.

Picking up the binoculars before he left was almost automatic. He was hardly aware he had them.

The beach, golden in the hazy evening, was deserted. It seemed years since he was down here in the early hours of the morning. He'd had a vague notion then of doing something to the boat to make it unseaworthy. The notion had remained vague. If a boat sank, it sank in its own good time. Unless you were a professional at this sort of thing. He was a professional solicitor—and what the hell good was that?

The rocks, covered with seaweed, had a strong, bitter smell, A mixture of iodine and salt. A hospital smell. He tried to ignore it. Gulls were flying silently, their wings strong and joyous. They were very high. Pleasant up there. Nice to be a bird. You hardly ever saw them dead. Perhaps they died over the sea in flight. Good way to go.

Duggie, approaching silently across the sand, saw the friend of his youth sitting on a rock and looking out to sea. He had binoculars beside him. Been watching the puffins, perhaps. They congregated along the cliff ledges looking like rows of pompous parsons. Jeremy's description. The lad had enjoyed the drive. More than he had, in a way. Today, for the first time, he had talked to him. Really looked at him. Got inside his mind, as much as he could.

And the myth had been dispelled. Which was a pity.

To be sexually active but with too small a sperm count to be able to make a child was shaming. When he had first seen Jeremy, aged six months or so, he had believed the tests carried out at the London hospital were wrong. It was possible, wasn't it, he had asked Brian? Brian, after arranging for further tests to be done, had been evasive and noncommittal about the results. Hope hadn't been quenched until today.

Duggie went and sat beside Alex, startling him. Why was everyone so worried, so relieved to see them back, he wondered? Anna had bitched him, her tongue sour with censure. Who did he think he was, she had demanded, taking the child without a by-your-leave? Next time—*ask*. He hadn't bothered telling her there wouldn't be a next time. It was unlikely he would ever come back. There was no point in it now. He had nothing to come back for. He would put Seawinds on the market and cut all links with the lousy town.

He noticed that Alex was sweating and that his face was gray. "Are you in pain?"

"A little." More than a little. It had come suddenly, making him focus all his attention on himself. Anxiety about Jeremy—rage against Duggie—were obliterated.

Duggie felt inadequate, embarrassed. He wanted to help, but didn't know how. "Is Brian being a good quack—dishing out enough dope? Trying to make it a bit easier for you?"

Alex nodded, turned away.

In that case, Duggie decided, you'd better not know. The lad's red hair has blinded you. It's a throwback. Skipped a generation or two. When he's older he'll have Brian's prominent nose. His height. He already looks like his half-brothers. Anna is aware of it. She must be. And Belle? A future explosion—or had the crater been grassed over long ago?

The two men sat in silence for several minutes. Alex, emerging slowly from a state of total self-absorption, turned back from the private land of pain and was aware that Duggie was looking at him. Duggie, unwilling to show compassion, an intrusive, unwanted emotion, looked away.

The tide was coming in, sending tentacles of foam over the pebbles. A rock like the snout of a sea lion, a little off shore, was being slowly submerged. Duggie reached for the binoculars. "Do you remember how we used to stand on that when we were lads and pretend we were Jesus walking on the water?" It was conversation for the sake of it.

They had pretended a lot of things in those days. Alex's imagination had been the most fertile. At times quite bizarre. Even bloody. But he'd never done anything very much—just stood back and watched him and Brian. He wouldn't even steal a golf ball. A cautious sod. It had been an odd gesture to invite him to the silver wedding celebration. He still couldn't make out why he'd been asked. Had Alex dreamed of shooting him, or something? Painted one of his lurid scenarios in his head, perhaps, and cast him in the role of villain?

Smiling, Duggie removed the binoculars from the case and adjusted them to his vision.

"Jeremy gave me those," Alex's voice was rough with the aftermath of pain, "a Christmas present."

The binoculars Anna had bought him had a case the wrong size. No way would the gun fit. Nothing had gone right in this venture. Or perhaps everything had. If he'd had the gun and shot Duggie now what the hell would he have done with the body? He tried to work out a course of action—purely hypothetical—in his head.

Duggie handed the binoculars back. "Wish I had a kid," he said, "who'd give presents to me."

Alex didn't hear him. Deliberately. He couldn't muster up enough energy for a confrontation—not even a mild verbal one. The Duggie of ten years ago—handsome, womanizing, intent on getting his own back in the town of his youth, wasn't the Duggie seated uncomfortably on the seaweed-covered rock beside him now. They were both middle-aged. Physically diminished. They no longer threatened one another. The trespass on matrimonial territory would never be repeated. Anna's expression had told him that. As for him—the urge to kill had gone.

Emotion, as from now, had better be positive. Peace must be made with Anna. Time was short and she had to be told.

He stood up and looked down at Duggie—small, fat Duggie—and took his leave of him politely.

Duggie, about to say something trite about Alex getting better—the quacks being wrong—refrained. This would be their last meeting. They both knew it.

Shadows crept over the beach as they went their separate ways.

Up at the house Anna put some coffee to percolate. Alex would be cold when he came in. Why did she love the wretched man so damned much? Why couldn't he leave the past *alone*?

She told Jeremy to go and meet him. "He'll be relieved to know you're back safe." He cares for you, she thought, as she looked at the tall, thin boy with the blazing, deceiving hair. In his reluctant, hurt, aggressive way, he really does.

SUE GRAFTON

SHE DIDN'T COME HOME

Sue Grafton published her first novel during the 1970s, but it was not until the appearance of her female private investigator Kinsey Millhone in "A" is for Alibi (1982) that readers really began to take notice. The second Millhone novel, "B" is for Burglar, won both the Private Eye Writers of America award and the Bouchercon award as the best mystery of 1985, and some critics felt "C" is for Corpse (1986) was even better. The author, who is the daughter of the late mystery writer C. W. Grafton, also found time to publish three Millhone short stories during 1986. This was the first of them, combining her solid writing with a strong plot and a uniquely feminine sort of clue.

September in Santa Teresa. I've never known anyone yet who doesn't suffer a certain restlessness when autumn rolls around. It's the season of new school clothes, fresh notebooks, and finely sharpened pencils without any teeth marks in the wood. We're all eight years old again and anything is possible. The new year should never begin on January 1. It begins in the fall and continues as long as our saddle oxfords remain unscuffed and our lunch boxes have no dents.

My name is Kinsey Millhone. I'm female, thirty-two, twice divorced, "doing business" as Kinsey Millhone Investigations in a little town ninety-five miles north of Los Angeles. Mine isn't a walk-in trade like a beauty salon. Most of my clients find themselves in a bind and then seek my services, hoping I can offer a solution for a mere thirty bucks an hour, plus expenses. Robert Ackerman's message was waiting on my answering machine that Monday morning at nine when I got in.

"Hello. My name is Robert Ackerman and I wonder if you could give me a call. My wife is missing and I'm worried sick. I was hoping you could help me out." In the background, I could

hear whiney children, my favorite kind. He repeated his name
and gave me a telephone number. I made a pot of coffee before I
called him back.

A little person answered the phone. There was a murmured
child-size hello and then I heard a lot of heavy breathing close
to the mouthpiece.

"Hi," I said, "can I speak to your daddy?"

"Yes." Long silence.

"Today?" I added.

The receiver was clunked down on a tabletop and I could
hear the clatter of footsteps in a room that sounded as if it didn't
have any carpeting. In due course, Robert Ackerman picked up
the phone.

"Lucy?"

"It's Kinsey Millhone, Mr. Ackerman. I just got your message
on my answering machine. Can you tell me what's going on?"

"Oh, wow, yeah. . . ."

He was interrupted by a piercing shriek that sounded like one
of those policeman's whistles you use to discourage obscene
phone callers. I didn't jerk back quite in time. "Shit, that hurt."

I listened patiently while he dealt with the errant child.

"Sorry," he said when he came back on the line. "Look, is
there any way you could come out to the house? I've got my
hands full and I just can't get away."

I took his address and brief directions, then headed out to my
car.

Robert and the missing Mrs. Ackerman lived in a housing tract
that looked like it was built in the forties before anyone ever
dreamed up the notion of family rooms, country kitchens, and
his 'n' hers solar spas. What we had here was a basic drywall
box; cramped living room with a dining L, a kitchen and one
bathroom sandwiched between two nine-by-twelve-foot bed-
rooms. When Robert answered the door I could just about see
the whole place at a glance. The only thing the builders had
been lavish with was the hardwood floors, which, in this case,
was unfortunate. Little children had banged and scraped these
floors and had brought in some kind of foot grit that I sensed
before I was even asked to step inside.

Robert, though harried, had a boyish appeal; a man in his early thirties perhaps, lean and handsome, with dark eyes and dark hair that came to a pixie point in the middle of his forehead. He was wearing chinos and a plain white T-shirt. He had a baby, maybe eight months old, propped on his hip like a grocery bag. Another child clung to his right leg, while a third rode his tricycle at various walls and doorways, making quite loud sounds with his mouth.

"Hi, come on in," Robert said, "We can talk out in the backyard while the kids play." His smile was sweet.

I followed him through the tiny disorganized house and out to the backyard, where he set the baby down in a sandpile framed with two-by-fours. The second child held onto Robert's belt loops and stuck a thumb in its mouth, staring at me while the tricycle child tried to ride off the edge of the porch. I'm not fond of children. I'm really not. Especially the kind who wear hard brown shoes. Like dogs, these infants sensed my distaste and kept their distance, eyeing me with a mixture of rancor and disdain.

The backyard was scruffy, fenced in, and littered with the fifty-pound sacks the sand had come in. Robert gave the children homemade-style cookies out of a cardboard box and shooed them away. In fifteen minutes the sugar would probably turn them into lunatics. I gave my watch a quick glance, hoping to be gone by then.

"You want a lawn chair?"

"No, this is fine," I said and settled on the grass. There wasn't a lawn chair in sight, but the offer was nice anyway.

He perched on the edge of the sandbox and ran a distracted hand across his head. "God, I'm sorry everything is such a mess, but Lucy hasn't been here for two days. She didn't come home from work on Friday and I've been a wreck ever since."

"I take it you notified the police."

"Sure. Friday night. She never showed up at the baby-sitter's house to pick the kids up. I finally got a call here at seven asking where she was. I figured she'd just stopped off at the grocery store or something, so I went ahead and picked 'em up and brought 'em home. By ten o'clock when I hadn't heard from her, I knew something was wrong. I called her boss at home and he said as far as he knew she'd left work at five as usual, so that's when I called the police."

"You filed a missing persons report?"

"I can do that today. With an adult, you have to wait seventy-two hours, and even then, there's not much they can do."

"What else did they suggest?"

"The usual stuff, I guess. I mean, I called everyone we know. I talked to her mom in Bakersfield and this friend of hers at work. Nobody has any idea where she is. I'm scared something's happened to her."

"You've checked with hospitals in the area, I take it."

"Sure. That's the first thing I did."

"Did she give you any indication that anything was wrong?"

"Not a word."

"Was she depressed or behaving oddly?"

"Well, she was kind of restless the past couple of months. She always seemed to get excited around this time of year. She said it reminded her of her old elementary school days." He shrugged. "I hated mine."

"But she's never disappeared like this before."

"Oh, heck no. I just mentioned her mood because you asked. I don't think it amounted to anything."

"Does she have any problems with alcohol or drugs?"

"Lucy isn't really like that," he said. "She's petite and kind of quiet. A homebody, I guess you'd say."

"What about your relationship? Do the two of you get along okay?"

"As far as I'm concerned, we do. I mean, once in a while we get into it, but never anything serious."

"What are your disagreements about?"

He smiled ruefully. "Money, mostly. With three kids, we never seem to have enough. I mean, I'm crazy about big families, but it's tough financially. I always wanted four or five, but she says three is plenty, especially with the oldest not in school yet. We fight about that some . . . having more kids."

"You both work?"

"We have to. Just to make ends meet. She has a job in an escrow company downtown, and I work for the phone company."

"Doing what?"

"Installer," he said.

"Has there been any hint of someone else in her life?"

He sighed, plucking at the grass between his feet. "In a way, I wish I could say yes. I'd like to think maybe she just got fed up or something and checked into a motel for the weekend. Something like that."

"But you don't think she did."

"Unh-uh and I'm going crazy with anxiety. Somebody's got to find out where she is."

"Mr. Ackerman . . ."

"You can call me Rob," he said.

Clients always say that. I mean, unless their names are something else.

"Rob," I said, "the police are truly your best bet in a situation like this. I'm just one person. They've got a vast machinery they can put to work and it won't cost you a cent."

"You charge a lot, huh?"

"Thirty bucks an hour plus expenses."

He thought about that for a moment, then gave me a searching look. "Could you maybe put in ten hours? I got three hundred bucks we were saving for a trip to the San Diego Zoo."

I pretended to think about it, but the truth was, I knew I couldn't say no to that boyish face. Anyway, the kids were starting to whine and I wanted to get out of there. I waived the retainer and said I'd send him an itemized bill when the ten hours were up. I figured I could put a contract in the mail and reduce my contact with the short persons who were crowding around him now, begging for more sweets. I asked for a recent photograph of Lucy, but all he could come up with was a two-year-old snapshot of her with the two older kids. She looked beleaguered even then, and that was before the third baby came along. I thought about quiet little Lucy Ackerman whose three strapping sons had legs the size of my arms. If I were she, I knew where I'd be. Long gone.

Lucy Ackerman was employed as an escrow officer for a small company on State Street not far from my office. It was a modest establishment of white walls, rust-and-brown-plaid furniture with burnt orange carpeting. There were Gauguin reproductions all around, and a live plant on every desk. I introduced myself first to the office manager, a Mrs. Merriman, who was in her sixties, had tall hair and wore lace-up boots with stiletto heels. She looked like a woman who'd trade all her pension monies for a head-to-toe body tuck.

I said, "Robert Ackerman has asked me to see if I can locate his wife."

"Well, the poor man. I heard about that," she said with her mouth. Her eyes said, "Fat chance!"

"Do you have any idea where she might be?"

"I think you'd better talk to Mr. Sotherland." She had turned all prim and officious, but my guess was she knew something and was dying to be asked. I intended to accommodate her as soon as I'd talked to him. The protocol in small offices, I've found, is ironclad.

Gavin Sotherland got up from his swivel chair and stretched a big hand across the desk to shake mine. The other member of the office force, Barbara Hemdahl, the bookkeeper, got up from her chair simultaneously and excused herself. Mr. Sotherland watched her depart and then motioned me into the same seat. I sank into leather still hot from Barbara Hemdahl's backside, a curiously intimate effect. I made a mental note to find out what she knew, and then I looked, with interest, at the company vice president. I picked up all these names and job titles because his was cast in stand-up bronze letters on his desk, and the two women both had white plastic name tags affixed to their breasts, like nurses. As nearly as I could tell, there were only four of them in the office, including Lucy Ackerman, and I couldn't understand how they could fail to identify each other on sight. Maybe all the badges were for clients who couldn't be trusted to tell one from the other without the proper IDs.

Gavin Sotherland was large, an ex-jock to all appearances, maybe forty-five years old, with a heavy head of blond hair thinning slightly at the crown. He had a slight paunch, a slight stoop to his shoulders, and a grip that was damp with sweat. He had his coat off, and his once-starched white shirt was limp and wrinkled, his beige gabardine pants heavily creased across the lap. Altogether, he looked like a man who'd just crossed a continent by rail. Still, I was forced to credit him with good looks, even if he had let himself go to seed.

"Nice to meet you, Miss Millhone. I'm so glad you're here." His voice was deep and rumbling, with confidence-inspiring undertones. On the other hand, I didn't like the look in his eyes. He could have been a con man, for all I knew. "I understand Mrs. Ackerman never got home Friday night," he said.

"That's what I'm told," I replied. "Can you tell me anything about her day here?"

He studied me briefly. "Well, now, I'm going to have to be honest with you. Our bookkeeper has come across some discrepancies in the accounts. It looks like Lucy Ackerman has just walked off with half a million dollars entrusted to us."

"How'd she manage that?"

I was picturing Lucy Ackerman, free of those truck-busting kids, lying on a beach in Rio, slurping some kind of rum drink out of a coconut.

Mr. Sotherland looked pained. "In the most straightforward manner imaginable," he said. "It looks like she opened a new bank account at a branch in Montebello and deposited ten checks that should have gone into other accounts. Last Friday, she withdrew over five hundred thousand dollars in cash, claiming we were closing out a big real estate deal. We found the passbook in her bottom drawer." He tossed the booklet across the desk to me and I picked it up. The word *VOID* had been punched into the pages in a series of holes. A quick glance showed ten deposits at intervals dating back over the past three months and a zero balance as of last Friday's date.

"Didn't anybody else double-check this stuff?"

"We'd just undergone our annual audit in June. Everything was fine. We trusted this woman implicitly and had every reason to."

"You discovered the loss this morning?"

"Yes, ma'am, but I'll admit I was suspicious Friday night when Robert Ackerman called me at home. It was completely unlike that woman to disappear without a word. She's worked here eight years and she's been punctual and conscientious since the day she walked in."

"Well, punctual at any rate," I said. "Have you notified the police?"

"I was just about to do that. I'll have to alert the Department of Corporations too. God, I can't believe she did this to us. I'll be fired. They'll probably shut this entire office down."

"Would you mind if I had a quick look around?"

"To what end?"

"There's always a chance we can figure out where she went. If we move fast enough, maybe we can catch her before she gets away with it."

"Well, I doubt that," he said. "The last anybody saw her was Friday afternoon. That's two full days. She could be anywhere by now."

"Mr. Sotherland, her husband has already authorized three hundred dollars' worth of my time. Why not take advantage of it?"

He stared at me. "Won't the police object?"

"Probably. But I don't intend to get in anybody's way, and whatever I find out, I'll turn over to them. They may not be able to get a fraud detective out here until late morning anyway. If I get a line on her, it'll make you look good to the company *and* to the cops."

He gave a sigh of resignation and waved his hand. "Hell, I don't care. Do what you want."

When I left his office, he was putting the call through to the police department.

I sat briefly at Lucy's desk, which was neat and well organized. Her drawers contained the usual office supplies; no personal items at all. There was a calendar on her desktop, one of those loose-leaf affairs with a page for each day. I checked back through the past couple of months. The only personal notation was for an appointment at the Women's Health Center August 2 and a second visit last Friday afternoon. It must have been a busy day for Lucy, what with a doctor's appointment and ripping off her company for half a million bucks. I made a note of the address she'd penciled in at the time of her first visit. The other two women in the office were keeping an eye on me, I noticed, though both pretended to be occupied with paperwork.

When I finished my search, I got up and crossed the room to Mrs. Merriman's desk. "Is there any way I can make a copy of the passbook for that account Mrs. Ackerman opened?"

"Well, yes, if Mr. Sotherland approves," she said.

"I'm also wondering where she kept her coat and purse during the day."

"In the back. We each have a locker in the storage room."

"I'd like to take a look at that too."

I waited patiently while she cleared both matters with her boss, and then I accompanied her to the rear. There was a door that opened onto the parking lot. To the left of it was a small restroom and, on the right, there was a storage room that housed four connecting upright metal lockers, the copy machine, and numerous shelves neatly stacked with office supplies. Each shoulder-high locker was marked with a name. Lucy Ackerman's was still securely padlocked. There was something about the blank look of that locker that seemed ominous somehow. I looked at the lock, fairly itching to have a crack at it with my little set of key picks, but I didn't want to push my luck with the cops on the way.

"I'd like for someone to let me know what's in that locker when it's finally opened," I remarked while Mrs. Merriman ran off the copy of the passbook pages for me.

"This, too," I said, handing her a carbon of the withdrawal slip Lucy'd been required to sign in receipt of the cash. It had been folded and tucked into the back of the booklet. "You have any theories about where she went?"

Mrs. Merriman's mouth pursed piously, as though she were debating with herself about how much she might say.

"I wouldn't want to be accused of talking out of school," she ventured.

"Mrs. Merriman, it does look like a crime's been committed," I suggested. "The police are going to ask you the same thing when they get here."

"Oh. Well, in that case, I suppose it's all right. I mean, I don't have the faintest idea where she is, but I do think she's been acting oddly the past few months."

"Like what?"

"She seemed secretive. Smug. Like she knew something the rest of us didn't know about."

"That certainly turned out to be the case," I said.

"Oh, I didn't mean it was related to that," she said hesitantly. "I think she was having an affair."

That got my attention. "An affair? With whom?"

She paused for a moment, touching at one of the hairpins that supported her ornate hairdo. She allowed her gaze to stray back toward Mr. Sotherland's office. I turned and looked in that direction too.

"Really?" I said. "No wonder he was in a sweat," I thought.

"I couldn't swear to it," she murmured, "but his marriage has been rocky for years, and I gather she hasn't been that happy herself. She has those beastly little boys, you know, and a husband who seems determined to spawn more. She and Mr. Sotherland . . . Gavie, she calls him . . . have . . . well, I'm sure they've been together. Whether it's connected to this matter of the missing money, I wouldn't presume to guess." Having said as much, she was suddenly uneasy. "You won't repeat what I've said to the police, I hope."

"Absolutely not," I said. "Unless they ask, of course."

"Oh. Of course."

"By the way, is there a company travel agent?"

"Right next door," she replied.

I had a brief chat with the bookkeeper, who added nothing to the general picture of Lucy Ackerman's last few days at work. I retrieved my VW from the parking lot and headed over to the health center eight blocks away, wondering what Lucy had been up to. I was guessing birth control and probably the permanent sort. If she were having an affair (and determined not to get pregnant again in any event), it would seem logical, but I hadn't any idea how to verify the fact. Medical personnel are notoriously stingy with information like that.

I parked in front of the clinic and grabbed my clipboard from the backseat. I have a supply of all-purpose forms for occasions like this. They look like a cross between a job application and an insurance claim. I filled one out now in Lucy's name and forged her signature at the bottom where it said "authorization to release information." As a model, I used the Xerox copy of the withdrawal slip she'd tucked in her passbook. I'll admit my methods would be considered unorthodox, nay illegal, in the eyes of law-enforcement officers everywhere, but I reasoned that the information I was seeking would never actually be used in court, and therefore it couldn't matter *that* much how it was obtained.

I went into the clinic, noting gratefully the near-empty waiting room. I approached the counter and took out my wallet with my California Fidelity ID. I do occasional insurance investigations for CF in exchange for office space. They once made the mistake of issuing me a company identification card with my picture right on it that I've been flashing around quite shamelessly ever since.

I had a choice of three female clerks and, after a brief assessment, I made eye contact with the oldest of them. In places like this, the younger employees usually have no authority at all and are, thus, impossible to con. People without authority will often simply stand there, reciting the rules like mynah birds. Having no power, they also seem to take a vicious satisfaction in forcing others to comply.

The woman approached the counter on her side, looking at me expectantly. I showed her my CF ID and made the form on the clipboard conspicuous, as though I had nothing to hide.

"Hi. My name is Kinsey Millhone," I said. "I wonder if you can give me some help. Your name is what?"

She seemed wary of the request, as though her name had magical powers that might be taken from her by force. "Lillian Vincent," she said reluctantly. "What sort of help did you need?"

"Lucy Ackerman has applied for some insurance benefits and we need verification of the claim. You'll want a copy of the release form for your files, of course."

I passed the forged paper to her and then busied myself with my clipboard as though it were all perfectly matter-of-fact.

She was instantly alert. "What is this?"

I gave her a look. "Oh, sorry. She's applying for maternity leave and we need her due date."

"Maternity leave?"

"Isn't she a patient here?"

Lillian Vincent looked at me. "Just a moment," she said, and moved away from the desk with the form in hand. She went to a file cabinet and extracted a chart, returning to the counter. She pushed it over to me. "The woman has had a tubal ligation," she said, her manner crisp.

I blinked, smiling slightly as though she were making a joke. "There must be some mistake."

"Lucy Ackerman must have made it, then, if she thinks she can pull this off." She opened the chart. "She was just in here Friday for a final checkup and a medical release. She's sterile."

I looked at the chart. Sure enough, that's what it said. I raised my eyebrows and then shook my head slightly. "God. Well. I guess I better have a copy of that."

"I should think so," the woman said and ran one off for me on the desktop dry copier. She placed it on the counter and watched as I tucked it onto my clipboard.

She said, "I don't know how they think they can get away with it."

"People love to cheat," I replied.

It was nearly noon by the time I got back to the travel agency next door to the place where Lucy Ackerman had worked. It didn't take any time at all to unearth the reservations she'd made two weeks before. Buenos Aires, first class on Pan Am. For one. She'd picked up the ticket Friday afternoon just before the agency closed for the weekend.

The travel agent rested his elbows on the counter and looked at me with interest, hoping to hear all the gory details, I'm sure. "I heard about that business next door," he said. He was young, maybe twenty-four, with a pug nose, auburn hair, and a gap between his teeth. He'd make the perfect costar on a wholesome family TV show.

"How'd she pay for the tickets?"

"Cash," he said. "I mean, who'd have thunk?"

"Did she say anything in particular at the time?"

"Not really. She seemed jazzed and we joked some about Montezuma's revenge and stuff like that. I knew she was married and I was asking her all about who was keeping the kids and what her old man was going to do while she was gone. God, I never in a million *years* guessed she was pulling off a scam like that, you know?"

"Did you ask why she was going to Argentina by herself?"

"Well, yeah, and she said it was a surprise." He shrugged. "It didn't really make sense, but she was laughing like a kid, and I thought I just didn't get the joke."

I asked for a copy of the itinerary, such as it was. She had paid for a round-trip ticket, but there were no reservations coming back. Maybe she intended to cash in the return ticket once she got down there. I tucked the travel docs onto my clipboard along with the copy of her medical forms. Something about this whole deal had begun to chafe, but I couldn't figure out quite why.

"Thanks for your help," I said, heading toward the door.

"No problem. I guess the other guy didn't get it either," he remarked.

I paused, mid-stride, turning back. "Get what?"

"The joke. I heard 'em next door and they were fighting like cats and dogs. He was pissed."

"Really," I said. I stared at him. "What time was this?"

"Five-fifteen. Something like that. They were closed and so were we, but Dad wanted me to stick around for a while until the cleaning crew got here. He owns this place, which is how I got in the business myself. These new guys were starting and he wanted me to make sure they understood what to do."

"Are you going to be here for a while?"

"Sure."

"Good. The police may want to hear about this."

I went back into the escrow office with mental alarm bells clanging away like crazy. Both Barbara Hemdahl and Mrs. Merriman had opted to eat lunch in. Or maybe the cops had ordered them to stay where they were. The bookkeeper sat at her desk with a sandwich, apple, and a carton of milk neatly arranged in front of her, while Mrs. Merriman picked at something in a plastic container she must have brought in from a fast-food place.

"How's it going?" I asked.

Barbara Hemdahl spoke up from her side of the room. "The detectives went off for a search warrant so they can get in all the lockers back there, collecting evidence."

"Only one of 'em is locked," I pointed out.

She shrugged. "I guess they can't even peek without the paperwork."

Mrs. Merriman spoke up then, her expression tinged with guilt. "Actually, they asked the rest of us if we'd open our lockers voluntarily, so of course we did."

Mrs. Merriman and Barbara Hemdahl exchanged a look.

"And?"

Mrs. Merriman colored slightly. "There was an overnight case in Mr. Sotherland's locker and I guess the things in it were hers."

"Is it still back there?"

"Well, yes, but they left a uniformed officer on guard so nobody'd walk off with it. They've got everything spread out on the copy machine."

I went through the rear of the office, peering into the storage room. I knew the guy on duty and he didn't object to my doing a visual survey of the items, as long as I didn't touch anything. The overnight case had been packed with all the personal belongings women like to keep on hand in case the rest of the luggage gets sent to Mexicali by mistake. I spotted a toothbrush and toothpaste, slippers, a filmy nightie, prescription drugs, hairbrush, extra eyeglasses in a case. Tucked under a change of underwear, I spotted a round plastic container, slightly convex, about the size of a compact.

Gavin Sotherland was still sitting at his desk when I stopped by his office. His skin tone was gray and his shirt was hanging out, big rings of sweat under each arm. He was smoking a cigarette with the air of a man who's quit the habit and has taken it up again under duress. A second uniformed officer was standing just inside the door to my right.

I leaned against the frame, but Gavin scarcely looked up.

I said, "You knew what she was doing, but you thought she'd take you with her when she left."

His smile was bitter. "Life is full of surprises," he said.

I was going to have to tell Robert Ackerman what I'd discovered, and I dreaded it. As a stalling maneuver, just to demonstrate what a good girl I was, I drove over to the police station first and dropped off the data I'd collected, filling them in on the theory I'd come up with. They didn't exactly pin a medal on me, but they weren't as pissed off as I thought they'd be, given the number of civil codes I'd violated in the process. They were even moderately courteous, which is unusual in their treatment of me. Unfortunately, none of it took that long and before I knew it, I was standing at the Ackermans' front door again.

I rang the bell and waited, bad jokes running through my head. Well, there's good news and bad news, Robert. The good news is we've wrapped it up with hours to spare so you won't have to pay me the full three hundred dollars we agreed to. The bad news is your wife's a thief, she's probably dead, and we're just getting out a warrant now, because we think we know where the body's stashed.

The door opened and Robert was standing there with a finger to his lips. "The kids are down for their naps," he whispered.

I nodded elaborately, pantomiming my understanding, as though the silence he'd imposed required this special behavior on my part.

He motioned me in and together we tiptoed through the house and out to the backyard, where we continued to talk in low tones. I wasn't sure which bedroom the little rugrats slept in, and I didn't want to be responsible for waking them.

Half a day of playing papa to the boys had left Robert looking disheveled and sorely in need of relief.

"I didn't expect you back this soon," he whispered.

I found myself whispering too, feeling anxious at the sense of secrecy. It reminded me of grade school somehow; the smell of autumn hanging in the air, the two of us perched on the edge of the sandbox like little kids, conspiring. I didn't want to break his heart, but what was I to do?

"I think we've got it wrapped up," I said.

He looked at me for a moment, apparently guessing from my expression that the news wasn't good. "Is she okay?"

"We don't think so," I said. And then I told him what I'd learned, starting with the embezzlement and the relationship with Gavin, taking it right through to the quarrel the travel agent had heard. Robert was way ahead of me.

"She's dead, isn't she?"

"We don't know it for a fact, but we suspect as much."

He nodded, tears welling up. He wrapped his arms around his knees and propped his chin on his fists. He looked so young, I wanted to reach out and touch him. "She was really having an affair?" he asked plaintively.

"You must have suspected as much," I said. "You said she was restless and excited for months. Didn't that give you a clue?"

He shrugged one shoulder, using the sleeve on his T-shirt to dash at the tears trickling down his cheeks. "I don't know," he said. "I guess."

"And then you stopped by the office Friday afternoon and found her getting ready to leave the country. That's when you killed her, isn't it?"

He froze, staring at me. At first, I thought he'd deny it, but maybe he realized there wasn't any point. He nodded mutely.

"And then you hired me to make it look good, right?"

He made a kind of squeaking sound in the back of his throat, and sobbed once, his voice reduced to a whisper again. "She shouldn't have done it . . . betrayed us like that. We loved her so much. . . ."

"Have you got the money here?"

He nodded, looking miserable. "I wasn't going to pay your fee out of that," he said incongruously. "We really did have a little fund so we could go to San Diego one day."

"I'm sorry things didn't work out," I said.

"I didn't do so bad, though, did I? I mean, I could have gotten away with it, don't you think?"

I'd been talking about the trip to the zoo. He thought I was referring to his murdering his wife. Talk about poor communication. God.

"Well, you nearly pulled it off," I said. Shit, I was sitting there trying to make the guy *feel* good.

He looked at me piteously, eyes red and flooded, his mouth trembling. "But where did I slip up? What did I do wrong?"

"You put her diaphragm in the overnight case you packed. You thought you'd shift suspicion onto Gavin Sotherland, but you didn't realize she'd had her tubes tied."

A momentary rage flashed through his eyes and then flickered out. I suspected that her voluntary sterilization was more insulting to him than the affair with her boss.

"Jesus, I don't know what she saw in him," he breathed. "He was such a pig."

"Well," I said, "if it's any comfort to you, she wasn't going to take *him* with her, either. She just wanted freedom, you know?"

He pulled out a handkerchief and blew his nose, trying to compose himself. He mopped his eyes, shivering with tension. "How can you prove it, though, without a body? Do you know where she is?"

"I think we do," I said softly. "The sandbox, Robert. Right under us."

He seemed to shrink. "Oh, God," he whispered. "Oh, God, don't turn me in. I'll give you the money. I don't give a damn. Just let me stay here with my kids. The little guys need me. I did it for them. I swear I did. You don't have to tell the cops, do you?"

I shook my head and opened my shirt collar, showing him the mike. "I don't have to tell a soul. I'm wired for sound," I said, and then I looked over toward the side yard.

For once, I was glad to see Lieutenant Dolan amble into view.

EDWARD D. HOCH

THE SPY'S STORY

As I frequently do, I have included one of my own stories from last year, relying upon the judgment of editors and friends.

It was a stormy night in January and Rand was seated by the fire with Leila, talking about the days before they were married. "How did you get started in Concealed Communications?" Leila asked suddenly. "I know about the Calendar Network in 1949, but what made you go into espionage work in the first place?"

Rand leaned back and closed his eyes, thinking about it. "I was at medical school briefly between King's School and Oxford, and that kept me out of the army until the war ended. I suppose I felt a bit guilty about it and decided to enter government service." He paused. "No, that's not completely true. Something happened in the late summer of '45, just after the war, that decided me."

"What was it?"

"I saw my father kissing a librarian."

Leila sat up on the sofa. "Now, you've really got to tell me about that!"

I suppose (Rand began) that not too many people today are aware of the denazification program conducted after Germany's surrender in 1945. My father, who'd been with the British embassy in Paris before the war, had joined the so-called Civilian Military Forces of the Control Commission, which was overseeing the Allied occupation of Germany. It was late August, shortly after Japan's surrender, and I'd just turned nineteen. I'd already decided a doctor's life wasn't for me and had arranged a transfer from St. Thomas Medical School in Lambeth to St. John's at Oxford. I had a few weeks of freedom in the meantime and decided to accompany my father to Germany as his unpaid clerical assistant.

135

He was one of a number of scholars, writers, and public servants chosen to inspect German libraries in the British zone of occupation. His job was to study the political background of the librarians, as well as the content of the books on their shelves. Once he ruled that a particular library had been denazified, it was allowed to reopen to the German public. My knowledge of German was limited but I knew enough to help weed out the sort of books we wanted to remove.

It was at a small community library just outside Düsseldorf that my father first made the acquaintance of Hannah Peters and Dr. Fredericks. They'd been the librarians there when the war came to its end. The library itself was quite nice, located in a former church building with a spire that could be seen for miles across the countryside. Inside, there was a little balcony at one end of the building that I suppose had once accommodated a choir and organ. It had been made into a small office and workroom for the librarians, and it was here that my father spoke with Hannah Peters.

She was a pale brown-haired young woman who still seemed stunned by the aftermath of a war her country had lost. She avoided my father's eyes and kept her own on the faded carpet, answering his questions with the briefest of German syllables. After several routine questions my father asked her, "In your opinion, is your co-worker Dr. Fredericks a Nazi?"

Her eyes came up for just an instant. "No."

My father sighed and rested his hands on the desk between them. His neatly trimmed moustache gave him the appearance of a handsome upper-class English gentlemen, but I suppose to the frightened young woman he appeared only as the enemy. "Look here, Miss Peters," he said, "it's my job to ask these questions. We'd like to get you back in business as quickly as possible, but you must cooperate. There's a file in Düsseldorf which lists Dr. Fredericks as a member of the Nazi Party."

For the first time, she was moved to speak at length. "A great many people were members of the party for one reason or another," she said. "That does not mean they were Nazis. The war took a terrible toll on the German people, on every aspect of our lives. Libraries did not escape merely because they held books rather than bombs. You see our building, luckily untouched by war, but in the city of Düsseldorf many libraries were hit. More than sixty thousand books were destroyed."

"I'm sorry about that, of course. But your cooperation is necessary to get this particular library open again."

"We have already removed all volumes of Nazi literature. They are stored in the basement."

"Very good. My son Jeff and I will inspect them, as well as the remaining books on your shelves."

She directed her gaze at me for the first time. My father was the only one who ever called me Jeff, and I never liked it. My mother didn't like it, either, and she often reprimanded him for it. But Mother was back in London.

Hannah Peters led us to the basement and showed us several cartons of books. Some were laudatory biographies of Hitler and the important Nazi generals. Others were anti-Jewish diatribes. I began to realize how necessary it would be to check the remaining books on the shelves. Almost anything might have slipped through.

We heard the upstairs door open and Hannah said, "That will be Dr. Fredericks now. You'll want to talk with him, to ask him if I am a Nazi." She turned and went up the steps.

Dr. Walter Fredericks was a little man with a frightened, rabbitlike expression. No doubt word of our mission had preceded us and he viewed my father as a threat to his freedom and his future. "You are Charles Rand?" he asked, squinting behind thick steel-rimmed eyeglasses.

"That's correct—and this is my son Jeff, who's assisting me. I believe you know the reason for our visit."

"The books have already been separated."

"We know. Miss Peters was just showing them to us in the basement."

"We have thrown out everything by Goebbels."

"That's a good start," my father assured him.

"And *Mein Kampf,* of course. Hannah and I know what you want removed. The offending books will be locked away, just as the books by Jews were locked away under the former government."

I didn't like the comparison he was drawing, but my father raised no objection. He allowed Fredericks to take us on a tour of the bookshelves, showing us a large collection of German textbooks and popular fiction dating from the pre-Nazi era. I saw Vicki Baum's *Menschen Im Hotel,* which I had read in English and seen as an American film. And *Im Westen Nichts Neues*—Erich Maria Remarque's *All Quiet on the Western Front.*

"We've been in limbo since the war ended," Fredericks explained. "I hope we can resume ordering books soon and get in some newer titles."

"Once you're open again, things will be back to normal," my father assured him.

We left the library, promising to return the following day for a more thorough inspection of the books and records. As we drove back toward Düsseldorf, past the steel mills where production was slowly being channeled to peacetime needs, I said, "That shouldn't take us long tomorrow. It looks fairly routine. Where do we go next?"

"Cologne." An army staff car had been provided for our transportation and my father drove it well, avoiding occasional craters that served as reminders of the wartime bombing.

We were billeted with the British occupation forces in an area near the Rhine River, and we ate dinner that evening at their mess hall. Strict regulations against fraternization with Germans were still in effect then, so none of the troops went into the city in the evenings unless on patrol. My father ate heartily but talked little during the meal. His mind seemed to be elsewhere, as if planning our future schedule.

After dinner they were showing a recent British film, *The Way to the Stars.* I stayed to watch it but my father excused himself, saying he wanted to catch up on his paperwork. The film was sort of a war story as seen from the home front, about the guests of a small hotel near an airfield, with John Mills and Michael Redgrave in the principal roles. In the opening sequence, the camera prowled through the abandoned air base, picking out details and objects that would become important when the film flashed back to tell its story.

But I was uneasy, and after several minutes I left the hall to join my father. The staff car outside our quarters was missing, but for some reason it didn't surprise me that he'd gone

somewhere, maybe into the city. I had a driver's license and my
ID card as a member of the Civilian Military Forces, so I was
able to borrow a jeep from the motor pool. I wasn't really
looking for him, but I figured if he could go out on the prowl so
could I.

There were a good many ruined buildings in the city, and as I
drove down Volkinger Strasse I began to realize for the first time
what those people must have lived through. Of course, we had
lived through it in London, too, but we were the victors. It
made a difference.

I was stopped once by a military-police vehicle and warned
against fraternization. When they asked what I was doing driving around alone, I told them I was on my way to pick up my
father after a meeting with city officials. That seemed to satisfy
them and I drove on, avoiding the glass and rubble that still
littered the roads in some sections. A tram rail twisted by a
bomb blast stuck up toward the sky on one street, illuminated
only by a single light down the block.

The streets were deserted in this area and I was sorry I hadn't
stayed more toward the center of the city. Once when I slowed
the jeep to avoid some rubble, a young man detached himself
from the shadows and spoke. "Cigarettes, mister?" he asked. I
tossed him a half-empty pack and drove on.

Before I knew it, I'd reached the outskirts of the city, on the
same familiar road I'd traveled with my father earlier that day,
the library we'd visited straight ahead. Perhaps that had been
my destination all along. I saw the staff car parked in front, its
lights out, and I knew I'd found my father.

Parking the jeep about a hundred yards down the road, I
approached the rest of the way on foot.

There was light burning on the second-floor balcony where
the office was located. Standing across the street, I could see
Hannah Peters pacing back and forth, talking to someone. Then
my father came into view, standing very close to her.

He took her in his arms and kissed her.

My eyes were blurred with tears as I drove away from there. I
felt he had betrayed me, as well as my mother back in London.
Just then I wanted to run away from them both, but there was
no place to run. I ended up returning the jeep to the motor pool

and climbing into my bunk. It must have been near dawn when I heard my father return, moving silently so as not to awaken me. I listened to the squeak of his bunk and wondered if I hated him . . .

At breakfast in the officers' mess, he acted as if nothing had happened, serving himself bacon and eggs from the buffet as he did every morning.

"I looked for you after the film," I said as we ate.

"I was restless. Went for a ride around the post, had a couple of drinks at the Officers' Club."

"I thought you might have driven into the city."

"No."

"What's on the schedule for today?" I asked.

"We have a meeting with the mayor and the chief librarian of Düsseldorf at ten o'clock at Military Government Headquarters."

"That should be exciting," I said sarcastically.

He raised his eyebrows. "You knew what this was going to be when you asked to come along, Jeff."

Not really, I almost replied, but kept silent instead. There'd be time enough later for voicing my opinions.

The HQ of Düsseldorf's Military Government was located in a huge red-brick building that stretched around three sides of a square near the center of the city. It was quite modern compared with the rest of the downtown area. Inside, there were polished stone floors and handsome chrome fixtures, setting off the warm walnut furnishings.

The mayor turned us over at once to the chief librarian, a tall Prussian type of man, with a withered left hand that must have kept him out of military service. His name was Carl Hesse, and his dislike of my father and me was obvious. "Frankly, gentlemen, I never expected to be sitting here negotiating for the reopening of our libraries and schools," he said at the outset.

"The schools will reopen next month," my father told him. "The libraries may open even sooner if you cooperate with us. We need the personnel files of your librarians and to inspect the libraries themselves. All Nazi titles must be removed."

"Surely we may keep them for study and reference."

"University libraries will have the books available if needed for such purposes."

"Very well," Hesse answered with some reluctance. "And the files? Do you want only the city libraries or those in the towns as well?"

"We are calling individually on regional libraries. My son and I met with Hannah Peters and Dr. Fredericks yesterday. We'll return there after lunch today."

"Ah, yes. What did you think of Dr. Fredericks?"

My father's eyes narrowed. "He seemed knowledgeable. I was more interested in Hannah Peters. What can you tell me about her?"

"I can tell you she has no love for the English. Her parents were killed in a bombing early in the war."

I shot my father a glance but his expression didn't change. "Is that so? I found her most cooperative."

"Will their library be allowed to open?"

"I expect so. We'll know better after today."

"And the city libraries?"

"If you can have those personnel files for me, we can begin checking them in the morning. We're especially anxious to weed out all Nazi Party members."

Carl Hesse nodded. "I understand. The mayor has instructed me to cooperate fully." His tone of voice indicated it was not his preference.

My father rose and shook hands, signaling an end to the meeting. At that moment the telephone rang on Hesse's desk. He answered it and frowned, then held up his withered left hand to keep us from leaving. "I will tell them," he said and hung up.

"Was that a message for us?" my father asked.

"It was the mayor. He has just heard from the military police that Dr. Fredericks has been found murdered, his body dumped on the side of a country road near here."

We drove there at once, escorted by a military-police jeep sent out from British headquarters. Our destination was a wooded area south of the city, along the east bank of the Rhine. I could see a number of official vehicles already at the spot as we pulled up. A criminal-investigation officer, Captain Bridlington, was in charge. "Thank you for coming so quickly," he told my father. "We're mainly interested in your identification of the body. I understand you met with Dr. Fredericks yesterday."

"That's correct," my father told him.

Captain Bridlington walked over to the side of the road and lifted the blanket that covered the body. It was Fredericks, all right. There were at least two wounds in his chest, but his face was untouched. "Shot at close range," the captain told us after my father had confirmed the identification. "We think it was the work of the Werewolf movement, the Nazi underground."

Although the war in Europe had been over less than four months, there were already reports surfacing about Werewolf activities. Heinrich Himmler had mentioned the movement in a speech the previous October, while the war still raged, and the suggestion was made that the SS should go underground rather than surrender, joining the Werewolf to fight the Allied invaders. Though the threat never amounted to more than a few random acts of terrorism and assassination, it was taken seriously by the occupying forces at that time in West Germany.

"Why would the Werewolf kill a party member like Dr. Fredericks?" my father wanted to know.

"Perhaps because he was no longer a loyal party member," Captain Bridlington suggested. "I understand he was cooperating with you in the reopening of his library. They killed the mayor of Aachen for cooperating."

We watched while the body was loaded into an army ambulance and taken away, then suddenly my father said, "We must get to Hannah Peters. Her life could be in danger, too."

Her car was parked in front of the library and we found her inside, dusting books and arranging them on the shelves. She smiled when she saw my father. "I have bad news," he announced gravely. He told her about Dr. Fredericks.

"My God! The poor man! When did it happen?"

"Sometime during the night, they think. They suspect the Werewolf underground. I came to warn you. They may have targeted both of you for cooperating with me."

She bent her head at his concern. "I can take care of myself."

I found myself shutting off the conversation and studying Hannah Peters with a new awareness. I knew from the personnel records that she was twenty-eight years old, and with her brown hair loose as it was today she looked even younger. She might have been someone with whom I'd shared a class at university.

"We should finish checking these books," my father said. "Once the library is open and we've moved elsewhere, the threat might lessen." He stepped close to her to read the titles and I saw her hand linger on his arm for just an instant. I walked around to the other side of the bookcase, unable to face my father.

On the way back to the base, driving a bit faster than he should, my father said, "I'm giving it my approval. They're certified for reopening."

"*They?*" I said, a bit harsher than I'd intended. "It's only her now. Fredericks is dead."

He glanced at me, then back at the road. "What's that supposed to mean, Jeff?"

"Maybe she killed him. Maybe she's part of this Werewolf underground."

"I don't think she could have killed him," my father answered carefully. "She was at the library about the time of the killing."

"How could you know that? Because you were with her last night?"

He seemed shocked at my words, and pulled the car over to the side of the road, "Jeff, I didn't realize—"

"I took one of the motor-pool jeeps and went out looking for you last night. I drove out to the library. I saw you kissing her near the window. Are you going to deny it?"

"No. I wish you'd understand, though. Sometimes there are things you have to do."

"Like sleeping with young German women? You did sleep with her, didn't you?"

"Jeff—"

"Just answer me, tell me the truth!"

He sighed and sat gripping the steering wheel, staring straight ahead. "Yes, I slept with her," he said at last. "I'm not excusing it. I hope someday you'll understand."

"Understand what? That there's a war on? In case you hadn't noticed, the war is over."

"Your mother—"

"Don't mention her!"

"All right," he said, starting the motor again.

Both of us were silent for the rest of the ride. There seemed nothing either of us could say without making matters worse. Finally, as we drew up in front of our barracks, I asked, "Are we through with her now?"

He ignored the implication of my remark. "I've certified the library for reopening. Tomorrow we'll work on the city libraries."

"All right." I climbed out of the car and walked away without another word. I felt like being alone just then. As I walked aimlessly about the camp, I gradually decided what I had to do.

There was no doubt in my mind that Hannah Peters was involved in the murder of Dr. Fredericks by the Werewolf underground. It was more than happenstance that he was dead and she was alive, when both had been cooperating with the occupying forces. Even if she hadn't pulled the trigger herself, she was involved—and I intended to prove it. I borrowed the jeep from the motor pool again and drove back into the city, heading for the Military Government Headquarters. This time I bypassed the mayor and sought out Carl Hesse, the chief librarian we'd seen earlier. He seemed surprised at my return and said, "Jeff Rand, isn't it?"

"Yes, sir. My father sent me to do a little more digging into the records. He's especially interested in Dr. Fredericks' library."

Hesse stroked his chin. "You understand that my regular office at the main library was destroyed in the bombing. They have given me a bit of space here only until other arrangements can be made. Many of my records no longer exist. However, the library that interests you was never part of the city system. I have no records of their operations because they were an independent repository funded directly by the state."

"It stands to reason that people working directly for the state would be more loyal to it," I suggested. "We know Dr. Fredericks was a party member—"

"But not a Nazi. Believe me, there was a difference."

"What about Hannah Peters? You said her parents were killed in a British bombing. Is she the sort to have ties to an underground resistance group like the Werewolves?"

"I doubt it very much," he said. "I've seen nothing to indicate she was politically active at any time in her career."

That wasn't what I'd been hoping for, but it didn't discourage me. After I left, I telephoned Captain Bridlington, pretending I was acting on my father's behalf. "He was wondering if you have the autopsy report on Dr. Fredericks?"

"It's too soon for anything but preliminaries. What was it that interested your father?"

"The time of death."

"Well, the doctor made a rough estimate of that. He thinks death occurred in the early evening, not more than two hours after Fredericks had dinner. However, the body could not have been dumped where we found it until shortly before dawn— the patrols would have spotted it earlier. It was at the edge of the highway, in view of car headlights."

"Thank you, Captain. I'll pass the word on to my father."

I hung up the phone and went back to the jeep. I had no intention of passing anything on to my father. I was going to confront Hannah Peters myself . . .

I parked some distance from the library, near where I'd left the jeep the previous evening. Now it was daylight, however, and I could see Hannah's battered pre-war car standing by the side of the building. If she were to look out the window, she could see me, too. The air was damp after a brief shower, and the grass beneath my feet was wet as I cut across the lawn to the library entrance.

When I knocked at the locked door, I heard her voice from within. "We're not open yet. Come back on Friday."

"This is Jeffery Rand," I called. "Charles's son."

There was silence and then I heard the bolt being slid open. "What brings you here?" she asked. "Where is your father?"

"I wanted to talk to you alone."

She seemed to be dusting and sorting books, as she'd been doing when we brought her the news of Dr. Fredericks' murder. Pushing the hair from her eyes, she faced me and asked, "What about?"

I tried to keep my mind on what I was there for, to forget that this was a woman who'd slept with my father. "I wanted to ask you more about the death of Dr. Fredericks. My father believes you couldn't have been involved because you were here at the library all evening. Is that correct?"

"Involved?" she repeated. "How could anyone think I was involved? Dr. Fredericks and I worked together for years. He taught me everything I know." She picked up a few books.

"The military command suspects the Werewolf underground."

"That's insane. There have been no Werewolf incidents in this area. And even if they are involved, how would that implicate me? My file must show that I'm a very nonpolitical person."

"Hear me out," I insisted. "Fredericks was killed within a couple of hours of eating dinner. But the body was not dumped at the side of the road until almost dawn. Why did his killer wait so long, risking discovery? And why was the body left so close to the road?"

"You seem to be doing the talking," she said.

"I know my father was here with you last night. I saw you together through the window. I think you shot Fredericks earlier, probably hiding his body in your car. But you couldn't drive it away while my father was here. You made love to him to lull his suspicions, then sent him home toward dawn so you could dispose of the body along the highway before daybreak. You didn't have the strength to carry it into the woods, so you had to leave it by the roadside."

"I see! You are a regular boy detective. Your mother must be so proud of you."

At the mention of my mother, all reason seemed to leave me. In a moment of blind anger, I lashed out at her, knocking the books from her hands. "What are you trying to do?" she gasped.

Suddenly the floor was strewn with money, British five-pound and ten-pound notes cascading from inside the books. I stared, unable to grasp what was happening. "What is this?" I said finally.

"I'm sorry you had to see it," she told me. "I didn't want to kill you, too."

Then I saw the little automatic pistol that must have been on the desk behind her. I saw the eye of its barrel pointed at me, saw her trigger finger whiten, and knew that I was going to die because I'd been stupid and foolish. I'd only partly solved the mystery and now I was going to die for my mistake.

Someone coughed gently from the next room and an expression of surprise spread over Hannah Peters' face. She died standing there, aiming her gun at my head. I saw it happen, my father in the doorway behind her. Then I doubled over and was sick to my stomach.

Somehow he got me out into the car and started driving. "The jeep—" I said.

"We'll have it picked up."

"You killed her! She's dead!"

"Don't think about it now, Jeff. Everything will be all right."

"All right? How will it be all right? How did you get there? What were you doing with that gun with a silencer on it?"

"There's a lot to explain, Jeff. We'll talk it over later when you're feeling better."

"I want to talk about it *now*," I told him, my voice shaking.

He pulled down a side road and parked.

"You can't just kill someone and go off and leave them like that," I said, trying to gain control of myself.

"Everything will be taken care of," he assured me. "I didn't intend to kill her, but it was your life or hers. I had no choice."

"She was the woman you loved!"

He shook his head. "No, Jeff. She was never that."

"But—"

"I'd better tell you exactly what happened. I arrived in time to hear you accuse her of Dr. Fredericks' murder, and your reconstruction was fairly accurate as far as it went. But this was not a Werewolf plot. Our first visit to the library yesterday revealed the most important clue, a German edition of *All Quiet on the Western Front*. A strong anti-war novel such as that is hardly the type of book you'd expect to find in a German library. In fact, Hitler ordered all of Remarque's books burned when he took office in 1933. He even stripped Remarque of his German citizenship in 1938. It's impossible that the book could have been there. You'll remember we were told that no new books had been received since the end of the war."

"But we saw it," I protested.

"We saw something that looked like a book. I went back last night to see what it really was. That's when Hannah Peters caught me. I had to have an excuse for being at the library, so I said I'd returned to see her. One thing led to another."

"You say it so—so—"

"Casually? Coldly? I had a job to do. Sometimes deceit is necessary to accomplish a serious goal. Much is permitted in the service of one's country."

It was beginning to dawn on me. "When you were at the Paris embassy, were you a spy?"

"I hate that word," he told me.

"That gun with the silencer—"

"It was issued to me. I carried it for many years, and I used it when necessary."

"You followed me to the library today."

"I had to. I had no idea what you might do."

"The money that was in the book—"

"Counterfeit, all of it. Hitler printed up millions of pounds in counterfeit money to use for an invasion of England. Later the money was used for other purposes—to pay agents in the field, to destabilize our currency. Hannah's library was one of the storehouses for this money, hidden inside fake, hollowed-out books. Since the books weren't real, someone must have decided it didn't matter what titles were on the spines. Somehow that one got out on the shelf and I suppose Fredericks noticed it, too. He must have spoken to Hannah about it after we left. Perhaps she had her own plans for all that money, counterfeit or not. Anyway, she shot him shortly before I arrived last night and hid his body in her car. After I left her early this morning, she dumped him along the highway. You were right about all that."

"How do you know she wanted the money for herself?"

"An educated guess. She was collecting some of the fake books when you arrived. But I didn't see the Remarque among them. I think she had already moved quite a few away, probably to her house or apartment."

"That really is a guess."

"Not so much as you'd think. When we went there earlier, her car was parked in front of the library. This time it was by the side of the building. She'd moved it, gone somewhere and come back, perhaps parked less obviously so she could load the books without being seen from the street."

I shook my head in wonderment. "How do you notice all these things?"

"Training. You could do it too."

"I could never deceive anyone. I could never make love to someone without meaning it." My words were cruel because I meant them to be. "I could never lie to my own son."

"I didn't mean to lie to you, Jeff."

"Does Mother know what you do? Does she know you're a spy? Does she know you use a silenced pistol?"

"Perhaps you'd better ask her those questions," he suggested.

Rand stopped talking and sat for a time staring into the fire.

"Did you ask her?" Leila said.

"No, somehow I never got around to it. When we returned to England, I went off to Oxford. Nothing more was ever said about Hannah Peters or what happened at the library. And to my knowledge nothing ever appeared in the newspapers about it. Someone did a good job of cleaning up the traces after our departure. By the time I finished Oxford my father had died. He didn't live long enough to see me go into intelligence work, but I know he would have approved."

"Did you keep your promise about never deceiving anyone? About never making love to someone without meaning it?"

"Come here," Rand said, gently pulling her down onto the rug by the fire. "I could never do the things my father did. Perhaps that's why I chose to work in London, rather than abroad. We were two different people, my father and I."

"But something about his life held a fascination for you or you wouldn't have gone into intelligence work. Perhaps you weren't as different as you thought."

Gazing into the fire, Rand knew that she was right.

CLARK HOWARD

SCALPLOCK

*For the second year in a row, the EQMM Readers Award
went to a story by Clark Howard, solidifying his position
as the most popular suspense writer of the 1980s in the
short story form. This year's winner, which you are about
to read, is quite different in plot and characters from last
year's, sharing with it only that moving and compassion-
ate sense of little people against the system that has
become a trademark of Howard's best stories.*

Rita saw the young man as he came out of the Las Vegas bus
depot and stood at the curb looking at the brilliant lights of the
Union Plaza Hotel and Casino. She was working across the street
because the Union Plaza security guards did not permit street
girls near the hotel. Normally Rita would have ignored the
young man; he looked too country to risk crossing the street
for: old faded Levis, worn Western boots, a khaki shirt like gas-
station attendants wore. He appeared to be deeply tanned
under a straw Western hat, so she figured he was a cowboy or
construction worker. Probably didn't have two twenties to fold
together. Still, you never knew. Business had been such a bitch
all night long. Plus which she was on her own now, had been for
a week, since Greg, her boyfriend, had taken off for San Francisco. She decided to take a chance and cross the street.

Keeping a wary eye out for Union Plaza security, Rita saun-
tered across Main toward the depot. She had lost some weight
the past few weeks—the heat of August in the desert, she
guessed. Her miniskirt did not fit as snugly as she would have
liked. For that same reason, she now had to open an additional
button on her blouse to show any cleavage at all. Still, she knew
she looked better than most girls on the street. Her main
problem was making sure her true age didn't show—she had to
appear at least eighteen or it spooked customers.

151

"Hi, there," she said, stopping next to the young man at the curb.

"Hello," he replied, with only a glance. Rita saw now that he wasn't suntanned at all; his skin was naturally clay-colored, and his hair under the straw hat, his eyebrows, even his eyeballs, were black and shiny. Maybe he's Mexican, she thought.

"Waiting for somebody?" she asked.

He glanced at her again. "No."

"Looking for a cab? A bus maybe?"

"No."

Rita nodded resignedly. "Okay. You're going to stand here all night, right?"

He fished a slip of paper out of his shirt pocket. "Do you know where this is at?"

Rita looked at the paper. On it was written the address of some cheap apartments on West Sahara Boulevard. "Sure, I know where it's at." Thinking quickly, she said, "Listen, if you're not in any big hurry to get there, I have an apartment a couple of blocks from here. Maybe you and I could—"

"I would like to go to this place as soon as I can," he said, taking back the slip of paper. "Will you tell me how to get there?"

Wonderful, Rita thought. She had taken a chance of being shagged by Union Plaza security to play Travelers Aid. "Okay," she said, a little exasperated. "Go down to the corner there and take a bus that has 'Las Vegas Strip' on the front—"

"Tell me how to walk there, please," he interrupted.

"*Walk* there? In this heat? This is the *desert.* It's six or seven miles."

"I will walk. Tell me, please."

Rita shrugged and gave him directions. Main to Wyoming and Highland to Sahara, then turn right and look for the number.

"Wyoming?" he said, looking surprised. "There is a street here named Wyoming? Is there one named Montana?"

"Not that I know of."

"Oh." He seemed disappointed. "Thank you for your help," he said and started to walk away.

"Listen," Rita said quickly, "you could leave your suitcase

here. I mean, it *is* a long walk. You could leave your suitcase in a locker in the bus depot."

He paused and turned back, frowning. "A locker?"

"Yeah, sure. Come on, I'll show you."

She led him into the brightly lighted waiting room and over to a bank of coin-operated baggage lockers. "You'll need two quarters." He picked two quarters out of some change from his pocket and Rita showed him where to deposit them. She held the locker door open while he put his bag inside and locked it for him. "You can leave it there twenty-four hours, then you have to put two more quarters in. And don't lose this key or they'll make you fill out all kinds of papers to get your suitcase back. I have to go now. It was nice meeting you."

She went into the ladies' room and held the door open a crack to watch him. For a moment he studied the key she had given him, then buttoned it securely in his shirt pocket and left the depot. Rita followed him outside, waited until he was down the block, then went back inside to get his suitcase. Every evening she invested fifty cents in a locker just to get a key she could switch with a likely victim if one should come along. Tonight she figured she had blown the fifty cents again. But you never knew. This guy had acted awfully funny. Maybe he was on something; there might be drugs in the suitcase she could sell. Or use. She could stand a little speed; lately she had been dragging. She was sure she was anemic. Tomorrow she had a doctor's appointment for a checkup.

As casually as if it were hers, Rita got the suitcase out of the locker and started home with it.

The young man with the key in his shirt pocket was not bothered by the temperature as he walked. Las Vegas was high desert, the heat was very dry, and he was accustomed to both higher humidity and longer walks. The distance to the address on West Sahara Boulevard was only half as far as the girl at the bus depot had said it was and the young man was there in less than an hour. It was a large, tacky apartment complex with uncut grass and tight little patios crowded with bicycles, portable barbecues, and forgotten toys. A variety of noises came through walls too thin for privacy. The manager, who occupied a corner apartment, was a heavyset man who looked as if he had a bad taste in his mouth. Before the young man even spoke he said, "We require first and last months' rent in advance, plus fifty dollars on utilities. An extra hundred deposit if you got kids. You got kids?"

"I don't want an apartment," the young man told him. "My name is George Wolf. I am the brother of Amalie Wolf. I have come for her belongings."

"Oh." The manager's eyes flicked over George's frame, assessing. "There's a week's rent owed. Eight days, actually."

George Wolf nodded. "I will pay. How much?"

The manager picked up a pocket calculator from his desk and pressed a few keys. "Make it seventy dollars. I won't charge you for utilities."

George paid him and the manager took a cardboard box from a closet and handed it to him. Suddenly the manager seemed uncomfortable. "That's all there was left. The guy she was living with took most of the big stuff: the TV and stereo and stuff."

George didn't open the box. He wanted desperately to see the things his sister had left behind, to touch something that she had touched, but he would not do it in front of a stranger, particularly a white stranger. "Where did he go, the man my sister lived with?" he asked quietly.

The manager shrugged. "If I was to tell you and you done some harm to him, why, I could get in trouble."

"Is there a reason for me to do harm to the man?" George asked. His eyes never left the manager's face and he did not blink once.

"Depends on how you look at it," the manager said, a little nervously. "Your sister died of a drug overdose. The cops didn't hold the guy she was living with, so it stands to reason they don't blame him for it. But the way the cops think and the way her own brother thinks, there could be a lot of difference. Especially since—" He shrugged again, letting his words trail off.

"Especially since I am an Indian, is that what you mean?"

"I didn't say nothing like that."

George smiled a slight, cold smile. "I may not be white, but I know some of the white man's ways." He put several bills in front of the manager. "Give me the name and address of the man my sister lived with. I will tell no one I found out from you. That is my promise."

The manager pushed a scratchpad and ballpoint at him, and told him what to write down. "It's about a mile from here, straight down Sahara. But you won't find him at home now. He works nights as a stick man at a craps table. He probably won't be home until morning."

"I will wait," George said.

His words expressed no emotion at all. The manager was afraid of him nevertheless and was relieved when he left.

Rita was back on the street when George returned to the bus depot. She had put his suitcase in another locker and had the new key in her purse. The suitcase, which she had carefully searched in her apartment, had contained nothing of value: a few changes of clothes, a magazine-sized leather pouch—empty, with some kind of Indian-looking markings on it—a long strip of rawhide or something similar, and a return bus ticket to Lame Deer, Montana. No money, no drugs, not even any jewelry she could hock.

When she saw George walking back into the bus depot, she hurried across the street to intercept him. Her intent was to tell him that she had given him the wrong locker key by mistake, the key he had was to a locker she was using, and she would trade keys with him. That way, he had no beef against her—his suitcase, with all its contents, was intact. But as she trotted into the depot, she saw that George wasn't headed toward the coin lockers at all; he had gone to a nearby bench in the waiting room and sat down. He had a cardboard box on his knees and was going through its contents. From where she stood, Rita could see that the young man's stolid, dark face had turned soft with sadness.

Edging around the side of the waiting room, Rita worked her way behind him and unobtrusively moved to where she could look over his right shoulder. Watching, she saw him take one article at a time out of the cardboard box and examine it thoughtfully, almost lovingly. There was an obviously cheap gold-colored bracelet that he turned over and over in his hands;

a hairbrush from which he drew a long black hair that he
caressed gently and then put back; a polyester scarf that he held
briefly to his nose; a makeup compact with a little mirror that he
opened and stared at for a long time. It was while he was staring
at the mirror that Rita moved around the bench and sat down
next to him.

"Hi again," she said.

George looked at her and then back at the mirror. "I heard a
story when I was a boy that if you stare at a mirror long enough,
you can see the last image that the mirror saw." The sorrow in
his face took on a melancholy smile. "It is not true."

"Whose image are you looking for?"

"My sister's. She is dead. I had not seen her in a long time." He
put the compact back and closed the box. "It doesn't seem right
that a piece of glass saw my sister before she died and I did not."

"Life is not always right," Rita said knowingly. She had the
other locker key in her closed hand—her palm was becoming
moist around it. "Are you going to take a bus back where you
came from now?"

George shook his head, his eyes narrowing a fraction. "No.
There is something I must do first. In the morning."

"Well," she said, seizing the opportunity, "you'll want your
suitcase so you can find a place to stay." Before he could protest,
Rita had unbuttoned the flap of his shirt pocket and fished out
the locker key she had seen him put there. "You wait here with
your sister's things and I'll get it for you."

She clicked across the waiting-room floor in her spike heels,
switching the keys as she went, found the right locker, and
removed his bag.

"Here you go," she said when she got back to the bench with
it.

"You have been very kind to help me," George said. "You are a
good person."

"Yeah, well," Rita said, feeling herself blush. She forced an
embarrassed smile. "Listen, I've got to run. You take care, hear?"

"Before you go, can you tell me which way it is to the nearest
woods?"

"The nearest what?"

"Woods. Forest. I will sleep among the trees tonight."

"I already told you once, this is the *desert,*" Rita replied. "There aren't no woods." She sighed dramatically. "There's a cheap hotel across the street, the Sal Sagev—that's Las Vegas spelled backwards. You better get a room there."

"I have no money for a room," George said. "I had to pay rent that my sister owed. And I had to give a man money to tell me where someone was."

"Who?"

"Someone I must see tomorrow."

"Well, lookit," Rita said, "there just aren't no woods and you can't sleep in the desert, it's full of scorpions." She began tapping one foot like an impatient mother. "If you try to sleep here in the bus depot, the cops'll bust you for vag."

"What's that?"

"Being broke. Don't you know it's a crime not having no money? Where do you come from anyway?"

George shrugged. "From a place where it's not a crime to have no money."

"Well, you'd better go back there as soon as you can," Rita advised cynically.

"I will. Tomorrow."

Rita tilted her head, studying him. "You have to stay until tomorrow?"

"Yes."

Looking up at the big waiting-room clock, Rita thought, what the hell, the night was shot anyway. She was too bushed to even think about another trick. Tomorrow, she was sure, she was going to find out she was anemic.

"Come on," she said, smoothing her skirt over her thin hips, "you can crash on my couch for the night. But you'll have to split early—I have a doctor's appointment at nine."

Chump, she thought as she led him out to the street. Getting soft in your old age. By the time you're seventeen, you'll be a real patsy.

Later that evening, Rita came into her postage-stamp living room wearing a ratty terrycloth robe and trying to comb wet tangles out of her hair. "You can use the shower now if you want," she told George, who was sitting on her tired velour sofa, once again going through the box of his dead sister's belongings.

"Thank you," he said. "I was hoping to find something of my sister's that I could give you for being so kind to me. But I am afraid there is nothing of value."

Peering into the box, Rita said, "That little bracelet looks like it might be worth something."

George shook his head. "If it was worth anything," he said darkly, "the man she lived with would have taken it." Then he added, "But if you would like it—"

"No, you better keep it, being your sister's and all," Rita said. Taking something that a dead person had worn gave her the creeps anyway.

She sat on the arm of the sofa, tugging at her hair with a large comb. "How'd your sister end up in Vegas?" she asked curiously.

"Because of something that happened more than a hundred years ago," George said. "Do you know the story of General Custer and the Little Bighorn?"

"The Custer massacre? When I was a little girl back in Milwaukee, my stepfather used to take me with him to this neighborhood tavern where they had a big picture of it behind the bar. What's that got to do with your sister?"

"There were many tribes that fought Custer at the Little Bighorn, and when it was over those tribes had to run away because the army sent thousands of soldiers to hunt them down and kill them. Sitting Bull, the great Sioux medicine man, took his people north into Canada where the white soldiers couldn't follow. Some of the Shahiyena tribe, which the whites called the Cheyenne, went with the Sioux. Crazy Dog took a band to Canada—so did Rock Forehead, Little Robe, Wolf Tooth, and others. Wolf Tooth was my great-grandfather. My full name is George Wolf Tooth."

Hell, Rita thought, he's not even a Mexican, he's an *Indian.* And I brought him home for the night. Your porch light's getting dim, kid.

"Many Shahiyena were not able to escape to Canada, to the north, and had to flee south," George continued. "They went down into what is now Wyoming and Colorado but were not part of the United States at the time. Some went over into

Nebraska, which *was* a state. Because the Shahiyena spread out
in so many directions, the tribe never got back together again as
one people. Even today we are known by the part of the
country in which we live. I am a Northern Cheyenne—we live
mostly in Montana. But those of us who live in the North have
uncles and cousins who are Southern Cheyennes or Western
Cheyennes."

He gazed off at nothing for a long moment, his clean features
dissolving into despair. He was really kind of nice-looking, Rita
thought. Not a hunk like Greg had been, but still not bad.

"My sister grew weary of our life in the North," George said at
last. "It is a very simple life and often young people my own age
find it dull and tiresome, so they go away. Amalie went to live
with our cousins in Ogallala, Nebraska. She got a job as a
waitress in a cafe on the big interstate highway that comes out
here to Las Vegas and goes on to California. One day a man came
through driving a big shiny car—"

"You don't have to say another word," Rita interrupted, "I
been there. I can even describe the guy for you. Nice tan,
sunglasses, gold chain around his neck, shirt unbuttoned halfway down. And he prob'ly told her he had 'connections' in Las
Vegas."

George shrugged. "I don't know what he told her. I only
know that she went with him. And now she is dead from using
drugs." He lowered his head. "We didn't even find out about her
until after the time had passed for claiming her body. She had
already been cremated. They didn't even keep the ashes for her
people."

Rita had stopped combing her hair.

"Our way of burial would have been different," George said.
"First she would have been wrapped in a cloak of white rabbit
fur and placed on a raised travois on the bank of the Rosebud
River. The travois would have been made of cedar and ash and
pine, all freshly cut so that their fragrances would surround her.
We would have prayed around the travois for a day and a night.
Then she would have been put on a bed of wildflowers—yellow
primroses, white wild lilies, red coralroot, and blue lobelias—in
a canoe made of white birch. Her body would have floated
down the Rosebud to our sacred burial ground. There the

women would have placed her in the ground and covered her resting place with the flowers from the canoe. When those flowers died, their seeds would have taken root and new blossoms would grow every spring."

Rita was enraptured. "That's beautiful," she said. "I never heard anything so beautiful before. I'm sorry you didn't get here before they cremated her." Then something occurred to her. "This thing you have to do in the morning—you're going to see the guy who brought your sister out here, aren't you?"

"Yes."

"Hey," she cautioned, "I hope you're not planning to do anything dumb. I mean, they've got a state prison up in Carson City that's like *ancient.* I know a guy that did time up there. The cells are like *dungeons,* you know what I'm saying? You don't want to end up in a joint like that."

George shook his head. "No."

"Okay. So you're not going to do anything dumb, right?"

He shook his head again. "No, nothing dumb."

"Smartest thing you can do," she lectured, "is forget that guy and get on a bus out of here in the morning. This town is a scab, believe me, and it never heals." She bobbed her chin toward the tiny bedroom and bath. "Go on now and take your shower like a good kid."

Listen to me, will you, she thought as George left the room. The guy's at least four or five years older than me and I'm playing mommy to him. I ought to be seeing a shrink tomorrow instead of an M.D.

While George was in the shower, Rita went to her stash and got a couple of joints to smoke after she had closed her bedroom door.

Closed it and *locked* it.

Just in case.

When Rita dragged out of the bedroom the next morning, feeling as if she had not rested at all, George was at the sink in the tiny kitchenette, slowly gliding the blade of a bone-handled pocketknife across the smooth surface of a four-inch-square whetstone. Every few strokes he would hold the blade under the faucet, which was running a thin stream of water. Rita mustered enough energy to become angry.

"Wonderful," she snapped. "You promised last night you weren't going to do anything dumb."

George looked at her, frowning. "I promised nothing."

"You're going over there to murder that man, aren't you?"

"No, I am not." George rinsed the blade, dried it on his shirttail, and closed the knife. "I am only going to take his scalplock."

Rita winced. "His what?"

"Scalplock." Turning off the faucet, George wrapped the whetstone in a square of soft leather and put it in his pocket. "It is a piece of his scalp. Four inches wide, from the top of his forehead in front to the top of his neck in back. That is all."

"That's *all?* You don't call that murder?" she asked incredulously.

"No. He will not die. It will be no worse than if he suffered a bad burn."

Rita grimaced, confused. "I thought when people got scalped it killed them."

The young Indian smiled tolerantly. "Only in the white man's movies. Usually a soldier, or a warrior—the white man scalped, too—was dead before his hair was taken, killed by a bullet or a saber, an arrow or a warclub. Scalps were taken when the fighting was over. There have been many instances when a man was thought to be dead and his scalp was taken—his whole scalp, not just the scalplock—and even after he was fully scalped he recovered to tell about it. My own great-grandmother, Wolf Tooth's middle wife, Fox Eye, was scalped by a soldier and survived. It is told that her hair grew back more beautiful than ever."

"I don't believe this conversation." Rita walked wearily into the living room and sat down. George, seeing he had upset her, followed and knelt on the floor in front of her.

"Let me try to explain something to you. In our tribe, we have an elder, a very old man, who is called the Keeper of the Sacred Arrows. In his home he has a section of buffalo hide that contains six arrows that have been used in battle against the

Shahiyena's six traditional enemies: the Crow, the Ute, the Shoshone, the Pawnee, the Blackfeet, and the white man. These arrows remain sacred, and our people maintain their tribal honor only as long as none of our traditional enemies commits an offense against us. If one of them does commit an offense, if one of them steals from us, cheats us, lures away one of our women—"

"Wait," Rita interrupted. "That's why you're going to cut off this man's hair? Because he lured your sister to Las Vegas? Don't you think *she* was partly to blame? I mean, she could've said no."

"Yes, the council of elders took that into consideration. Amalie went with the white man of her own free will. That is why I've been sent for his scalplock instead of his life. It was felt that this man took advantage of my sister's free will. He was much wiser and more worldly than she and influenced her beyond a point which was acceptable. Had it not been for him, she wouldn't have become involved with the drugs that killed her." George studied Rita closely for a moment. "Do you understand?"

"No, I don't. But what difference does it make?"

"It makes a lot of difference." He took her hands in his. "You have been kind to me; it's important to me that you do not feel that I have lied to you or broken a promise. You are my friend— I want you to understand."

"The only thing I understand is that you're about to get yourself into something very heavy." She sniffed as if trying to hold back tears. "I just hate to see you do it, that's all."

George squeezed her hands. "There will be no trouble," he assured her. "It will be over very quickly and I will be gone like the morning mist when the sun rises. You are good to worry about me." Suddenly he frowned. "Rita, why are you all alone? You are so young to be alone."

She shrugged and sniffed again. "I had a boyfriend until last week. He took off."

"Where are your people?"

"Milwaukee. That's in Wisconsin." She became embarrassed. "I don't keep in touch no more. The stepfather I told you used to take me to the neighborhood tavern with him? Well, he used to take me other places, too. Like into the bedroom when my old lady was at work. I didn't know how to tell her. So I just left."

"Will your boyfriend come back?" George asked with obvious concern.

Rita forced herself to brighten up. "Oh, sure, he'll be back any day now. Probably bring me a nice present." What the hell, she thought, why let the guy worry about her when he had problems of his own. As for Greg, he was gone for good. Guys like Greg never came back. They just drained all a person had, then went on to the next one.

"I am happy you will not be alone for long." George stood up. "I must go now."

She managed a smile. "Yeah—me, too. I can't be late for the doctor. Listen, you take care."

"I will. You, too." At the door, with his suitcase and the cardboard box, George paused. "Thank you for everything," he said.

He went to the bus station and put the suitcase and box in a locker, then he walked back through the increasing morning heat to Sahara Boulevard and started following the numbers on the apartment buildings, carrying in one hand the slip of paper on which he'd written the name—Nick Gordon—and address of the man his sister had been living with. From time to time, waiting to cross a street, George would look at the name, wondering what Nick Gordon would be like. How big would he be, how strong? Would he fight hard or give up easily? In the pocket with his knife, George carried a slip-tie of the kind used to capture wild ponies. The previous night, while Rita slept, he had fashioned it out of the length of rawhide from his suitcase. It resembled a lariat made of leather. With a quick jerk, the intricate slipknot could hold a man's wrist or foot as tautly as a steel chain. George had been using slip-ties since he was eight—he was very good with them.

When he found the right address, he looked on a bank of mailboxes and located Nick Gordon's apartment number: 308. All apartment doors were outside, on walkways that ringed the building on each floor. It was a large building and George saw a

few people coming and going, but no one paid any attention to
him. Unobtrusively, he made his way up two flights of cement
steps and along the walkway to 308. At the door, he took the
slip-tie from his pocket and enlarged the restraining loop to
about twice fist-size. Holding it at his side, he knocked.

The door was opened by a man about thirty-five who had a
nice suntan and thick black hair with long sideburns. Except for
his eyes, he was handsome. His eyes were somehow offensive—
they flicked over George, top to bottom.

"Mr. Nick Gordon?" George asked.

"Yeah, what do you want?"

"I was told to give you this." George held out the rawhide
slip-tie.

Nick Gordon instinctively reached for it, and when his right
hand was at the proper angle George expertly flipped the loop
around his wrist and jerked it tight. "Hey, what the hell?"

That was all the protest Gordon could voice before George
spun him around, twisting his arm behind him, and pushed him
back inside the apartment. Elbowing the door shut after them,
he put a foot in front of Gordon and tripped him to the floor.
Grabbing the other man's left foot, he bent it up behind him and
looped the thong once around the ankle. Drawing it tight, he
had him face down with his right hand held to his left foot.

"What the hell are you doing, man!" Gordon said, half in
anger, half in fear. "You want money, it's on the dresser!"

"I'm not a thief," George said with quiet indignation. Drawing
the thong upward, he threw a loop around Gordon's neck, and
with one knee in the middle of the helpless man's back he held
it firmly in place across his throat, cutting off his voice. The next
instant, he had his pocketknife out and with his teeth opened its
honed blade. Closing his eyes, he silently intoned the Shahiyena
scalping prayer. When his lips stopped moving, he held the
blade at the top of Nick Gordon's head, entwined the fingers
holding the thong in Gordon's thick black hair, and pulled it to
taunten the scalp for slicing.

But it did not tauten. The hair, all of it, came off in George's
hand—a great round mass of it—leaving the top of the man's
head bald and shiny.

George got to his feet, staring at the thing in his hand. On the floor, the loop slipped from around Gordon's neck and he twisted and struggled until his foot was loose. "You crazy son of a bitch!" he said.

George looked at him, then back at the bowl of hair in his hand. He didn't understand. This man was wearing a scalp!

"Try to choke me, will you?" Gordon sputtered. "I'll kill you!" Jerking open an end-table drawer, he snatched out a small revolver and pushed the cylinder free. From a box of cartridges, he fumbled to load it. At the sight of the gun, George's eyes widened in fear. Still holding the patch of hair, he wrenched open the apartment door and fled.

In his examining room, the doctor, whose name was Franken, asked, "How old are you really, Rita?"

"Twenty-one—like the form says," Rita replied with practiced annoyance. She chastised herself for not wearing more makeup. She had tried to dress like some of the young women she saw pushing shopping carts with toddlers in the child seat in the supermarket. They always seemed to be wearing slacks, blouses, sandals, and shoulder-strap bags. They were all scrubbed-looking—the effect Rita had wanted today—but apparently she had not achieved it.

"Do you have any identification that proves your age?" the doctor wanted to know.

"You sound like a bartender," Rita grumbled.

The doctor, a short man with a beard, said, "Rita, we've got a problem, you and I. If you're under eighteen, and I suspect you are, I'd like to get in touch with your parents."

"Forget it," she told him firmly. She studied the look of concern on the doctor's face. "Is there something wrong with me?"

"You have gonorrhea, Rita."

She looked relieved. "Is *that* all? Oh, look, I've had it twice before. It's no big deal. Just start me on penicillin shots."

"I'm afraid it *is* a big deal this time, Rita," he said gravely. "Do you know what AIDS is?"

The color drained from her face. "Oh, no."

"You can understand why it's imperative that your family be notified," Dr. Franken said. "We also have to contact your school so that any boys you've been intimate with can be referred to their own doctors."

"I don't go to—school," Rita said, her mouth suddenly dry. Her confidence was gone now, her eyes wide with fright. "I'm a hooker, see? A runaway and a hooker."

The doctor's expression reflected a fleeting moment of incredulity, but he quickly composed himself. "I see. Well, it's important that we contact as many of your clients as possible, Rita."

She shook her head. "I work the street, Doc. My tricks don't leave calling cards. But I can tell you where I probably got the AIDS." She gave the doctor Greg's full name. "He's bi. We lived together for about six months. He took off for San Francisco last week with some guy who was down for the weekend." She swallowed tightly and asked, "What's going to happen to me?"

"There's a Public Health Service hospital in Phoenix I could send you to," the doctor said. "It wouldn't cost you anything and they have the personnel and facilities to work up a complete prognosis on your condition."

"AIDS kills people, doesn't it?" she asked bluntly. Tears were trying to escape her eyes but she wouldn't let them.

"AIDS itself doesn't kill people," Dr. Franken explained. "AIDS is a condition known as Acquired Immunodeficiency Syndrome. It's a condition that helps other conditions kill people. The gonorrhea you have that was so simply cured for you twice before, for instance, could develop this time into meningitis that could affect your spinal column and brain, or endocarditis that could affect the membranes of your heart."

"Okay, okay," Rita interrupted. "I don't want to hear no more. How do I get into that hospital you mentioned?"

"I'll telephone and arrange admittance. Do you have bus fare to Phoenix?"

"Sure I do. I'm not a charity case, you know. I got my own checking account."

"Fine," Dr. Franken said. He circled Greg's name on his pad. "The San Francisco health authorities will have to look for your boyfriend."

"*Ex*-boyfriend."

"All right, ex-boyfriend. Now, before you go there's one thing

I'd like you to do for me. Let me call the county health department to send a representative over to get you. They'll want to take your photograph and show it around areas where you worked to try and find some of the men you've been with."

Rita shrugged. "Why not? I'm not going to be around no more anyhow."

"Good." Dr. Franken rose. "You wait here in the examining room while I make arrangements."

After he left and Rita was alone in the quiet stillness of the cubicle, she lay back down on the examining table, closed her eyes, and sighed as wearily as if she were a tired old woman. Finally she let the tears come.

It was just after noon when Rita got back to her apartment and found George sitting outside her door. "Oh, no," she said. "Look, man, I've got a big problem right now, okay?" Seeing the hairy object in his hand, she looked away. "Is that what I think it is?"

"He was wearing a scalp," George told her incredulously. "It came off in my hand."

Rita looked back at it. "That's a *toupee,* you dummy. Oh, I don't need this." She put the key in the lock and opened the door.

"What is a two-pay?" George asked. "Not a scalp?"

"No." Snatching it from him impatiently, she turned it inside-out and showed him the sewn lining. "It's for guys that lose their hair."

"From scalping?"

"No—for guys whose hair falls out!" Thrusting it back at him, she said, "Look, I'm sorry but you gotta go. I'm trying to deal with something really heavy right now."

"I'll go," George said. "I'm sorry, I didn't mean to upset you again." From his shirt pocket he took the scrap of paper and looked at the address again. "I must go see this man again."

"What? Are you crazy?" She glared at him. "He's probably got the cops over there waiting for you."

George shook his head. "He's not the kind who calls the police. He has his own gun."

"Wonderful. Look, you've *got* his hair—that's what you came for, isn't it?"

George glanced scornfully at the toupee. "It isn't really his
hair. I must take his scalplock—"

"But he doesn't *have* one! Gimme a break here!"

"He has hair in back and on the sides, and in front of his ears,"
George said stubbornly.

Rita shook her head in amazement. "You're crazy, you know
that? Look, read my lips: *You—are—crazy.*"

"I do what is necessary," George informed her. He started to
turn away.

"Wait a minute," she said quickly. "Look, it's your business,
okay? Who am I to stop you. But I want you to do me a favor
first. You owe me a favor, am I right?" He nodded. "Okay. I have
to go out of town, see, on personal business. Wait for me to pack
and carry my suitcase to the bus depot for me, will you? It's
right on your way. I mean, it's so hot out there I don't think I can
make it by myself. Will you help me?"

"Of course," said George.

"Super. Go in and sit down while I run get my suitcase from
the landlady. I let her borrow it last week to visit her brother in
Reno."

George sat and waited, folding and unfolding the scrap of
paper with Nick Gordon's address on it. Rita was gone nearly
twenty minutes. When she returned, she had two uniformed
policemen with her.

"That's him," she said, pointing at George. "He tried to rape
me."

George stood up, bewildered, as the officers swiftly descended on him, one of them pinioning his arms behind him
and handcuffing his wrists, the other patting him down in a body
search and relieving him of his pocketknife. George stared at
Rita in wide-eyed disbelief, but she refused to look at him.
Presently one of the policemen took George down to sit in the
caged back seat of the radio car while the other officer remained with Rita to do the paperwork. It took ten minutes to fill
out the arrest form and complaint, both of which Rita signed.
The officer, handing her a copy, said, "Be at the address on the
form for arraignment court at nine in the morning."

"Right."

She watched out the window as they drove George away.

When the car was out of sight, she went to her stash and rolled a joint. Smoking it, she dragged out an old Samsonite overnighter and started packing. It occurred to her that the assortment of things she was carelessly tossing into the bag weren't a whole lot different from the things in the cardboard box that had belonged to George's sister. Too bad we didn't know each other, she thought. Maybe I could have helped her, given her a few tips. As soon as the thought manifested, she grunted softly. Listen to me. The blind leading the blind.

She finished the joint and her packing, and started to leave. On the way out, she noticed a scrap of paper on the floor. It was the address George had had with him. He must have dropped it when the police grabbed him. Rita picked it up and studied it. She pursed her lips and tapped the toe of one sandal. Then she shrugged and thought, Why not? Why the hell not?

Sixty days later, George walked out of county jail and stood indecisively for a moment on the hot Las Vegas sidewalk. In one hand he had his suitcase, in the other the box containing his sister's belongings. The police, finding the key when George was booked, had gone to the bus depot and opened the locker. Finding nothing incriminating, they had put the suitcase and box in the jail property room to be held for his release. He had been given back the rest of his things, even his pocketknife, which was under the legal blade length. In a shirt pocket, he had his return bus ticket to Lame Deer, Montana. He no longer had the piece of paper with Nick Gordon's address on it, but that didn't bother him. He was sure he could find the place again.

As he started down the street toward the bus station to check his suitcase and the box in a locker again, he heard a voice behind him call, "Hey, wait a sec!"

Turning, he saw Rita hurrying toward him. His first reaction was anger. Then, as she got closer, a sudden pity came over him. She looked terrible: pale, very thin, her eyes hollow. Nevertheless, when she reached him he said stiffly, "You should not have done what you did. I almost went to prison."

"You didn't either," she retorted. "There was no complaining witness 'cause I didn't show up. I never intended to."

"Well," he said sullenly, "they put me in jail for two months for vagrancy."

"They didn't either. They gave you thirty days for vag. The other thirty you got for trying to make a break from the courtroom. Hot head."

He looked away. "You shouldn't have done it anyhow," he muttered.

"Come on"—she pulled on his arm—"let's get out of the sun."

They walked to the bus depot, got two glasses of iced tea in the self-service coffee shop, and sat at a tiny table.

"Guess where I've been," she said. George shrugged. "In the hospital," she told him. "Down in Phoenix, Arizona. I've been part of some experiments. Very important *medical* experiments.—I've got Kaposi's sarcoma," she added almost aloofly.

"What's that?"

"Well, let's just say it's not the twenty-four-hour flu. It's here to stay." She found it too embarrassing to describe the ugly purple lesions growing on the surface of her thighs, stomach, and lower back. "Anyway," she went on excitedly, "I was the very first one picked to test a new drug called Ribavirin, which was previously used only on some kind of fever down in Africa. It didn't work, but it was kind of an honor to be picked first."

George nodded gravely. "It is always an honor to be picked first for something important."

She bit her lower lip. "You're probably wondering why I'm here, right?"

George shook his head. "You're still my friend. I know why you did what you did. But it does not change what *I* must do."

"But it does," Rita told him anxiously. "That's what I ran away from the hospital for and came here to tell you. That guy Nick Gordon is down there in the same hospital I was in, only he's over in the men's building. He checked in about five weeks ago. He's almost dead. Seems he had sex with someone who had the same thing I've got."

She remembered for a fleeting moment how easy it had been. He'd opened the door and she had said, "Hi, there. Listen, could I trouble you to use your phone? My girlfriend and I want to rent an apartment here and she was supposed to meet me with the deposit, you know, but she hasn't showed. I want to call and

see if she's left yet." She had pulled the top of her blouse out and
fanned herself. "It's so hot! I can't wait to get my hands on a nice
cold beer." He had invited her in and from there on it had been
a piece of cake.

"You say he's dying? How do you know?" George asked
suspiciously.

"He was a cocaine user," Rita explained. "Over the years, the
lining of his nose weakened from snorting the stuff. After he
picked up what I've got, he developed something called *Can-
dida albicans,* which is like a fungus, really gross, that grows in
the nose, mouth, and throat. There's no way to stop it. The man
is practically *finito."* She saw mistrust in George's eyes. "Don't
you believe me?" she asked indignantly.

"I wonder if you are only trying again to keep me out of
trouble."

Rita reached across the table and took his hand. "I'm not," she
said, the simple phrase coming out with a quaver. "I'm dying,
too," she told him. "I wouldn't lie to you, not now. The man
can't speak, can't swallow, can't breathe through his nose or
throat. He's got a dozen tubes in him. If you want to, you can go
to Phoenix and see for yourself, but he'll probably be dead
before you get there. He might be dead already."

George's direct, penetrating black eyes studied her across the
table for several long moments, his intense concentration mut-
ing for him the sounds of the coffee shop around them. When
he finally spoke, he said, "I believe you, Rita."

Relief showed in her hollow eyes, her drawn expression.
Sniffing, she took back her hand and dabbed at her eyes with a
paper napkin. "Look at me, will you?" she said. "Blubbering like
some dumb kid. No shame at all."

"Where will you go now?" George asked. "Back to the
hospital?"

"Not on your life," she announced. "Me and that place are
quits. I'm in my final stage, so they won't use me for no more
experiments. All's I'd do is live in a separate ward until—well,
you know."

"What will you do?" he asked with concern. "Who will look
after you?"

"I can look after myself," she assured him. "I'm not no charity

case. I got my own checking account. I'll get a room some-
wheres. No problem."

Now it was he who took her hand. "Would you like to come
back home with me?"

She had thought to play coy if he asked her, but it was too
important. She seized on the offer as if it were salvation. "Could
I?" she asked, like a desperate child pleading. "Could I, please?"

"Yes. I will take you. You will be my sister for the time you
have left."

"And when it's all over?" she asked. "Will I have the cloak of
white rabbit fur and the bed of wildflowers and float down the
river in a canoe made of white birch?"

"Yes," he said solemnly, "you will have that." He rose and
picked up his suitcase and the box. "Come, sister," he said.

NELL LAMBURN

TOM'S THATCH

*Nell Lamburn is a new name to most American readers,
though she has been widely published in British magazines. With this especially well-written story she stakes
her claim to an area once the exclusive preserve of male
writers like Stanley Ellin, John Collier, and Roald Dahl.
"Tom's Thatch" finished third in the voting for the EQMM
Readers Award.*

Mrs. Spreadbury was a very particular woman. She was particular about her person, her cottage, and her husband. But most of
all, she was particular about her garden.

Mr. Spreadbury used a stronger word. "My wife is ob-sessed,"
he would announce to anyone who would listen, dividing the
word in order to squeeze every particle of meaning from it.
"Quite ob-sessed. Never leaves it alone. Out there, tinkering
about, whatever the weather. It's a brave weed that shows its
face in Alice's garden."

They rarely did. Out had gone the creeping buttercup, the
couch grass, and the ground elder. Out, too, the bindweed and
the convolvulus, plucked, poisoned, and burned.

"Heretics. She's at it, burning heretics," Mr. Spreadbury would
murmur as the gray-blue smoke rose straight and true from
behind the wattle fencing at the bottom of the garden. And if he
dared venture down there, he'd see her prodding and poking
the smoldering mound, the light of fanaticism concentrated on
her round and rosy face.

It was a very pretty garden, just what a cottage garden should
be. Lupines, delphiniums, heavy-headed roses. Hollyhocks, can-
terbury bells, cornflowers and pansies, they grew and blos-
somed in succession, obeying like some floral orchestra the
harmonizing of her green fingers. There was always the music of
color in Alice's garden, even in winter.

Tourists, quartering the scent to Stonehenge and Salisbury

173

Cathedral, paused in the village of Chilton Magna to photograph
and admire, and in Mrs. Spreadbury's desk there was an album
of prints sent from all over the world. There was also a postcard,
available, albeit in black-and-white, at the Chilton Magna Post
Office and General Stores. In it, Mrs. Spreadbury stood smiling
and apple-cheeked at the cottage gate, the roses about the
porch yearning toward the deep snug-cap of thatch. You
couldn't quite see her eyes, though, eyes like little chips of blue-
gray Wiltshire flint. That would have quite spoilt the image.

Mr. Spreadbury was not in the photographs. Sometimes, in
fact, he wondered if he were anywhere at all. Sometimes he
thought that all he was was a pair of Wellington boots at the
back door, two hands at the driving wheel, a porter of shopping
baskets. Sometimes he felt so superfluous, so insubstantial, that
he was surprised his wife didn't bustle right through him.

It hadn't always been like this. At the Reliable Insurance
Company, before he retired, he had been a man of authority,
commanding a personal office, a secretary, and luncheon vouch-
ers. Then, April Cottage had seemed an extension of the orderli-
ness, routine, and security that prevailed at work. He'd prided
himself on teamwork, and he and Alice made a fine, disciplined
team. It was only on his retirement that he discovered that his
place in that team had never really existed. He was required
neither in the garden nor the house—yet so necessary was he to
the image of Mrs. Spreadbury's life that she would rarely allow
him from her vicinity. He decorated her existence like her
seventeenth-century bible box and her rosewood tea caddy,
whose original uses were long passed away.

He took to going for walks, something he'd never cared for
very much, and spending more money than he could afford at
The Green Man. A whiskey or three dulled the burgeoning
realization that this was to be the order of his life, this living
nonexistence. He sat on the black-oak settle, smoking his only
pipe of the day, and a sort of bewilderment would encompass
him, a vague resentment at the unfairness of it all. Had the past
sixty-odd years really been moving toward this nothingness? It
seemed to Mr. Spreadbury, pondering in the snug of The Green
Man, that God had played him a terrible trick.

They had no friends, because to entertain made clutter and

untidiness, and Mrs. Spreadbury said they had no time to visit.
He would have liked a dog. His father had had a dog. He'd
always planned to have a dog one day. He'd have enjoyed
walking then. A spaniel perhaps, all enthusiastic ears. Or a
labrador, honey-colored, melting eyes. Even a mongrel, quivering intelligence. But there were no dogs, no animals at all.

There were no children, either. He would have liked those,
too, but Alice had never been very enthusiastic. In fact, in little
scenes that he preferred to forget, she had demonstrated both
vocally and physically just how unenthusiastic she had been. In
the face of such antagonism, his desire to procreate had splut-
tered and faded, becoming an intermittent ache that occurred
less and less frequently.

There should be grandchildren now. But instead there was a
full stop after the sentence of his life. No subparagraphs, no
postscripts. Now and then, when the bonds fretted too sharply
and the whiskey lubricated his dreams, he entertained crazy
ideas of escaping to some fruitful girl who would surround him
with little, loving replicas, who would let him potter in the
garden and smoke his pipe in bed and play his records. There
was, after all, for him, still time.

But the ideas passed like summer storms, like the occasional
flutterings of a bird against its confining bars. Ashamed, he knew
that if the cage door were opened he was too conditioned to
captivity to escape.

So the dissatisfaction and frustration of his life would be
stilled and he would assume again the mien of a contented man.

And so it might have continued if it hadn't been for the winter
of the great rains, as it came to be known. . . .

At first it fell gently and unassumingly, washing the spikes of
winter wheat to an emerald brilliance, muddying the shallow
chalk streams and teasing the tracks across the plain to toffee.
No one took it very seriously, and so, affronted, a viciousness
edged it, cutting the earth like little knives, filling the streams
and soaking the thin topsoil so that the natural reservoirs
beneath the chalk burst their veins and the springs gushed
furiously early. To the villagers of Chilton Magna and thereabouts, it seemed to be raining above and below them, they
seemed to be squeezed in a great wet sandwich of water.

At April Cottage, the thatch darkened and dripped, the bonfire rotted unburnt, and curious molds and fungi latticed stalks
and leaves and trunks.

Mrs. Spreadbury drew in her apple cheeks and buttoned her
little thin lips, darting about the garden in increasing anxiety
while tawny, slime-shiny slugs taunted her and mottle-shelled
snails trailed their glistening threads to tease her.

"Don't worry so, my dear," Mr. Spreadbury counseled ill-
advisedly. "Nature will right itself. It always does." Thus irritating his wife still further.

As if to refute his advice, the winds curled their tongues
about the rain and spewed it venomously upon the thatched
roofs of Chilton Magna and those other villages that trickled like
narrow streams themselves amongst the ancient valleys of the
Plain.

The bathroom eaves were the first to surrender, the leisured
dripping of the leak hardly noticeable amongst the normal
activity of pipes and cisterns. But the rich dark stain in the spare
bedroom was obvious enough and within twenty-four hours the
breach was complete, the saturated thatch had yielded.

With difficulty, Mr. Spreadbury eased his stubby body through
the trapdoor into the loft while Mrs. Spreadbury hovered,
incensed face uplifted, on the landing below, an armory of
buckets and bowls beside her. The chill dampness struck him
unpleasantly as he balanced on the network of rafters, the
inadequate beam of his torch stabbing the darkness with rings
of pale light. It was a long time since he'd been up here.

When they'd first bought the cottage, he'd had such plans for
this loft—he'd peopled it with sons and daughters—their own
playroom. He'd even designed it down to the last lightbulb. A
ball of resentment pushed at him. It was Alice's fault it was
empty. All Alice's fault. It was a pity he'd never converted it
anyway, because he could have used it himself, pulling up the
ladder like a drawbridge. He could have smoked up here, worn
his old gray cardigan, made those soldier models he'd been so
fond of, and listened to the old records Alice refused to have
played.

As he placed the bowls and buckets beneath the leaks, a
sudden surge of determination emboldened him. There was

absolutely nothing to stop him converting it now. He could do most of it himself, he'd enjoy that. For a moment, the clouds of his life parted—he saw a celestial vision of solitude and peace before reality obscured it. Alice's reality. She would never allow the cottage to be disrupted to such a degree. The struggle would be exhausting, every stage a wounding encounter that would bleed him dry of ambition and courage. The conversion would become his penance, she would never miss an opportunity to flagellate him with it. And as swiftly as the plan was born, it died. But, unaccustomedly, the bruise of resentment remained.

"Well? Is it all right now? Have you fixed it?" Mrs. Spreadbury pecked the questions at him as he eased himself slowly down the ladder.

"For the moment." He went into the bathroom to wash his hands. "We'll need the thatcher come spring, though. That north slope is bad, got very patchy. You don't see it from the outside. Some of it must be four foot thick, other bits you can almost see through." He began to sound important. This was something for him to decide, Alice hadn't seen the roof, she'd have to take his word for it. "I'll mention it to Tom Molyneaux, he'll be in The Green Man tonight, he always is on a Friday." He looked at himself in the mirror, jutting his chin a little as he dried his hands on the pink-flowered towel. "Have to book him early, you see."

"Tom Molyneaux? I'm not having that man near my house." Mrs. Spreadbury stood in the doorway, her back deliberately turned to him as if he were performing some intimate ablution. "He's filthy."

"He's an excellent thatcher, my dear. That's all that matters. He's the best thatcher hereabouts." He narrowed his eyes at himself, patting the thickened line of his chin. "Everyone will be after him."

"Then let them." Her voice began to shrill. "The council shouldn't let him keep that terrible hut he lives in, it's a disgrace to the village. They should make him go into a council house, the health people should make him. It's full of rats and—and disease."

"I think you exaggerate, my dear. You can't possibly know."

"You only have to look at the place—and goodness knows it's near enough for us to see." Mrs. Spreadbury darted past him, replacing the once-used hand towel with a fresh one. "Mrs. Ellison has seen rats there, ones as big as cats. They didn't run away, either—just sat and looked at her. Petrified her. You just find some other thatcher, not Tom Molyneaux."

And as far as Mrs. Spreadbury was concerned, the matter was closed.

But not, to his own surprise, for Mr. Spreadbury.

Tom Molyneaux was a long man, long and narrow like the hazel spars he worked with. Nose and chin, arms and hands, even his feet. But particularly his hands. Dark, calloused, stubby-nailed, knob-jointed, they splayed across his knees as he sat in the snug of The Green Man that Friday night.

His father had been a shepherd, his grandfather, too—and now his home was the wheeled hut they'd once summered in on the Plain, parked, unassailably, on his own plot of land across the field behind April Cottage. But his uncles had been thatchers and, reckoning the fashion for thatch being more stable than that of sheep, young Tom had apprenticed himself to his uncles instead, to become, as Mr. Spreadbury pronounced, the best thatcher thereabouts.

Mr. Spreadbury admired him greatly. Here was a man who was his own master, answerable only to himself, a free man, a dark and secret man. Often on his solitary walks, he would pause to wonder at his skills and, to his satisfaction, Tom Molyneaux would sometimes come down his ladder to share a noisome pipe with him and comment on this and that. There was little in Chilton Magna or thereabouts that escaped his narrow eyes.

Mrs. Spreadbury always knew. "You've been near that Tom Molyneaux again!" she'd accuse him, wrinkling her little nose accusingly. "I can smell him—go and wash, go and change!" Obediently, he would scrub his hands and face and hang his jacket on the line. Until the next time.

Now he got up from the oak settle and crossed the stone-flagged floor to the bar. (In the lounge bar there were vinyl flooring and draloned seats. Mrs. Spreadbury would much have preferred him in the lounge bar.) There was a ritual to be observed, a slow, measured ritual: through the weather, a fresh pint, the Chilton Magna football team, work, the weather again, and, finally, the roof of April Cottage.

Tom Molyneaux refilled his pipe before he answered, stabbing down the black tobacco with his long stained forefinger.

"Your missus won't like it." He drew the words out slowly in his soft, Wiltshire voice with each suck of smoke. "She don't like me."

"You're the best. I want the best." Mr. Spreadbury rolled his shoulders back importantly. "I think your uncle thatched it—must be over twenty years ago. But I never realized it had got so bad, not until all this rain."

"Patchy. Been watching it. Some of it four foot thick, I reckon. Some not. Needed ridging five years back. Surprised it's not gone before now."

Mr. Spreadbury didn't feel aggrieved that he hadn't warned him. Just pleased that not only had he been correct about the thickness of it, but that Tom'd been keeping an eye on it, as if the roof were singled out for Divine favor.

"Then you'll do it?"

"Cost you."

"The best always does." Mr. Spreadbury was on firmer ground, commercial ground now. "I wouldn't want anyone else."

Tom Molyneaux flared one narrow nostril, slitting his pale eyes against the pipe smoke.

"Reckon the missus won't like it."

Mr. Spreadbury began to feel affronted, as if his manhood had been called into question.

"There's not much she does like," he said excusingly. "But she'll come round to the idea. She doesn't like mess, that's all, doesn't like her surroundings untidy, particularly the garden."

"Thatchin's a mucky business. Reckon she'll agree?" Tom Molyneaux was looking at him sideways, slyly, and Mr. Spreadbury had the uncomfortable feeling of being mocked.

"She won't have a choice." He puffed out his cheeks. "I shall

tell her that you are going to do it—that is, if you will. It's got to
be done and I want the best. She'll see the sense in that. She
always wants things to look their best."

Tom Molyneaux scratched the back of his head, tipping his
flat stained cap forward on his straggling hair, and Mr. Spreadbury held his breath.

"I'll do it, then. Be the spring, mind you. But I'll come, I'll
come."

Fear and elation effervesced in Mr. Spreadbury's breast as he
bought a further round of drinks. A fourth whiskey would not
come amiss, not with what he had to face at home. Tom
Molyneaux was a man of his word. If he said the spring then the
spring it would be. A bond as binding as anything in law.
There'd be time enough for Alice to accept the idea.

Later, stepping gingerly along the dark and puddle-sodden
road, it seemed a ridiculous idea to court her rage so prema-
turely. As the whiskey bravery seeped out of his nerve ends, he
argued that it would be actively foolhardly to encourage her
anger at this stage. Weeks of recriminations stretched ahead,
exhausting and bowing him, perhaps even breaking him so that
he'd have to cancel Tom Molyneaux.

He shuddered. No one cancelled Tom Molyneaux. No one
crossed Tom Molyneaux, either. Mr. Spreadbury's feet stumbled
with his thoughts and he had to stand for a minute, breathing
deeply, while the whiskey waltzed about his head.

They said Mrs. Grantley Patterson hadn't paid him, despite
her acres, and all Chilton Magna knew what had happened to
her. Mr. Dowset, too, who'd shortchanged him on the straw—
no good had come to him, either. That young couple from
London who'd thought they were so clever—coincidence perhaps. Perhaps not. All he did know was that he wouldn't like
Tom Molyneaux's anger directed at him, not at all. Better to
surprise Mrs. Spreadbury—shock tactics, and while she was
adjusting and absorbing, the job would begin. A nice case of fait
accompli, as the French so neatly put it.

Mrs. Spreadbury left April Cottage only once a week, and that
was on Tuesday market day in Salisbury. At 8:30 sharp, Mr.
Spreadbury would bring the Ford to the front gate, arrange the

baskets and bags on the back seat, and hold open the door while his wife admired, for the statutory few minutes, the splendors of her garden.

And on this particular spring morning there was a great deal to admire. Patches of purple crocuses stippled the lawn. Clumps of daffodils and narcissus, like crusty yellow cream, lay thick on the brown earth of the beds. Pdyanthus buds dared to show their hues, bright eyes through their masks of green. The skeletons of the climbing roses latticed the whitened flint-and-brick walls and yellow starred forsythia bunched by the garden shed. It was an orderly and contented garden, a garden that knew exactly where it was going. You could almost say a well-adjusted and self-satisfied garden. No muddle or confusion here. And it was a measure of Mrs. Spreadbury's ability that so much had been salvaged from the savage rains of the winter.

"Come along, don't dilly-dally!" Every week, as if the delay were his fault, she said the same, plumping down on the front seat, a hen fluffing out her feathers, and every week Mr. Spreadbury felt the nerves at the back of his head tighten and quiver. Sometimes, he thought, he felt like a violin, each ensuing, predictable remark of Mrs. Spreadbury's stringing him tighter and tighter until one day he felt he would snap.

On market days he became porter and baggage carrier, walking two paces behind while his wife rooted out the bargain truffles, one of the band of husbands who, after a working life of independence, were trapped into this servitude. While he was still at the office, they'd go to the Saturday market and there he'd never felt so conspicuous. But on Tuesdays he was pinpointed, a marked man, slide-eyeing the others of his ilk.

They lunched, as always, at the same black-beamed restaurant—£2.80 set menu—and afterward Mr. Spreadbury enjoyed his hour and a half freedom while his wife pursued her personal shopping. Sometimes he walked down to Victoria Park and sat by the river. At others he strolled about The Close—he liked that when the tourists were there, they were a funny lot. Then there were the book shops and the library—the time went only too quickly. Sometimes, after a particularly trying morning, he would contemplate flight. For a few moments he would relish the thought of Mrs. Spreadbury's growing impatience, her anger and consternation, her distress and remorse, her ultimate prayers for forgiveness if only he'd come back. But it was never more than a dream, the impracticalities hedging him in, bomalike, his own character the most impenetrable thorn of all.

On that Tuesday afternoon, as always, the same desire goaded his mind, daring him, and as always he backed away, returning slowly to the car and servitude. He was, he thought in disgust, like those laboratory rats so conditioned to run a certain distance that when the partition was removed they still could not exceed that length.

But oh! on their return to April Cottage, how he wished that he had!

Nothing during their journey home intimated the catastrophe that awaited them. No gathering of clouds, no rumblings of divine thunder, no single magpie or solitary crow perched on the rooftop.

Tom Molyneaux had finished for the day, but the evidence of his presence was only too clear.

Mrs. Spreadbury, her hand on the white slatted gate, screamed sharply, once, and Mr. Spreadbury, bending into the boot, straightened too quickly, wrenching his back. But the pain was banished by what he saw. Rusted roof wire mottled the lawn, crumpling the crocuses. New straw was stacked in sheaves by the shed, carelessly crushing the forsythia. A ladder rested against the roof, and over the flowerbed was cast a mantle of old straw pulled from the roof, through which the daffodils, like drowning men, upthrust their desperate faces.

It was, in reality, no more than disorder. But for Mrs. Spreadbury, it was disaster.

Wordlessly, she darted through the gate, plucking the straw with little incoherent cries, trying to prop up the drooping heads, tugging the sheaves from the forsythia. But it did not, strangely, touch Mr. Spreadbury's heart. There was no love in her concern, and he waited, bracing himself for the inevitable accusation.

The attack lasted the entire evening. He did not defend himself, only murmuring at intervals.

"Tom Molyneaux is the best. You'd want the best, wouldn't you?"

It was the wisest course he could have taken. Sustained attack against nonaggression is difficult to maintain and by bedtime her fury had coagulated into solid antagonism.

"I'll not have him in the house, you just make that clear! He's not stepping inside my house—horrid, filthy man." She scrubbed viciously at the hot-milk saucepan. "He stays outside and I'll bill him for every plant he harms, you just tell him that."

Of course, Mr. Spreadbury didn't. He wouldn't have dared. And to his surprise, neither did she. Instead, she scuttled from window to window, staring, her little lips pursed and angry, her eyes persecuting. But if Tom Molyneaux so much as glanced toward her, she curled up her lip in a sneer and with a flounce of her shoulders was gone.

It occurred to Mr. Spreadbury then, with the sort of wondering realization reserved for the witness of miracles, that Mrs. Spreadbury was intimidated. Not physically, but mentally. He had never seen her so before and he wasn't quite sure that she was aware of it. She was like some small, venomous thing, fluttering at the window, darting out at night to glean the loose straw, inspect the flowers, trample the old wire into even squares which Mr. Spreadbury must stack behind the wattle fence.

Tom Molyneaux never said a thing, but he knew—he knew all right. Each morning he would look around the tidied garden from under his hooded lids and then, gathering his tools with a slow deliberateness, climb his ladder and begin to cast down the old brown straw so that it lapped the cottage like a muddied tide. Mr. Spreadbury had never seen him make so much mess at any of the other houses he had thatched, and the thought that perhaps he was being quite deliberate in his actions made Mr. Spreadbury horribly nervous. A confrontation between the two of them would inevitably mean that he would be trapped in the middle, and he perspired at the very thought. He would be destroyed. He didn't know how, but he would be, and deep inside him, all amongst the soft center of acquiescence and placation, there stirred a worm of survival. His monotonous and featureless life suddenly began to seem overwhelmingly attractive, and in his anxiety he abased himself before both of them, attempting to anticipate any confrontation like some plump, middle-aged go-between. Instead, it only increased Mrs. Spreadbury's impatience, venting on him her revulsion against Tom Molyneaux, snapping and snarling at him throughout the day so that he spent an increasing time in the garden, hovering in the thatcher's protective shadow.

He'd placed an old table and two chairs in the shed and he'd carry two mugs of tea down there several times a day.

"Tea!" he'd call in a jovial voice, and Tom Molyneaux would glance down from his high ladder and nod imperceptibly, following in his own time to the brown depths of the shed.

Mr. Spreadbury liked it there. The smell of compost and creosote and earth comforted him, backed like an animal into its lair. They didn't talk much, but, daringly, Mr. Spreadbury brought out his pipe, too, so that soon the familiar earth smells were soaked up by a heavy miasma of tobacco smoke that permeated the walls of the shed itself.

Mr. Spreadbury was very careful never to be in there alone. Sometimes he saw his wife venture from the kitchen, her little tip-tilted nose he'd once thought so charming sniffing the air, all the world like a venturing vole. She would dart a few steps toward them and then, casting about, seem to think better of it and retreat to the house again. When he took the mugs into the kitchen, she would scrub them out with soda and invent little irritating jobs for him to keep him from the garden.

But it could not loosen his pleasure in the thick crust of crisp golden thatch that was edging across the roof. He watched Tom Molyneaux's great grimed hands twisting the hazel spars, driving them through the new straw with his wooden mallet, evening the bundles with his legget—the heavy, square, handled board with its wooden studs that had belonged to his uncles. And watching as the days passed, he felt that he, too, was working there, his own hands stung from the sharp straw, his knees aching from pressing upon the ladder rungs, and he felt, in the evening, the satisfaction of a good day's work. He began to think of it as a joint creation, his and Tom's, and would talk of

"us" and "we" and "our." For the first time since he left the
Reliable Insurance Company, he felt he had a purpose, felt he
was achieving something, was a man again. He began to look
forward to each day, there seemed a point now to getting up,
and if Tom Molyneaux resented his plump, balding, self-ap-
pointed assistant, he never showed it.

But as Mr. Spreadbury found a curious contentment, so his
wife, in ratio, became less so. Each evening when he returned
indoors, she whittled away at him with the chisel of her
nagging, her criticizing, her objections, until he expected to see
little flakes of himself like stone chips scattered upon the floor.
And nearly all the pleasure of the day would be debased. Nearly,
but not all.

Until the dreadful morning came when Tom Molyneaux
found his legget gone.

It was such a fresh, silvery morning, as if the Plain had been
dipped in some clear spring-fed pool and then laid to dry in the
sun's strengthening warmth. Not a morning for disaster, and Mr.
Spreadbury felt cheated as he hurried from the kitchen at Tom
Molyneaux's cry.

" 'Twas here! I left 'n here!" He stared, perplexed, at the spot
where the legget had been as if it would materialize under his
gaze. His shears lay tucked beneath the ladder, with his mallet
and hooks and the fat roll of orange binder-twine. But the legget
was gone.

"Is it on the roof? Perhaps you left it on the roof." Mr.
Spreadbury backed quickly from the ladder foot, staring upward, his eyes yearning for the square, studded board. But it
was not there.

"Did you—perhaps you took it home?" Mr. Spreadbury
clasped his hands in mute supplication and then shook his head
violently at Tom Molyneaux's look of scorn. "No—no, of course
not, you wouldn't do that."

" 'Twas here." Tom Molyneaux pointed to the ground, insist-
ing. "Just as I alus leave 'n."

And then Mr. Spreadbury, striving against the disintegration
of his contented morning, said a very foolish thing:

"I'll ask my wife. Perhaps she's seen it!"

A slow dark rage suffused Tom Molyneaux's face. He swiveled his pale eyes to stare at Mr. Spreadbury.

"The woman—her took 'n!"

"Oh, no! No—no—no!" Mr. Spreadbury raised up and down on his toes in his gross anxiety. "Mrs. Spreadbury wouldn't do a thing like that—please, you must believe me."

But Tom Molyneaux stood, neck thrust forward, head weaving, his pale and angry eyes casting about the garden like some chase-thinned hound.

Above the wattle fence the very finest of smoke columns penciled the sky. With a grunt, he loped across the grass, Mr. Spreadbury pattering in distress behind him.

The bonfire was a blackened, dismal thing, but some tiny wayward draught must have sought out an ember, betraying the faint life in it.

Distractedly, Tom Molyneaux thrust at it with the old fork until, with a moan, he fell on his knees. For buried at the heart lay the charred remains of the legget.

He snatched it to him, cradling it in disbelief.

"Yourn missus, yourn missus done it!" he groaned. "Yourn missus burned me legget!"

But Mr. Spreadbury was staring past him, his mouth hanging open. "She's burned my pipe, my favorite pipe!" The words dribbled from his slack lips as he bent for the bare bones of the old briar. "Why would she do that? She knows I loved it!" And answered his own question.

"Her's wicked, wicked. A wicked woman." Tom Molyneaux rose, muttering, casting the now useless tool down, his gaze after it. "Her'll destroy us. Her's evil."

Mr. Spreadbury found he was trembling. Revenge. Alice had deliberately taken those two cherished articles and destroyed them. It was a terrible, terrible thing she had done. They were not pieces of wood, they were molded for work and pleasure, patinaed by the satisfaction they had given, to be rewarded with honor and acclaim. Not to be burned at the stake. For Tom Molyneaux, his tools were more than that—they were his livelihood, an extension even of himself, his skill.

The trembling mutated to a shudder. Tom Molyneaux was still and silent, but his lips were working about unheard words, his long hands clenching and unclenching by his sides. Mr. Spreadbury could not move, although he would very much have liked to. How often in his life he had read of "impending doom," marking it as a vague and blanketing phrase, favored by indolent authors. Now he knew absolutely and exactly what it meant. Nothing had changed outwardly about him: the gentle blue of the sky, the golden-patched roof, the glorious outpourings of the thrush in the walnut tree, the hoarse barking of the Merediths' old dog down the lane. Yet into it all, soaking slowly like a dark stain, was impending doom.

He was helpless. He could feel whatever strength of mind he'd ever had drain from him, sucked out by the terrible will of the man beside him. He became a shell, a gourd, a puppet. Alice's action had delivered him into Tom Molyneaux's huge, angled hands, because to defend her would be to condone and thus be condemned by him.

Condemn. That was a strange word to be using, Mr. Spreadbury thought miserably, yet that was the only description he could think of as he looked into Tom Molyneaux's black angry face. The face of the hanging judge. Alice was condemned but he did not know how.

Yet nothing changed. There were no thunderbolts, no ravens croaking portents, no trees flowering out of season. Tom Molyneaux continued to work regularly and steadily, and if he became even more monosyllabic Mr. Spreadbury did not blame him. Indeed, the weight of his own loss leadened his heart and thoughts so that he, too, found conversation difficult. That pipe had been more than a conveyor of smoke. It had been his first pipe, a present from his father, the companion of his youth and maturity, his comfort in times of stress and anxiety, the smooth, polished bowl a reassurance to his hand when times were trying. It had been a friend, a comforter, a companion. And Alice, knowing that, had destroyed it, deliberately and malevolently.

Like a poison, his resentment festered beneath the surface of his good temper, erupting in little pustules of irritability and impatience. Mrs. Spreadbury did not like it, not one little bit, but it was as if her wicked action had armored him against her

vituperation, emboldening him. As if he might shelter beneath
the bitter black shadow of Tom Molyneaux's resentment. He no
longer attempted to protect the garden, he even once wore his
Wellington boots in the kitchen. There was a subtle shifting of
power, so slight as to be almost imperceptible. But for Mr.
Spreadbury, it was heady stuff.

It was on the second Friday in April that Mrs. Spreadbury
developed a nasty cold. By market day she had taken to her bed
and Mr. Spreadbury was ordered to proceed to Salisbury alone.

"No need to stay to lunch," Mrs. Spreadbury instructed
thickly. "You come straight back here." She glared at him, her
little tip-tilted nose all red and shiny, her gray hair spindly from
the pillow, her fingers, like paws, gripping the edge of the sheet
to her chin. And Mr. Spreadbury wondered yet again, in quiet
astonishment, that he could ever have found her desirable.

Not that it really mattered, because when he returned at
dusk, disobedient and more than a little inebriated after a
lengthy and jolly lunch with the rakish Mr. Crosswell from the
office, she was not there.

With the concentration of the not-quite-sober, Mr. Spreadbury searched every room and cupboard, the garden, and the
shed not once, not twice, but three times. She was not there,
she was not anywhere at all.

But Tom Molyneaux said, coming out from the oil-lit interior
of his hut:

"She be there. She be there when I left. I seed her."

"I can't understand it, it's so unlike her." Mr. Spreadbury stood
in a maze of bemusement and Wadsworths. "Perhaps—the
police. Perhaps I should tell the police—"

Tom Molyneaux cracked the joints of his long fingers, staring
out across the dim field, lace-edged by the hawthorns' black
branches.

"Her'll be angry. Her's tricking again. Wants to torment, like
with the pipe. You tell police and her'll flay you." He moved his
foot as something scampered past them from beneath the hut.
"Police don't care. Her's adult."

"But it's so unlike her, don't you see? She's never done such a
thing in her life!" Up and down Mr. Spreadbury went on his
toes, in an ecstasy of anxiety. "Perhaps she became very ill—lost
her memory—went outside—"

"I'd've seen her. Never moved from the garden all day. Her'd be brought back—wandering in her nightdress. No, you leave her be. You just wait."

He stared out across the night-black fields, disinterested now, and Mr. Spreadbury hesitated in an agony of indecision, the lunch fumes blurring his judgment. Perhaps if he waited until the morning—yes, he'd wait until the morning. And then, when Alice returned, he'd show that he'd taken it all quite calmly, her little tormenting ruse hadn't worked at all. Why, even her cold had probably been false! He began to feel quite indignant. She was trying to humiliate him again, upset him. She was being very unkind, very unkind indeed. She'd have him running about all over the country and then blame him for the furor.

"Very well." Mr. Spreadbury puffed out his chest. "Very well. I'll wait and see. Thank you. Thank you, Tom. Goodnight to you."

He walked carefully away from the hut, his steps rustling through the cool grass. Then he stopped. Yet the rustling went on, as if he were not alone, as if other things might be escorting him back to April Cottage. His heart gave a little nervous leap. He stumbled into a half run, his foot touching something that bounded sharply from his path, so that he was quite out of breath with agitation by the time he reached the cottage.

He slept uneasily that night, his head aching. Above him, there was a scratching and a squealing and a quarreling, a scampering such as he'd never heard in the cottage before. It was a good thing, he thought through the little hammers in his brain, that Alice was not there to hear. She'd have had him up in the attic in no time at all. He'd tell Tom Molyneaux in the morning. Tom would know what to do.

"They'll not stay. 'Tis the spring. They'll settle sooner, you just see."

"But my wife—she'll have a fit! When she comes back from— wherever she is." Mr. Spreadbury's voice faded off and Tom Molyneaux showed his yellowish, infrequent teeth.

"Then 'tis lucky her's away. Count yer blessings, that's what I'd say." And he began to whistle, something Mr. Spreadbury had never heard him do before.

But Mrs. Spreadbury never did come back, and somehow, as the

days slid comfortably and enjoyably by, Mr. Spreadbury felt less
and less inclined to go to the police. After all, if Alice wished to
leave home it was really no one's business but hers. And the
longer he postponed it, the more curious a complaint might
seem. Certainly no one inquired for her, no one missed her at
all. Least of all Mr. Spreadbury himself.

And Tom Molyneaux was quite right, the rats didn't stay long.
Just a few weeks. But there must have been quite a dust-up
because for quite some time there was a most curious and
unpleasant smell, a sweet sour pungent smell that stirred long-
buried memories of the war.

"Very savage, rats is," Tom Molyneaux volunteered when
consulted. "Little murderers—cannibals, too."

Mr. Spreadbury didn't bother to take the mugs of tea to the
shed any longer. They sat at the kitchen table instead. He took
to wearing his old gray cardigan whenever he wanted, and he
even began to smoke in the lovely solitude of the bed.

That summer no one stopped to photograph the garden of
April Cottage. Like lurking miscreants, the couch grass, the
ground elder, and the convolvulus slunk back. But Mr. Spreadbury didn't mind at all. He thought it all looked very wild and
typically English.

When at last Tom Molyneaux was done, they stood together
on the daisy-dotted lawn and Mr. Spreadbury said in quiet
satisfaction:

"Well, Tom, that's a splendid job done. It's good to know I
shan't have to have it touched again in my lifetime."

Beside him, Tom Molyneaux nodded, a long slow smile
creasing the rough dark skin of his face, and if Mr. Spreadbury
had been attending he might have found exceedingly curious
the expression of acute satisfaction that constituted that smile.

"No, you'll not have to touch it. 'Tis good and thick now.
That'd quite spoil it. You want anything, you ask Tom. 'Tis Tom's
thatch now."

"Oh, I will, I will. I don't know what I'd have done without
you, Tom." And, beaming, Mr. Spreadbury led the way indoors
for tea.

JOSH PACHTER
THE NIGHT OF POWER

The exotic area of Bahrain on the Persian Gulf is well known to Josh Pachter, who lived and worked there before moving to his present home in West Germany. Pachter's name can be found these days in all the American mystery magazines, and I think his most successful stories to date have been those involving his sleuth Mahboob Chaudri in the mysteries of a region still too little known and understood by the Western world.

The burning in his lungs was a hawk with sharpened claws and it tore at his flesh with cruel anger.

Ana aouz cigara, he thought, his throat parched, his breathing hoarse. I *must* have a cigarette!

But it was Ramadan, the month of Saum, and the Holy Quran commanded all able-bodied adult Muslims to "eat and drink until so much of the dawn appears that a white thread may be distinguished from a black, then keep the fast completely until night." The sick were temporarily exempt from fasting, as were nursing and pregnant women and travelers making long journeys, though they were all obliged to make up any of the thirty days they missed for such reasons as soon after the end of the month as they were able. Only the very young and the very old were fully excused from participation.

He had no reason not to fast, so he tasted no food in spite of his hunger, his cracked lips touched no water in spite of the heat of the day, and—worst of all—the packet of cigarettes in the pocket of his *thobe* remained unopened, and its cellophane wrapper crinkled in laughter at his suffering as he caressed it with longing fingers.

He looked out the plate-glass windows of the great Presidential Hotel, past the green-tiled roofs and golden central dome of the Guest Palace to the sea, where the sun's nether rim flamed but a centimeter above the slate-gray waters of Gudabiyah Bay.

He watched without appreciation as the fireball extinguished itself in the Gulf and brilliant streaks of salmon and orange and brightest yellow washed across the ivory sky. He clenched his teeth and waited impatiently as darkness fell and the *imams* peered solemnly at their white and black threads in the gathering dusk.

Then at last, at 8:07 P.M., the signal canon sounded. Almost instantly there was a cigarette between his lips and he was drawing its soothing smoke deep within himself, blessing the Almighty for having given him the strength to conduct himself faithfully throughout the day. Praise Allah, he thought, only three days more and I am free of this torture for another year!

When he had smoked his cigarette down to the filter, he stubbed it out in an ashtray and crossed the lobby to the doors of the Al-Wazmiyyah Coffee Shop. The room was already crowded, but he filled a plate with *mezzah* and *ouzi* and *kofta* kebabs from the Iftar buffet and found an empty table by the window. He ate slowly and sparingly and drank three glasses of cool spring water, then he left the restaurant and, after a brief stop to pick up the object he needed, rode the elevator to the fourth floor of the hotel.

The corridor was deserted—all the Presidential's guests but one, he felt certain, were downstairs at the buffet, even the Westerners, who had been cautioned not to eat in public during the daylight hours as a sign of respect to Ramadan and to the Muslims observing the fast. He walked quickly down the hallway to the fire door, let himself through it, and climbed the last two flights of stairs to the hotel's top floor.

Here, too, there was no one to be seen, no one to see him as he crept along the thick brown carpeting to the door marked 613.

He put his left ear and the fingertips of his right hand to the wood and listened intently. There was nothing to be heard from within. His hand darted into the pocket of his *thobe*—not for his cigarettes this time but for the ring of keys, which he clasped tightly in his fist to keep them from jangling as he drew them forth. He selected one key from the dozen on the ring and fitted it soundlessly into the lock set into the doorknob. He held his breath as he turned the key, turned the knob, and swung the door inward just enough to allow himself to slip through the opening and ease it shut behind him.

The room was dark, illuminated only by the faint glow of the hotel's exterior lighting that filtered in through the drapery covering the single window.

He waited. The only noises in the room were the gentle hum of the air-conditioner and the deafening pounding of his heart. When his eyes had adjusted to the almost-blackness, he was able to make out the shape in the left-hand bed, imagined he could actually see the one thin blanket rising and falling with the breathing of the figure who lay there asleep.

He stole across the room to the side of the bed and reached once more into his *thobe's* deep side pocket.

When his hand reappeared, he was holding neither cigarettes nor keys.

He was holding a small black revolver which glittered evilly in the diffused light admitted by the curtains, and his hand was steady as he touched it to the temple of the sleeping man in the bed.

Mahboob Chaudri's temples throbbed and his pulse raced with exasperation as he stood looking down at the dead man. "Where in the name of the Prophet is his *clothing*?" he demanded of no one, though there were four other people in the room to hear him. There were angrier words in Chaudri's mind, but he was able to bite them back before they escaped his lips. Fasting is only one half of faith, he reminded himself. During the month of Saum, hostile behavior was also to be avoided—as were lying, backbiting, slander, the swearing of false oaths, and the glance of passion. So it was written, and—a devout believer—so Mahboob Chaudri would comport himself, the better to avoid distraction from the pious attention to God which was the meaning of Ramadan. It was not easy for him to calm his thoughts, but he held them inside his mouth with the tip of his index finger as he returned his gaze to the bed.

The dead man was completely naked, covered only by a light blanket of a blue several shades paler than his eyes. He was a Westerner, a Caucasian, but his skin was richly tanned. He had close-cropped blond hair, a fine Roman nose, and what Jennifer

Blake under happier circumstances would have called a dishy moustache. There was a small black hole just above his left temple and the blood that drenched his pillow was still damp.

The Pakistani turned away in disgust. In spite of the air-conditioning, he was hot and sticky in his olive-green Public Security uniform. There was a line of perspiration on his upper lip. "Where are his trousers?" he exclaimed, fighting to keep his voice below a shout. "His shirt? His shoes and stockings? Where is his billfold? Where are his papers?"

"The murderer—" Abdulaziz Shaheen began, but Chaudri cut him off.

"Yes, yes, of course. The murderer has taken everything away with him, including the gun and the keys he used to let himself into this room."

"But *why?*" said Jennifer Blake, a willowly brunette in a trim gold-and-white suit with a nametag on one lapel that identified her as the hotel's night receptionist.

"So that we would not be able to determine the victim's identity, of course." Chaudri had been called away from his Iftar meal at the Juffair police barracks to investigate a report of a gunshot at the Presidential Hotel, and he was tired and hungry after a long day of fasting.

"That's not what I meant." The Blake woman frowned, her cultured British tone beginning to broaden under the strain of the evening's events. "It's bloody well obvious that's why his kit was taken off, excuse my French. What I meant was, why was he here?"

"Yes," said Mirza Hussain from a straight-backed chair by the low couch where the receptionist, Shaheen, and an elderly woman bundled up in a terrycloth bathrobe were all sitting. "That is exactly what I have been asking myself all along. Why was this man sleeping in room 613 in the first place? Why, for that matter, was he in here at all?"

"He was not a guest of the hotel?" asked Chaudri.

"*I* never checked him in," Jennifer Blake said firmly. "Not tonight nor any other night."

"Mr. Hussain? Mr. Shaheen?"

Although the Presidential was part of a large American chain, it was—like all major hotels in the emirate—run by Bahrainis

and staffed by a mixture of British expatriates, Indians, and
Pakistanis. Mirza Hussain was general manager; Abdulaziz Shaheen, chief of security. Both men were native Bahrainis, both
now wore the traditional Arabic long white *thobes* and red-and-
white-checkered *ghutras,* but there the resemblance between
them ended. Hussain was built along the lines of the country's
ruler, Sheikh Isa bin Sulman al-Khalifa; he was small in height
but rather portly, with golden skin, a graying moustache and
chin-beard, and wise black eyes behind the glittering lenses of a
pair of spectacles with thin golden rims. Shaheen was muscu-
larly built and cleanshaven and olive-complected, a decade
younger and a full head taller than his superior.

"I have never seen him before," said Hussain with an uncomfortable glance at the lifeless figure on the bed. "Perhaps Miss
Ramsey or Miss Messenger checked him in during one of the
other shifts."

The security chief shook his head. "I don't think he was a
guest," he said, and paused to draw deeply on the cigarette held
between the thumb and index finger of his right hand. When he
spoke again, wisps of smoke puffed from his mouth along with
his words. "But of course I can't be certain. It should be easy
enough to find out."

"You yourself do not recognize him?" Chaudri persisted.

"No. I have no idea who he was. But whether he was a guest
here or not, he had no business in this particular room, that
much is certain."

"And why is that?"

It was Mirza Hussain who answered. "Standard hotel practice,
mahsool. Sometimes important visitors drop in on us unexpectedly. We must always have space available to accommodate
them. So no matter how fully booked up we may be, we keep
this one room vacant in case of an emergency. It is never rented
out in the ordinary way."

Chaudri made an irritated grimace and turned back to the
dead man in the bed. "Then what were you doing here sleeping?" he muttered. "What is it you were doing in room 613,
where you ought not to have been at all, asleep so early on a
Ramadan evening? And who is it who shot you, by all that is
holy? Why were you here, and why were you killed, and by

whom?" He curled his nut-brown hands into fists and rubbed wearily at his eyes. "All right," he sighed, "let us begin at the beginning. Frau Jurkeit?"

The older woman in the bathrobe stirred restlessly on the green-leather sofa. "I am in ze room next door," she said, her English heavily accented. "Room 611. I am here in Manama wiss ze trade delegation from Bonn. We were to meet in ze coffee zhop downstairs for dinner at 8:30 but I twisted my ankle as I was dressing and decided to dine alone in my room. I ordered a—how do you say it?—a cutlet from room service." She glared disapprovingly at Mirza Hussain. "It was undercooked. Tomorrow I shall recommend zat we try ze Hilton instead. Just after nine o'clock I heard ze shot from zis room."

Chaudri took a pad from the pocket of his uniform jacket and made a note. "And what did you do then?"

"I called down to ze desk and reported what I had heard to, I assume, zis young woman."

"You did not look out into the corridor?"

"Certainly not!"

"Ah, yes," Chaudri remembered. "Your ankle."

"*Mein Gott,* it had nuzzing to do wiss my ankle! Someone is shooting a gun, do you sink I am sticking my head outside for a better look?"

"No, no," he said quickly. "Of course not. Miss Blake?"

The receptionist brushed a stray lock of hair into place and took up the story. "It was three past nine when I spoke with Frau Jurkeit, I checked the time as I hung up the phone. I immediately rang Mr. Shaheen's office, but he wasn't there at the moment. Then I tried Mr. Hussain, but he didn't pick up, either. So I did what I ought to have done straightaway, I expect—"

"You rang up the Manama Directorate," Chaudri completed the woman's sentence for her. "And the officer you spoke with reported to the investigation officer, and the investigation officer sent for me. And by the time I arrived here at the hotel you had located Mr. Shaheen and Mr. Hussain, and you gentlemen had already come up to this room and let yourselves in, and discovered—"

He let his voice trail away and indicated the body in the bed with a wave of his hand. He worked his jaw thoughtfully from side to side and went on. "And discovered a naked man in a room where he ought never to have been, shot to death by an unknown assailant who then took all the victim's clothing and other belongings away with him when he left."

"It seems incredible," said Abdulaziz Shaheen. "What will you do now, *mahsool?*"

The Pakistani clapped his hands together decisively. "Now," he said, "I will begin to earn the salary which the Public Security Force is so generously paying me."

It was almost midnight and Mahboob Chaudri was alone in the room with Abdulaziz Shaheen. Mirza Hussain had gone down to his second-floor office, where he had promised to keep himself available in case his further presence should be required. Jennifer Blake was back at her post. In a few moments she would be relieved by Gillian Messenger, who would be on duty at the reception desk until 8:00 A.M. Frau Jurkeit had long since returned to her own room next door. Even the body of the murder victim was gone.

Much had happened during the last two hours. Two and three at a time, the Presidential Hotel's entire night staff and those members of the daytime and graveyard shifts the security chief had been able to reach by phone had paraded in and out of room 613 for a look at the dead man. Yousif Albaharna, the daytime doorman, thought he might have seen him entering the hotel that afternoon, but all Westerners looked more or less alike to him, he admitted sadly, and he could not be sure. No one else could remember ever having seen the man before, and both Gillian Messenger and Leslie Ramsey were certain they had not checked him in as a guest.

The forensic medical officer had arrived shortly after eleven, had examined the body, had confirmed that death had resulted from a single shot to the head from a small-caliber weapon, had grudgingly agreed that the victim had most probably been asleep at the time the shot was fired, had stood around impatiently while the final groups of hotel employees filed past the corpse, and then at last had instructed two uniformed *natoors* to carry it away on a stretcher. He would perform an autopsy in the morning, he announced, and then he was off.

Mahboob Chaudri had been kept almost continuously busy. He had interrogated the staff. He had conferred with the F.M.O. He had supervised the activities of the team of photographers and fingerprint men sent out by the Criminal Investigations Division. He had gone down to the lobby and verified that both of the keys to room 613 were present in the room's mail slot on the wall behind the reception counter where they belonged. There were several sets of passkeys available to the maids, and the manager and security chief each had a set of their own, of course, but these, too, he had been able to account for. It seemed improbable that the dead man and his murderer had entered the room together. A more likely explanation of the sequence of events was that the victim let himself in, either with a skeleton key or by springing the lock with a strip of celluloid, and had then undressed and gone to sleep. The murderer had followed sometime later on, had committed his crime and gone away with the dead man's belongings, unaware that there was anyone next door to hear the fatal gunshot and report it.

Thus far Mahboob Chaudri had proceeded with his investigation and with his thinking, and now he sat with Abdulaziz Shaheen and sipped gratefully at the strong Arabic coffee that Mirza Hussain had sent up for their refreshment. There was a bowl of fresh dates next to the fluted *qraishieh* on the room-service dolly, and the fruit had happily dulled the edges of Chaudri's hunger.

The security chief lit a cigarette from the butt of his last one and slipped the almost-empty packet back into the pocket of his *thobe*. "If only we could put a *name* to the man," he grumbled. "If we knew who he was, that might tell us why he was here in the hotel, in this room. And if we knew why he was here, that might tell us why he was killed, and who it was who shot him."

"In the morning," said Chaudri, "we will circulate his photograph around the embassies, the banks, the Western companies, and hopefully someone will recognize him. But all that must wait for business hours. If only there was something else we could be doing *now*."

"What a night to feel powerless," Shaheen growled. "On this, the most powerful night of the year."

Mahboob Chaudri looked up from his thoughts. In the flurry of activity surrounding the murder he had forgotten that this twenty-seventh night of Ramadan was Lailat al Qadr, "The Night of Power," when the first teachings of the Holy Quran were revealed to the Prophet of Islam for the guidance of his followers.

" 'This night better than a thousand months,' " Chaudri quoted, " 'when angels and spirits descend to the earth, and it is peace until the rising of the dawn.' " He got impatiently to his feet and began to pace the deep golden carpet, his hands clasped fitfully behind his back. "Well, for once the blessed book is mistaken," he said. "There has been no peace for me this night, oh, dearie me, no. And there will *be* no peace for me, not until I locate the gun and identify the villain whose finger pulled its trigger, not even should all the angels and spirits in heaven choose this very moment to begin their descent."

And at that very moment, Mahboob Chaudri ceased his restless pacing. "To begin their descent to earth," he said slowly, staring down at the faint impression in the empty bed that showed him where the dead man had lain.

Then, to the amazement of Abdulaziz Shaheen, he grabbed up his peaked uniform cap from the nightstand between the two beds and dashed from the room without another word.

Milling crowds of men in long white *thobes* and women in veils and long black *abbas* thronged the Baniotbah Road as Chaudri wheeled his dusty Land Rover out of the Presidential Hotel's parking lot and headed north toward the Muharraq causeway. Andalus Park was filled with picnickers, and children splashed in the fountains as wide-awake and gleeful as if it were the middle of the afternoon rather than the middle of the night. But this was Ramadan, and Bahrain's Islamic population would celebrate with food and drink and gaiety till long after dark, then sleep for several hours and arise to celebrate again until Sahari, when the first light appeared in the east and the *muezzin's* call to dawn prayer announced that it was time to resume their fasting with the ritual of Niyya, the renewal of intention.

The crowds thinned out as he swung across the Khawr al Qulayah waterway, then picked up once more when he reached

Muharraq Island. He left the Land Rover in a no parking zone at the entrance to the International Airport's main terminal building and welcomed the rush of cool air that greeted him as he stepped through the glass doors.

As always, the terminal was buzzing with activity. Day and night had no meaning here: Bahrain was a refueling point for flights connecting the Western world with the Far East and there was a constant ebb and flow of transit passengers whiling away the hours between legs of their journeys, in addition to the frequent takeoff and landing of planes beginning or terminating their runs in the emirate. As Chaudri paused in the teeming passenger hall to get his bearings, the information boards above his head showed the arrival of a Korean Airlines flight bringing construction workers from Seoul and the imminent departure of an Air France 727 returning bankers, corporate executives, and diplomats to Paris.

When he found the small glass-walled checkpoint he was looking for, a solicitous *natoor* listened to his request and handed him a thick bundle of white cards. He went through the stack carefully, and when he had examined them all he shuffled back to the middle of the pile and removed a single card. He read it again, and a third time, and then he put it in his pocket and returned the rest of the cards to the *natoor* and drove back to Manama to the Police Fort at Al Qalah, where he closed himself up in a tiny investigator's cubicle and placed a long-distance telephone call to a distant city where it was still late the previous afternoon.

"I appreciate your staying on so late," said Mahboob Chaudri, as they stepped off the elevator into the quietly tasteful lobby of the Presidential Hotel. "So early, I suppose I should be saying— it will be dawn in another few hours. Which way is it we are going?"

"This way." Mirza Hussain led him past the entrance to the Al-Wazmiyyah Coffee Shop (still open, but practically deserted now), past the reception desk (where Gillian Messenger stood diligently at her post), and down a broad corridor lined with boutiques, a newsstand, a hairdresser, all dark and long since closed for the night. "I am responsible for whatever happens at this hotel," he said as they walked. "Never before has such a terrible thing taken place here. Naturally I stayed."

"It is almost over now," Chaudri told him reassuringly. They were at the end of the corridor, facing a heavy wooden door marked "Abdulaziz Shaheen, Chief of Security" in both Arabic and English.

Chaudri knocked loudly, then twisted the doorknob and walked in without waiting for a response. The Presidential's security chief was seated behind a cluttered desk, a half-smoked cigarette in his hand. He had apparently been reading through the contents of the file folder lying open on the desk before him, but he closed it at their entrance and pushed it casually off to one side. His dark face was drawn and tired, and there were shadows beneath his deep-set black eyes.

"Mr. Shaheen," said Chaudri, "we've come to talk with you about the murder."

Shaheen nodded silently and waved them to a pair of chairs. He put his cigarette to his lips and inhaled deeply.

"According to the stories of Frau Jurkeit and Miss Blake," Chaudri began, "the death shot was fired at approximately nine o'clock last evening. Now, of all the puzzling questions this crime presents, the question which has been interesting me the most is this one: why was this man in bed, probably asleep, at that rather early hour of the evening? The simplest answer would be that he was in bed because he was tired. But why was he tired? During Ramadan, both Arabs and nonbelievers keep late hours as a rule—and even were it *not* Ramadan, nine o'clock is rather early for a man of that age to be sleeping, isn't it?"

"Not necessarily." Mirza Hussain frowned. "If he had had a busy day, he might well have decided to go to sleep early. But why here in my hotel? He was not a guest. He had no business here. He most certainly had no business in room 613."

"Yes, yes," said Chaudri. "But still the question bothered me. Then, an hour ago, you said something which supplied a possible answer, Mr. Shaheen."

"About The Night of Power, you mean?"

"Indeed. You reminded me that tonight, the twenty-seventh night of Ramadan, is Lailat al Qadr, and it struck me that perhaps our victim had just recently descended to earth, like the angels and spirits written of in the Holy Quran—not in a winged chariot from heaven, no, but in a silver bird from some other time zone. Though it was only nine in the evening to us when he died, if he was a new arrival from, say, the United States or Canada, his inner clock would have insisted that it was, for him, the middle of the night. Perhaps that was why he was in bed when his murderer found him in room 613."

Abdulaziz Shaheen stubbed out his cigarette carefully and took a fresh packet from the top drawer of his desk. He left the drawer open, Chaudri noticed, stripped off the cellophane and peeled back the foil, and tapped the packet against his forefinger. "So you think he was a newcomer to Bahrain?" he asked as he flicked a thin gold lighter into flame.

"I know he was. When I left you in such a rush, I drove out to the airport and found the officer in charge of Customs and Immigration. He gave me all of the disembarkation cards filled out by the passengers who arrived in Bahrain yesterday afternoon. Those cards are containing quite a bit of information: name of arriving passenger, home address, employer, reason for visit to the emirate, and so on. One of yesterday's cards caught my eye. It was made out in the name of Stephen Kimble, an American, and his employer was given as Presidential Hotels International, with an address in California, in the USA."

Abdulaziz Shaheen breathed out a cloud of smoke that masked the expression on his face for a moment.

"I placed a phone call to the Presidential chain's Los Angeles headquarters," Chaudri went on. "It was still daytime there, and I was able to speak with a Mr. Deming, who recognized my description of our unfortunate corpse and identified him as a company executive named Stephen Kimble and told me exactly why Mr. Kimble had been sent to Bahrain."

It happened so swiftly that, had Mahboob Chaudri not been waiting for the movement, he would certainly have missed it. Abdulaziz Shaheen's hand darted into his opened desk drawer and came out holding a .25-caliber Browning automatic pistol. His dark face was cold and hard as he jumped up from his chair with the gun in his fist.

"I must insist that you both keep your hands in sight," he said, his voice tight and strained. "I'm sorry, Mr. Hussain, but I really must insist."

Mirza Hussain sat very still, one hand in the pocket of his *thobe*. His eyes told a tale of infinite weariness and sorrow. At last, with a deep sigh, he took his hand from his pocket. He was holding a packet of cigarettes and a plastic lighter. He lit a cigarette for himself and held out the packet to Chaudri.

"No, no," the Pakistani shook his head. "I am not a smoker. It is, I think, an evil habit. But it does not seem to have interfered with your reflexes, Mr. Shaheen. I'm glad I stopped in to see you on my way to the second floor and warned you of what to expect from this visit. Now, if you will give me your pistol I will hold it while you are seeing what else is to be found in Mr. Hussain's cavernous pockets."

"You are thinking of the murder weapon?" Hussain smiled grimly. "I don't have it here, gentlemen. Perhaps I should have brought it with me, after all. But it is back in my office, in my closet—in Stephen Kimble's suitcase."

"You were embezzling money from the hotel," said Chaudri flatly, when Abdulaziz Shaheen had confirmed that the manager's pockets were indeed empty, save for a ring of passkeys and a handkerchief.

"Yes. Never very much at a time. Always small amounts, small amounts. But over the last three years I have diverted almost fifty thousand dinars into my private account. I was very careful. I thought it would be impossible for anyone to discover what I had done. Apparently I was wrong."

"Embezzlement," remarked Mahboob Chaudri, "is also an evil habit. More evil than smoking, since it does harm not only to oneself but to others as well. But I am interrupting. Please forgive me and go on with what you were saying."

Hussain told his story matter-of-factly. There was nothing in his manner to indicate that he saw anything out of the ordinary in the events he was describing. "Kimble flew in yesterday afternoon," he said. "He took a taxi from the airport and came directly to my office without stopping at the reception desk. We spoke for a few moments only. He was exhausted from his journey, and I took him up to 613 and let him in with my passkey. He did not tell me why he had come—we would talk further in the morning, he said—but I knew. The home office had found out about the missing money. He had come to investigate, and he was sure to learn that I was the thief. If only I could have another few days, I thought, I could get my affairs in order and get out of the country before anyone was the wiser."

"So you killed him," said Abdulaziz Shaheen.

Hussain looked down at the glowing tip of his cigarette. "Yes. I waited until Iftar was well under way, when I could be certain that the sixth floor would be deserted, then I went upstairs and let myself back into the room. It was dark, he was sound asleep. I shot him. Then I gathered his belongings and put them in his suitcase with the gun and brought it down to my office."

"You realized that if we knew who he was," Chaudri suggested, "we would quickly learn the reason for his visit to Bahrain. And that would tell us it was you who had the only motive for killing him."

"I thought I was safe. Unless room 613 is in use, the maids clean it only once a week. It would be days before the body was discovered, I felt certain, and by then I would be safely away. It never struck me that there might be anyone else on the sixth floor when I fired the shot. I never stopped to consider that you would be able to trace him through Customs and Immigration without his papers. I must have been mad. If I had thought of that, I would never have killed him. I would have dropped everything and fled."

Mahboob Chaudri got to his feet. "But criminals never think of everything," he said. "Not even wise men think of everything. Perhaps it is their remembering that fact that makes them wise."

"In another hour it will be Niyya," said Mirza Hussain, lighting a cigarette. "I'd better smoke now, while it is still permitted."

Chaudri marveled at the state of the man's mind, at the idea that he felt it acceptable to embezzle money during the month of Ramadan, felt it permissible to commit murder then or at any other time, but would be careful to avoid food, drink, and tobacco during the daylight hours as if he were truly a devout Muslim.

They were standing in the warm night air in front of the Presidential Hotel's main entrance, waiting for a Public Security van to come and take Hussain away. The streets were almost empty, the city was asleep. But shortly the Islamic population would begin to awaken, in time to enjoy another meal before the time of fasting began.

"Listen to me, *mahsool*," said Mirza Hussain softly. "I have perhaps ten thousand dinars hidden away at my home. If we were to go there, you and I, I could give you half of that money and use the other half to make my escape. You could say that I broke away from you, that you chased after me but lost me in the darkness. No one would ever know the truth."

Chaudri did not respond.

"Five thousand dinars," the murderer continued. "That is a great deal of money, *mahsool*. It is, I imagine, more than your beautiful green uniform earns you in an entire year. Does my proposal not even tempt you?"

Chaudri considered the question. In fact, five thousand dinars was slightly more than he earned as a policeman in *two* years. It was enough to make the down payment on the bungalow in Jhang-Maghiana he was planning to build for Shazia and the children. It was enough to allow him to return to Pakistan much earlier than he had ever dreamed possible. *Was* he tempted? Was he resisting temptation now, or was his mind truly pure?

The answer came to him with the clarity of polished crystal.

"No," he said firmly, truthfully. "Your proposal is not tempting me, Mr. Hussain. It is not tempting me at all."

It was still quite dark, but soon the sky would begin to lighten. Soon it would be possible to distinguish a white thread from a black, soon the *muezzin* would call the faithful to the renewal of their fast, soon the Night of Power would draw to a close.

Mahboob Ahmed Chaudri took in a deep breath as he stood there before the great hotel with his prisoner at his side. He could feel the power enter his body, his lungs, his very being— the power of a thousand months. He raised his gaze to the heavens and offered up a silent prayer of thanksgiving and joy. As his lips formed the unspoken words, a shooting star arced across the sky and lost itself in the velvet infinity of the night.

A great sense of peace descended around him and into him, a peace Mahboob Chaudri knew would last until—no, *beyond*— the rising of the dawn.

BILL PRONZINI

ACE IN THE HOLE

Is it possible for a private eye to function as an armchair detective, solving a seemingly impossible crime while conversing with friends over a poker table on a Friday night? It's a tough challenge, and Bill Pronzini's popular "Nameless" detective is the only one I know who could have brought it off, in a story that will be appreciated by connoisseurs of both mystery genres.

I was twenty minutes late to the poker game that Friday night, but the way Eberhardt and the other three looked at me when I came in, you'd have thought I was two hours late and had sprouted tentacles besides. The four of them were grouped around the table in Eberhardt's living room—Eb, Barney Rivera, Jack Logan, and Joe DeFalco—and I could feel their eyes on me as I shrugged out of my overcoat and took the one empty chair. I put twenty dollars on the table and said, "All right, who's banking?" I said, "Well? Come on, you guys, are we going to play poker or what?" I said, "For Christ's sake, why do you keep *staring* at me like that?"

"You're on the spot, pal," DeFalco said, and grinned all over his blocky face. He was a reporter for the *Chronicle,* but he didn't look like a reporter; nor, for that matter, did he look Italian. He looked like Pat O'Brien playing Father Jerry in *Angels with Dirty Faces.* People told him things they wouldn't tell anybody else.

"Meaning what?"

"Meaning Eb and Barney have a hot bet on you. Your exalted reputation as a detective is on the line."

"What the hell are you talking about?"

Eberhardt said, "I bet Barney twenty bucks you can make sense out of the Gallatin thing within twenty-four hours."

"What Gallatin thing?"

"The shooting this noon. Jack's baby. Don't tell me you didn't hear about it?"

"As a matter of fact, I didn't."

"You see, Eb?" Barney Rivera said. He was a tubby little Chicano, Barney, with a mop of unruly black hair, big doe eyes, a fondness for peppermints, and a way with women that was as uncanny as it was unlikely. He didn't look like what *he* was, either: chief claims adjuster for the San Francisco branch of Great Western Insurance. "Your partner just won't read the newspapers or listen to news programs. When it comes to current events, he lives with his head in a hole like an ostrich."

I told him which hole he could put his ostrich in. Everybody laughed, including Barney. He's not a bad guy; he just likes to use the needle. But he's got a sense of humor, and he can take it as well as dish it out.

Jack Logan hadn't said anything, so I turned to him. He was in his mid-fifties, Eberhardt's and my age—a quiet, hard-working career cop who had been promoted to lieutenant when Eberhardt retired a couple of years ago. Now that I was looking at him up close, I saw that he seemed a little worn around the edges tonight.

"What's this all about, Jack?"

He sighed. "Frank Gallatin . . . you know who he is, don't you?"

"Westate Trucking?"

"Right. This morning we thought we finally had him nailed on racketeering and extortion charges, maybe even a mob connection. This afternoon we thought we had him nailed on something even better—a one-eight-seven. Tonight we don't have him on either score."

One-eight-seven is police slang for willful homicide, as defined in Section 187 of the California Penal Code. I said, "Why not?"

"Because even though we know damned well he shot an accountant named Lamar Trent a little past noon," Logan said, "we can't prove it. We can't find the gun he used. Nor can we find an incriminating file we know—or at least are pretty sure— Trent had in his possession earlier. Without the file, now that

Trent is dead, the D.A. can't indict Gallatin on the racketeering and extortion charges. And without the gun, Gallatin's cockamamie version of the shooting stands up by default."

"How come you're so positive he killed this Trent?"

"I was there when he did it. So was Ben Klein. Not fifty feet away, outside Trent's locked office door. We piled in on Gallatin inside of fifteen seconds; there's no way he could have got the gun out of the office in that length of time, just no way. Only it wasn't anywhere *in* the office when we searched the place. And I mean we did everything but pry up the floorboards and strip the plaster off the walls."

"Just your kind of case, paisan," Eberhardt said happily. "Locked doors, disappearing guns—screwball stuff."

I gave him a look. There were times, like right now, when I was sorry I'd taken him into my agency as a full partner. "Thanks a lot."

"Well, you've worked on this kind of thing before. You're good at it."

"Not good," Barney the Needle said, "just lucky. But this one's a pip. If the rest of us can't figure it, neither can he."

"Hey," I said, "I came here for poker, not abuse."

"So you're not even interested, huh?" DeFalco asked. He was still grinning. But behind the grin and his Father Jerry facade, his journalistic zeal was showing; *his* interest in all of this was strictly professional.

"Did I say I wasn't interested?"

"Ah," he said. "I thought so."

Rivera said, "Wait until you hear the rest of the story," and rubbed his pudgy hands together in exaggerated anticipation.

"I'm sure I'll hang on every word."

Eberhardt was firing up one of his smelly pipes. "So am I," he said between puffs. "Jack, lay it out for him."

I said, "All right, but can we play cards while I'm listening?"

Nobody objected to that. So we played a few hands of five-card stud, none of which I won, while Logan told the story. It was a pip, all right. And in spite of myself, just as Eberhardt had predicted, my own professionalism had me hooked from the start.

This morning, one of the SFPD's battery of informants had

come through with the tip that Lamar Trent was Gallatin's
private accountant—a fact that Gallatin had managed to keep an
ironbound secret until now. The word was that Gallatin and
Trent had had a falling out, either over money or some of the
nastier aspects of Gallatin's operation, and that Trent had grown
so afraid of his employer he might be willing to sell him out in
exchange for police protection and immunity. And what he had
to sell was a complete and documented file on Westate Trucking's illegal enterprises, which it was rumored he kept in his
office safe.

So as soon as they got the tip, around noon, Logan and Ben
Klein had gone over to the Wainright Building, a relic of better
days on lower Market, for a talk with Trent. When they came
into the lobby, they found both of the ancient and sometimes
unreliable elevators in use; instead of waiting they took the
stairs up, since Trent's office was only one flight up. They were
moving along the empty second-floor hallway when they heard
the shot.

"It came from inside Trent's office," Jack said, "there isn't any
doubt of that. Then there was some kind of commotion, followed by a yell and a thud like a body hitting the floor. We were
already at the door by then. It was locked, but it wasn't much of
a lock; Ben kicked it open first try.

"First thing we saw when we barreled inside was a man we
later IDed as Trent lying face down across his desk. Shot once in
the middle of his face, blood all over the remains of his brown
bag lunch. Gallatin was down on the floor, holding his head and
looking groggy. The window behind him was open—looks out
onto a fire escape and down into an alley that intersects with
Market. It's a corner office; the other window, the one at right
angles that overlooks Market, was jammed shut."

"Let me guess," I said. "Gallatin claims somebody came up or
down the fire escape, shot Trent through the open window,
knocked him to the floor when he tried to interfere, and then
went back up or down."

"That's about it. He says he went there to see Trent on a
routine business matter. They were talking while Trent was
eating his lunch; the window was open because Trent was a

fresh-air nut. Then this phantom with a gun showed up out of nowhere on the fire escape. Gallatin's story is that he didn't get a good look at him, it all happened so fast—the usual crap. But the odds of it having gone down that way are at least a couple of thousand to one.

"In the first place, the Wainright Building has six floors; two of the corner offices on the four floors above Trent's were occupied at the time. None of the people in those two offices saw anybody go up or down the fire escape past their windows. Nobody except Klein, that is, on *his* way to the roof. He didn't find a trace of anyone up there; and no one could have got *off* the roof except by way of the fire escape because the closest building is only four stories high—too far down to jump—and the door to the inside stairwell was locked tight.

"It's not any more likely that this phantom assailant came up from the alley or went down into it afterward. A teamster was unloading his truck down there, not fifty yards away, and he didn't see or hear anybody on the fire escape; and he sure as hell would have because the lower section is weighted and hasn't been oiled in twenty years, if ever: it makes plenty of noise when you swing on it. I know that for a fact because Klein played Tarzan after he came down from the roof. We also checked the teamster out, just to make sure he has no connection with Gallatin. He hasn't; he's a model citizen.

"And if that isn't enough, we had a doctor examine Gallatin. His claim—Gallatin's—is that the assailant whacked him on the side of the head to knock him down, but there's not a mark on him."

"What about a nitrate test to determine if he fired a gun?" I asked.

"Negative. He must have used gloves or something and got rid of them the same way he got rid of the gun."

"Didn't the people in the offices near Trent's see or hear anything?"

"No, because the only two offices close by were empty at the time. The elevators are directly across the hall from Trent's office, and the stairs are next to them, so there aren't any offices on that side. The one adjacent to Trent's belongs to a CPA, who was out to an early lunch; the one next to that is occupied by a mail-order housewares outfit that was closed for the day. Nearest occupied office was halfway to the rear of the building and off another corridor, and the woman holding it down is half deaf."

"You search the two empty offices?"

"Damn right we searched them," Logan said. "Got a passkey from the janitor and combed them as fine as we combed Trent's. All the other offices on that floor, too, just to be safe. Nothing. Not that we expected to find anything; like I told you, Klein and I were in on Gallatin within fifteen seconds after he shot Trent. He just didn't have time to get out of that office and hide the gun somewhere else."

"There's no chance of some clever hiding place in Trent's office that you might have overlooked?"

"None—I'll swear to that. And that's the hell of it. He couldn't have made that damn gun disappear, yet he did. Just as if he'd thrown it down a hole somewhere."

"Maybe he ate it," Barney said.

"Ha ha. Very funny."

"No, I'm serious. I read about a case like that once. Guy used a zip gun, knocked it down into its components after the shooting, and then swallowed the pieces. He was an ex-carnival sideshow performer—one of those dudes with a cast-iron stomach."

"Well, Gallatin's not an ex-carnival sideshow performer, and I'd like to see anybody eat a Beretta in fifteen seconds or fifteen *hours.*"

I asked him, "How do you know it's a Beretta?"

Logan smiled grimly. "Gallatin just happens to have one registered in his name. Same caliber as the bullet that killed Trent."

"Which is?"

"Twenty-five."

"One of those small, flat pocket jobs?"

"Right. Not much of a piece, but deadly enough."

"Any way he could have got rid of it through the open window?"

"No. If he'd chucked it into the alley, we'd have found it. And the teamster unloading his truck would have heard it hit; even a little gun makes plenty of noise when you drop it twenty feet onto pavement."

"How about if Gallatin chucked it straight *across* the alley?" I said. "Through an open window in the facing building, maybe?"

"Nice try, but no dice there, either. The first two floors of that building belong to a men's haberdashery; windows are kept locked at all times, and there were sales personnel and customers on both floors. Third and fourth floors are offices, most of them occupied and all with their windows shut. It was pretty cold and windy today, remember. I had the empty offices checked anyway: no sign of the Beretta."

He made an exasperated noise and shook his head. "Even as weak as Gallatin's story is, we can't charge him without hard evidence—without the gun. It's his ace in the hole, and he bloody well knows it."

I folded another lousy hand and ruminated a little. At length I said, "You know, Jack, there's one big fat inconsistency in this thing."

"There's more than one," he said.

"No, I mean the shot you heard, the commotion and the yell and the thud. It has a stagey ring to it."

"How do you mean?"

"As if he put it all on just for your benefit."

Jack scowled. "He couldn't have known it was Ben and me out in the hallway."

I said musingly, "Maybe he could. Had he ever seen either of you before today? Had any dealings with either of you?"

"No."

"Was it just you and Ben? Or was anyone else with you?"

"Couple of uniformed officers, as backups. They stayed down in the lobby."

"Well, he could've spotted them, couldn't he, through the window that overlooks Market Street? The four of you coming into the building together?"

"I guess he could have," Logan admitted. "But hell, if he *did* know police officers were on the scene, it doesn't make sense he'd have shot Trent. Gallatin is a lot of things but crazy isn't one of them."

Eberhardt, who was raking in a small pot with a pair of queens, said, "Could be he didn't intend to shoot Trent. Maybe there was a struggle, the gun went off, and Gallatin decided to improvise to cover up."

"Some fast improvisation," I said.

He shrugged. "It's possible."

"I suppose so. But it still doesn't add up right. Why was the door locked?"

Rivera said, "Gallatin wanted privacy when he confronted Trent. He might not have gone there to kill him, but he did go there to get that file; otherwise, why bring the gun with him?"

Logan nodded. "We figure he picked up the same information we got about Trent's willingness to sell him out. He just didn't expect us to get it and come after Trent as fast as we did."

"I still don't like that door being locked," I said. "Or that window conveniently being open."

Barney gave me a sly look; he had the needle out again. "So what's your theory, then? You must have one by now."

"No. Not yet."

"Not even a little one?"

"I'm as stymied as you are."

Eberhardt said, "Give him time, Barney. He can't come up with an answer in fifteen minutes; he's not a goddamn genius." He sounded disappointed that I wasn't.

"I'm beginning to wish I'd stayed home," I said. "Eb, is there any beer?"

"Fridge is full. Help yourself. Maybe it'll help you think."

I went and got a bottle of Schlitz, and when I came back we settled down to some semi-serious poker. Nobody said much about the Gallatin business for the next two and a half hours, but we might as well have been talking about it all along: the events as Jack Logan had described them kept running around inside my head, and I couldn't concentrate on the flow of cards. It all seemed so damned screwy and impossible. And yet, if you looked at it in just the right way . . .

Five-card stud was what we played for the most part—strict

traditionalists, that was us; anybody who even suggested a wild-card game would have been tossed out on his ear—and DeFalco was dealing a new hand. My up card was the ace of hearts. I lifted a corner of my hole card: ace of clubs. Wired aces. The best start of a hand I'd had all night.

Joe nodded at me and said, "Your bet," and I said, "Open for ten," and pushed a dime into the middle of the table. Then I looked at my down card again, my ace in the hole.

Eberhardt called my dime; he had a king showing. Jack and Barney folded. Joe called with an eight up, and then dealt me a deuce of something and Eb and himself cards that I didn't even notice.

Ace in the hole . . .

I sat there. Then somebody—Barney—poked me with an elbow and said, "Hey, wake up. We're waiting."

"Huh?"

"For you to bet. What are *you* waiting for?"

"Nothing. I was just thinking."

Eberhardt perked up. "About the Gallatin thing?"

"Yeah. The Gallatin thing."

"You're onto something, right? I know that look. Come on, paisan—spill it."

"Give me a minute, will you?"

I got up and went into the kitchen and opened another bottle of Schlitz. When I came back with it, the poker game had been temporarily suspended and they were all watching me again, waiting. Time for the Big Dick to perform, I thought sourly. And maybe do a comical pratfall like Clarabelle the Clown. Bah.

I sat down again. "All right," I said, "I've got an idea. Maybe it's way off base, I don't know, but you asked for it. It fits all the facts, anyhow. Just don't anybody make any smart cracks if it fizzles."

Eb said, "Go, boy. Go."

I ignored him. To Logan I said, "The key isn't what Gallatin did with the murder weapon, Jack. It's that shot you and Ben heard."

"What about it?"

"Well, suppose it was a phony. Suppose Gallatin staged it and everything else to make you think that was when Trent was killed, when in reality he'd been dead from two to five minutes—shot *before* the two of you were even in the building."

Frown lines made a puckered V above Jack's nose. "You mean Gallatin fired a second shot out the window?"

"No. He didn't have the gun then. I mean a phony all the way—it *wasn't* a gunshot you heard."

DeFalco said, "How do you fake a gunshot?" He had his notebook out and was scribbling in it.

I didn't answer him directly. Still talking to Logan, I said, "You mentioned that Trent was eating a brown bag lunch when he was killed or just before it. You meant that literally, right?" He nodded. "Okay, then. Where was the paper bag?"

"Wadded up in the wastebasket—" He broke off abruptly, and his frown changed shape.

"Sure," I said. "An old kids' trick. You blow up a paper sack, hold the opening pinched together to keep the air in, and then burst the sack between your hands. From a distance, from behind a closed door, it would sound just like a small-caliber gun going off."

There was silence for a few seconds while they all digested that. Then Rivera said, "Wait a minute. I'll grant you the possibility of a trick like that being worked. But why would Gallatin get so fancy? He's not some amateur playing games. If he killed Trent before Jack and Ben came into the building, why did he hang around? Why didn't he just beat it out of there?"

"Circumstances. And some bad judgment."

"All right, what's your scenario?"

"Try it like this. He arrives at Trent's office while Trent is eating his lunch; he waves his gun around, gets Trent to open his safe and hand over the incriminating file, and then shoots him for whatever reason. Afterward he pokes his head out the office door; the hallway's deserted, nobody seems to have heard the shot. So far, so good; he figures he's in the clear. Now . . ." I paused. "Jack, is there a window at the end of the hallway, overlooking Market?"

"Yeah, there is."

"I thought there might be. Back to the scenario: Gallatin pockets the Beretta, goes out with the file tucked under his arm, and pushes the button for the elevator. While he's waiting for it, he happens to glance through the window; *that's* when he sees you and Ben and the uniformed officers entering the building. Gives him quite a jolt. He's got to figure you're there to see Trent, the man he's just killed. And he's got both the murder weapon and the file in his possession. If he hangs onto them and tries to take them out of the building, he runs the risk of capture—too big a risk. For all he knows, cops are swarming all over the place. He's got to get rid of them, and fast. That's his first priority."

"But where, for God's sake? Not in the hallway; we searched it, just like we searched the offices and everything else on that floor."

"The gun and file weren't *on* that floor when you searched it. Not anymore."

"Where the hell were they, then? Where are they now?"

"I'll get to that in a minute," I said, and watched the four of them grumble and squirm. A little payback for putting me on the spot the way they had. "Let me lay out the rest of it first. Gallatin dumps the gun and the file in a matter of seconds. . . . *Now* what does he do? The smart thing is to play it cool, take the elevator down to the lobby, and try to walk out unobserved; but he doesn't see it that way. He's afraid he'll be recognized and detained; that it'll look like he's trying to run away from the scene of the murder. Maybe he hears you and Ben coming up the stairs just then; in any case, he gets a bright idea, and bad judgment takes over. Why not stay right where he is, right *on* the scene, and divert suspicion from himself by making it look as if somebody else shot Trent? After all, he's already dumped both the gun and the file; as long as you don't find either one, he's in the clear. And he doesn't believe you're going to find them.

"So he ducks back into Trent's office, locks the door to give himself a little extra time, opens the window, and then goes into his act. He hasn't had time to think it through or to check who might be down in the alley; the result is that the whole thing comes off weak and stagey. Still, as you said before, without the murder weapon . . ."

"Will you quit dragging it out? What did he do with the gun?"

I let them stew another few seconds while I drank some of my beer. Then I said, "You supplied the answer yourself, Jack: you said he made it disappear as if he'd thrown it down a hole somewhere. Well, that's just what he *did* do. The file, too."

"Hole? What are you talking about?"

"I was in the Wainright Building once, about six months ago. At that time those cranky old elevators didn't always stop flush with the level of each floor, going up or down. If they've been fixed since then, my whole theory goes down a different kind of hole. But if they haven't been fixed, if they still sometimes stop a couple of inches above or below floor level . . ."

Logan sat up straight and stiff, as if somebody had just goosed him. "Well, I'll be damned. They *don't* stop flush, no."

Eberhardt said, "The elevator shaft!"

"Why not?" I said. "One of those flat .25-caliber Beretta pocket jobs is about an inch and a half wide. Even a thick file of papers probably wouldn't be any wider. It would only take a few seconds, once the elevator doors opened, for Gallatin to spot the opening between the car floor and the shaft, wedge both the gun and the file through it, and then push one of the buttons inside to close the doors again and start the car."

DeFalco was scribbling furiously now. He said without looking up, "So Gallatin *literally* had an ace in the hole all along. I love it."

"Well, I don't," Barney the Needle said. He sounded pissy, but he wasn't; he was still playing devil's advocate, a role he enjoys almost as much as that of Grand Seducer. "I don't believe a word of it."

"No? Why not?"

"It's got too many holes in it."

Eberhardt glared at him. "Is that supposed to be a pun?"

"I don't make puns," Barney said, straight-faced. "On the whole, I mean."

Logan was on his feet. "We'll see about this," he said, and hurried off to use the phone. Three minutes later he was on his way to the Wainright Building downtown.

The rest of us were still hanging around Eberhardt's living room, drinking beer and playing desultory four-handed poker, when Logan telephoned a few minutes before midnight. Gallatin's Beretta had been at the bottom of one of the elevator shafts, all right. Along with the papers from Trent's file and a pair of custom-made doeskin gloves with the initials F. G. inside each one. They had Frankie boy but good.

Murderers, especially the ones who think they're clever, are all damned fools.

So Barney paid off to Eberhardt, with a great show of grumbling reluctance. Eb said, grinning, "I told you, didn't I? I told you the paisano here was a whiz when it comes to this kind of screwball stuff. Three hours, that's all it took him. *Three,* Barney, not twenty-four."

"Luck," Barney the Needle said. "Pure blind luck. He's the luckiest private eye on the face of this earth."

Sure I am. Eberhardt collected on his twenty-buck bet and won gloating rights in the bargain. Barney won twenty-nine dollars on the poker table, which left him nine bucks up for the evening. Jack Logan won five dollars early on, got to put the blocks to a nasty bastard like Frank Gallatin, and had a large burden lifted from his shoulders. Joe DeFalco won three dollars and got a story that he didn't dare print as straight news—it would have embarrassed Jack and made the SFPD look bad; but he'd find a way to turn it into a feature or something. And what did I get? I got a headache from too much beer, an empty wallet—I won exactly two hands all night and ended up thirty-seven dollars poorer—and the privilege of plying my trade and overworking my brain for no compensation whatsoever.

Mr. Lucky, that's me . . .

ROBERT SAMPSON

RAIN IN PINTON COUNTY

Robert Sampson is the last of our eight "new" writers to be presented in this volume. Though he's the author of some two dozen mystery stories and a five-volume study of pulp magazines, Yesterday's Faces, *until now he has not been widely known as a mystery writer. All that changed this year when the Mystery Writers of America awarded this story from* The New Black Mask #5 *its Edgar as the best short story of 1986.*

Fat raindrops rapped circles across puddles the color of rusty iron. Ed Ralston, special assistant to the sheriff, said, " 'Scuse me," and pushed through the rain-soaked farmers staring toward the house. Ducking under the yellow plastic strip—CRIME SCENE, KEEP OUT—that bordered the road, he followed the driveway up past a brown sedan, mud-splashed and marked "Sheriff's Patrol."

Behind him, a voice drawled, "He's her brother."

The house, painted dark green and white, sat fifty feet back from the country road. That road arced behind him across farmland to hills fringed darkly with pine. Black cattle peppered a distant field. The air was cold.

In the rear parking lot, a second patrol car sat beside a square white van with "Pinton County Emergency Squad" painted across the state outline of Alabama. On the shallow porch, a deputy in a black slicker watched rain beat into the yard.

Ralston said, "Punk day, Johnny. Fleming get here yet?"

The deputy shook his head. "They're still calling for him. Broucel's handling things inside." And, as the door opened, "I'm sure as hell sorry, Ed."

"Thanks."

He entered a narrow kitchen, went through it to a dark hallway that smelled faintly of dog, turned left into the front room. There a handful of men watched the photographers put away their gear.

When he entered the room, their voices hesitated and softened, as if a volume control had been touched. Men stepped forward, hands out, voices low: "Sorry. Sorry. Ed, I'm real sorry."

He crossed the familiar room, keeping to a wide plastic strip laid across the beige carpet. He shook hands with a little, narrow-faced man who looked as if he had missed a lot of meals. "Morning, Nick."

"Sorry as hell about this, Ed," Nick Broucel said.

Ralston nodded. His glasses had fogged, and he began rubbing them with a piece of tissue that left white particles on the glass. Without the glasses, his eyes seemed too narrow, too widely separated for his long face. His dark hair was already receding. Scowling at the flecks on his glasses, he said, "Well, I guess I better look at her."

A gray blanket covered a figure stretched out by the fireplace. Ralston twitched back a corner, exposing a woman's calm face. Her hair was pale blond, her face long, her lipstick bright pink and smudged. On the bloodless skin, patches of eye and cheek makeup glared like plastic decals.

He looked down into the face without feeling anything. There was no connection between the painted thing under the blanket and his sister, Sue Ralston, who lived in his mind, undisciplined, sharp-tongued, merry.

He stripped back the blanket. She was elaborately dressed in an expensive blue outfit, earrings and necklace, heels; nails glittered on hands crossed under her breasts. "Well, now," he said at last. "It's Sue. What happened?"

Nick said, "She went over backward. Hit her head on the corner of the fireplace. Pure bad luck. Somebody moved her away. Smoothed her clothes. Folded her hands. Somebody surprised, I'd say."

"Somebody shoved her and she fell?"

"Could be."

"Or she just slipped."

"Could be."

Rain nibbled at the windows. The investigative work had started now, and the room squirmed with men standing, bend-

ing, looking, methodically searching for any scrap of fact to
account for that stillness under the gray blanket.

Ralston asked, "Why the full crew? How'd we hear about
this?"

"Anonymous call. Male. Logged at 5:32 this morning. Gave
route and box number. Said the bodies were here."

"Bodies? More than one?"

"Not so far." Broucel looked sour and ill at ease. "This is
Fleming's job, not mine. I'm just marking time here. I don't
know where the hell he's got to. Where's the sheriff?"

Ralston said carefully, "He's taking a couple of days' vacation."
He slowly scanned the room. Money had been freshly spent
here, money not much controlled by taste. New blue brocade
chairs bulked too large for the room. The couch seethed with
flowered cushions. The lamps were fat glass creations with
distorted shades. Tissues smeared with lipstick scattered a
leather-topped coffee table.

"And there's something else," Broucel said.

He gestured toward the shelves flanking the fireplace. Cassettes of country music littered the bottom shelves. On upper
shelves clustered carved wooden animals, ceramic pots, weed
vases. Centered on the top shelf was the photograph of a
grinning young man. It was inscribed "To Sue, With Ever More
Love, Tommy."

"You recognize that kid?" Broucel asked.

"Isn't that Tommy Richardson? His daddy owns the south half
of the county."

"That's the one."

"Daddy's going to enforce the dry laws, jail the bootleggers,
clean up the sheriff's department—come elections. That's a
mike, isn't it?"

"Yes, sir, that's a mike."

A fat wooden horse had tumbled from the second shelf. Its fall
had exposed the black button of a microphone, the line vanish-
ing back behind the shelves.

In a slow, reflective voice, Ralston said, "Sue never had a
damn bit of sense."

"Let's go down in the basement," Broucel told him.

Steep wooden stairs took them to a cool room running the

length of the house. Windows along the east foundation emitted
pallid light. Behind the gas furnace, a small chair and table
crowded against the wall and black cables snaked out of the
ceiling to connect a silver-gray amplifier and cassette tape
recorder. On the table, three cassette cases lay open and empty,
like the transparent egg cases of insects.

Broucel said, "We found three mikes. About any place you
cough upstairs, down it goes on tape."

Ralston gestured irritably at the equipment. "I don't understand this. She didn't think this way. She couldn't turn on the TV.
Why this?"

Broucel fingered his mouth, said in a hesitant voice, "I sort of
hoped you could help me out on that."

"I can't. I don't know. We didn't speak but once a year."

"Your own sister?"

"My own damnfool sister. She had no sense. But she had more
sense than this."

"Somebody put this rig in. She had to know about it."

"Must have," Ralston agreed. "Must have. But what do I know?
I'm no investigator. I'm a spoiled newspaper man. My job's
explaining what the sheriff thought he said."

Feet hammered down the stairway. A deputy in a dripping
slicker thumped into the basement, excitement patching his
face red. He yelped, "Nick, we found Fleming."

Broucel snapped, "Where the hell's he . . ."

"He's in his car, quarter of a mile down the road. Tucked in
behind the brush. Rittenhoff saw it. Fleming's shot right through
the head."

Broucel sucked in his breath. He became a little more thin, a
little more gray. "Dead?"

"Dead, yeah. He's getting stiff."

"Oh, my God," Broucel said. His mouth twitched. He put two
fingers over his lips, as his eyes jerked around to Ralston.

Who said, with hard satisfaction, "I guess we're going to have
to interrupt the sheriff's vacation."

He drove his blue Honda fast across twelve miles of back-
county road. A thick gray sky, seamed with deeper gray and

black, wallowed overhead. Thunder complained behind the pines.

He felt anger turn in him, an orange-red ball hot behind his ribs. Not anger about Sue. That part remained cold, sealed, separate. It's Piggott's doing, he thought. Piggott, Piggott, Piggott the beer runner and liquor trucker, the gambler, briber, the sheriff's poker-playing buddy. Now blackmailer. What else? And Sue's very particular good friend, thank you.

Whatever Piggott suggested, she would, bright-eyed, laughing, follow. No thought. No foresight. Do what you want today, ha ha. More fun again tomorrow.

When he last visited her, they had quarreled about Piggott.

"He's lots of fun," she said loudly. Her voice always rose with her temper. "He's interesting. He's different all the time. You never know with him."

"You always know. He'll always go for the crooked buck. He handles beer for six dry counties. He owns better than two thousand shot houses. He's broke heads all over the state. Even a blond lunatic knows better than to climb the sty to kiss the pig."

It ended in a shouting match. She told Piggott the next day, with quotations, and Piggott told Ralston and the sheriff the day after.

"A full-time liar and a postage-stamp Capone." Piggott pushed back in his leather chair and yelled with laughter. "I swear, Ed, I didn't know I was that good."

"Hardly good," Ralston said.

The sheriff's eyes, like frosted glass, glared silence.

Ralston said, "Look, Piggott, Sue's just a nice, empty-headed kid. She sees the fun, but she don't smell the dirt. She's got no sense of self-protection. She's different."

Piggott swabbed his laughing mouth with a handkerchief and straightened in his old leather chair. Amusement warmed his face. "I know she's different. I'm going to marry her, Ed."

The Honda reeled on the road. He jerked the wheel straight. It was not quite nine o'clock in the morning and cold, and the road twisted as complexly as his thoughts.

Two miles from the highway the fields smoothed out, bordered by white fencing that might have been transplanted from a Kentucky horse farm. When the fence reared to an elaborate entrance, he turned right along a crushed-gravel road gray with rain. A square, big house loomed sternly white behind evergreen and magnolia. In the parking lot, two Continentals and a dark green BMW sat like all the money in the world. Rain sprinkled his glasses. As he walked across the road to a porch set with frigid white ornamental-iron chairs, the front door swung open to meet him. A slight man with very light blue eyes and a chin like a knife point waved him in.

"Out early, Ed."

Ralston nodded. "I need the sheriff bad, Elmer."

"He just got to bed."

"Tough. Tell him it's official and urgent."

The man behind Elmer snorted and showed his teeth. "Official and urgent," he said, arrogantly contemptuous. He was thick-shouldered, heavy-bodied, round-faced, and scowled at Ralston with raw dislike.

Elmer said, "I can't promise. The game lasted all night. You and Buddy mind waiting here?"

He stepped quietly away down a high white hallway lined with mirrors and horse paintings. The hall, running the length of the house, was intercepted halfway by a broad staircase. Beyond lounged a man with a newspaper, his presence signifying that Piggott was in.

A sharp blow jarred his arm. He turned to see Buddy's cocked fist.

"We got time for a couple of rounds, Champ."

Ralston said, "Crap off."

Buddy, hunched over shuffling feet, punched again. "Ain't he bad this morning." Malice rose from him like visible fumes. "The sheriff's little champ's real bad. Couple of rounds do you good. You lucked out, that last time."

"You got a glass jaw," Ralston said.

Elmer appeared on the stairway to the second floor. He jerked his hand, called, "Come on up."

Ralston walked around Buddy, not looking at him. Buddy,

clenching his hands, said distinctly, "You and me's going to have a little talk, sometime."

The second floor was carpeted, dim, silent, expensive, and smelled sourly of cigars. Elmer pointed to a carved wooden door, said, "In there," wheeled back down the hall.

Ralston pushed open the door and looked at Tom Huber, sheriff of Pinton County, sitting on an unmade bed. The sheriff wore a white cotton undershirt, tight over the hairy width of his chest, and vivid green and yellow undershorts. Hangover sallowed his face. He was a solid, hard-muscled old roughneck, with a hawk-nosed look of competence that had been worth eighty thousand votes in the last four elections.

He said, "Talk to me slow, son, I'm still drunk."

Easing the door shut, Ralston said, "Last night, Fleming was shot dead. In his own car. In the country. With his own gun, couple of inches from the right temple. Gun in car. Wiped off. Far as we know, he wasn't on duty. You need to show up out there. Broucel's in charge, and he's got the white shakes."

"Fleming shot?" A slow grin spread the sheriff's mouth. "So that grease-faced little potlicker went and got himself killed. That's not worth getting a man out of bed for. Let Broucel fumble it."

"Fleming was your chief deputy," Ralston said sharply. "You have to make a show. The media's going to crawl all over this. You got to talk to the TV—sheriff swears vengeance. Hell, we got an election coming."

"There's that." The sheriff touched his eyes and shuddered. "Lord a'mighty, I didn't hardly get to sleep. Cards went my way all night."

In a neutral tone, Ralston said, "You don't ever lose, playing at Piggott's."

"That why I play at Piggott's." He got up carefully. "God, what a head. Well, now, that's one less candidate for the high office of Pinton County Sheriff. Ain't it a shame about poor old Lloyd Fleming?"

He moved heavily into the bathroom to slop water on his

head and guzzle from the faucet. Ralston drifted around the bedroom, face somber, peering about curiously, fingering the telephone, light fixtures, pictures.

The sheriff emerged, toweling his head. "I'm scrambling along, Ed. Don't prance around like a mare in heat."

Ralston said, "I need to tell you a little more. But I'll save it. Too many bugs here."

"I counted one," Huber said pleasantly.

"Two, anyhow." He knelt to reach under the airspace of a dresser and jerked. His fingers emerged holding a microphone button and line. It seemed a twin of the one on Sue's shelf. "These may be dummies to fake you off an open phone tap."

The sheriff sighed. "It's hard for an old fellow like me to bend over to squint in every hole. You know, you got to like Piggott. He don't trust nobody."

They returned unescorted to the first floor. "I best make my good-byes," the sheriff said. "Not fit for a guest to leave without he thanks his host for all those blessings."

Ralston followed him to the rear of the white hall. The watcher there, a burly youngster with a face like half a ham, stared at them eagerly. The sheriff asked, "Piggott up?"

"Oh, Lordy, sure," the youngster said. "He don't hardly ever sleep."

He clubbed the door with his fist, opened it, saying, "Mr. Piggott, it's the sheriff."

A cheerful voice bawled, "You tell him to bring himself right in here."

It was a narrow, bright room stretched long under a hammered-tin ceiling. The walls were crowded with filing cabinets and messy bookshelves, stuffed with as many papers and magazines as books. A worn carpet, the color of pecan shells, led to an ancient wooden table flanked by straight-backed chairs. Behind the table, Piggott lolled in an old leather chair.

He bounced up as they entered. He burst around the table, vibrating with enthusiasm, grinning and loud. He had curly black hair over a smooth face, deeply sun-burned, and he looked intelligent and deeply pleased to see them. "Didn't expect you up till noon, Tom." He smiled brilliantly. "Lordy, you're tough."

He pounded nervously on the sheriff's shoulders, then seized Ed's arm. "Now you come over here and look at this picture. You'll like this."

He extended a large color photograph. Sue Ralston beamed from it. She stood close to Piggott, arms clutching each other, heads together, delighted with themselves.

Through rigid lips Ralston said, "Nice photo." He felt nauseated.

Piggott burst into his rolling laughter. "That's our engagement photo, Ed. Listen, don't look so sour." His arm slipped around Ralston's shoulders. "It's okay. I'll make a great husband. I grow on you."

Ralston swallowed, standing stiff within the embrace. "Piggott . . ."

" 's all right, Ed. I know." He smacked Ralston's shoulder amiably. "It's a funny world. Who wants a postage-stamp Capone for a brother-in-law?"

He emitted a howl of joy, throwing back his head, opening the deep hollow of his mouth. "Even us booze merchants fall in love, Ed. We even get married. Ain't it a crime?"

Ralston forced, "Congratulations, then," from his closed throat. It was now imperative to tell them about Sue. But he could not. He listened to Piggott and the sheriff bantering. He could not.

Piggott had set it up, sometime, for some purpose. And she was dead because of it. Somehow. Set a trap and what dies in it is your responsibility.

"Fleming!" Piggott was saying. "I can't believe it. Who's Moneybucks Richardson going to run for sheriff now?"

Laughter. The sheriff edged toward the door.

The need to tell them about Sue, the urgency of it, tore at him. At the door, he blundered to a halt, said, "Piggott . . ." Terrible pressure locked his throat. He said, instead, "Piggott— what about that ancy-fancy recording stuff in Sue's basement?"

Fleeting hardness in Piggott's face softened to laughter. He flung out joyous arms. "Wasn't that something. We told some friends we were engaged. Then I went out to the car and let them warn her about me. Then we played the cassettes back to them. Funny! Hell, they'll never speak to me again. Hey, you got to hear those tapes. And they're my good friends."

Joy wrinkled his big face. He bellowed with laughter like a furnace. "I mean, funny."

They sat in the sheriff's car behind Piggott's house. Rain rattled on the hood and glass.

Ed asked, "What are they doing with Tommy Richardson?"

"Son, you probably don't want to know anything about that."

"I got to. It's important." Their eyes met, held, strained, force against force. "Yes," Ralston said. "I mean it's important. It's important to me."

The sheriff shrugged. " 'Tain't but a trifle. They're just roping the boy a little. Just a little business insurance."

"Business insurance?"

"Why sure. Here's a nice respectable boy gaming around with beer runners. Well, shoot, people game and people have a drink now and then. Least I've known them to do it in Pinton County. Don't expect they'll change. No harm in it, less they get mean. The mean ones is what sheriffing is about. But you can't never tell when sin's going to get a bad name. So maybe Old Richardson goes and gets a hard-on against sin. Then they got something for him to listen to while he gets calm. Or maybe not. You can't ever know."

"That's all?"

"All there is. Nothing a'tall."

"Merciful God," Ralston said. "Is that all?"

He got out into the rain. He stood staring blankly, hunching up his shoulders, rain smearing his glasses, distorting the world so that it appeared twisted and in strange focus. He circled the car and tapped the sheriff's window, and rain ran in his hair, wet his forehead, ran from his chin.

The sheriff's window rolled down.

Ralston said, "Sheriff, Sue's dead. At home. Fell and hit her head. I couldn't tell Piggott."

He turned away and walked toward the front parking lot. The cement driveway danced with silver splashes.

Behind him, a car door slammed and heavy footsteps hurried back toward the house.

The Honda streaked toward Pintonville. He had, perhaps, a ten-, even fifteen-minute start on them. More if Piggott delayed. The road flew at him, glistening like the back of a wet serpent. Soon they too would think of questions to ask Tommy Richardson.

If it had been Tommy who was with Sue last night.

If he had read the evidence correctly.

If Sue had got herself up, polished and shining, to dazzle the son of Old Man Richardson, the fun and indiscretion funneling into the cassette's hollow maw.

If the boy had found the mike. If his suspicions blazed . . .

But Fleming. He could not understand Fleming's presence.

The Honda slid on the shining asphalt, and the back end fought to twist around. He corrected the wheel, iron-wristed, jabbed the accelerator.

First, talk to Tommy Richardson. Before Piggott.

The car leaped. The rain came down.

"I'm Tommy Richardson," the boy said in a low voice, affirming that being Tommy Richardson was futile and burdensome. His head drooped, his shoulders slumped, his body was lax with self-abasement.

"I'm Sue Ralston's brother Ed. I'm with the sheriff's department. I'd like to talk with you."

"I guess so." He pushed open the screen door separating them, exposing his consumed face. He was unshaven, uncombed, unwashed. He smelled of sweat and cigarettes, and despair had drawn his young face and glazed his eyes. "Dad says you guys are incompetent, but you got here quick enough."

He looked without hope past Ralston's shoulder at the rain sheeting viciously into the apartment complex. Lightning snapped and glared, blanching the pastel fronts of the apartments and rattling them with thunder. "Come in. You're getting soaked."

Ralston stepped into the front room, saturated trousers slopping against his legs. Tension bent his tall frame.

Stereo equipment, lines of LPs, neat rows of paperbacks

packed the cream-colored walls. A table lamp spilled light
across a card table holding a typewriter and a litter of typed
pages, heavily corrected.

"I've been up all night," Richardson said. He gestured toward
the typewriter. "Writing out my incredible . . . stupidity."

He turned away, reaching for a typed page. As he did so,
Ralston saw, behind the boy's left ear, a vivid pink smudge of
lipstick.

The room convulsed around him, as if the walls had clenched
like a fist.

"Mr. Ralston?"

He became aware that Tommy was holding out typewritten
pages to him, eyes anxious. "This explains it."

"Sit down," Ralston said.

"Thank you. Yes, I will." The boy collapsed loosely on a tan
davenport, long legs sprawled, head back, eyes closed, hands
turned palms uppermost, the sacrifice at the altar. On the wall
behind, two fencing foils crossed above the emblem of the
university team.

Tommy added, without emphasis, "I thought really serious
things were more formal. You expect personal tragedy to have
dignity and form. But it doesn't. It's only caused by trivialities—
stupid mistakes, misjudgments. Nothing of weight. All accident." He might have been whispering prayers before sleep.

Ralston, set-faced, read:

CONFESSION
of
Thomas Raleigh Richardson

I am a murderer.

Last night, I murdered two people that I cared for.

One I loved and loved deeply. The other was my friend.
But it was wholly by capricious and accidental chance,
which now seems inescapable, that I murdered both of
them. That it was essentially accidental does not excuse
me.

The balance of the paragraph was crossed out. There were
four pages, scarred by revision, ending with his full signature.

Ralston took out his pen and laid the pages in Tommy's lap. "Sign your usual signature diagonally across each page." He watched, immobile, as the boy wrote. Then he folded the sheets and thrust them into his breast pocket.

"Now tell me what happened," he said.

"I loved her. We were planning to get engaged. At first I thought she was a criminal with Piggott. But she was sensitive and warm. You're her brother. You know. She didn't know about Piggott, what he did. We fell in love. We were going to get engaged after I graduated."

"How did you get involved with Piggott?" Ralston asked. The tremor shaking his legs and body was not reflected in his voice.

"It was Fleming. Dad had a Citizens' Committee for Law and Order meeting at the house. Fleming came. He said that the sheriff and the bootleggers were cooperating. But he needed more evidence. He said that Piggott would try to blackmail me to make it seem like I was participating in his business. He called it a business. Dad didn't like it, but he agreed that I would let them try to blackmail me."

"So then Fleming introduced you to Sue."

"I met her at his house. Twice. He said that she knew Piggott. Then I went to her house, and Piggott was there a couple of times. He doesn't look like a criminal, but he laughs too much. It makes you distrustful."

"Why was Fleming there last night?" He glanced at his watch, and anxiety crawled in him.

"I told him I loved her. That we were almost engaged. Fleming wouldn't believe me. I told him to wait outside, last night, I could prove it easily. He thought that if I were right, she could help us.

"I walked down to his car. This was after the accident. There was lightning on the horizon, like a bad movie. I told him they'd been recording everything I said. He laughed and said he knew it. I asked to see his gun. I didn't tell him about Sue. When I shot, there was all this light. I thought lightning had struck by us. Then it smelled like blood and toilets. I wiped off the gun. I wrote it all down. You just have to read it."

Ralston asked gently, "I don't understand. Why did you shoot Fleming?"

"He would have known right off I killed her. He said she was working for Piggott."

His head shook blindly, and he jerked forward in his seat.

"He would have been sorry for me. I couldn't have faced him if he had known. Isn't that a dumb reason? It doesn't even make sense. But she told me she wouldn't have given the cassettes to Piggott. She told me. She loved me. We were almost engaged.

"You and I," he said, "would have been brothers-in-law."

He lifted his head.

"Are you corrupt, Mr. Ralston?"

"Not always," Ed said at last. He glanced again at his watch, and his heart pulsed. "Will you come with me and make a formal statement?"

"I wrote it down."

"We still need a statement."

"Okay."

He rose slowly, a sleepwalker awake in his dream. He looked slowly around the room. "This is real, isn't it? I keep thinking that I'm going to wake up, but I am awake."

Ralston said, "You better hurry. I think Piggott knows you were there last night. He knows Sue . . . had an accident. He'll want to ask you about it."

"I pushed her away from me and she fell."

"He doesn't know that."

"It's just that simple. I pushed her away and she fell."

"We have got to get moving."

He followed the boy into the bedroom, watched him find a coat, pick up wallet, keys, money from the dresser.

"Not that." He took a fat pocketknife from Tommy's fingers.

"Dad gave me that."

"You'll get it back. Better give me the cassettes, too."

"Sure."

They left the apartment. Driving rain lashed their faces. As they came into the parking lot, a black sedan jerked to a stop before them. Its doors opened, like an insect spreading its wings, and Buddy and Elmer bobbed out.

Ralston whispered urgently, "You left the house early. Nothing happened."

"But that's a lie," Tommy said.

The two men splashed toward them. Buddy's mouth was opened. He stopped before Ralston, hunching in the rain, hands jammed into his pockets. "Goin' somewhere, Champ?"

Elmer said, "Hello, Tommy. I think we met once at Sue's. Mr. Piggott would appreciate it if you could stop by and see him."

Tommy nodded gravely. "I'd like to see him. I have a lot to say."

Elmer looked respectfully at Ralston. "Mind if we borrow him, Ed?"

Ralston looked at Buddy's weighted pocket. He said, "I was just going that way, myself. Might as well join you."

They sat in the rear seat of the rain-whipped car. Elmer drove. Buddy, in the front seat, sat turned, looking at them.

Tommy lay back on the brown leather upholstery, his unshaven face wan in the pale light. His eyes were closed. His lips twitched and jerked with internal dialogue.

When they had driven for a quarter of an hour, he said unexpectedly, "Mr. Ralston?"

"Yes?"

"It feels—it's rather complicated to describe. It's as if I had been walking along someplace high and it fell apart under my feet. I feel as if I am in the act of falling. I'm suspended. I haven't started to fall yet. But I will. I don't understand how I feel. Is that guilt?"

"It's lack of sleep."

"I think it is the perception of guilt."

"Get some sleep if you can. Keep quiet and get some sleep."

Buddy said sharply, "Nobody asked you, Ralston. Let the kid talk. What'd you do, kid?"

Tommy's unkempt head threshed right and left.

Ralston jerked hands from pockets as he said, "Tommy, keep quiet," in a savage voice.

"Can it, Ralston," Buddy said.

"Screw you."

Buddy's arm flashed across the seat. He hit Ralston on the side of the head with a revolver. Ralston grunted and, trying to turn, was struck twice more.

He let himself fall loosely into Tommy's lap. To his surprise, he felt himself rising very swiftly up a shimmering incline. As he rose, he thrust the knife he had taken from his pocket into Tommy's hand. Light turned about him in an expanding spiral, and his speed became infinite.

He awoke almost at once. His nose and cheek were pressed against Tommy's coat. Elmer was snarling at Buddy with soft violence. Tommy was saying, "Mr. Ralston, Mr. Ralston," his voice horrified. The blows, Ralston decided, had not been hard. He reasoned methodically that the angle for striking was wrong, and therefore insufficient leverage existed for a forceful blow. This conclusion amused him. Tommy's coat faded away.

When it returned, he heard Tommy saying: "You're bleeding."

"Let it bleed," he muttered.

He levered himself erect. His stomach pitched with the movement of the automobile and, when he moved his head, pain flared, stabbed hot channels down his neck. He closed his eyes and laid his head back against the seat and bled on Piggott's upholstery until the car stopped. He felt triumphant, in an obscure way.

The door opened. Ralston worked his legs from the car, gingerly hauled himself out. Rain flew against his face. Pain hammered his skull, and nausea still worked in him. He stood swaying, both hands clamped on the car door until his footing steadied.

Buddy stood smirking by the open door.

Ralston hit him on the side of the jaw. The effort threw white fire through his head. He fell to his knees. Buddy tumbled back against the side of the car, striking his head on the fender. He lay in the rain, eyes blinking.

Ralston staggered up, got his hand in Buddy's pocket, removed a heavy .38 with a walnut handle, a beautiful weapon. He stood swaying as Elmer glided around the side of the car.

Looking down at Buddy, Elmer said, "He never got past the third round, any time."

"Let him lay," Ralston said, with effort.

"Gotta take him in," Elmer said. He and Tommy hoisted Buddy between them, hauled him loose-legged, foul-mouthed, into the white hall. They flopped him into a chair, walked toward Piggott's office. The ham-faced youngster bumbled up from his chair, stared round-eyed at them.

"Mr. Piggott's busy, " he said.

"Go back to sleep," Ralston said, and pushed the door open.

Piggott was working at his table, shuffling papers with two other men. He looked sharply up as Ralston came in, then began to chuckle. "Ed, it must have been a strenuous morning." He glanced at the two men. "Boys, let's chase this around again in half an hour, okay?"

They left silently, not looking around, their arms full of paper.

Tommy, at the table now, looking down on Piggott, asked, "Mr. Piggott, why did you feel it necessary to involve Sue?" His voice was formal and mildly curious. "I mean—I should say, in your efforts to entrap me."

Glee illuminated Piggott's face. "Lordy, Tommy, there wasn't a thing personal. You're a real nice boy. Sue just completely enjoyed it."

Amusement shook his shoulders. He added, "Now, don't you take it too hard. Women just fool men all the time. It's their way."

Tommy said in a clipped voice, shoving hands into his pockets, "I blamed her at first. I made a serious mistake. I should have realized that you were responsible. I was most certainly warned. But she would never have turned those cassettes over to you. She loved me, and she wouldn't have countenanced blackmail."

Incredulous delight lifted Piggott's shoulders. "Tommy, my friend, you are one of a kind. You really are."

"She loved me. We were going to get engaged."

Piggott's laughter poured into Tommy's face, a stream of sound. "Son, she did a real job on you. Not that she didn't like you. She thought you were grand. You just look here."

He tossed the engagement photograph across the table.

He said, "I was marrying her next month, Tommy. You were just a mite late."

"I love her," Tommy said, looking at the photograph. His voice began breaking up. "You never did."

The hall door came open hard, and Buddy came into the room, taking neat little steps. In his plaster face the eyes were terrible things. He called, "You, Ralston." A silver pistol jetted from his clasped hands.

Laughter stiffened on Piggott's face. In an unfamiliar voice, the texture of metal, he said, "Buddy, did I call . . ."

"I love her," Tommy said again.

He executed a fencer's flowing movement, an arc of graceful force that glided up the leg to the curved body to the extended right arm. His knife blade glinted as it entered Piggott's throat. His shoulders heaved with effort as he slashed right.

Incoherent noise tore from Piggott and a sudden scarlet jetting. He fell back in his chair, his expression amazed. His feet beat the floor. The chair toppled over with a heavy noise.

Gunfire, sudden, violent, repetitious, battered the room.

Tommy was slammed face forward onto the table. Papers cascaded, and a single yellow pencil spun across the pecan carpet.

The gunfire continued.

Pieces jumped out of the tabletop as Tommy's legs collapsed. He sprawled across the table, right arm extended, body jerking.

Buddy darted forward, the revolver bright in his brown hand, concentration wrinkling his face. He fired into Tommy's back.

Ralston shot him in the side of the head. Buddy fell over sideways and his gun, bounding across the floor, thudded against a gray filing cabinet.

Ralston whirled, knelt, looked down his gunsights into the enormous hollow hole of the .45 in Elmer's hand.

Confused shouting in the hallway.

Elmer said, white-lipped, "There's not five-cents profit for more shooting, Ed."

"No."

"We'd best put the guns up."

"All right."

The thumping of feet behind the table had stopped.

Men poured into the room.

Ralston sucked air, roared, "I'm Ed Ralston of the sheriff's department. This is police business, and I want this room cleared." He paced savagely toward them, face rigid, eyes gleaming, the horror in him intolerably bright.

Their faces glared anger, fear, shock. His voice beat at them.

Elmer pushed at them, a confusion of voices and shoving bodies.

After one lifetime or two, the room emptied. Ralston shoved the gun away, said, "I'll call the sheriff."

"You might want to give us maybe half an hour. Some of the boys might want to fade. Give them a chance to get packed."

"Fifteen minutes. It'll have to be fifteen minutes."

Elmer nodded. "See you around, Ed."

The door closed and he was alone with the dead.

The strength leaked out of his body. He dropped into a chair and began to shake. His head blazed with pain. He could not control the shaking, which continued on and on.

Outside, engines began to roar, and he heard automobiles begin to go.

As last he wavered up on fragile legs, took a tissue from his pocket, and approached the table. Splinter-rimmed holes pocked the wood. He removed Tommy's wallet, took thirty of the sixty-two dollars. When he replaced the wallet, the body shifted and he thought that it would slip from the table to press its torn back against him. He wrenched back, white-faced. The body did not move again.

Piggott's wallet contained nearly six thousand dollars. Ralston removed four thousand in fifties and hundreds, counting them out slowly. He returned the wallet to a pocket the blood had not touched.

"They can both help bury her," he said.

His voice sounded stiff and high.

"We're all dead together," he said. He began to laugh.

When he heard himself, he became suddenly silent. Hard rain whipped the windows.

At last, his hand reached for the telephone.

THE YEARBOOK OF THE MYSTERY & SUSPENSE STORY

Directory of Mystery Publications

(Compiled with the assistance of Ruth Cavin and Sara Ann Freed)

Professional Publications

Alfred Hitchcock's Mystery
Magazine
Davis Publications, Inc.
380 Lexington Avenue
New York, NY 10017

Ellery Queen's Mystery
Magazine
Davis Publications, Inc.
380 Lexington Avenue
New York, NY 10017

Espionage Magazine
Leo II Publications, Ltd.
PO Box 1184
Teaneck, NJ 07666

A Matter of Crime
Bruccoli Clark Publications,
  Inc.
2006 Sumter Street
Columbia, SC 29201

Semi-Professional & Fan Publications

The Armchair Detective
129 West 56th Street
New York, NY 10019

As Crime Goes By
Anaheim Public Library
500 West Broadway
Anaheim, CA 92805

Bloodhound
The Burgho Press Ltd.
5a, 66 Fairhazel Gardens
London NW6 3SR
England

CADS
9 Vicarage Hill
South Benfleet, Essex SS7 1PA
England

Clues, A Journal of Detection
Bowling Green University
  Press
Bowling Green, OH 43404

The Crime File
PO Box 1321
Bonita, CA 92002

Crime Prints
704 E. 63rd Terrace
Kansas City, MO 64110

The Drood Review of Mystery
Box 8872
Boston, MA 02114

Hardboiled
903 #8 West Jackson Street
Belvidere, IL 61008

I Love a Mystery
PO Box 6009
Sherman Oaks, CA 91403

Mystery and Detective
  Monthly
14411-C South C Street
Tacoma, WA 98444

The Mystery Fancier
1711 Clifty Drive
Madison, IN 47250

Mystery Loves Company
809 Caldwell Avenue
Union, NJ 07083

Mystery News
PO Box 2637
Rohnert Park, CA 94928

Mystery Readers of America
  Journal
PO Box 8116
Berkeley, CA 94707

Mystery Scene
3840 Clark Road SE
Cedar Rapids, IA 52403

The Poisoned Pen
50 First Place
Brooklyn, NY 11231

The Short Sheet
Josh Pachter
Erlangen Elem. School
APO NY 09066

Stephen Wright's Mystery
  Notebook
PO Box 1341, FDR Station
New York, NY 10150

Publications Devoted to a Single Author

(Agatha Christie)
Woman of Mystery
PO Box 1616, Canal Street
  Station
New York, NY 10013

(Arthur Conan Doyle)
The Baker Street Journal
Fordham University Press
University Box L
Bronx, NY 10458

Baker Street Miscellanea
Sciolist Press
PO Box 2579
Chicago, IL 60690

(R. Austin Freeman)
The Thorndyke File
121 Follen Road
Lexington, MA 02173

(Stephen King)
Castle Rock
PO Box 8183
Bangor, ME 04401

(Elizabeth Linington)
Linington Lineup
1223 Glen Terrace
Glassboro, NJ 08028

(Rex Stout)
The Rex Stout Journal
212 Follen Road
Lexington, MA 02173

(Arthur W. Upfield)
The Bony Bulletin
5719 Jefferson Blvd.
Frederick, MD 21701

(Edgar Wallace)
The Edgar Wallace Society
    Newsletter
4 Bradmore Road
Oxford OX2 6QW
England

Newsletters From Publishers & Bookstores

Bantam Deadline
666 Fifth Avenue
New York, NY 10103

The Butler Did It Newsletter
2020 North Charles Street
Baltimore, MD 21218

Crime After Crime
Walker & Company
720 Fifth Avenue
New York, NY 10019

Crime Times
PO Box 10218
Stamford, CT 06904

From Our Inspector's File
Dell Publishing Co.
One Dag Hammarskjold Plaza
New York, NY 10017

Grounds For Murder
    Newsletter
Old Town Mercade, 2707
    Congress St.
San Diego, CA 92110

Kate's Mystery Books
    Newsletter
2211 Massachusetts Avenue
Cambridge, MA 02140

Murder Ink Newsletter
271 West 87th St.
New York, NY 10024

Mysterious News
129 West 56th St.
New York, NY 10019

The Purloined Letter
Rue Morgue Mystery
   Bookstore
942 Pearl St.
Boulder, CO 80302

Scribner's Mystery Newsletter
115 Fifth Avenue
New York, NY 10003

Whodunit
201 East 50th Street
New York, NY 10022

THE YEAR'S BEST
MYSTERY & SUSPENSE NOVELS

Chosen by Edward D. Hoch & Martin H. Greenberg

Peter Ackroyd, *Hawksmoor* (Harper & Row)
Robert Barnard, *Bodies* (Scribners)
Lawrence Block, *When the Sacred Ginmill Closes* (Arbor House)
Simon Brett, *Dead Romantic* (Scribners)
Robert Campbell, *In La-La Land We Trust* (Mysterious Press)
John William Corrington & Joyce H. Corrington, *So Small a Carnival* (Viking)
Bill Crider, *Too Late To Die* (Walker)
Peter Dickinson, *Tefuga* (Pantheon)
Kinky Friedman, *Greenwich Killing Time* (Beech Tree/Morrow)
Sue Grafton, *"C" Is For Corpse* (Henry Holt)
P. D. James, *A Taste For Death* (Knopf)
Thomas Keneally, *A Family Madness* (Simon & Schuster)
John le Carré, *A Perfect Spy* (Knopf)
Robert Littell, *The Sisters* (Bantam)
Ed McBain, *Another Part of the City* (Mysterious Press)
Marcia Muller & Bill Pronzini, *Beyond the Grave* (Walker)
Francis M. Nevins, Jr., *The 120-Hour Clock* (Walker)
Ruth Rendell, *Live Flesh* (Pantheon)
Patrick Süskind, *Purfume* (Knopf)
John Trenhaile, *The Mah-Jongg Spies* (Dutton)
Barbara Vine, *A Dark-Adapted Eye* (Bantam)

BIBLIOGRAPHY

I. Collections & Single Stories

1. Asimov, Isaac. *The Best Mysteries of Isaac Asimov*. Garden City, NY: Doubleday. Thirty-one stories from various sources, 1966–1984, seven previously uncollected, with introductions by the author.
2. Ballard, W. T. *Hollywood Troubleshooter*. Bowling Green, OH: Bowling Green State U. Popular Press. Five novelettes from *Black Mask*, 1933–1942, about tough sleuth Bill Lennox, edited with an introduction and bibliography by James L. Traylor. (1985)
3. Brown, Fredric. *Pardon My Ghoulish Laughter*. Belen, NM: Dennis McMillan Publications. Seven stories from the pulps, 1942–1944. Introduction by Donald E. Westlake.
4. ———. *Thirty Corpses Every Thursday*. Belen, NM: Dennis McMillan Publications. Eight stories from the pulps, 1940–1943. Introduction by William Campbell Gault.
5. Dahl, Roald. *Two Fables*. London: Viking. Two short stories, one of which—"Princess Mammalia"—concerns a murder.
6. Davis, Frederick C. *The Night Nemesis*. Bowling Green, OH: Purple Prose Press. Nineteen stories from *Ten Detective Aces*, 1933–1936, about a masked crime-fighter called the Moon Man. Edited and published by Garyn G. Roberts & Gary Hoppenstand. (1984)
7. Highsmith, Patricia. *The Animal-Lover's Book of Beastly Murder*. New York: Penzler Books. Thirteen stories about animals in a collection first published in England in 1975.
8. ———. *Little Tales of Misogyny*. New York: Penzler Books. Seventeen stories, some criminous, in a collection first published in England in 1977.
9. Marlowe, Dan J. *The Devlin Affair*. Belmont, CA (19

Davis Dr.): Fearon. The author's final short story, in a small 60-page booklet.

10. McBain, Ed. *And All Through the House*. Garden City, NY: Nelson Doubleday. A 32-page book-club edition of a single 87th Precinct Christmas story, originally published in *Playboy*.

11. O'Donnell, Peter. *Pieces of Modesty*. New York: Mysterious Press. Six novelettes about Modesty Blaise in a collection first published in England in 1972.

12. Sanders, Lawrence. *Tales of the Wolf*. New York: Avon Books. Thirteen stories about insurance investigator "Wolf" Lannihan, from *Swank* magazine, 1968–1969.

13. Slesar, Henry. *Murders Most Macabre*. New York: Avon Books. Twenty-seven stories from various publications, from 1956 to the present.

14. Wallace, Edgar. *The Death Room*. London: William Kimber. Fourteen previously uncollected stories, 1909–1929, some fantasy but many criminous, including a novelette about the Just Men. Edited by Jack Adrian.

II. Anthologies

1. Adams, Lois & Gail Hayden, eds. *Alfred Hitchcock's Words of Prey*. New York: Davis Publications. Twenty-nine stories from *AHMM*, 1960–1980.

2. Adler, Bill, concept by. *Murder In Manhattan*. New York: Morrow. Eight stories and novelettes by well-known New York mystery writers, two previously published in magazines. Introduction by Bill Adler.

3. Adrian, Jack, ed. *Sexton Blake Wins*. London: Dent. Nine stories and novelettes by various authors, about British pulp sleuth Sexton Blake, 1925–1941.

4. Asimov, Isaac, Charles G. Waugh & Martin Harry Greenberg, eds. *Tin Stars*. New York: New American Library. Fifteen science fiction stories about robot detectives, guards and judges.

5. ————. *The Twelve Frights of Christmas*. New York:

Avon Books. Thirteen horror and fantasy tales, some criminous.

6. Bainbridge, Beryl, introduction by. *Unnatural Causes*. Poole, England: Javelin Books. Seven stories of violence and murder, by Bainbridge and other writers, based upon a British television series.

7. Breen, Jon L. & Rita A. Breen, eds. *American Murders*. New York: Garland Publishing. Eleven novelettes from *American Magazine*, 1934–1954, with a checklist of all mystery novelettes published by the magazine.

8. Bruccoli, Matthew J. & Richard Layman, eds. *The New Black Mask #4*. San Diego: Harcourt Brace Jovanovich. Fourth in a series of original anthologies.

9. ————. *The New Black Mask #5*. San Diego: Harcourt Brace Jovanovich. Fifth in a series of original anthologies.

10. ————. *The New Black Mask #6*. San Diego: Harcourt Brace Jovanovich. Sixth in a series of original anthologies, concluding a two-part publication of Dashiell Hammett's screen treatment for *After the Thin Man*, begun in *NBM #5*.

11. ————. *The New Black Mask #7*. San Diego: Harcourt Brace Jovanovich. Seventh in a series of original anthologies.

12. Drew, Bernard, ed. *Hard-Boiled Dames*. New York: St. Martin's Press. Fifteen stories from the pulps, 1930–1938, about female detectives and criminals. Preface by Marcia Muller.

13. Etchison, Dennis, ed. *Cutting Edge*. Garden City, NY: Doubleday. A short novel and nineteen new stories of horror and fantasy, some criminous.

14. Green, Richard Lancelyn, ed. *The Further Adventures of Sherlock Holmes*. New York: Penguin Books. Eleven Holmes adventures written by authors other than Conan Doyle, 1911–1982.

15. Greenberg, Martin & Bill Pronzini, eds. *Locked Room Puzzles*. Chicago: Academy Chicago. Volume 3 in the Academy Mystery Novellas series, reprinting four novelettes and novellas by Carr, Rawson, Pronzini, and Hoch.

16. Hale, Hilary, ed. *Winter's Crimes 18*. London: Macmillan.

Eleven new British stories in an annual anthology series. (U.S. edition: St. Martin's Press, 2/87)

17. Hardinge, George, ed. *The Best of Winter's Crimes*. London: Macmillan. A two-volume edition of forty-one stories chosen from the first seventeen years of the British annual *Winter's Crimes*.

18. Hoppenstand, Gary, Garyn G. Roberts & Ray B. Browne, eds. *More Tales of the Defective Detective in the Pulps*. Bowling Green, OH: Bowling Green State U. Popular Press. Eight pulp stories concerning handicapped detectives, from 1939 issues of *Dime Mystery Magazine*.

19. Jordan, Cathleen, ed. *Alfred Hitchcock's A Mystery By the Tale*. New York: Davis Publications. Twenty-eight stories, mainly from *AHMM*, 1956–1979.

20. ———. *Five Classic Stories*. New York: Davis Publications. A promotional booklet containing five stories from *AHMM* which were adapted for Alfred Hitchcock's television series. See also #31 below.

21. Mcdonald, Gregory, ed. *Last Laughs*. New York: Mysterious Press. Fourteen humorous crime stories, two of them new, in the annual anthology from Mystery Writers of America.

22. Meadley, Robert, ed. *Classics In Murder*. New York: Ungar. Fifteen accounts of true crimes by well-known writers in the field, from 1854 to the present.

23. Mulhallen, Karen, ed. *Descant #51: The Detection Issue*. Toronto (PO Box 314, Station P): Descant. Winter 1985/86 issue of a literary quarterly containing twenty-four stories, plays, and poems about crime and detection.

24. Peyton, Richard, ed. *Deadly Odds*. London: Souvenir Press. Twenty-three mystery and crime stories about horse racing, from 1849 to the present, by well-known British, American, and Australian writers.

25. Pronzini, Bill & Martin H. Greenberg, eds. *Great Modern Police Stories*. New York: Walker and Company. Twelve stories, one of them new, 1940–1986.

26. ———. *101 Mystery Stories*. New York: Avenel Books. One hundred and one mystery and crime stories, mainly short-shorts, from a variety of sources.

27. Pronzini, Bill, Barry N. Malzberg & Martin H. Greenberg, eds. *Mystery In the Mainstream*. New York: Morrow. Twenty-one crime stories by well-known mainstream authors, past and present.

28. Randisi, Robert J., ed. *Mean Streets*. New York: Mysterious Press. Twelve new stories by members of the Private Eye Writers of America.

29. Russell, Alan K., ed. *The Book of the Sleuth*. New York: Sterling Publishing. Fourteen classic detective stories, mainly from the nineteenth century.

30. Sullivan, Eleanor, ed. *Alfred Hitchcock: Tales of Terror*. New York: Galahad Books. Fifty-eight stories from *AHMM* and prior Hitchcock anthologies.

31. ————. *The Best Short Stories of 1983*. New York: Davis Publications. A promotional booklet containing all five Edgar nominees published by *EQMM* during 1983. See also #20 above.

32. ————. *Ellery Queen's Blighted Dwellings*. New York: Davis Publications. Twenty-three stories, mainly from *EQMM*.

33. ————*Ellery Queen's Prime Crimes 4*. New York: Davis Publications. Twenty-five new stories in an annual anthology series.

34. Waugh, Charles G., Martin H. Greenberg & Frank D. McSherry Jr., eds. *Strange Maine*. Augusta, ME (Box 2439): Lance Tapley. Fourteen horror and fantasy stories, some criminous, set in the state of Maine.

III. Nonfiction

1. Barley, Tony. *Taking Sides: The Fiction of John le Carré*. Milton Keynes, England: Open University Press. A study of le Carré's novels.

2. Barnes, Melvyn. *Dick Francis*. New York: Ungar. A study of the author's novels, with a bibliography of novels, short stories, and other works.

3. ————. *Murder in Print*. London: Barn Owl Books. An

expanded and updated edition of the author's 1975 book, *Best Detective Fiction.*

4. Billman, Carol. *The Secret of the Stratemeyer Syndicate.* New York: Ungar. A study of Nancy Drew, the Hardy Boys, and other popular mystery series for young readers.

5. Bourgeau, Art. *The Mystery Lover's Companion.* New York: Crown. Brief descriptions and ratings of more than 2,500 mystery novels and short story collections.

6. Budd, Elaine. *13 Mistresses of Murder.* New York: Ungar. Interviews with thirteen women mystery writers from America and England, with a study of a typical novel by each of them.

7. Dale, Alzina Stone & Barbara Sloan Hendershott. *Mystery Reader's Walking Guide: London.* Lincolnwood, IL: Passport Books. Eleven walking tours of London, with mention of several hundred mystery novels and short stories set in the vicinity.

8. Eyles, Allen. *Sherlock Holmes: A Centenary Celebration.* New York: Harper & Row. An illustrated study of the total Holmes phenomenon.

9. Granovetter, Pamela & Karen Thomas McCallum. *A Shopping List of Mystery Classics.* New York: Copperfield Press. A checklist of 609 classic mystery novels published through 1950, together with a list of mystery bookshops.

10. Green, Richard Lancelot, ed. *Letters to Sherlock Holmes.* New York: Penguin Books. A selection of letters written over the years to 221B Baker Street.

11. ———. *Sherlock Holmes Letters.* Iowa City: U. of Iowa Press. Letters to *The Strand* and other publications regarding Holmes.

12. Haining, Peter. *The Television Sherlock Holmes.* London: W. H. Allen. A study of Holmes on television.

13. Hardwick, Michael. *Complete New Guide to Sherlock Holmes.* London: Weidenfeld & Nicolson. Another centenary volume.

14. Hogarth, Paul. *Graham Greene Country.* London: Pavilion/Michael Joseph. Paintings by the artist Hogarth of places mentioned in Greene's novels, together with the artist's diary entries, a synopsis of each of Greene's novels and

short novels, with excerpts, and brief comments by Greene himself.

15. Homberger, Eric. *John le Carré.* London: Methuen. A brief study in the publisher's series on Contemporary Writers.

16. Jute, Andre. *Writing a Thriller.* London: A & C Black. Tips on writing and selling thrillers.

17. Keating, H. R. F. *Writing Crime Fiction.* London: A & C Black. Tips from a leading British mystery writer.

18. Knudson, Richard L. *The Whole Spy Catalogue.* New York: St. Martin's Press. An "espionage lover's guide," containing bibliographies of leading spy novelists, descriptions of film and TV spies, and accounts of real spies and how they operate.

19. Kobayashi, Tsukasa, Akane Higashiyama & Masaharu Uemura. *Sherlock Holmes's London.* San Francisco: Chronicle Books. A photographic guide to places mentioned in the Holmes adventures, as they appeared in Victorian times and as they are today. First published in Japan in 1984.

20. Menendez, Albert J. *The Subject Is Murder.* New York: Garland Publishing. A selective subject guide to nearly four thousand mystery novels and short story collections in twenty-five categories.

21. Milward-Oliver, Edward. *Len Deighton: An Annotated Bibliography 1954–1985.* London: The Sammler Press. A complete bibliography, plus an interview with Deighton. Introduction by Julian Symons.

22. Morselt, Ben. *An A to Z of the Novels and Short Stories of Agatha Christie.* Canaan, NH: Phoenix Publishing. Brief plot outlines of all Christie novels and stories, with an appendix listing the name of the villain in each case.

23. Norville, Barbara. *Writing the Modern Mystery.* Cincinnati: Writer's Digest Books. Instructions from a well-known New York editor.

24. Nown, Graham. *Elementary, My Dear Watson.* London: Ward Lock. A centenary book about Holmes and his world. (U.S. edition: Salem House)

25. Pronzini, Bill & Marcia Muller. *1001 Midnights.* New York: Arbor House. Critical evaluations of 1001 mystery and

suspense novels and collections, classic and modern, by the two authors and other experts in the field.

26. Riley, Dick, Pam McAllister & Bruce Cassiday, eds. *The New Bedside, Bathtub & Armchair Companion to Agatha Christie.* New York: Ungar. An enlarged edition of a guide first published in 1979.
27. Scheper, George L. *Michael Innes.* New York: Ungar. A study of the author's life and major novels.
28. Winks, Robin W., ed. *Colloquium on Crime.* New York: Scribners. Essays on their work by eleven well-known mystery writers.

AWARDS

Mystery Writers of America

Best novel: Barbara Vine (Ruth Rendell), *A Dark-Adapted Eye* (Bantam)

Best first novel: Larry Beinhart, *No One Rides For Free* (Morrow)

Best paperback original: Robert Campbell, *The Junkyard Dog* (Signet)

Best short story: Robert Sampson, "Rain in Pinton County" *(New Black Mask)*

Best fact crime: Carlton Stowers, *Careless Whispers* (Taylor)

Best critical/biographical work: Eric Ambler, *Here Lies* (Farrar Straus & Giroux)

Best juvenile novel: Joan Lowery Nixon, *The Other Side of Dark* (Delacorte)

Best motion picture: *Something Wild,* screenplay by E. Max Frye (Orion)

Best telefeature: *When the Bough Breaks,* teleplay by Phil Penningroth (NBC-TV)

Best episode in a television series: "The Cup" from *The Equalizer,* teleplay by David Jackson, story by Andrew Spies & Carleton Eastlake

Grandmaster: Michael Gilbert

Ellery Queen Award: Eleanor Sullivan

Robert L. Fish Memorial Award: Mary Kittredge, "Father to the Man" *(AHMM)*

Crime Writers Association (London)

Cartier Diamond Dagger: P. D. James

Gold Dagger: Ruth Rendell, *Live Flesh* (Hutchinson)

Silver Dagger: P. D. James, *A Taste for Death* (Faber)

John Creasey Memorial Award: Neville Steed, *Tinplate* (Weidenfeld & Nicholson)

Gold Dagger for Non-fiction: John Bryson, *Evil Angels* (Viking)

Private Eye Writers of America (for 1985)

Best novel: Sue Grafton, *"B" Is For Burglar* (Henry Holt)

Best paperback novel: Earl Emerson, *Poverty Bay* (Avon)
Best short story: Loren D. Estleman, "Eight Mile and Dequindre" *(AHMM)*
Best first novel: Wayne Warga, *Hardcover* (Scribners)
Life achievement award: Richard S. Prather

Anthony Awards (Bouchercon XVII, for 1985)

Best novel: Sue Grafton, *"B" Is For Burglar* (Henry Holt)
Best paperback novel: Nancy Pickard, *Say No To Murder* (Avon)
Best short story: Linda Barnes, "Lucky Penny" *(New Black Mask)*
Best first novel: Jonathan Kellerman, *When the Bough Breaks* (Atheneum)
Grandmaster award: Barbara Mertz (Elizabeth Peters, Barbara Michaels)
Best TV series: *Murder, She Wrote* (CBS-TV)
Best movie: *Witness* (Paramount)

Ellery Queen's Mystery Magazine Readers Award

Clark Howard, *Scalplock*

The Maltese Falcon Society (Japan)

Best novel: Lawrence Block, *When the Sacred Ginmill Closes* (Arbor House)

NECROLOGY

1. Virginia Cleo Andrews (?–1986). As V. C. Andrews, author of seven bestselling suspense paperbacks, notably *Flowers in the Attic* (1979).
2. Martha Axelrod (?–1986). Short story writer and novelist, contributor to *Mystery* magazine and other publications.
3. Mel Arrighi (1933–1986). Playwright and novelist whose work included more than a half-dozen mystery and suspense novels, 1968–1986.
4. Jean L. Backus (1914–1986). Author of three intrigue novels as "David Montross," as well as short stories and articles under her own name.
5. William E. Barrett (1900–1986). Author of mainstream novels who began his writing career in the mystery pulps and published at least one suspense novel, *The Shape of Illusion* (1972).
6. Jorge Luis Borges (1899–1986). Famed Argentine author of short stories, many criminous, collected as *Six Problems For Don Isidro Parodi* (1942, with Adolfo Bioy-Casares), *Ficciones* (1962), *Labyrinths* (1962), etc.
7. John Braine (1922–1986). Well-known British author of *Room at the Top* who wrote two intrigue novels, *The Pious Agent* (1975) and *Finger of Fire* (1977).
8. Michael Butterworth (1924–1986). British author of more than a dozen crime novels, 1967 to the present, notably *The Man in the Sopwith Camel* (1974).
9. Victor Canning (1911–1986). British author of more than thirty novels of mystery and intrigue, notably *The Rainbird Pattern* (1972), filmed by Alfred Hitchcock as *Family Plot.*
10. Thomas B. Dewey (1915–1981). Highly regarded author of three dozen mystery novels and some short stories, 1944–1970, many about private detective "Mac." Also published a few paperbacks as "Tom Brandt" and "Cord Wainer" in the 1950s. (Died April 23, 1981)
11. Fred Dickenson (1908?–1986). Reporter and editor who

authored the "Rip Kirby" comic strip and a single mystery novel, *Kill 'Em With Kindness* (1950).

12. Richard Dougherty (1921–1986). Author of five mainstream novels, one of which—*The Commissioner* (1962)—was the basis for the film and television series *Madigan.*

13. Stanley Ellin (1916–1986). Famed author of short stories and novels, winner of three Edgar awards, whose first story "The Specialty of the House" became an anthology favorite. Notable among his fourteen novels were *The Key to Nicholas Street* (1952), *The Eighth Circle* (1958), *Mirror, Mirror on the Wall* (1972), and *The Dark Fantastic* (1983). Thirty-five of his stories were collected in *The Specialty of the House and Other Stories* (1979). Past president of Mystery Writers of America and Grand Master recipient.

14. J. M. (Jay) Flynn (1927?–1986). Author of more than twenty novels, mainly paperback originals.

15. Ray Gaulden (1914–1986). Author of Westerns and some crime fiction, including *A Good Place to Die* (1965).

16. Elizabeth Gresham (1904–1986). Author of eleven novels, starting with *Puzzle in Porcelain* (1945) and *Puzzle in Pewter* (1947), first published as by "Robin Grey."

17. John Buxton Hilton (1921–1986). British author of a score of novels, sixteen about Superintendent Kenworthy of Scotland Yard. A few of his books appeared as by "John Greenwood."

18. Romilly John (1906?–1986). British author of a single mystery novel, *Death by Request* (1933), with his wife Katherine.

19. Gwenyth Little (1903–1986). Australian author, with her late sister Constance, of twenty-one mystery novels, 1938–1953, notably *The Black Coat* (1948) and *The Black Dream* (1952), published in England as by "Conyth Little."

20. John D. MacDonald (1916–1986). Best-selling author of twenty-one Travis McGee novels, notably *Darker Than Amber* (1966) and *The Green Ripper* (1979), and forty-six other novels, notably *Dead Low Tide* (1953), *Slam the Big Door* (1960), *A Flash of Green* (1962), *The Girl, the Gold*

Watch, and Everything (1962), and *A Key to the Suite* (1962), as well as five collections of short stories. Past president of Mystery Writers of America and Grand Master recipient.

21. Dan J. Marlowe (1914–1986). Edgar-winning author of more than twenty-five paperback mystery and crime novels, many about Earl Drake, notably *The Name of the Game is Death* (1962) and *Flashpoint* (1970). Also published short stories as by "Jaime Sandaval."

22. Dudley Dean McGaughey (?–1986). Western writer who authored at least six paperback mystery novels, 1956–1973, as by "Dudley Dean" and "Owen Dudley."

23. Mary McMullen (1920–1986). Sister of mystery writer Ursula Curtiss, and daughter of Helen Reilly, she authored nearly a score of detective novels beginning with *Strangle Hold* (1951).

24. Robert P. Mills (1920?–1986). Short story writer, literary agent, and managing editor of *EQMM,* 1948–1959.

25. Nigel Morland (1905–1986). British author of more than sixty mystery and crime novels, many unpublished in America, under his own name and as by "John Donavan," "Roger Garnett," "Neal Shepherd," "Mary Dane," "Norman Forrest," and "Vincent McCall." Co-founder of the Crime Writers Association in 1953, he edited *Edgar Wallace Mystery Magazine,* 1964–1967.

26. Henning Nelms (1900–1986). As "Hake Talbot," author of two novels and a novelette about gambler sleuth Rogan Kincaid, notably the classic locked-room mystery *Rim of the Pit* (1944).

27. John Nieminski (1929–1986). Co-founder of *Baker Street Miscellanea* and compiler of two important mystery magazine indexes, *EQMM 350* (1974) and *The Saint Magazine Index* (1980).

28. William Dale Smith (1929–1986). Author of five mystery novels, 1969–1979, as by "David Anthony," notably *The Midnight Lady and the Mourning Man* (1969).

29. Wendell Hertig Taylor (1905–1985). Co-author, with Jacques Barzun, of *A Catalogue of Crime* (1971), highly regarded reader's guide to crime literature.

30. Manly Wade Wellman (1903–1986). Well-known fantasy writer who authored a few mystery novels and short stories. First-prize winner in *EQMM*'s first contest, 1946.
31. Helen Wells (1909?–1986). Author of juvenile mysteries and long active in Mystery Writers of America.
32. Audrey Williamson (1913–1986). British author of a few theatrical mystery novels, unpublished in America, and of several nonfiction works including the CWA Gold Dagger winner, *The Mystery of the Princes* (1978, U.S. edition 1986).
33. Gertrude Mary Wilson (1899–1986). British author, as G. M. Wilson, of some twenty-two mystery novels, 1957–1977, all but one unpublished in America.
34. Lee Wright (1904?–1986). Well-known mystery editor at Simon & Schuster and Random House who edited four notable paperback anthologies starting with *The Pocket Book of Great Detectives* (1941).

HONOR ROLL

Abbreviations:
AHMM—*Alfred Hitchcock's Mystery Magazine*
EQMM—*Ellergy Queen's Mystery Magazine*
ESP—*Espionage Magazine*
NBM—*The New Black Mask*
*(Starred stories are included in this volume. All dates are
1986.)*
Adcock, Thomas, "Christmas Cop," *EQMM*, March
———, "New York, New York," *EQMM*, July
*———, "Thrown-Away Child," *EQMM*, October
———, "Zero Man," *EQMM*, December
Alexander, Gary, "Rambaugh and Ye Olde Bookshoppes, Inc.,"
AHMM, October
Allyn, Doug, "Wolf Country," *AHMM*, September
*———, "The Puddle Diver," *AHMM*, October
———, "Homecoming," *AHMM*, Mid-December
Arden, William, "Clay Pigeon," *ESP*, October
Asimov, Isaac, "Sunset on the Water," *EQMM*, June
Barnard, Robert, "Blown Up," *EQMM*, June
———, "Hardacre Hall," *EQMM*, September
*———, "Happy Christmas," *Prime Crimes 4*
———, "The Injured Party," *EQMM*, Mid-December
Bean, Spaulding, "What Have You Done Now?" *EQMM*, October
*Block, Lawrence, "As Good as a Rest," *EQMM*, August
*Braly, David, "The Gallowglass," *AHMM*, August
Burch, Russ, "Robbery by Robot," *Woman's World*, September 2
Callow, Jessica, "Trouble at Tillingford," *AHMM*, May
Charyn, Jerome, "The Blue Book of Crime," *NBM* #7
Clark, Mary Higgins, "Lucky Day," *Ladies' Home Journal*,
August
———, "The Lost Angel," *Woman's Day*, December 2
Collins, Lorraine, "Only Clay," *EQMM*, December
Collins, Max Allan, "House Calls," *Mean Streets*
Collins, Michael, "Killer's Mind," *NBM* #6
Crenshaw, Bill, "World Enough and Time," *AHMM*, April

Davidson, Avram, "Louie and the Library," *EQMM*, August

Davis, Dorothy Salisbury, "Till Death Do Us Part," *Murder In Manhattan*

Dirckx, John H., "Algorithm 512," *AHMM*, December

Dobbyn, John F., "Deadly Score," *ESP*, August

DuBois, Brendon, "Driven," *EQMM*, November

Dundee, Wayne, "Body Count," *Mean Streets*

Fraser, Antonia, "Boots," *Prime Crimes 4*

*Gill, B. M., "A Certain Kind of Skill," *Winter's Crimes 18*

*Grafton, Sue, "She Didn't Come Home," *Redbook*, April

———, "The Parker Shotgun," *Mean Streets*

Gray, Robert, "If There's Anything We Can Do," *AHMM*, Mid-December

Haldeman, Linda, "Shabby Little Shocker," *AHMM*, July

Hamlin, Fred, "The Clam Soup Connection," *AHMM*, August

Harness, Charles L., "Crossings," *ESP*, Feburary

Hoch, Edward D., "Leopold and the Thunderer," *EQMM*, August

———, "The Theft of McGregor's Skunk," *EQMM*, November

*———, "The Spy's Story," *EQMM*, December

———, "The Problem of the Invisible Acrobat," *EQMM*, Mid-December

Howard, Clark, "Harmonic Interlude," *EQMM*, January

———, "The Last One to Cry," *EQMM*, June

*———, "Scalplock," *EQMM*, July

———, "The Wide Loop," *EQMM*, October

Kanter, Rob, "The Man Who Called From Tomorrow," *AHMM*, September

Kittredge, Mary, "Father to the Man," *AHMM*, November

LaCour, M. M., "The Case of the Lost Collie," *AHMM*, August

*Lamburn, Nell, "Tom's Thatch," *EQMM*, July

Long, Virginia, "The Man in the Chair," *Woman's World*, April 1

Loomis, Greg, "Postcards," *Woman's World*, May 27

Lovesey, Peter, "The Corder Figure," *EQMM*, January

Marlett, Melba, "The Second Mrs. Porter," *AHMM*, November

Mayhar, Ardath, "No Olive Branch," *ESP*, April

Moore, Richard A., "The Last Bank Robbery," *EQMM*, June

Naccarato, Charles, "Who Dares Tell the President?" *ESP*, December

Newton, B., "Simple Minds, Simple Tasks," *AHMM*, September

OCork, Shannon, "Mifflin Must Go," *EQMM,* June
Olson, Donald, "The Scarlett Syndrome," *EQMM,* January
Pachter, Josh, "The Qatar Causeway," *AHMM,* January
*———, "The Night of Power," *EQMM,* September
Peirce, J. F., "The Spy Who Came in With a Cold," *ESP,* June
Petrin, Jas. R., "Early Summer," *AHMM,* December
Powell, James, "The Singular Bird," *EQMM,* April
*Pronzini, Bill, "Ace in the Hole," *Mean Streets*
Reynolds, William J., "Guilt Enough to Go Around," *AHMM,*
  September
Romun, Isak, "Letter From Moscow," *ESP,* February
———, "Eagles," *St. Anthony Messenger,* August
———, "Love Is Here to Stay," *ESP,* October
*Sampson, Robert, "Rain in Pinton County," *NBM #5*
Simenon, Georges, "The Man Behind the Looking Glass,"
  NBM #6
Smith, Pauline C., "The Dog," *AHMM,* August
Sproul, Dan A., "Madame Ruby," *AHMM,* Mid-December
· Story, Quenda Behler, "Do Garnets Glitter Like Gold?" *AHMM,*
  August
Strieber, Whitley, "Vaudeville," *Murder In Manhattan*
Stuart, Ian, "Roberta," *Prime Crimes 4*
Symons, Stuart, "The Visiting Professor of Estonian," *ESP,* August
Turnbull, Peter, "The Sort of Man He Was," *EQMM,* August
Twohy, Robert, "Another Dead Nobody," *EQMM,* July
Walsh, Ann, "Child Support," *Woman's World,* July 1
Wellen, Edward, "Backup," *ESP,* June
Youmans, Gilbert, "Mrs. Hudson Stays for Tea," *EQMM,* January